By J. A. Jance

J. P. Beaumont Mysteries

UNTIL PROVEN GUILTY • INJUSTICE FOR ALL
TRIAL BY FURY • TAKING THE FIFTH
IMPROBABLE CAUSE • A MORE PERFECT UNION
DISMISSED WITH PREJUDICE • MINOR IN POSSESSION
PAYMENT IN KIND • WITHOUT DUE PROCESS
FAILURE TO APPEAR • LYING IN WAIT
NAME WITHHELD • BREACH OF DUTY
BIRDS OF PREY • PARTNER IN CRIME
LONG TIME GONE • JUSTICE DENIED
FIRE AND ICE • BETRAYAL OF TRUST
RING IN THE DEAD (NOVELLA)
SECOND WATCH • STAND DOWN (NOVELLA)
PROOF OF LIFE • STILL DEAD (NOVELLA)

Joanna Brady Mysteries

DESERT HEAT • TOMBSTONE COURAGE
SHOOT/DON'T SHOOT • DEAD TO RIGHTS
SKELETON CANYON • RATTLESNAKE CROSSING
OUTLAW MOUNTAIN • DEVIL'S CLAW • PARADISE LOST
PARTNER IN CRIME • EXIT WOUNDS • DEAD WRONG
DAMAGE CONTROL • FIRE AND ICE • JUDGMENT CALL
THE OLD BLUE LINE (NOVELLA) • REMAINS OF INNOCENCE
RANDOM ACTS: A JOANNA BRADY AND
ALI REYNOLDS NOVELLA • DOWNFALL • FIELD OF BONES

Walker Family Novels

HOUR OF THE HUNTER • KISS OF THE BEES
DAY OF THE DEAD • QUEEN OF THE NIGHT
DANCE OF THE BONES: A J. P. BEAUMONT AND
BRANDON WALKER NOVEL

Ali Reynolds Novels

EDGE OF EVIL • WEB OF EVIL • HAND OF EVIL
CRUEL INTENT • TRIAL BY FIRE • FATAL ERROR
LEFT FOR DEAD • DEADLY STAKES • MOVING TARGET
A LAST GOODBYE (NOVELLA) • COLD BETRAYAL
NO HONOR AMONG THIEVES: AN ALI REYNOLDS AND
JOANNA BRADY NOVELLA • CLAWBACK
MAN OVERBOARD • DUEL TO THE DEATH

Poetry

AFTER THE FIRE

J. A. JANCE

FIELD OF BONES

A BRADY NOVEL OF SUSPENSE

WILLIAM MORROW

An Imprint of HarperCollinsPublishers

This is a work of fiction. Names, characters, places, and incidents are products of the author's imagination or are used fictitiously and are not to be construed as real. Any resemblance to actual events, locales, organizations, or persons, living or dead, is entirely coincidental.

First William Morrow premium printing: May 2019
First William Morrow trade international printing: September 2018
First William Morrow hardcover printing: September 2018

Print Edition ISBN: 978-0-06-265758-9
Digital Edition ISBN: 978-0-06-265759-6

Cover design by Richard L. Aquan
Cover photographs: © Glass House/Getty Images (desert landscape);
© Cressa Cruzan/Shutterstock (sky); © Natalia Kuzmina/
Shutterstock (vultures); © Maria Jeffs/Shutterstock; © FotoRequest/
Shutterstock; © Bruce MacQueen/Shutterstock
Author photograph by Mary Ann Halpin

19 20 21 22 23 QGM 10 9 8 7 6 5 4 3 2 1

To Carl and Barbara, you know why

FIELD OF BONES

❦ PROLOGUE

AS SHERIFF Joanna Brady and her reelection committee gathered in the social hall at the Tombstone Canyon United Methodist Church in Old Bisbee to await the results, everyone expected it would be an election-night nail-biter, one that would end with either a victory celebration or a concession speech.

This was the third time she had stood for election, and this battle had been by far the toughest. For one thing, her opponent, Donald Hubble, was a well-heeled good old boy who had money to burn. He had paid for his run for office out of pocket without having to do any outside fundraising, either. He had outspent Joanna three times over, papering the whole of Cochise County with thousands of yard signs and buying spots on Tucson television channels that broadcast throughout southern Arizona. His favorite tagline, "Cochise County needs a full-time sheriff as opposed to a part-time one," was a not-so-subtle reference to Sheriff Brady's very obvious and advancing pregnancy. The one thing his paid-for commercials couldn't paper over was Hubble's well-deserved reputation as a bully of both people and animals, a reputation he had earned during the years he'd been in charge of running his father's massive cattle ranch south of Willcox.

Being both pregnant and outspent hadn't been Joanna's only stumbling blocks during this election cycle, not by a long shot. Late in August her world had been shattered when her mother, Eleanor, and her stepfather, George Winfield, had both fallen victim to a freeway shooter on I-17 south of Flagstaff, Arizona. The tragic loss of Joanna's parents should have been more than enough to derail her reelection effort. Unfortunately, fate had much more in store.

Back home in Cochise County, what started out as a routine homicide investigation had revealed that one of her longtime officers, Deputy Jeremy Stock, despite showing a "good guy" face to the world, had actually been an abusive and ultimately murderous husband and father. When the truth finally came out, he turned his wrath on Joanna herself. Only the timely intervention of Joanna's K-9 unit—Deputy Terry Gregovich and his dog, Spike—had saved her life, but not before the dog had been gravely injured. Three months later he was still recovering and had been medically retired from his K-9 duties. As for Jeremy Stock? Rather than be taken into custody, he had taken his own life, plunging to his death off a rock-bound cliff.

The fact that Joanna had been totally bamboozled by someone she thought she knew well had shattered her confidence in her ability to read people and made her wonder how many more troubled souls might be hiding in plain sight inside her department. For a time she'd seriously considered dropping out of the race. She might well have done so had not members of her department rallied behind her.

Both her sworn officers and civilian staff members had urged her to stay in contention. Most of them had worked with her for the better part of eight years, and they'd come to trust her. Although she could often be a demanding boss, she required as much of herself as she did of others, and she made every effort to be fair.

With their backing she fought the good fight. After her parents' funeral and once the ink had dried on the paperwork surrounding the Jeremy Stock homicides, Joanna had gone back to campaigning with renewed effort and purpose. And now here they were—nine o'clock on election night with the results just starting to trickle in.

Using a bottomless checkbook to fund his run for office, Don Hubble had been able to hire a professional campaign manager and campaign workers, while Joanna's effort had relied on an army of volunteers mobilized by two of her greatest cheerleaders, her first in-laws—Jim Bob and Eva Lou Brady, the parents of her long-deceased husband, Andy. When it came time to undo the pause button on the campaign, and once Joanna made the decision to continue her run for office, they had stepped up in a big way, functioning as her campaign co-chairs.

Jim Bob might have been a novice when it came

to local politics, but he knew almost everyone in town, if not in the county as a whole, and he wasn't afraid to ask for help. Eva Lou had served as the campaign's volunteer coordinator and was a killer when it came to door-to-door canvassing. She had also stepped in as a pinch-hitting grandmother and babysitter, looking after five-year-old Dennis when late-night campaign events in far-flung corners of the county had kept Joanna, and sometimes her husband, Butch Dixon, as well, out on the road far past their son's bedtime.

One item that had escaped Jim Bob's attention until the last minute was lining up a location for a post-election party, something that should have been done well in advance. By the time the novice campaign manager figured it out, the preferred venues in town—the ones at the Copper Queen Hotel and in the basement of the Convention Center—were already booked, which explained why tonight's post-election gig was being held in the parish hall of the Tombstone Canyon United Methodist Church.

The intention was to collect incoming election results in real time and immediately upload them to a PowerPoint display projected onto a screen. So far that process wasn't going well. While Jim Bob and Butch fought to get the balky hardware and software to work together, Eva Lou coordinated setting up the kitchen to serve coffee and refreshments. As for the candidate herself? Joanna sat at a cloth-covered table near the front of the room, keeping an eye on Denny, who was deep into the Lego project that Eva Lou had wisely brought along to keep him occupied.

This was not Joanna Brady's best night ever. The waistband of her latest uniform had undergone several discreet expansions. Nonetheless, it no longer fastened. A strategically placed safety pin three inches below the top of the zipper was all that was keeping the placket more or less in place. Unfortunately, her equally snug-fitting jacket could no longer be trusted to keep the resulting gap from showing. In other words, her clothes didn't exactly fit, and neither did her shoes.

Tonight her ankles were swollen. Under the cover of the tablecloth, she'd managed to slip off her heels in order to give her sore feet a rest. Her back hurt. Any minute now she'd need to put the shoes back on and make a quick trip to the restroom. In the meantime her baby girl—due to make her first appearance three weeks from now in early December—was kicking up a storm.

As guests began to meander into the room, the PowerPoint display finally went live, and numbers began coming in. That was also the same moment when Joanna's phone rang with her daughter's photo showing in the ID window. "Hey, Mom," Jenny said. "How's it going?"

This was not the time to mention either the swollen feet or the aching back. "Fine," Joanna said.

"How are the returns looking?"

Jenny had been intimately involved in both of her mother's previous campaigns. She knew about keeping election-night vigils. Tonight, however, as a freshman at Northern Arizona University, she was three hundred fifty miles away in Flagstaff.

"Just starting," Joanna replied. "According to the screen, some of the smaller precincts have already reported in, mostly up around the northeast corner of the county—Bowie, San Simon, and Kansas Settlement." She paused. "Results from Elfrida and Portal just came in."

"And?" Jenny prodded.

"We've got a small margin so far," Joanna said. "Only about a thousand votes, but still a margin. The problem is, Hubble is a big deal out in Sierra Vista, his home base, and Sierra Vista alone accounts for almost a quarter of the county's voters."

"So if Sierra Vista goes for Hubble . . ." Jenny began.

"Right," Joanna said, glancing at the screen where the display was now showing final tallies from precincts in Willcox, Bisbee, Douglas, Tombstone, and Benson. So far that thousand-vote differential seemed to be holding steady.

"How's Denny doing?" Jenny asked. "You brought him along, didn't you? I always loved getting to stay up late on election night."

Yes, Joanna thought, *but both those other times we won. This time we might not.*

"He's here all right. Grandma Brady brought along a new Lego set to help keep him occupied."

"What about Marliss Shackleford?" Jenny asked. "Is she there, too?"

Marliss, a reporter for the local paper, the *Bisbee Bee*, had been a burr under Joanna's saddle for as long as she'd been sheriff. She had also been an unapologetic supporter of Joanna's opponent.

"No sign of her so far," Joanna answered. "I'm guessing she's making herself at home at someone else's post-election party."

"I'm sure," Jenny grumbled. "I wonder whose. Do you have your victory speech ready to deliver?"

"Not a speech so much," Joanna said, "just a few words thanking the people who've done all the work."

In actual fact Joanna had prepared two separate sets of remarks, one for a win and the other for a loss. She was still a Girl Scout at heart, and Girl Scouts are always prepared.

A couple of women, two of her loyal volunteers both proudly displaying their BRADY FOR SHERIFF buttons, approached the table. Joanna knew them both—they were old friends of her mother's from the Presbyterian church who had also shown up at Eleanor and George's post-funeral barbecue, but right that moment a weary Joanna couldn't for the life of her come up with either of their names. Despite almost eight years in elected office, Joanna Brady had yet to master the one essential task that is the mark of a true politician—the ability to remember names.

"Some of the guests are here, so I have to go," Joanna told Jenny quickly. "But I'll call you when we have a final tally."

"You promise?" Jenny asked.

"I promise."

"No matter how late it is?"

"No matter how late."

"Sorry," Joanna said to the new arrivals, stowing the phone and hoping to cover her momentary failure in the name department. "It was my daughter checking in from Flagstaff."

"I can't believe Jenny's already away at college," said one. "Eleanor was just as proud as punch over her. Bragged about her constantly, like she was the greatest thing since sliced bread."

If Eleanor Lathrop Winfield had bragged about her granddaughter to others, very little of that praise had ever made it back to Joanna's ears.

Dennis chose that moment to slip away from his Lego project. He came over to where Joanna was sitting and snuggled up to her. "Are we still winning?" he asked.

Joanna glanced at the screen. The vote count had increased, so results from some of the more populous precincts must have come in. The difference between her votes and Hubble's was now under a thousand—only a few votes under, but under nonetheless.

She gave her son a hug. "So far so good," she said.

"Are we going to go home soon?" he wanted to know.

Joanna glanced at her watch and saw that it wasn't quite ten. "Probably not very soon," she told him. "Are you tired?"

Denny nodded and snuggled some more, a sure sign that he was right at the end of his endurance.

There was a seating area in one corner of the social hall that held a sofa and two matching chairs.

"Why don't you go over there and rest on that couch for a while?" she suggested, pointing.

"You'll wake me up if anything happens?"

"I will."

Without a murmur of objection, Denny headed for the sofa. "What a good boy," one of the two women exclaimed, watching him go.

"Thank you," Joanna said. "And yes, he is a good boy."

"Come on, Alva," the other said. "They're putting out the coffee. Let's go get some."

That's when the name surfaced: Alva—Alva Bullard. "Thank you both for all your help," Joanna said.

"You're most welcome, Sheriff Brady," Alva replied with a smile. "It's the least we can do."

Joanna glanced up at the screen. Another 5,000 votes had been added to the total, and it looked as though her lead was slowly being whittled away. Now there was an 830-vote difference. Yes, once her lead disappeared completely, she'd be more than happy to let Denny sleep through the outcome.

More of her supporters filed in. As the room began to fill up, Joanna realized that aching back or no, it was time for her to put a smile on her face, pull on her big-girl panties—to say nothing of her shoes—and start working the room. She had located the stray shoes and was in the process of forcing her feet back into them when it happened— the sudden, undeniable gush of liquid as her water broke, accompanied by the pressure of that first full-on contraction. The baby didn't give a whit that she was three weeks early or that her mother was up to her ears in election-night festivities. It was Sage's time, and she was coming now!

The jolting intensity of the first contraction took Joanna's breath away. When it finally passed, she turned around and tried to catch Butch's eye. It seemed to take forever before he noticed her frantic wave.

"Don't worry," he said, hurrying over to her. "We're still ahead."

"It's not the election," she told him through gritted teeth. "It's the baby!"

"The baby?" Butch repeated. "What, she's coming now? Are you sure? Isn't it too soon?"

"It may be soon, but yes, I'm sure. This isn't my first rodeo. My water just broke," she said. "I left a mess under the table, but we need to get me to the hospital now."

"Where's Denny?" Butch demanded. "I thought he was right here."

"He's over in the corner, sleeping, and let's leave him there. If you tell Jim Bob what's going on, I'm sure he and Eva Lou will look after him."

"Okay," Butch said. "I'll go get the car."

Except that was when the next contraction hit, and it was another surprisingly forceful one. With the second contraction coming so close on the heels of the first, Joanna knew that the baby was coming in one hell of a hurry.

"No car," she gasped. "Call 911. We're going to need an ambulance and an EMT!"

For a second it looked as though Butch was prepared to argue, but then he thought better of it and reached for his phone. Just then Marianne Macul-yea appeared beside him. "Is something wrong?"

Not only was the Reverend Marianne Maculyea the pastor of the Tombstone Canyon UMC, she had been Joanna's best friend since junior high.

"My water just broke," Joanna told her. "Butch is calling 911."

A minute or so later, when Butch and Marianne led Joanna outside, she was still barefoot and wrapped head to toe in a flowing robe of borrowed tablecloth. No doubt the party would continue without them, but regardless of how the final voting tallies came out, Joanna had other fish to fry that night and wouldn't be on hand either to declare victory or face down defeat.

It turned out that summoning an ambulance was the right call, because Eleanor Sage Dixon refused to be kept waiting. She made her appearance just as the EMTs were wheeling Joanna's gurney into the ER at Bisbee's Copper Queen Community Hospital. They never made it anywhere near the delivery room. Dr. James Lee, Joanna's longtime GP, didn't make it to the hospital in time. Dr. Mallory Morris, the recently appointed head of ER in the hospital's newly remodeled emergency unit, later joked that he needed a catcher's mitt more than latex gloves when they rolled her in from the ambulance.

An hour later, having been pronounced early but healthy, the six-and-a-half-pound baby girl was wrapped in blankets and sleeping in a bassinet in her mother's room, blissfully unaware that her parents were in the process of sorting out birth-certificate paperwork. Joanna and Butch had been seesawing back and forth on the name issue for weeks. Sometimes the preferred name was Eleanor Sage, and sometimes it was the other way around.

"Maybe we should call her Electra Sage in honor of election night," Joanna suggested.

"Not a good idea," Butch said at once.

"Why not?" Joanna asked. "Isn't Electra some kind of Greek goddess?"

"Sort of," Butch allowed, "but not necessarily in a good way. She joined forces with her brother, Orestes, to murder both their mother and their stepfather. Orestes got punished for the crime, while Electra pretty much got away with it. So let's just stick with naming the baby after your mother, shall we?"

"All right, then," Joanna agreed. "She can be Eleanor Sage as far as officialdom is concerned, but I plan on calling her Sage no matter what."

"That's not exactly news from the front," Butch told her with a grin.

Jim Bob Brady showed up about then. The fact that he was all smiles pretty much gave away the game.

"So did we win?" Joanna demanded.

"We certainly did," a beaming Jim Bob replied, "by a total of sixty-seven votes. Hubble was on the air giving his concession speech as I left the church. Now let me get a look at this brand-new grandbaby of ours. If this isn't a red-letter night, I don't know what is!"

ONE

THE FIRST time Latisha Marcum had awakened in darkness in that house-of-horrors dungeon, she thought she'd gone blind. She was lying on a bare mattress on what seemed to be an earthen floor. When she tried to get to her feet, she discovered two things—she was completely naked, and her leg was secured to the wall with a heavy-duty chain. That's when she started to scream.

"Help!" she pleaded. "Somebody help me! Get me out of here."

"Shut up," said a voice out of the darkness—a woman's voice or a girl's, Latisha couldn't tell which. "No one's going to help you. If you keep making all that racket, you might make him mad, and he'll come back down. Believe me, you don't want that to happen."

"Who will come back down?"

"The Boss," she said, "from upstairs."

"Who's he?"

"The devil," said a second voice, another female speaking in a soft southern accent. "And in case you're wondering, you're in hell."

"How many people are here?" Latisha asked.

"Three, counting you," the first voice said. "I'm Sandra Locke, but people call me Sandy."

"And I'm Sadie Jennings," the other voice said. "Who are you?"

"Latisha Marcum."

"With a name like that, are you black?" Sadie asked.

"Does it matter if I am?"

Sadie laughed. "Just wondering," she said. "In this hellhole you could be deep purple for all I care, and it wouldn't make a bit of difference."

"But where is here?" Latisha wanted to know. "Where are we?"

"In the desert somewhere," Sandy said. "One day when I was upstairs, one of the blackout curtains wasn't all the way shut. I saw some old buildings that looked like they might have been part of a movie set from one of those old westerns. I could see some mountains in the distance, but everything between here and the mountains looked like desert."

"A desert, then, but where?"

"Who knows?" Sadie answered. She might have shrugged or not. It was impossible to see. "In Arizona maybe, or Texas or New Mexico—all those places look alike to me, although there aren't many mountains in Texas."

As far as Latisha was concerned, the words Arizona, Texas, and New Mexico meant nothing to her. She had no idea what those states might be like. Until Trayvon had taken her to New Orleans, she had never set foot outside Missouri except for the East St. Louis corner of Illinois.

Latisha fell silent for a moment, and so did the others. The urge had been coming on for some time, and now she was desperate. "I need to go to the bathroom," she said.

"See that spot of light over in the corner?" Sandra asked.

Latisha looked around. Now that her eyes had adjusted to the gloom, she realized it wasn't completely dark. There was a bit of murky light coming into the space from a row of three glass blocks set high in what had to be an outside wall.

"That's where the toilet is," Sandy said. "When you go, take your cup along. If you want water to drink, you'll have to get it out of the flushing tank."

"From the toilet?" Latisha repeated.

"The water in the flushing tank is clean," Sadie said. "Since it's the only water there is, get used to it."

Latisha reached out and felt around the head of her mattress. Eventually her fingers closed on a cup of some kind—a metal cup with a handle—and a plastic storage container with a lid on it. When she picked it up and shook it, something rattled inside.

"What's this?"

"That's your dinner," Sadie said. "It's also breakfast and lunch. Don't spill it, because if you do, the rats will come looking for it."

"But what is it?" Latisha insisted.

"Purina Dog Chow would be my first guess," Sandy suggested, "or maybe a brand that's not as good."

"Dog food?" Latisha echoed in disbelief. "We're supposed to eat dog food? I can't. I won't."

"You'll be surprised," Sadie told her. "Once you're hungry enough, you'll eat most anything."

Taking the cup with her, Latisha struggled to her feet. The cumbersome chain around her ankle made it difficult to walk. She'd taken only two steps when she tripped over something on the floor. The next thing she knew, she had tumbled onto another mattress, one as empty and bare as her own.

"Whose mattress is this?" she asked, picking herself back up and retrieving the cup she'd dropped when she fell. It had fallen to the floor. If she'd been wearing any clothes, Latisha would have wiped the lip of the cup on her clothing. Since she wasn't, she couldn't.

"That one still has a Vacancy sign posted on it," Sadie said. "At least so far."

Latisha struggled to her feet once more. Feeling her way through the gloom, she was finally able to make out the ghostly presence of a toilet.

"Before you go to the bathroom, it's always a good idea to check and make sure no one else is using it," Sandy said. "If the chains get tangled up in the dark, it's hell getting them loose again."

"You have chains, too?" Latisha asked.

"No," Sadie said. "We stay down here in the dark because we wanna be here, right?"

"Right," Sandy agreed. "In reality we're all off on some fancy cruise ship, and these are deck chairs."

They both laughed then, as though they were sharing some hysterically funny joke.

Not laughing, Latisha located the toilet and used it. When she flushed it, the toilet made a funny

sound, like there was some kind of machinery involved. But there was no sink, nowhere to wash
her hands afterward, no soap and water, no towel.
After filling the cup and returning to her mattress,
she learned that a scratchy woolen army blanket,
that metal cup, and the plastic container of food
were the sum total of her possessions. There was
no pillow for her head, no comb or brush, no eating
implements, and no toothbrush, either.

She started to ask about that, but then she stifled
it. She had seen movies and TV shows about what
went on in prisons. Given enough desperation, a
comb or a toothbrush or an ordinary kitchen fork
could be turned into a lethal weapon.

Time passed. The other girls had fallen silent.
Maybe they'd both fallen asleep. Maybe Latisha
had, too. But then a door opened and an electric
light flashed on, burning so brightly that Latisha
had to cover her eyes. Once she could see again, she
realized that the only light fixture was a bare bulb
hanging from a frayed brown cord in the middle of
the room. There were four mattresses positioned
foot to foot in the room with a narrow earthen
pathway running between them. Latisha's eyes adjusted to the sudden light in time to see two sets of
grimy bare feet disappear beneath khaki-colored
army blankets just like hers.

"What's happening?" she whispered. "What's
going on?" No one answered. Sadie and Sandy had
gone completely silent.

She looked around the room, trying to get her
bearings. At one end was a concrete slab where

the toilet was located. At the other end was an old-fashioned chest-style freezer. Behind that was a plank stairway that seemed to lead upstairs.

She watched as a pair of work-boot-clad legs slowly descended the stairs. When the hulking figure of a man finally came into view, she immediately recognized his face. He was the john who had approached her in New Orleans; the same guy who'd lured her into his vehicle and then drugged her somehow. Sitting up, Latisha glanced questioningly at the two occupied mattresses, hoping for a clue about what was going on, but all she saw was the outline of two figures, lying still as death under the blankets. There would be no help for her from that quarter, nor any answers, either.

The man heading toward her was white, most likely in his fifties or sixties, heavyset, with wavy graying hair. He gave her a wolfish grin that showed off a set of crooked, yellowish teeth.

"Time to give the new girl a try," he said, leaning down with a key at the ready to unlock the clamp around Latisha's ankle. "Time to see whether or not you were worth hauling all the way home from New Orleans."

As soon as the clamp let loose, Latisha scrambled away from him on the mattress, kicking as she went, but she wasn't nearly fast enough. Grabbing her naked thigh with a bruising, iron grip, he dragged her back to him.

"So that's how it's gonna be, is it?" he said with a chuckle. "I can see that I've got myself a fighter on my hands. Well, good enough. Come on, girl, let's us go upstairs and have ourselves some fun."

Latisha was still struggling to get away when he slapped her with a tooth-jarring blow that left her seeing stars and rendered her momentarily unconscious. When she came to, she was being carried upstairs. Latisha was no lightweight. She weighed more than a hundred and fifty pounds, and yet he carried her on his shoulder as though she were no trouble at all.

Upstairs he lugged her through a ramshackle room where holes in the peeling linoleum revealed the bare wooden planking of the underlying floor. The walls were made of rough plaster. At one end of the room was an old-fashioned electric stove, an antique-looking fridge, and a small kitchen table. At the other end was an iron-framed double bed—one with another bare mattress and no bedding.

In this room, as in the one downstairs, the only light came from a single bare bulb dangling on a tan cord. There were windows in the walls, but they were covered by thick curtains made up of what looked like black plastic garbage bags. They were positioned in such a way that it was impossible to catch a glimpse of what was outside.

The man carried Latisha into a bathroom, lifted her off his shoulder, and then stood her upright in the middle of the room. "Everything you need is right here," he said. "You get yourself all spiffed up now, and then we'll see what you've got."

Going out and closing the door, he left her standing there alone. A moment later she heard the sound of a key turning in the lock.

She looked around. There was a rust-stained lavatory, a creaky toilet, and an old-fashioned claw-foot tub. Next to the tub sat a wooden stool loaded with body soap, shampoo, and a thin bath towel, along with a brush and a comb. Latisha didn't want to do what he said, but there wasn't really any choice. Besides, she felt utterly filthy, so she ran water into the tub and then climbed in. Despite the circumstances she was able to lean back in the hot water, close her eyes, and relax. Maybe this wouldn't be so bad after all. After shampooing her filthy hair, she climbed back out and used the towel to dry off.

Standing in front of the mirror over the sink, she was shocked to see how much her face had swollen from that one terrible blow. The comb and hairbrush he'd provided for her use had never been intended for hair like hers, and she finally had to give up trying to sort out the tangles. Behind the pockmarked mirror of the medicine chest, she located a tube of toothpaste and a single toothbrush—a used toothbrush to be sure, but it was better than no toothbrush at all.

Finally she was done, and she tapped on the door to let him know she was ready, although she wasn't, not really. When she was working the streets, Latisha had dealt with some rough customers from time to time, but nothing had prepared her for the Boss. What he dished out was far worse than anything she'd ever experienced.

It seemed as though the torment lasted for hours. The more he hurt her, the better he liked it. When he finally had his fill, he grabbed her upper arm and propelled her back downstairs, turning on the overhead light as he did so. He threw her onto her mattress and then reached for the chain. She was too exhausted to fight anymore or try to get away. While he fastened the clamp around her leg, she looked at the others. Sandy and Sadie still lay unmoving and silent under their respective blankets.

The light went off. The door slammed shut. There was the sound of a bolt of some kind being latched. Heavy footsteps pounded across the plank flooring upstairs before another door slammed shut, followed a few minutes later by the sound of a vehicle starting up.

"He's gone now," Sandy said. "He probably won't be back for a day or two."

"Are you okay?" Sadie asked.

Latisha was not okay. She was anything but okay, but she didn't want to admit it. "I'll live," she said. "But you were wrong. This isn't hell. Upstairs is."

She heard the sounds of chains clanking. Then, to her surprise, she felt her mattress shift underneath as though people had sat down next to her, on either side. An invisible hand patted her shoulder.

"I'm sorry for what he did to you," Sadie said. "But there's nothing we could do to help."

It was small comfort, but comfort nevertheless. And much to Latisha's further surprise, it was the beginning of an unlikely but abiding friendship.

TWO

SAGE'S UNSCHEDULED early arrival had put a fly in any number of ointments. Based on a December due date, the release of Butch's next book, *Just the Facts*, and the accompanying book tour had been rescheduled. It was now set to occur starting the week after the election. Butch immediately offered to call his publisher and cancel the two-week tour for his upcoming murder mystery, but Joanna nixed that idea.

Years earlier, when Butch had sold his restaurant in Peoria, Arizona, he had come to Bisbee intent on pursuing two very different things—Joanna and his lifelong ambition to become a writer. He had won big on both counts. His first book, a cozy called *Serve and Protect*, featured Kimberly Charles, the fictional chief of police in Copper Creek, a tiny fictional Arizona town. Did Kimberly bear any resemblance to Joanna Brady? When people asked him that question, he would smile and say, "You be the judge."

In marketing that first book, Drew Mabrey, his agent, had advised him against using his real name—F. W. Dixon.

"Hey," he had told her, "I always loved the Hardy Boys."

Drew was not amused, and since Butch was writing cozies, she suggested a more "gender-neutral name," which is how his *nom de plume* became Gayle Dixon as opposed to F.W. The book about to hit the shelves, *Just the Facts*, was the fourth book in the Kimberly Charles series, and at every booksigning event he had to deal with someone, usually an opinionated LOL, who couldn't quite believe that a "man can write these books."

"Look," Joanna said, "we both know that tours for midlist authors are hard to come by these days. The fact that your publisher was kind enough to readjust the pub date in order to take both the election and my projected due date into consideration was a huge concession on their part, and we need to treat it as such. You go out there and do your job, and I'll stay here to keep the home fires burning. As long as you're home in time for Thanksgiving, it's not a problem."

"You're sure?"

"Yes, I'm sure."

The truth is, they both knew that even with Butch out of town she'd have plenty of help. For one thing, Carol Sunderson would be there to assist her with looking after Dennis as well as Sage. Years earlier Carol and her husband had been living nearby and raising their two grandsons when their mobile home had burned to the ground. Carol's husband had died in the fire. Not only was she left alone, she and her grandsons had nowhere to live.

At the time Joanna and Butch had moved into their new place just up the road, and Joanna's old place, High Lonesome Ranch's original ranch house, was sitting empty. They'd been able to offer Carol a place to live rent-free along with a part-time paid gig as housekeeper/nanny—a job that suited Carol Sunderson to a tee.

With Butch off on the road, Carol came to the house early enough each day to help get Denny fed, dressed, and down to the end of High Lonesome Road in time to catch the school bus. Eva Lou Brady showed up on an almost daily basis, often bringing along a casserole or two, as did Marianne Maculyea. And both of them were more than happy to take over baby-holding duties when called upon to do so. Having all those helping hands around left Joanna feeling truly blessed that she wasn't having to look after both a newborn and a five-year-old on her own.

Butch's publicist had organized a short but intense two-week book tour that had launched on time, while most of the items on Joanna's to-do list had taken a direct hit. Expecting to be off work most of December and part of January, she had originally planned to spend November's spare time focused on wrapping up election issues—finishing the legally mandated paperwork that follows an election campaign and sending out personal thank-you notes to her many supporters. Once her maternity leave started, she would have had all of December to get ready for Christmas.

Now, though, with the prospect of being back at work in early December, everything got lumped together in a hodgepodge November. Yes, she had time for cuddling and caring for her newborn infant, but in order to get everything else accomplished, too, Joanna lived a twenty-four-hour cycle—sleeping only by fits and starts and nursing every couple of hours. Luckily, Eva Lou came over and helped get the thank-you notes written and sent. Carol went out and bought a set of Christmas cards that Joanna managed to get signed and addressed in short order.

A week and a half into her maternity leave and long before either Black Friday or Cyber Monday, Joanna had gotten most of her Christmas shopping done online, with UPS stopping by the house on an almost daily basis, dropping off gifts that showed up at the door prewrapped.

In other words, Joanna was busy and productive, but was she happy? Not exactly. Halfway through the second week of her leave, she was antsy and restless. For one thing, she wasn't used to spending so much time at home. She missed the office. She missed the job and the responsibility. Most of all she missed the people. Tom Hadlock, Joanna's current chief deputy, was the man in charge during her maternity leave. She resisted the temptation to drop by the office and check on things, because it was important not to second-guess the acting sheriff or undercut his authority. Nonetheless, he called her often, giving her updates on what was happening.

There had been another high-speed chase between the Border Patrol and a coyote smuggling undocumented aliens. The unfolding incident had ended in a fiery crash near Willcox in which seven illegal immigrants and their would-be smuggler, another illegal, had all perished. Joanna's team of homicide investigators had devoted the better part of the past two weeks to tracking down the victims' real identities so that their survivors—in Mexico, El Salvador, and Honduras—could all be properly notified.

It was frustrating, time-consuming, thankless work. There were other cases that they should have been investigating. Instead a big portion of Joanna's sworn officers had spent precious hours and effort doing a job which by all rights should have been the responsibility of the federal government. That was a part of the "migrant crisis" that the open-borders folks and the news media seldom noticed or acknowledged—the added costs that accrued to local law-enforcement agencies left to pick up the pieces when the federal government failed to do its job of maintaining and policing the borders.

While the department's homicide investigators had been preoccupied with that, Acting Sheriff Hadlock, true to his jail-commander roots, had managed to see to it that the inmates' Thanksgiving dinner plans, under the auspices of the jail's recently hired chef, Wendell Marks, were laid out well in advance.

Tom Hadlock had been around long enough to remember the time, early in Joanna's tenure as sheriff, when the turkeys intended for the inmates' holiday dinner had been siphoned off by a previous jail cook who'd left town in the dark of night. No one wanted a repeat of that challenging episode.

On Friday afternoon Joanna found herself pretty much caught up with everything on her to-do list. With Sage down for her afternoon nap, Joanna had sorted through the mail that Carol had brought from the post office when she went to town to get groceries. In among the Bed Bath & Beyond coupons and the home-improvement catalogs was a first-class envelope from Butch's publisher.

At this point Butch had been a published author for a number of years. Over time Joanna had learned that authors are paid on an irregular basis. Advances on royalties are paid on signing a contract, on delivering a manuscript, on hardcover publication, and again on paperback publication. With Butch still off on tour and due back on the Wednesday before Thanksgiving, this envelope most likely contained the pub payment for his current book.

Wanting to guarantee that the important missive didn't go AWOL, Joanna ventured into Butch's office and placed it on the keyboard of his desktop computer. As she turned away, she came face-to-face with the shelves containing her father's leather-bound diaries, although "journals" probably would have been a better term. At least that was the word written in gold leaf on the spine and front cover of each volume.

The books had arrived at Joanna and Butch's home in a roundabout fashion many years after her

father's death. D. H. Lathrop had come to law enforcement later in life, having spent his early years
working as an underground miner. As first a deputy and later a sheriff, he had never been more
than a two-finger typist. Joanna remembered him
spending night after night, sometimes long after
her mother had shut off the TV and gone to bed,
laboring over the books in longhand while seated at
the dining-room table. Joanna never remembered
asking him what he was doing. She had simply
assumed it was something to do with work. Her
father had made it clear on numerous occasions
that he didn't like discussing work at home under any circumstances, except in vague good-guy/
bad-guy terminology that had charmed his daughter and made his job sound not at all dangerous
or threatening—more like a game of cowboys and
Indians than anything else.

When her father died in an incident long presumed to be an accident, Joanna saw no sign of his
books. His personal effects had been packed up and
sent home, and her mother had stowed the many
boxes in her garage. For almost two decades, they
had sat unopened on makeshift platforms on the
rafters of Eleanor's garage.

No one had been more surprised than Joanna
when her long-widowed mother had fallen in love.
Even more startling was the fact that the object of
her affections was a relatively new arrival in town,
George Winfield, the medical examiner. They
had merged households, with George moving into
Eleanor's home. As part of that process, he had
cleaned out the garage and stumbled upon the jour-

nals written by his long-dead predecessor, D. H. Lathrop. Eleanor had been of only one mind concerning those journals—get rid of them. George respectfully disagreed.

Prior to marrying Eleanor and in his role as the Cochise County medical examiner, he had worked with Joanna for years. Eleanor saw Joanna as her headstrong, opinionated daughter, while George regarded her as a respected colleague. Since she had followed in her father's law-enforcement footsteps, George felt she deserved to have access to her father's personal history.

Against his new wife's wishes, George had turned the journals over to Joanna, and Butch had taken charge of them. He shelved them in his study in strict chronological order, and there they'd remained. Twice in dealing with cold cases, Joanna had searched through the applicable volumes. Other than that, however, the books had simply languished there, gathering dust and mostly forgotten.

In Joanna's view her father had always been larger than life. She regarded him as perfection itself. Even before D. H.'s death, Joanna's unrelenting hero worship of the man had been a bone of contention between her and her mother, and once he was gone, things got worse. It was only after Eleanor's marriage to George that she had finally revealed her first husband's feet of clay, disclosing to Joanna that prior to his death her father had been involved in a longtime affair with Mona Tipton, his secretary from work.

At the time Butch had already unpacked D. H.'s

journals. In full denial, shaken by what her mother had told her, and hoping to disprove what she thought to be an unfounded allegation, Joanna had turned to the journals in search of the truth, and once she found it, the truth hurt. In among the last journal's concluding entries, Joanna learned that Eleanor was right. Her father and Mona Tipton had indeed been romantically involved. Once Eleanor became aware of her husband's infidelity, she had given him the basic her-or-me ultimatum.

The book's final entry, scribbled in Joanna's father's distinctive handwriting, indicated that he had reached a decision of some kind, but there was no accompanying hint as to what that decision might have been, because he had died right after that. With no additional entries to supply the missing information, eventually Joanna had gone to Mona Tipton herself in search of answers. In the unlikely conversation that followed—a conversation between D. H.'s grown daughter and his still-grieving mistress—Joanna had learned that the night before he died, her father had told Mona that he was breaking up with her. He had decided to cast his lot with his wife and daughter.

Joanna had vivid memories of Eleanor's tight-lipped fury at the funeral and in the days, months, and years after her husband's passing. As a teenager Joanna had attributed her mother's anger and apparent lack of grief to a lack of caring. After talking to Mona, Joanna began to suspect that Eleanor had been more crushed by her late husband's betrayal than she had been by his death.

Would things have been different if Eleanor had known that D. H. had decided to give Mona up in favor of hearth and home—in favor of staying with his wife and daughter? Joanna was left to wonder. Perhaps Eleanor had known the truth and it had made no difference. In any event it was something Joanna and her mother never discussed. The topic of how and when Eleanor had learned of her husband's affair was never broached between them. Had they been allowed more time together, a few more years maybe, they might have found a way to have that conversation, but Eleanor's unexpected death had precluded any such outcome.

Now, with Butch away, Joanna stood in his office, staring at the shelf containing her father's journals. Other than those three occasions when she'd gone looking for answers, Joanna had maintained a hands-off policy toward the books. Butch had read through them—he'd told her so—but she herself had not.

Why? she wondered now. Had she done so out of some kind of loyalty to her mother? Or maybe a sort of misguided allegiance to her father had been at work. Perhaps she suspected that there were other betrayals on her father's part lurking in those pages and hadn't wanted to uncover them.

But now Joanna's parents were both dead and gone. She was the only one left to be the actual grown-up in the room. Maybe it was time for Joanna to finally come to terms with all three versions of her own history—as her father told it, as her mother told it, and as Joanna herself told it.

And so, with trembling hands, Joanna Brady went to the first volume on the shelf, pulled the book out of its designated slot, and carried it out to the living room. There, settled in her favorite chair, while Sage slept and while Denny was safely stowed at school, Joanna turned the first page and promptly fell into a rabbit hole.

1967

I hate swing shift. I get off work and come home in the middle of the night. Usually Ellie's left something on the back of the stove for me to eat, but by then she's already in bed. I'm done with my day, ready to relax and maybe have a conversation, but like I said, Ellie's in bed. The TV stations are already off the air by then, so what am I supposed to do? Haul out the booze and drink myself into oblivion every damned night? Nope, that's what my old man did, and it's no way to live. It's also the whole reason I left West Texas, so I wouldn't turn out to be like him. Not ever.

I told Ellie I can't just sit around in the middle of the night twiddling my thumbs and waiting to get sleepy, and that's why she gave me this book for my birthday. She bought it from the stationery department at the company store. She says when it's late at night and I don't have anyone to talk to, I can talk to the book. And that's what I'm doing right now—talking to the book—and it's just as well, because what's going through my head isn't something I can talk about with anyone else, most especially her.

Because it's always the middle of the night when the house is quiet that it gets to me—when I sit around wondering where is he? What happened to our little boy, our baby? Is he in a good family? Are his adoptive parents taking proper care of him? Do they love him? He's five now and probably in kindergarten. Does he like school? Is he smart? Is he learning to read?

Most of all, does he know he's adopted? If he does, what do the people raising him tell him about us—that we didn't want him? That wasn't the case for either one of us, but Ellie's mother was and is a bitch on wheels! If Ellie didn't agree to give up the baby, her mother was going to go to the cops, have me arrested, and brought up on charges of statutory rape. So Ellie caved. She gave up the baby—and she did it for me. And the whole first year we were married, she cried herself to sleep every single night.

By the time the baby was born, Ellie's father had been transferred to Fort Benning, Georgia. She went there long enough to get her high-school diploma, but on the day she turned eighteen, she ran away from home, caught a Greyhound bus, and came straight back to Bisbee. She was waiting for me on the sidewalk one day when I came off shift at the Campbell shaft. "What are you doing here?" I asked her when she got into my truck.

"My parents can go to hell," she told me. "I

*came back to marry you, and nobody's going to
stop me. I'm eighteen now, and I've got my birth
certificate along to prove it."*

*We drove over to Lordsburg that very weekend
and got married in front of the justice of the peace.
It was the best day of my life.*

THREE

THE BOSS often went away for days at a time, leaving his prisoners chained but otherwise unguarded. The girls had discussed his absences among themselves—first just the three of them, and later, once Amelia joined them, all four of them together—theorizing about where he went and what he did while he was gone. This time, however, he had made his intentions clear. He was off hunting—but where? Latisha had no idea. Soon some other poor girl would be cast into this hellish nightmare with her, and eventually one or the other of them would die.

But for now Latisha was alone. Sandy had disappeared first. Maybe she'd gotten away, or maybe the Boss had let her go. That's what Latisha hoped. One day Sandy went upstairs and never returned. Sadie was the next to leave. Now Amelia was gone, too, with no question whatsoever about what had happened to her. Amelia hadn't escaped. There was no one left in the basement for Latisha to talk to—no stories to tell, no histories to share, only endless stretches of time where one day bled into the next, or maybe not. She sometimes awakened from sleep thinking that a whole day had passed, or a night, and maybe that wasn't true. All she had to do—all she *could* do—was think about how much she missed the others—Sandra Ruth Locke, Sadie Kaitlyn Jennings, and Amelia Diaz Salazar. She repeated their names aloud each time she thought of them, almost like a sacred chant. She didn't want to forget them, because someday, if she ever got away and lived to tell the story, Latisha wanted to let the world know about her friends and what had happened to them.

In many ways all their histories were unsurprisingly similar—fractured families and lives complicated by poverty, drug use, and other criminal activity. To begin with, and more than anything else, they talked about food. Given their stark circumstances, that was hardly surprising.

Sandy had been thirteen when her mom, Margo—a divorced, single mother—had gone to prison for writing bad checks. Sandy's father had never been "in the picture," and with Margo incarcerated, he didn't step forward then, either. Instead Sandy had gone "into the system" and had ended up in foster care. Thanks to a series of unfortunate circumstances, she'd gone through a series of foster homes.

Sandy's first placement, with Ben and Andrea Thompson, had been a revelation. Ben and Andrea were a married couple in their early forties. Ben worked long hours selling medical equipment, but he made good money. Andrea was an architect who worked out of their home, a sweet little bungalow in Van Nuys, California. Unable to have children of their own, they had signed up for foster care with the ultimate intention of adoption.

Throughout Sandy's young life, Margo hadn't come close to being Mother of the Year. She had worked sporadically, but working or not, she was seldom at home when school let out. From a very early age, Sandy was a latchkey kid with very little adult supervision. She came home from school, ate whatever was available, and then spent the evenings watching cartoons rather than doing homework. By the time she landed in foster care, she was a freshman in high school and reading at a fifth-grade level.

Once Sandy moved in with the Thompsons, Andrea set out to change all that. When Sandy came home from school, Andrea was there, more often than not with a batch of freshly baked cookies—chocolate chip or peanut butter—cooling on the kitchen counter. Then she would sit Sandy down at the kitchen table and help her with homework until Ben came home for dinner.

The idea of eating the evening meal as a family was also strange. Margo's idea of a balanced diet had been a Big Mac and a Diet Coke. For her a home-cooked meal was a Papa Murphy's bake-at-home pizza. Andrea actually cooked food for dinner each night—grilling pork chops or steaks, serving them with salads and fresh vegetables—combinations Sandy had encountered before only in school cafeterias.

"That musta been weird," Sadie had observed.

"It was," Sandy agreed. "I didn't know that things like broccoli and cauliflower could actually taste good. And I didn't know that real people ate like that, either, sitting down in an actual dining room so they could all eat together. I thought that was a thing that only happened on TV. It made me feel sort of like Cinderella. My grades started getting better. I thought I was going to be okay."

In the dark of the basement, her voice faded into silence.

"So what happened?" Latisha wanted to know.

"One day when I came home, Andrea wasn't there, and there weren't any cookies."

"How come?"

"There'd been a wreck on the 405—a multi-car wreck. Ben's car was rear-ended by a semi. He ended up with a broken neck—a quadriplegic. It's bad of me, but sometimes I found myself wishing that he'd died. Maybe that way I could have stayed with Andrea, but she told me she couldn't take care of him and me, too, so I ended up back in the system."

"And then what?"

"The next place wasn't a foster family so much as it was a foster farm. As far as the Millers were concerned, taking in foster kids was strictly a moneymaking proposition. It turns out Mr. Miller was especially fond of little girls. I was almost fifteen, so I was too old for him, but someone finally blew the whistle on him, and they ended up shutting the place down."

"And then?"

"They sent me someplace else, but by then my

grades were crap again. The dad was retired military. When he told me to shape up or ship out, I shipped. I was seventeen. I hit the streets, hooked up with a pimp, and was doing okay until I ended up here. But if I could make a wish and have it come true, I'd be back in Andrea's kitchen, stuffing my face with chocolate-chip cookies."

"What about you, Sadie?" Sandy had asked. "If you could eat anything in the world, what would it be?"

"My grandma's fried chicken," she answered at once. "No doubt about it."

"And you, Latisha?"

"Lyle's pancakes," she answered.

"Who's Lyle?"

"My stepfather," Latisha said.

"Whoa, you got a stepfather who actually cooks? I got one of those, too. Problem is, the only thing he cooks is meth, and that's how both he and my mom ended up in the slammer. But about these pancakes," Sadie continued, sticking to the topic at hand. "Buttermilk or plain?"

"Plain."

"Thick or thin?"

"Thin—really thin—with peanut butter and maple syrup."

While Sadie and Sandy went on talking about food, Latisha withdrew from the conversation. It was odd to realize how much she missed Lyle and his pancakes. When he had first shown up in her mother's life, she'd regarded Lyle Montgomery Richards as a threat and the source of all evil.

For one thing, through most of Latisha's life it

had been just her mother, Lou Ann, and her. What Latisha knew of her father came from the gold-framed photo of him in his marine dress uniform that had always sat on the chest of drawers in her mother's bedroom next to the presentation box containing the folded flag from his coffin. Corporal Samuel Honoré Marcum had perished in an IED blast near Mosul, on December 21, 2005. He was twenty-four at the time of his death and left behind a twenty-two-year-old widow and a four-year-old daughter. Latisha's first memory was of the man in the uniform kneeling in front of her mother and handing her that carefully folded flag—all blue and white, her mother had told her, with no red showing.

After the funeral they had gone to live with Lou Ann's mother, Granny Lou, in her shotgun house on Gaty Avenue in East St. Louis. Granny Lou wasn't your basic sweetness-and-light kind of grandmother. A diabetic who had lost both legs, she was a wheelchair-bound, mean-spirited, and cantankerous old woman, one who needed her daughter's help every bit as much as Lou Ann and Latisha needed a place to stay.

Lou Ann had some widow's benefits coming in, and she contributed most of that to the household expenses. She also looked after her mother, doing the bulk of the cooking and cleaning. But Lou Ann was also determined to improve herself in order to provide a better life for Latisha. To that end she had enrolled in the four-year nursing program at St. Louis University. The fact that she could leave

Latisha at home with Granny Lou was the only thing that made the two-hour commute and long days of classes remotely possible.

And then one day, when Latisha was nine, Lou Ann had come home with Lyle. He was more than ten years older than her mother—thirty-nine to Lou Ann's twenty-seven—and a lifelong bachelor. Like Latisha's father, Lyle had served in the Middle East—U.S. Army rather than Marine Corps. Now out of the service, he drove the #10 bus, and they had met in the course of Lou Ann's daily commute. He was the driver on the #10 bus that took her from Seventeenth and Missouri to the MetroLink. Over time they had become friends. Now they were about to become more than friends, and Latisha was less than thrilled.

During the long hours when Lou Ann was at school, Granny Lou had ostensibly been in charge, but her babysitting skills were minimal. She was much more engaged in watching whatever was on TV than she was in watching Latisha, who was allowed far greater freedom of action than was probably good for her.

By the time Lyle appeared on the scene, Latisha was in the fifth grade at Dunbar Elementary, the neighborhood's perennially underachieving school. The fact that Latisha was bringing home indifferent grades from a failing school was a problem for Lou Ann and an even bigger problem for Lyle. He had grown up in University City, another area not known for its outstanding public schools, but his devoutly Catholic parents had seen to it that he attended Christ the King School, and he came away with a solid education, one that had served him well when he went on to University City High School.

When it came to courting Lou Ann Marcum, Latisha's education was one of Lyle's big selling points. He had inherited his parents' two-story, three-bedroom home on Amherst Avenue in University City, and that's where he continued to live. He assured Lou Ann that if she married him, he'd see to it that Latisha got into Christ the King, too.

By then Lou Ann had been a widow for close to a quarter of her life, and she had spent almost that whole time caring for her mother. Over time Granny Lou's situation had deteriorated. Now, in addition to being wheelchair-bound, she was virtually blind. Not only did she require more care than Lou Ann could provide, she was almost useless when it came to supervising the headstrong Latisha.

So Lyle, a fixer at heart, had asked Lou Ann to marry him and had come out with all guns blazing, suggesting a nearby assisted-living facility for Granny Lou in addition to a better education for Latisha. It should have been no contest, but he hadn't taken into consideration that Granny Lou, a lifetime Baptist, would raise holy hell not only about her daughter's marrying a Catholic but also about his idea of putting Latisha into one of those "dirty papist" schools.

The battle lines had been drawn—with Lyle Richards and Lou Ann on one side and Granny Lou and Latisha on the other. When Lou Ann converted so she and Lyle could have a church wedding, Granny Lou threw a hissy fit and refused to attend. She also insisted that she'd rather die than be stuck in some bedbug-infested nursing home. While Lyle and Lou Ann went off on their honeymoon, Latisha had stayed with Granny Lou, listening to her rant and rave. When the newlyweds returned and it was time for Latisha to move to her new home on the far side of the river, she wasn't exactly a willing participant.

Lyle had never been married. He'd never had kids. He thought children were to do as they were told and to be seen but not heard. He wanted Latisha to go to school, pay attention, study, and get good grades. He wanted her to keep her room clean and respect her elders. Latisha wanted none of it, except for Saturday-morning breakfasts. That was when Lyle Richards routinely made and served his incredibly wonderful pancakes.

But now, from the vantage point of Latisha's solitary cot, with her leg chained to the wall and with dry kibble her only food, she thought about Lyle Richards a lot. He was someone who couldn't help himself. He was always saying dorky things to her and giving her what she thought was stupid advice: What's to be done is best begun. By the inch it's a cinch; by the yard it's hard. If it is to be, it is up to me. God helps those who help themselves.

She could see now that he'd been a kind man who had wanted only the best both for her and for her mother, and she wished she could tell him that she was sorry—sorry for everything.

In the background Sandy and Sadie were still talking about food, while Latisha thought about the people back home. When Lou Ann and Latisha moved out, Granny Lou had disdained her daughter's suggestion about moving into assisted living. Just because Lou Ann had her nursing degree, that didn't mean Granny Lou had to listen to her. Assuring Lou Ann that she'd have no trouble hiring someone to take over Lou Ann's caregiving responsibilities, Granny Lou had insisted on staying on in her own place. Not surprisingly, when the new hired help arrived, they didn't amount to much. Less than two months after Lou Ann and Latisha moved out, Granny Lou had died alone in her bed after falling into a diabetic coma. Her funeral at Southern Missionary Baptist Church on State Street had been sparsely attended. It was also the last time Latisha had set foot in East St. Louis.

But what about her mother and Lyle? Were they worried about her? Did they suspect that something bad had happened to her? Did they even know she'd gone missing? Did they still care? And what were they doing now? Just before Latisha ran away with Trayvon, her mother had gotten a job working the night shift in the ER at Kindred Hospital. Was she still working there? And what about Lyle? Latisha supposed he was still driving a bus, but was he still making those wonderful pancakes on Saturday mornings?

FOUR

ACTING SHERIFF Tom Hadlock leaned back in his chair, put his hands over his eyes, and closed them. It was four thirty on Friday afternoon. He had almost made it through his second week of being in charge of the Cochise County Sheriff's Department. That meant he had to live through a little more than two weeks and survive two more board of supervisors meetings before Joanna came back from maternity leave. Compared to sitting through those meetings, running the jail had been a breeze.

Kristin Gregovich—Joanna's secretary and currently filling that role for Tom—popped her head in the door. "They're here," she said. "Are you ready to come meet Mojo? I just took Spike outside so the two of them could meet."

On the night of Jeremy Stock's suicide, it had been Joanna's K-9 unit—Kristin's husband, Terry, and his dog, Spike—who had risen to the occasion. Joanna might well have died of gunshot wounds herself had Spike not lunged to her rescue. The brave dog had taken a bullet intended for Joanna and had suffered severe injuries. Four months later Spike had recovered better than anyone thought possible, but his days of active-duty K-9 work were over, and that was where Mojo came in.

Years earlier Joanna's department had taken down a pit-bull puppy mill that had been in operation near Bowie in the northeast corner of the county. Joanna had brought the starving, mistreated animals home to Bisbee and had put her jail inmates to work fostering the animals. The mommy dogs especially had required extensive socializing before they were ready for adoption.

Joanna's participation in that case had put her and her department in the crosshairs of any number of animal-rescue organizations. The Pit-Bull Brigade was an organization located outside Dallas that specialized in taking abandoned pit bulls from shelters, rehabbing them, and preparing them to perform law-enforcement duties. Some were trained to do drug interdictions. Others specialized in bomb or cadaver sniffing. Still others, the top dogs, were deemed worthy of K-9 training.

Spike and Terry had come to Joanna's department as a matched set, having served together in the military. When it became apparent that the severity of Spike's injuries made it unlikely that he would ever be able to return to duty, Joanna had gone looking for a replacement. Spike was a purebred German shepherd, but the cost of finding an exact substitute was prohibitive. That was when she had stumbled across the Pit-Bull Brigade. While the organization was mostly involved in training dogs, it also trained people, giving them the necessary qualifications to be hired as K-9 officers themselves. The dogs came from shelters and were mostly free; the people paid tuition. That meant that a dog trained at PBB could be purchased for a fraction of the price charged by other K-9 dog-training entities.

With an eye on her budget, that's where Sheriff Brady had gone looking. The director had suggested a dog named Mojo as a possible candidate, and she had dispatched Terry to Texas to meet the dog and see what he thought. After declaring all things a go, he had spent the past two weeks in Texas, working and training with Mojo before driving the dog home to Bisbee.

"Where are they?" Tom asked, pushing back his chair.

"Out in the parking lot," Kristin said.

By the time Tom and Kristin made it out to the parking lot, Terry was crouched down on one knee with a dog on either side of him. If there had been any stiff-legged interaction between the two animals when they met, that was over.

"Looks just like Petey," Tom said.

"Petey?" Terry asked. "Who's Petey?"

"Didn't you ever see the Little Rascals on TV? I think Petey was a Staffordshire terrier instead of a pit bull, but Mojo looks just like him."

"I was thinking he's more like the dog on the Target commercials," Kristin said.

"That, too, I suppose," Tom allowed. "How'd he do in the car?"

"Slept most of the time," Terry answered. "He's a good traveler. Loves Burger King."

"That makes two of us," Tom said.

"Chief Deputy Hadlock?" Sunny Sloan's voice came through the radio attached to the shoulder of the chief deputy's uniform. Some people called him "Acting Sheriff." Some called him "Chief Deputy." Tom Hadlock answered to both.

"I'm out back in the parking lot, Sunny. What's up?"

Sunny was the widow of a fallen deputy, Dan Sloan. She had come to work as a clerk for the department in the aftermath of her husband's death and following the birth of their baby. Believing that her department should take care of its own, Joanna had hired Sunny to work the reception desk out in the public lobby.

"There's someone here to see you," Sunny said.

"Can you tell me who it is and what it's about?"

"It's a Mrs. Carver from Douglas—June Carver and her son, Jack. All she would say is that it's urgent and they need to speak to you directly."

Tom glanced at his watch. The idea of leaving work at five had just gone out the window. "Okay," he said. "Give me a minute to get back to my desk."

Minutes later Sunny escorted the new arrivals into his office. June Carver was a tall, slender woman with ash-blond hair and generous curves in all the right places. The permanent scowl imprinted on her face made her look as though she was mad enough to chew nails. She was trailed by an even taller, half-grown kid. He was lanky and scrawny and appeared to be somewhere in his midteens. The boy paused uncertainly in the doorway as if reluctant to enter.

"Come on," his mother ordered. "Get your butt in here!"

Jack Carver shuffled into the room, staring at his feet rather than looking anyone in the eye. It wasn't until he approached the desk that Tom noticed Jack was lugging what appeared to be a worn leather bowling bag.

"Put it there," his mother commanded, pointing to an empty spot on Tom's otherwise cluttered desk.

When the kid placed the bag on the desk as he'd been told, it landed with an alarmingly heavy thud.

Tom had risen to his feet in order to welcome the new arrivals. "I'm Acting Sheriff Thomas Hadlock," he said, offering his hand. "I'm standing in for Sheriff Brady, who's currently on maternity leave. And you are?"

"I'm June Carver." The woman responded to his greeting with a surprisingly firm handshake of her own. "This is my son, Jack."

The kid's limp, halfhearted handshake was nothing at all like his mother's.

"Won't you both please have a seat?" Tom invited.

June sat down, perching primly on the front edge of her chair, while her son flopped loosely into his, as though his legs had suddenly turned to jelly.

"How can I be of service?" Tom asked.

"Tell him," June ordered. "Tell him now."

"We didn't mean to do anything wrong," Jack began in a self-effacing whimper, but his mother wasn't having any of it.

"Cut the excuses and tell him," she snapped.

"Me and my friend Randy went out hunting," he began.

"My friend and I," June corrected. "And you need to get real. They weren't out hunting—they were out poaching. They ditched school, made off with Randy's father's shotgun without permission, and then went after quail without either one of them having a hunting license! Their harebrained plan was for Randy to shoot and clean the birds while Jack was supposed to cook 'em. What a joke! The most this dork has ever managed to cook in his life is mac and cheese—and he only makes that work because it comes straight out of the box."

"We looked up how to do it on the Internet," Jack whined. "We watched the video and everything."

"Hah," his mother snorted. "Sure you did."

"Besides," Jack continued, "we didn't get anything. We didn't see any quail. In fact, Randy never even fired the gun."

"Tell him why," June urged.

Jack hesitated for a moment before he answered. "Because we found something else," he said meekly.

"When did all this happen?" Tom asked. "Today?"

"No," Jack said. "It was early in October during quail season. We thought there would be other hunters out there, and the place we went was so far out of town we didn't think we'd get caught."

"Did you get caught?" Tom asked.

"No," Jack answered.

"Then what's so urgent about talking to me today?" Tom asked.

June butted in with an answer before her son had a chance. "My husband works for the Border Patrol," she explained. "He's being transferred to Tucson. He lives in an apartment up there during the week while Jack and I stay on here in Douglas so he can finish out his senior year and I can get the house ready to sell. We were planning on painting his room this weekend. This morning when I went to clean out his closet, that's what I found." She nodded accusingly toward the offending bag.

"And that is?"

"Well," she urged her son, "what are you waiting for? Open up the damned bag and show him."

"Do I have to?" Jack whined.

"Yes, you have to," June snarled back at him. "You don't have the option of going all squeamish on me now. It's a little late for that."

Reluctantly, Jack leaned forward, unzipped the bag, and dug inside with both hands. What he pulled out was a human skull—or at least what was left of a human skull. Even from across the desk, Tom could see the single bullet hole in the rounded back of the sun-bleached bone. The front of the skull was a shattered mess—entrance wound, exit wound. The victim, whoever he or she was, had been shot in the back of the head at what was likely point-blank range.

"Where the hell did you get that?" Tom demanded.

"We found it," Jack said miserably, carefully returning the skull to the bag. "Out in the Peloncillos east of Douglas. It was just lying there out in the open, all by itself. I thought maybe we'd stumbled on an old Apache burial ground or something. I didn't think anyone would care about some old dead Indian, so we brought it home—sort of like those steer heads people put on their fence posts sometimes."

"You kept it as a trophy, you mean?"

"I guess," Jack admitted, squirming uncomfortably in his seat.

"Do you realize that in the state of Arizona interfering with a human corpse is a class-C felony?" Tom asked.

Jack nodded. "I do now," he said. "Mom told me."

Tom glanced back toward June Carver. "Are you an attorney?" he asked.

"Hardly," she said. "I looked it up on the Internet. But I'm a mother, and I know a little something about how this game is played."

"What game?"

"Long ago, on a planet far away, I used to be a stripper, so I know how law enforcement works. Jack's already signed up with a recruiter to join the army once he graduates from high school next May. His grades aren't good enough to get him into college right now. His father and I are hoping the military can help him get his act together.

"The problem is, if he ends up with some kind of juvenile conviction hanging over his head, that's not going to happen. We're here. We brought you evidence of a homicide. You haven't read Jack his rights, so none of what he just said to you is admissible. And if you want him to show you where this skull came from, you won't be charging him, and you won't be charging Randy, either. Deal?"

Tom looked back and forth between June Carver and her son. Jack sat with his head bowed and in such a state of abject misery that Tom couldn't help but feel sorry for him. His impression was that there was nothing the justice system could hand the kid that would come close to measuring up to what his mother was prepared to dish out, and with June Carver, Tom suspected, there would be no room for legal loopholes or appeals.

"I think I can live with that," he said. "So where was this?"

"On the far side of the San Bernardino Valley in the Peloncillos, on the way to Paramore Crater. I can't tell you where we were exactly, but I can show you."

Tom glanced out the window. The Peloncillos, the "Little Baldies," were a forty-mile-long mountain range standing astride the Arizona–New Mexico border. Getting to that remote area of the county would take the better part of two hours at least and would entail driving on extremely primitive roads.

This far into November, it was already nearly sunset—much too late to send a group of investigators on a nighttime trek out into the desert in search of human remains. Had the homicide been recent—one that had occurred this very day, for instance—there would have been a need to track down valuable evidence before it was lost. In that case it would have been easy to justify hauling in generators and light stanchions. But this crime had been cold long before Jack Carver and his pal stumbled across that skull.

Hadlock turned away from the window and focused on the boy. "Did you have anything to do with what happened to this individual?" he demanded.

"God n-no," the boy stammered in an anguished whisper. "I wouldn't do something like that. I couldn't."

The poor kid looked as though he was going to puke on the spot, but Tom waited a little longer before putting him out of his misery.

"I think there's a good chance you're telling me the truth," Tom said after a pause, "so here's what we're going to do. I'm going to take charge of this bag and drop it off where it belongs—which happens to be at the M.E.'s office up in Old Bisbee. Tomorrow morning I'll have one of my homicide investigators come by your place, pick up both you and your mother, and we'll all take a little field trip out to the Peloncillos. Since you're a minor, you can't be interviewed in any fashion without a parent present. Your mother will be along in the car with you as a safeguard for her and for us—so we can demonstrate that there was no wrongdoing on our part or on yours."

"Will we be, like, in handcuffs or something?" Jack asked.

"No handcuffs," Tom said, "and you will not be in custody, because I'm a man of my word. If my officers find evidence that later suggests there was some connection between you and the victim, then all bets are off. Should that happen—should you become an actual suspect—that's when investigators will be required to read you your rights. In the meantime your mother is correct. Nothing you have said in this office today and nothing you say in a car tomorrow can be used against you in a court of law. Is that clear?"

"Yes, sir."

"But if you renege on your part of the deal and don't take my investigators back to the place where you found this—"

"Believe me," June Carver interrupted. "Jack will keep his end of the bargain. I'll see to it."

"I'm sure you will," Tom Hadlock replied.

That's what the acting sheriff said aloud, but his thoughts were elsewhere. It occurred to him that if Jack Carver ever did make it into the military, basic training would be a breeze. The poor kid had been raised by a drill sergeant and didn't even know it.

FIVE

LATISHA MARCUM awakened to darkness and to the blessing of absolute silence. Even in her sleep, she had been haunted by the quiet thumping that she'd at first mistaken as the sound of an approaching thunderstorm and by the faint scratchings that she had assumed to be the plague of a new generation of rats. It wasn't until the next day that she learned the awful truth.

The day before, the Boss had come downstairs and selected Amelia as his current choice of amusement. While he used the key from his pocket to unlock the chain around the girl's thin ankle, Latisha had lain on her own filthy mattress, fully awake under her blanket but feigning sleep and all the while uttering a silent prayer of gratitude that he'd chosen Amelia instead of her.

Latisha had gone upstairs on numerous occasions, and she knew exactly what went on. First she heard the water running in the old claw-foot bathtub overhead. When he took one of the girls upstairs with him, that's what he always demanded first—that she bathe. He wanted them to be clean. Afterward they were required to do whatever he wanted. If they did well, they were rewarded by being brought back downstairs and clamped back into their chains. On occasion, presumably when they didn't do well, they didn't return.

So when Latisha heard the water running, she knew what that felt like—wanting desperately to be clean instead of filthy but knowing that the price of that bath was what would come later. It was what Lyle, her stepfather, would have called "damned if you do, damned if you don't."

To her surprise, however, while the water was still running in the bathroom upstairs, the basement door banged open, the bare bulb came back on again, and planks of the stairway groaned under the weight of the Boss's lumbering tread. Thinking he was coming for her, too, Latisha shrank beneath her blanket. When she didn't feel his hand on her ankle, she peered out from under the edge.

He seemed to be doing something at the bottom of the stairway. She heard a rustling sound and a series of thuds, as if something heavy were falling against something else. At last the lid of the freezer slammed shut. Moments later he slung two bulky and seemingly weighty garbage bags over his shoulder and marched back upstairs.

It seemed like an odd time to decide to empty a freezer. The old appliance had been there all along. Often, in the long silences of the night, the sound of the freezer compressor switching on and switching off was the only thing to be heard in the darkened dungeon. But until now the Boss had never taken anything out of it, at least not to Latisha's knowledge.

After a while the awful sounds resumed upstairs. The bath was over now, and Latisha knew what came next. It was all a game to him, starting slowly enough before escalating into the frenzied sounds of bare fists hammering on yielding flesh. There would be shouts of unspeakable demands followed by first cries and later whimpers of pain. Finally the unmistakable squealing of the box springs of the old double bed in one corner of the room and the thudding as the iron bed frame pounded the wall would indicate that the session was at last coming to its soul-shattering conclusion.

To keep from listening, Latisha threw off her single blanket and rose from her filthy mattress. Then, taking her tin drinking cup with her, she limped her way through the gloom, as far as her chain would stretch, to the concrete slab in the back corner where the surprisingly modern toilet had been installed. A row of three thick glass blocks near the top of the outside wall just over the toilet allowed a tiny bit of light into this one section of the basement during daytime hours. Now, though, as the sun set outside, the gloom inside the dungeon was thickening. Soon the basement prison would once again be cloaked in total darkness.

Latisha knew she was weak and getting weaker. It took all her strength to pry the lid off the flushing tank so she could fill her cup with water. She set the lid on top of the toilet and somehow managed to keep it balanced there while she gulped down three cups of water. Early on she had asked the other two prisoners in the room why they couldn't just leave the lid off to begin with. Wouldn't that be easier?

"We tried that once," Sandra had explained. "The next day there was a drowned rat floating in the flushing tank."

Latisha hadn't wanted to drink the water at all after that, but by then the dead rat was long gone, and besides, she didn't have a choice. It was either drink the water from the tank or die of thirst.

Still trying to shut out whatever was happening upstairs, Latisha limped back to her mattress. The clamp around her ankle was too tight, and the flesh underneath had been rubbed raw. She used some of the precious water from her cup to try to clean the wound. She didn't want to develop some kind of terrible infection and die, because Latisha Marcum didn't want to die. She wanted to live.

Once again in her corner of the room, she sank down onto the mattress. It was full-on dark now. She felt around blindly until she located the covered plastic storage container that held her food. Back home her mother had always kept the fridge stocked with Ziploc containers, all of them full of leftovers. Here the covered dishes were necessary for the same reason the toilet tank had to be closed—to keep the rats out.

Latisha pried off the plastic lid, plucked out a single piece of kibble, and put it into her mouth. Even now she had to fight back the impulse to gag. Dog kibble wasn't supposed to be suitable for humans. It tasted horrible. Eating it often left Latisha with agonizing stomach cramps and painfully difficult bowel movements, to say nothing of at least one broken tooth, one that ached constantly now and made it impossible for her to chew on the right side of her mouth. All that aside, though, there was enough nourishment in the dog food to keep her alive, and that was what Latisha had decided. No matter what, she would live. Somehow she would live.

She'd been sitting there slowly chewing on a piece of kibble when, after a period of relative quiet, things upstairs had suddenly gotten much worse. First she heard a dull thud, as though someone had fallen to the floor. Then, without warning, the door at the top of the stairs opened once more. As the single bare bulb dangling in the middle of the room flashed on, Latisha did the same thing Sadie and Sandy had done. She covered her face with her blanket and lay there waiting to hear the sound of the clamp being fastened around Amelia's ankle—waiting for him to leave.

But this time the chain didn't rattle. There were odd sounds from the far end of the room, but that was it. Once the door at the top of the stairs slammed shut, she reached out toward the neighboring blanket and whispered Amelia's name, but there was no answer. Alone in the basement for the very first time, Latisha cried herself to sleep.

She had awakened much later to what she thought was the distant sound of thunder and the scratching of the rats. At least that's what she told herself in the middle of the night when she first heard them, but now she knew the truth about those awful sounds. The Boss had locked Amelia inside that freezer and left her to die. The dull poundings and frantic clawings that had awakened Latisha had been Amelia's desperate attempts to escape. Eventually the sounds had faded away to nothing—at least in the basement, but not in Latisha's heart and soul, because she heard them still, every time she closed her eyes, and they haunted every moment of Latisha's restless sleep.

All of that had happened days ago now. The next morning, or maybe the one after that, when the door at the top of the stairs opened once again, Latisha had shivered with dread, expecting that the Boss was coming for her this time. Instead he stopped beside the freezer, dropped a tarp on the earthen floor, and spread it open.

With Latisha peeking out from under her blanket, he unlocked the padlock and then wrestled Amelia's crouching, frozen body out of the freezer. Once he had her loose, he dropped her onto the tarp and then rolled it into a bundle. When he picked up the tarp, the shape of her frozen flesh made for an unwieldy, awkward load, and it was a struggle for him to lug it upstairs. That time he left the basement without bothering to turn off the light. A few minutes later, he returned, coming back down the stairs with another Ziploc container loaded with kibble.

"I'll be gone for a couple of days, so you need to make this last," he told her, placing it at the end of Latisha's mattress. "I'm going hunting. I'll be bringing back a new friend for both of us."

And then he was gone. He disappeared upstairs, the light went off, and Latisha heard the door being bolted shut. Heavy footsteps trod across the plank flooring, and another door slammed shut. A few minutes later, she heard the sound of a vehicle starting up and driving away.

Long after the Boss had left, Latisha lay on the bed drowning in despair and wallowing in grief. She wept for herself and for Amelia, for Sandra and for Sadie and for however many others there might have been before and however many others might come later. When her tears were finally exhausted and the racking sobs subsided, just one sound remained in her universe—the nightmare hum of the freezer, still plugged in and still running— switching on, switching off. In the overpowering darkness that was the only thing still there—the sound of the freezer. It had killed Amelia, and Latisha was pretty sure it would kill her, too.

SIX

THAT FRIDAY evening Joanna managed to have both kids down and asleep before Butch called after his Friends of the Library dinner event in Oklahoma City. He was off on what most people would regard as an exotic book tour, but as he and Joanna talked about the kids and what was happening at High Lonesome Ranch, Joanna could tell he was homesick. The tour was going fine, but Butch was ready to be home, and the time between Friday and Wednesday, when he was scheduled to return, seemed like forever away.

"How are things going at work?" he asked finally.

"After all that mess with the carload of dead illegals, Tom Hadlock got hit over the head with another homicide case just this afternoon."

"What happened?"

"A kid from Douglas turned up at the Justice Center late today lugging an old bowling bag with a skull inside it—a human skull showing signs of a single bullet hole. According to the kid, he and a buddy found it a couple of months ago when they were out in the Peloncillos shooting quail. Rather than reporting what they'd seen, the kid brought the skull home and hid it in his closet. That lasted until this morning, when his mother found it and frog-marched her son into the department to report it."

"Good mom," Butch breathed in clear admiration.

Joanna laughed. "I guess," she said. "According to Tom, the mother is a piece of work. She brought the kid in and had him confess to finding the skull before Tom had any idea about what was going on. Since he had no way of knowing that a crime had been committed, he hadn't bothered to read the kid his rights."

"Shrewd move on the mother's part, because that makes whatever the kid said to him totally inadmissible."

"Exactly," Joanna agreed. "Tom's having Deb Howell take the lead on the investigation, because he thinks she'll be able to handle the mother in a way Ernie Carpenter and Jaime Carbajal probably couldn't. Deb is supposed to pick up the kid and his mother and drive them out to the scene tomorrow to get a better idea of what's there. Tom says he's making arrangements for the M.E. and the crime-scene folks to tag along."

"I trust none of this is making you feel as though you need to jump right back in the saddle?" Butch asked.

"Not so far," Joanna answered with a laugh. "I think Tom has a pretty good handle on things. It all happened late this afternoon, but he's already delivered the skull, bowling bag and all, to the M.E.'s office uptown. Kendra Baldwin will be bringing her team along to the Peloncillos tomorrow in case there are more remains out there in addition to the skull. But don't worry about me. I have no intention of going. Lugging an infant around a crime scene just isn't in the cards."

"Glad to hear it," Butch said, sounding relieved. "You had me worried for a minute."

There was a sudden pause in the conversation, something Butch picked up on. "Is there anything else?" he asked.

Joanna took a deep breath. "Actually, there is," she said at last. "I had no idea both my dad and my mother grieved so much over giving that first baby up for adoption."

"You've started reading your father's diaries." It was a statement—a confirmation rather than a question.

"Yes," Joanna answered. "From the way Mother reacted when Bob Brundage finally came looking for his birth family, I knew how much she must have grieved over having to give him up, but until now I never knew that my father grieved, too. I can't help but wish that Dad had had the chance to meet that long-lost boy of his."

"Why wouldn't your father grieve?" Butch asked. "Isn't it a little sexist on your part to think he wouldn't have been as affected by the loss of his son as she was?"

"Guilty as charged," Joanna admitted, "but I still wish you had mentioned some of it."

"It was a part of your history I didn't think you were ready to hear."

"And I may not be even now," Joanna added. "I'm still on the first volume—the one from 1967. Obviously Dad didn't get the diary-writing memo that says you're supposed to keep track of the dates. So it's just stream of consciousness, and you have to pick up from context what time of year it is. His birthday was in April, and the journal was a present from my mom, so I guess he started writing sometime after that. But it's weird. Reading the journal entries, I feel like I'm doing time travel and eavesdropping on my parents' private lives long before I was even a blip on their radar."

"Is that so wrong?"

"It's just . . ."

"Look," Butch said. "Your father died when you were fifteen—just a kid. He had no way of knowing that years in the future you'd follow him into law enforcement. Yes, if you read the journals, you'll learn a lot about him, but you know what else? You'll also learn a lot about you. In addition, you'll have the benefit of some very wise fatherly advice, not only about how to be a parent but also about how to be a cop. So here's what I say—keep on reading. And you know what else? I may just take a page out of your father's book and start doing the same thing—keeping a journal. Not in a leather-bound book—more likely on the computer. And why would I do that? Because one of these days, once I'm gone and you're gone and there's no one left to tell our story, Sage and Denny and maybe even Jenny will be able to learn something about us that they didn't know before."

Butch paused then, as if to take a breath. "Oops," he added, finally noticing from Joanna's long silence that he'd been in full-on rant mode. "Did I go too far and step in it?"

Butch seldom had that much to say, but on those rare occasions when he did, Joanna had learned to pay attention.

"No," she told him. "I don't think you went too far at all."

When I was growing up, what I wanted more than anything was to be a Texas Ranger, because being a Texas Ranger was the exact opposite of anything my worthless father would ever be or do.

When I left home and came to Arizona, hoping to work in the mines, that's one of the reasons I settled on Bisbee—because this is where Texas John Slaughter came. Cochise County felt like the Old West to me. Tombstone was here—the town too tough to die. The shoot-out at the O.K. Corral was here, and so were Wyatt Earp and the Clanton Gang. I wanted to be part of it.

Last week I saw an ad in the paper that the sheriff's department is hiring. I'm close to the top of the age bracket to get in, so it's pretty much now or never. When I checked out the pay scale, I can see it would mean a big drop in pay compared to what I make working underground. Ellie and I would have to cut corners, of course, but we could probably make it. When I mentioned it to Ellie, she hit the roof. Why would I even think of giving up a sure thing like working in the mines to go to work as a cop?

Except that's what I've always wanted to do—be a cop, and if I can keep the bills paid and food on the table, why the hell not? Yes, Ellie's my wife, but why should she get to say where I spend eight hours a day of my life for the next umpteen years? Because working underground in the dark is not a walk in the park. It's a dirty, mind-numbing, soul-killing job. Sure, there's a lot of high jinks and joking around and banter and stuff, but the guys in the stopes sure as hell don't want their kids working underground. They want them to go on to college and get an education and make something of themselves. Do as I say, not as I do.

If we still had our son, I'm sure I'd feel exactly the same way and do everything in my power to keep him from choosing "the sure thing." I'd want to encourage him to go after what he wants to do—what makes him happy rather than what pays the bills.

But of course we don't have our son. He's forever lost to us. We don't have any kids at all and most likely never will, so again, why shouldn't I do what I want to do?

I don't think this is the kind of discussion Ellie expected me to have when she gave me this journal and told me to "talk to the book." But it turns out that talking to the book is helping me. It's making

*me think about stuff that I might not think about
otherwise.*

The deadline for applications is next week.
We'll see what happens.

Unable to read any further, Joanna closed the
book, turned off the lamp, and sat in the quiet
darkness of the living room, thinking. Lady, Joanna's rescued Australian shepherd, lay on the sofa
beside her while Jenny's deaf black Lab, Lucky,
sprawled at her feet. With Jenny away at school,
Lucky now literally dogged Joanna's heels wherever
she went.

Absently stroking Lady's soft coat, Joanna realized that in reading that passage she had just caught
a glimpse of her father on the cusp of making a
life-and-death decision, and one that had indeed
cost him his life years later. It was the same decision
Joanna herself had made nine years earlier, and the
circumstances of their separate decision-making
processes couldn't have been more different.

At the time her father had been a married
man—for all intents and purposes a childless married man—with no hint that another child, Joanna,
would ever come into his life. He had entered
law enforcement as the fulfillment of a lifelong
ambition. His working underground had been a
chore, one he had done out of duty—to support the
woman who'd given up so much to marry him—and
he'd gone into law enforcement over her express
objections. Being a deputy was something D. H.
Lathrop had wanted, something Eleanor had not.

Joanna had landed in law enforcement almost by accident—not because it was what she'd always wanted to do. She hadn't chosen that profession because her father had been a cop, and not exactly because her husband had been a cop, either. Her first husband, Andrew Roy Brady, had been a deputy sheriff who had gone to war with his boss at the time, Sheriff Walter McFadden. Andy had decided to run for office against what he regarded to be a corrupt administration. Joanna had supported his effort without really understanding how deep the corruption ran or how dangerous it could be.

When candidate Andrew Brady was gunned down in a hail of bullets and subsequently died, Joanna hadn't even considered the idea that she might run for office in his place. She didn't remember for sure if it was at Andy's funeral or at the reception afterward when someone had first broached the subject of her taking up Andy's cause and running for office in his place.

At first it seemed like a joke to her. She was a widow—a single mother with a nine-year-old child. And yet after more and more people asked her, she finally agreed—not because she thought she'd win, not because she had wanted to win, and certainly not out of an overriding desire to be sheriff. It had simply seemed right somehow. And when she finally did win, that had seemed right, too.

Now she was sheriff in the same way her father, D. H. Lathrop, had been sheriff. He'd earned it, and so had she—by doing the job. And that's how she thought of herself now—as a sheriff rather than as a wife or a mother or a woman or anything else for that matter. Where had that come from? Was it in her DNA? Had D. H. Lathrop bequeathed his own law-enforcement ambitions to his daughter? Was that her inheritance?

And that being the case, what kind of inheritance was Joanna leaving her own children?

A tiny wail of protest from Sage's nursery indicated it was time for one final round of nursing and diaper changing before Joanna could go to bed. It was also time for her to stop ruminating about being a sheriff or a wife or a daughter and concentrate on being a mother.

SEVEN

THE VOICES of the other girls had offered some small measure of comfort in the darkness. They told one another stories; kept one another company. After Amelia showed up, she sometimes sang to them. Her songs were always in Spanish. She said they were ones she had learned from her grandmother. Latisha hadn't understood a word of them, but Amelia had a pretty voice, and Latisha liked hearing her sing.

Sadie, who managed to make jokes out of almost everything, had said it was like sitting around a campfire telling ghost stories, only there was no fire and no marshmallows. With Latisha on her own, there was still no fire, and instead of ghost stories or songs there were only ghosts.

She remembered that one of her teachers at Christ the King—a nun named Sister Martha who hadn't worn a habit—had told the class that all civilizations had their origin stories—tales that told where they came from and why. The same thing was true of the girls in the basement.

"I don't think I was the first," Sandra had told Latisha early on. "I think someone else was here before I got here, but she was gone before I came along."

"But where did you come from?" Latisha had asked. "And when?"

"From California," Sandy replied. "It was winter and raining. I was living with a couple of girls in a tent in a homeless camp in Orange County when a guy came through recruiting for a PHT."

"A what?"

"A panhandling team. He said he'd give us a place to stay and something to eat. Each morning he would drive us around in a van, drop us off at various locations with handmade signs, and then come back to pick us up late in the afternoon. Once we divided up that day's take, he'd give us a ride back to the crash pad. There were nine of us squatting in a bank-owned two-bedroom house, but we all had beds and running water, so it beat sleeping on the beach. It beat being here."

"How did you meet him?" Latisha asked.

They all knew who "him" was—the Boss. They didn't know his name, but he was the man who had brought them here, the lord of their universe, the one in control, the one with the power of life and death.

"The house was in Valencia, but we mostly worked freeway entrances, gas stations, truck stops along I-5. I liked the truck stops best. Most of the drivers were good guys. It was a really cold day in January, and I was working the entrance to a Flying J. There had been snow on the Grapevine, so there were lots of trucks parked and waiting for the weather to clear. I was standing outside, shivering—not having a decent coat and looking cold and miserable always made for better money. So this guy comes out of the restaurant and hands me a cup of hot chocolate—at least that's what he said it was. I was cold, and the cocoa was warm, so I drank it. And it tasted good, but right after I drank it, I started feeling funny. The next thing I knew, I woke up in a bed behind the cab of his truck, tied hand and foot with duct tape over my mouth."

"And you?" Latisha asked, facing toward the sound of Sadie's voice even though Sadie herself was invisible.

"I was hitchhiking in Oregon," came the answer. "I'd gone to Oregon with a guy I knew. Charlie was older than me, but he had a car, a job offer in Portland, and he was willing to take me along for the ride. I wanted out of North Carolina in the worst way, and off we went. I didn't find out until days later that he was into drugs big time. When we got to Oregon, naturally the job offer didn't pan out. We were living in a homeless camp in Portland when Charlie died of an overdose. It was cold as hell, and I didn't know anyone there, so I decided to head back home—hitchhiking. I didn't get far. The Boss offered me a ride somewhere south of Eugene. And here I am."

"When was this?" Latisha asked.

"Charlie died on Valentine's Day. The Boss picked me up a few days later."

"So we were about a month apart, then," Latisha said. "He got me the middle of March."

"Where?"

"New Orleans."

"How'd it happen?"

For a time Latisha didn't answer. She hadn't been a Catholic when she attended Christ the King, but she had learned a lot about what was a sin and what wasn't. Begging wasn't a sin, and neither was hitchhiking. Working as a whore on the streets? That was a sin, all right.

And how had it happened? At Christ the King, they'd given her an achievement test and then had put her back a whole grade. Even with kids a year younger than she was, school had been a struggle. If she'd started there earlier, it might have worked, but by middle school she was already so far behind that she just couldn't catch up.

So she attended Christ the King, but she didn't make friends there. She preferred hanging out with kids from the neighborhood. When it came time for her to start high school, Lyle pretty much gave up trying to fix her, and he let her go to University City High School with her friends. The other freshmen were fourteen. She was a year older, and that's when she met Trayvon Littlefield. He was a really cool guy, a friend of a friend of a friend, who happened to be a gangbanger visiting from out of town. He had a fancy car—a black Camaro— several gold teeth, plenty of money, and lots of tattoos. He treated Latisha like a queen, promised to give her whatever she wanted, and told her everything she wanted to hear—including the idea that her parents were out of line and holding her back. He said he wanted to take her far away from University City and give her the life of her dreams.

Naturally, Lyle and Lou Ann had hated the guy. They told her that Trayvon was scum—a no-good, useless excuse for a human being. Latisha fought with them over that, arguing that they were wrong, wrong, wrong about him, but of course it turned out they hadn't been wrong at all. Soon after running away with Trayvon, she learned that the guy she'd thought of as Prince Charming wasn't. He was nothing more than a pimp who took her to New Orleans, threw her out on the streets in the French Quarter in the middle of Mardi Gras, and expected her to earn her keep.

And that was how she had come to be here. A year later she was a seasoned pro, and that's when the Boss had found her—still working the streets. He'd pulled up next to her in a big black SUV. They had conducted their business in the usual fashion, negotiating terms through his open passenger window. As she climbed inside the vehicle, Latisha had wondered what would happen if the john turned out to be an undercover cop. Unfortunately, she wasn't that lucky.

No sooner had she slid onto the passenger seat and shut the door behind her than she felt the sharp prick of a needle biting into her bare thigh. That was the last thing she remembered for days on end. She had vague memories of being confined to a bed, a bunk of some kind, in a moving vehicle—a big truck, most likely. However long the trip had taken, it had been just like Sadie's. Latisha had been bound, gagged, and sedated for most of it.

By the time she landed in the dungeon, Latisha was seventeen years old and had already had two abortions. She knew what her mother would say about that. And Lyle, not to mention the nuns at Christ the King.

"I was turning tricks," Latisha admitted aloud at last.

"Hey," Sadie said. "Are you still here? You were quiet for so long that I thought you'd gone to sleep—or maybe Scotty had beamed you up."

"Who's Scotty?"

"You don't know Scotty? You mean to tell me you never watched reruns of *Star Trek* on TV?"

"Never."

"Your loss, then," Sadie said. "Stick with us, girl. We'll teach you everything you need to know."

But Sadie with her funny jokes was gone now. So was Sandy with her talk of chocolate-chip cookies, along with Amelia and her sweet-voiced songs.

Amelia Salazar, the last to arrive, had landed in the basement months after Latisha and sometime in the summer, since a thunderstorm had been raging outside. When the Boss carried her downstairs that first time, they'd both been soaking wet.

Amelia was sixteen at the time, and the youngest of any of them. Orphaned at an early age, she'd grown up living with her grandmother, Cecilia Diaz, on a desolate plot of land located on an unnamed road west of Juárez, Mexico. Everyone knew that many of the young girls who went to Juárez to find jobs were never heard from again. It was what had happened to Amelia's mother. Fearing that history might repeat itself and out of concern for her granddaughter's safety, Cecilia had sent Amelia to El Paso to live with her aunt, Rosa Moreno.

Rosa, Cecilia's older daughter, was lucky enough to have a green card. Antonio, the husband who had made her green card possible, had long since disappeared, but Rosa remained in the States. She had a job as a maid at a marginal motel on the outskirts of town and assured her mother that the owner would give Amelia a job, too, once she turned sixteen.

A week after her sixteenth birthday, Amelia turned up at the border crossing. She'd had enough documentation to be allowed to walk through customs and into her auntie's arms, where she promptly became yet another illegal immigrant in a population of illegal immigrants. The under-the-table wages that the motel manager paid her were far greater than she would have been able to earn in Juárez, and she was thrilled to be able to send money home to her grandmother.

On the Fourth of July, she had left Aunt Rosa's trailer and walked a few blocks away to where some of the neighborhood kids were setting off fireworks. Later, walking home along Castner Drive, she'd been approached by a man in an SUV who pulled up beside her and asked directions. When she went to talk to him, he grabbed her by the arm and hauled her into the vehicle.

"There's a pattern here," Sandra said. "He did

this in January, February, March, and July. What about the other months? Or maybe there were others before he found us."

"Maybe they got away," Latisha suggested.

"I don't think so," Sadie said. "Maybe he just didn't bring them back here."

But Latisha wasn't buying it. "I still think they got away," she insisted.

It's what she wanted to believe. It's what she had to believe.

EIGHT

THE CARAVAN of vehicles that left Bisbee heading for the Peloncillos bright and early on Saturday morning might well have been dubbed a criminal-justice parade. Detective Deb Howell led the motorcade in her Tahoe, intent on picking up June and Jack Carver from their home in Douglas. That way, with Jack along to provide directions, she could lead the other investigators to the crime scene.

Dave Hollicker, Joanna's chief CSI, was next in line, behind the wheel of the county's new Ford Transit evidence van. Next up came the medical examiner, Dr. Kendra Baldwin, driving her all-wheel-drive Honda CRV. Dr. Baldwin had two morgue assistants, officially known as dieners. One of the two, a guy named Ralph Whetson, followed his boss in the morgue's official vehicle, a Dodge Caravan, a minivan everyone in the department routinely referred to as "the body wagon."

Acting Sheriff Hadlock brought up the rear of the procession, driving the Yukon that had once been Joanna's. That had been passed along to him in anticipation of the delivery of a new Ford Interceptor SUV, which was due to make its appearance about the time Joanna was scheduled to return from maternity leave.

Tom was one of the veterans in the department, and he looked the part of an Arizona sheriff. The man had a middle-aged girth to him. The Stetson he customarily wore concealed a receding hairline and his sparse gray comb-over. He had hired on as a deputy back in the day when D. H. Lathrop was still running the show. Hadlock had moved out of patrol and into jail management early on in the four-term administration of D. H.'s successor, Walter McFadden.

Hadlock had been aware of much of the underhanded dealings going on back then. Although he hadn't been part of any of it, he hadn't had nerve enough to come out publicly against it, either. When Deputy Andrew Roy Brady had decided to go up against their mutual boss, Hadlock had quietly supported Andy's attempt to oust McFadden from office and had been left heartsick by Andy's untimely and brutal murder.

Even so, when people started broaching the idea of asking Andy's widow to run for office in her murdered husband's place, Hadlock had considered that to be a bridge too far. Just because Joanna's father had been a sheriff and her husband had been a deputy running for the office of sheriff, this didn't mean that Joanna herself was qualified to do the job. In that original three-way contest, Tom had actually backed and voted for another candidate, Cochise County deputy, Frank Montoya. Then, when Joanna won, Tom, as the newly appointed jail commander, had sat back on the sidelines watching and waiting for her to fail—something that hadn't happened.

Most of the people who'd voted against Joanna and even some of her supporters had expected Andy Brady's widow to function as sheriff in name only—as a placeholder rather than as a real officer of the law. Almost no one had expected that she would transform herself into a consummate professional. People both inside and outside the department had been surprised and gratified when she took the time and effort to put herself through the rigors of police-academy training, and they were amazed by the seriousness with which she conducted herself on the job.

She brought the rank and file around by running her department in an open, honest, and evenhanded fashion. The fact that she had taken her two opponents—deputies Dick Voland and Frank Montoya—and made both of them her co-chief deputies had settled the hash for many of the folks who'd originally supported them. She won over hearts and minds by being a hard worker and putting herself on the line. She wasn't someone who sat at her desk and phoned the job in. When something happened, Joanna was present and accounted for. Cochise County was a vast square, almost eighty miles wide by eighty miles long. If a homicide occurred somewhere within those jurisdictional boundaries, Sheriff Brady's officers went, and so did she.

And that was why on this bright Saturday morning in mid-November, rather than sleeping in or watching golf on TV, Acting Sheriff Hadlock, standing in for Joanna, was on his way to the crime scene, too.

The vehicles formed up on the shoulder of Geronimo Trail, just east of the Douglas city limits and waited for Detective Howell to arrive on the scene. When she did so, Tom was surprised to note there were three passengers riding along with her rather than the expected two. As soon as the Tahoe came to a stop, the front passenger door swung open and a man stepped out. As he strode over to where Tom was parked, there was enough of a family resemblance for Tom to realize this had to be Jack Carver's father.

He was approaching in such a purposeful fashion that it seemed reasonable to expect there would be some kind of hell to pay. Not one to dodge a confrontation, Tom emerged from his own vehicle and stepped forward to meet whatever was coming. Rather than throwing a punch, the new arrival surprised Tom by extending his hand.

"Chief Deputy Hadlock?" he asked.

"That's me," Tom said, returning the proffered handshake.

"I'm Nathan Carver," the man said, "Jack's dad. I wanted to meet you before we got started."

In the old days, Tom would have known most of the Border Patrol guys in the county on sight and probably on a first-name basis as well, but that was no longer true. Border enforcement was a growth industry in Cochise County, and Nathan Carver was a complete stranger.

"Glad to meet you, too," Tom replied.

"Thanks for giving my boy a break," Nathan added. "You didn't have to do that, and I appreciate it."

Tom couldn't help but chuckle. "Turns out I didn't have a choice. That wife of yours pretty much painted me into a corner."

"She's a pistol, isn't she?" Nathan said with a wry grin.

"She is that," Tom agreed. "Shall we get started?"

They loaded up again and headed out, this time driving east on a rough dirt track that skirted the Mexican border. With each of the vehicles billowing rooster tails of dust, it was necessary to maintain a fair amount of distance between them. They drove through the San Bernardino Valley in a forest of winter-bare mesquite, past the turnoff to John Slaughter's ranch, and past Silver Creek as well. Finally, just beyond Sycamore Creek, Deb turned off onto a primitive forest service road that ran into the foothills of the Peloncillos toward Paramore Crater before eventually hooking up with Skeleton Canyon Road. It was rugged terrain. The high-profile all-wheel vehicles were fine, but Tom could see that the poor guy driving the morgue's low-ground-clearance minivan had his work cut out for him.

Eventually Deb pulled over and stopped once more. She and her three passengers piled out of the Tahoe and stood waiting until the trailing vehicles caught up. Once they did, Jack set off toward the north, heading into a sea of brittle yellow grass and low-lying brush, with the others trailing along behind. On the way they passed more than one NO HUNTING sign. A hundred yards or so from the road, a startled covey of quail shot into the air and flew off to the west. Tom Hadlock couldn't help but smile at that. If Jack and his shotgun-wielding buddy had been better hunters, those birds probably wouldn't be here right now.

It was no mystery why this would be a good place for birds. When Anglos first arrived on the scene, the wide valleys in what would eventually become southern Arizona—the San Pedro, Sulphur Springs, San Bernardino, Santa Cruz, and San Simon Valleys—had consisted of lush grasslands. Overgrazing cattle soon depleted the grass. When that was gone, hungry stock had foraged on low-hanging mesquite. Over time, digested and fully fertilized mesquite beans had performed their own kind of magic. Unfortunately, where mesquite trees flourish, grass does not. Thirsty mesquite roots sucked all the moisture out of the surrounding soil, turning lush valleys into hard-packed desert dotted with mesquite.

Over the past twenty years, some of the cattle ranchers in the foothills of the Peloncillos had banded together to get rid of the mesquite and bring back the native grasses by chopping down and removing hundreds of long-entrenched trees. When the grass returned, other things came back as well, including a now much-photographed jaguar—long thought to be extinct in the United States—along with a thriving population of deer, birds, and other wildlife.

As they topped a small rise, a single bird—an immense vulture—spread his massive wings and vaulted into the air, circling briefly above them before soaring away. The presence of the buzzard sent a chill message to Tom Hadlock and to almost everyone else in the group. Up ahead of them, something was dead.

Jack, seemingly unaware of the bird, continued to press forward. Then, a few steps later, he stumbled to a stop and dropped to the ground. By the time Tom reached the stricken boy, he was on his hands and knees, heaving his guts out, and the distinctive odor of death was all around them.

Jack had stopped on the lip of a dry creek bed. Lying in the sandy wash below them was the bloody mess of what had to be a partially consumed human being. There was no clothing present and there was nothing recognizable in the damaged face, but the long black hair fanning out across the sand suggested that the victim was a woman who had been left in the desert, face-up and naked. Her legs were folded under her in an unnatural pose that made her look as though she'd been kneeling at the time of her death and had remained locked in that same position.

Based on his finding of that desiccated skull, Jack Carver's story had led Tom to believe that they would come upon a collection of sun-bleached, ancient bones, but there was nothing ancient about the body. This was a relatively fresh kill.

It was time for the acting sheriff to take charge. "Everyone stop right where you are," he said, reaching down to help an ashen-faced Jack Carver to his feet. "Are you all right?" Tom asked the boy.

"I guess," Jack mumbled, but he was swaying so dangerously that Tom beckoned for Nathan to step forward to help keep his son upright.

"Can you show me approximately where you found the skull?"

"Over there," Jack said, pointing a trembling hand in the direction of a clump of scrub oak on the far side of the wash. "It was hot that day. I was going over there to sit in the shade, and that's where I found the skull—twenty yards or so on this side of that grove of trees."

"Okay, then," Tom said. "This is now an active crime scene. Mr. and Mrs. Carver, we can't have unauthorized civilians interfering with our investigation. I'm going to ask Detective Howell to take you and Jack here back home. If we need anything else from you, we'll be in touch."

"Thank you," Jack said in a strangled whisper, backing away from the grisly scene.

"Go home and take care," Tom told him. "Thanks for your help."

As the Carvers and Detective Howell took off, Tom turned back to the others. "Okay, folks," he said. "I'm guessing you all know what needs to be done. Let's secure the scene. Keep a sharp eye out for any kind of evidence, especially footprints or tire tracks."

Tom knew as he said the words that looking for tracks of any kind was useless. The cars parked along the shoulder of the road would have obliterated any visible tire tracks, and the simple act of having that group of people tramp through the desert would have done the same to any footprints that might have been left behind.

While Dr. Baldwin sent Whetson to retrieve both her bag and a gurney, Tom Hadlock pressed the button on his shoulder radio in an attempt to summon Tica Romero in Dispatch. Unsurprisingly, this far from civilization, the first transmission didn't go through.

"Okay, guys," he announced. "Radios don't work out here. I'm going to have to go to the car and call this in, either on the car radio or on the satphone. I'll be right back."

He walked out to where the cars were parked accompanying Ralph Whetson.

Once in the Yukon, Tom punched the mic button on the car's radio. Nothing happened. In the far-flung corners of Cochise County, communications problems were an ongoing, mostly budgetary issue. In outlying areas where low-band radios didn't work, deputies were assigned satellite phones. Joanna usually kept one in her own vehicle as well, but it was always the least reliable of the current crop and the one next in line for replacement.

That was the phone Tom was using now. When he dialed into Dispatch, he was relieved to hear Tica's voice coming through loud and clear.

"We've got a homicide out here in the Peloncillos," he told her. "Get hold of the Double C's for me," he said, referring to detectives Ernie Carpenter and Jaime Carbajal. "It's urgent. The crime scene is off Geronimo Trail—first road to the left after Sycamore Creek, on the way to Paramore Crater. I need everybody on deck. Tell them to get their asses to Douglas ASAP so they can meet up with Deb Howell. That way she can guide them back to where we are. Got it?"

"Copy that," Tica replied. "I'll get right on it."

When it was time to return to the others, Tom took a slightly different route, twenty or so yards to the east of where they'd walked earlier. On the way in, he'd kept an eye out for any additional bones and had seen nothing. The same was true this time, too, until he was beyond the creek bed and heading for the scrub oak. There he hit pay dirt. The remains of a human rib cage, picked clean and bleached white, lay half hidden in the grass.

"Hey, Dave," he called to the CSI. "I've got something over here. I'll need an evidence marker—" He broke off in midsentence when he spotted another skull. "Make that two evidence markers," he said. "Looks like we're up to at least three separate bodies."

As Tom waited for Dave to show up, the grim reality finally dawned. This was most likely a dump site—a place where a serial killer had come to dispose of his dead prey.

At that point Tom reached into his pocket to pull out his phone. The gesture was done strictly out of force of habit. It was also completely pointless. This far out in the wilderness, the satellite phone worked, but there was no cell service of any kind.

As for the satphone? Because it was having trouble holding a charge, he had left it plugged in in the Yukon.

Dave Hollicker showed up and started laying down a series of evidence markers. "I need to go back to the car and call Sheriff Brady," Tom said as he hurried past. "She may be on maternity leave, but this is a big deal, and she needs to know what we're up against."

NINE

LATISHA'S EYES opened in the gray gloom that meant the sun was shining outside. In the days since she'd been alone—and she wasn't sure how many there had been—she began each one with a prayer, not one of Granny Lou's hellfire-and-brimstone prayers but a variation on the ones she'd learned secondhand when she was a reluctant student at Christ the King.

"Holy Mary, Mother of God, pray for us sinners now and at the hour of our death. Amen. God bless Sandra Ruth Locke, Sadie Kaitlyn Jennings, and Amelia Diaz Salazar. Take them home with you and grant them peace, now and forever, amen."

Saying that simple prayer aloud somehow made Latisha feel less alone, although she *was* alone—absolutely alone. If you were in prison, she realized, this was what solitary confinement had to be like, except in prison there would be guards and someone coming by during the day and passing you trays of food. Obviously this was far worse than prison.

She got up and hobbled to the bathroom. There was no longer any need to ask if anyone else was already there and no danger of crossing chains with anyone else and creating a tangle. She used the toilet. While she was sitting there, she touched her leg. It felt hot and feverish. So when she filled her cup the first time, she sat back down and ran water across the wound, hoping to clean it. What would happen if it got worse? Granny Lou had told her that was how she'd lost her legs—with sores that wouldn't heal and that had turned into gangrene.

With all four girls there, they'd had to be stingy about using too much toilet paper, because there was always a worry about running out. Now, though, left on her own, Latisha wrapped layers of toilet paper around the shackle on her leg to provide some cushioning and maybe give the wound a chance to heal. She already knew that the Boss didn't tolerate imperfection. If he came back and noticed the sore, Latisha worried that might be the end of things—that he'd get rid of her the same way he'd gotten rid of the others, but for a different reason.

Latisha suspected that the other three had all been pregnant at the time they disappeared—first Sandra, then Sadie, and finally Amelia. When Trayvon had come to pick Latisha up after her second abortion, the doctor at Planned Parenthood warned them that she'd suffered some internal damage as a result of the procedure and that it was unlikely she'd ever be able to have children. And now the fact that she'd gotten rid of that baby and the one before it—both mortal sins, she was sure—was the thing that was sparing her life, or at least keeping her alive at the moment. Not that being alive was any favor.

Walking back from the toilet with her cup of water, Latisha discovered that the makeshift bandage she'd made actually helped. The clamp didn't chafe quite as much. On her mattress again, she set the cup of water beside her and groped around until she located the food dish. The kibble was easier to swallow if you had water to wash it down.

With the others gone, Latisha had appropriated their three blankets and their food containers as well. She had rolled up one blanket and used that as a pillow and appreciated the warmth those other two layers of blanket offered. She didn't think Sandra and Sadie and Amelia would have minded. After all, the three of them had been her friends, and she was sure they would have been glad to share.

But even with extra rations added into the mix, Latisha found the level of kibble in the container alarmingly low. For the first time, she wondered what would happen if the Boss was gone and wasn't coming back—not ever.

"That was the worst part," Sandra had told them one day. "The first time he went off and left me here by myself, I worried about what would happen if he never came back. I'd be lying here dead and no one would ever find me. No one would ever notice."

"Do you think anyone is looking for us?" Latisha had asked.

"I doubt it," Sadie had said with a laugh. "We're your basic no-deposit, no-return kind of girls."

Sadie was always cracking jokes that Latisha didn't quite get. "What's that supposed to mean?"

"In Oregon, on some pop bottles, you have to pay a deposit, which you get back when you return the empty bottles to the store. There are other bottles that are marked 'no deposit, no return.'"

Latisha didn't like being compared to a pop bottle, but it made sense. Trayvon wouldn't have gone out of his way to look for her. He'd just go out and find himself some other stupid girl. As for her parents? No, Lou Ann and Lyle for sure would have given up on her long ago.

But that brought Latisha to the core problem. What if the Boss didn't come back? What if he was gone for good? How long would her food last? She had water to drink, but the toilet made that strange sound when you flushed it—as if there was what sounded like an electric motor inside it. What if the Boss didn't come back and somebody turned off the water and the electricity because he wasn't paying the bills? What would happen to Latisha then?

And of course there was the chain clamped to her ankle. What about that? She remembered hearing of animals with their legs caught in traps who had gnawed through their own limbs in order to escape. That wasn't possible here. Latisha could barely touch her head to her knee.

And then she remembered the book. What was the name of it again? Something about a rock and a hard place. She'd done a book report on it once and had gotten a good grade, too, even though she'd never actually read the book. She had never read any books. One of the boys at University City High School had shown her how to look up book titles on the Internet and then write book reports based on what the Internet said about them. Once she knew about that, her grades in English had improved remarkably.

But that book in particular was about a guy whose name she couldn't remember. Alan, maybe? Anyway, he'd been out hiking by himself in the wilderness somewhere out west. There'd been an avalanche, and a big rock—a boulder that was far too heavy for him to move—had landed on his arm.

So there he was, trapped and alone, with no one to help him. He was there for a period of time—Latisha didn't remember exactly how long—before his water ran out. That was when he realized that if he didn't get loose, he was going to die, so he tied a tourniquet around his arm and then used a pocket knife to cut off his lower arm to save his life.

But Latisha didn't have a knife. She had water, kibble, four blankets, and darkness—and that was it. Oh, and maybe God, too—in case He was still listening. And so she prayed again, without benefit of a rosary, whispering the words into the silent gloom.

"Holy Mary, Mother of God, pray for us sinners now and at the hour of our death. Amen."

After asking another blessing for Sandra and Sadie and Amelia, Latisha found herself oddly at peace. In the darkness that prayer she hadn't wanted to learn, just like Lyle's remembered pancakes, offered her comfort. And in that moment of hopefulness, she made herself a promise. She swore that if she ever did get out of here, if someone came to her rescue and she somehow managed to live, she would track that book down and read the whole thing, from cover to cover, because she now understood that man on the mountainside. He'd been left alone with nothing but his thoughts and prayers, and so had she.

TEN

After almost two weeks of being stuck at home with the kids and feeling more than a little stir-crazy, Joanna had jumped at the offer when Marianne Maculyea called, inviting her to their customary Saturday lunch at Daisy's Café. She had wanted to get Denny into the barbershop for a pre-Thanksgiving haircut, and going to lunch afterward sounded just about right.

With her grandsons home from school, Carol usually didn't come in on Saturdays, so getting ready to go out fell to Joanna on her own. Two kids instead of one made the process more complex than she remembered. First she had to transfer Denny's car seat from Butch's Subaru, where he usually rode, to the middle seat in Joanna's Enclave. Then, with her purse over her shoulder, a diaper bag in one hand, and Sage's infant seat in the other, Joanna headed for the car. Denny fastened his own seat belt, but by the time Joanna managed to get Sage's backward-facing seat properly secured, she was starting to wonder if going anywhere at all was worth it.

The Enclave's sound system connected up to Joanna's cell automatically. She was expecting to hear from Butch. This was a two-appearance day, with a noontime event in Tulsa and an evening one in Dallas. The phone rang before she even turned off High Lonesome Road onto the Double Adobe Highway. The caller-ID display led back to one of the department's aging and sometimes temperamental satellite phones.

"Good morning, boss," Tom said. "Hope I'm not interrupting."

"No, what's going on?"

"I'm out at the crime scene in the Peloncillos."

"Where Jack Carver picked up the skull?"

"That's the one, but it's a whole lot more serious than we first thought. We've got one body that's maybe only a couple of days old and another that's been there long enough for the grass to grow up through the rib cage."

"So maybe the ribs you found belong to the skull Jack Carver dragged home," Joanna offered.

"No such luck," Tom told her, "because I just found another one."

"A second skull?"

"Affirmative, so it looks to me like we've got a serial killer on our hands and we've just stumbled onto his dump site."

Joanna's heart fell. She looked back at Denny to see if he was paying attention to the conversation coming through the speaker. Fortunately, his face was buried in a book.

"Are you sure—a serial killer is operating in Cochise County?"

"That's how it looks," Tom said, "and that's why I'm calling. I need your help."

"I'm in the car right now, but I've got both kids with me. I can't possibly come to the crime scene."

"I'm not asking you to," Tom said, "but here's the deal. A few weeks ago, there was something on the news about a couple up in Phoenix who had just come back from working the aftermath of that big earthquake down in Costa Rica. They run a nonprofit with dogs that are cross-trained to function as both rescue dogs and cadaver dogs, depending on the situation. I'm thinking that if we've got bones scattered all over hell and gone, using cadaver dogs might just fill the bill."

"Call them up," Joanna said. "Find out what they charge."

"I was hoping I could get you to do that," Tom told her. "There's no Internet service out here in the boonies. Besides, I'm just your stand-in here. With all the work you've done in animal control and with various dog organizations around the state and the country, you're the one with the brand name, which makes you the one with the pull. If I were to call them up and ask, we'd likely get the brush-off. If you're the one making the call, people might sit up and take notice."

"What about Mojo?" Joanna asked. "You told me that he and Terry showed up yesterday afternoon. Is this something he could do?"

"Nope," Tom said. "I already asked. Cadaver sniffing isn't part of Mojo's bag of tricks."

"Okay," Joanna said. "I'll see what I can do. Do you have any idea what the organization is called?"

"I don't remember—Canine something."

"How soon do you want them there?"

"Dr. Baldwin and Ralph Whetson are here to take charge of the most recent body. Dave Hollicker is laying down evidence markers, doing crime-scene photos, and collecting bones. Deb left here a little while ago to take the Carvers back home. She's supposed to meet up with the Double C's in Douglas and bring them here. I'm guessing it'll take the rest of today and maybe part of tomorrow to finish processing the scene around this most recent body. Once that's handled, we'll need to bring in the dogs to see if they can locate any additional remains that aren't immediately obvious. There's a lot of dead grass out here and a lot of ground to cover. If you could get them to show up tomorrow or Monday maybe, it would be great."

"Okay," Joanna said. "I'll see what I can do and get back to you."

"Thanks," he said.

As the call ended, Joanna was turning in to the parking lot. Denny's first trip to the barbershop at age three had been a traumatic, screaming mess for all concerned. Now, two years in, he and Eddie were old pals. While Denny's hair got trimmed, Joanna sat in the lobby with Sage's infant seat on a chair next to her, scrolling through the Internet. She finally found Canine First Responders, CFR for short, by Googling dogs and earthquakes. Within minutes she was on the phone with a woman named Patricia Paxton, who, along with her husband, Dwayne, was at the helm of CFR.

"What's this all about?" Patricia asked when Joanna called.

"My officers have stumbled on what appears to be a serial killer's dump site," Joanna explained after introductions were out of the way. "We're talking about the remains of a very recent victim as well as partial skeletal remains of at least two others, so three victims for sure and maybe more."

"Where is this, exactly?" Patricia asked.

"At a very remote location in the foothills of the Peloncillo Mountains on the far side of Douglas."

"So we're talking the middle of nowhere?"

"Correct," Joanna told her, "with miles of very bad roads between there and civilization."

"What made you call us?"

"My chief deputy saw a piece someone did about the work you did after the earthquake—that you had dogs trained to locate living survivors and ones that could search for deceased victims. And that's what we need—help in locating human remains that have most likely been scattered over a wide area. I was calling to see if you might be available to come give us a hand and to ask what you charge."

"We're always on call," Patricia answered, "and we're also nonprofit. We accept donations, of course, but we don't charge for our services. Most of the time, we're dealing with people who've lost everything. Since we couldn't justify charging them, we decided not to charge anybody. We do what we do as a public service. Usually it turns out to be disaster relief, but this sounds intriguing. When would you want us there, Sheriff Brady?"

"Would tomorrow be too soon?" Joanna asked.

"My people are there right now processing the crime scene."

"Any idea how much territory we're talking about?"

"Not really," Joanna answered. "I'm currently on maternity leave, so I haven't been to the crime scene in person, but the way it was explained to me, we're probably talking about several acres. And we need to do this as soon as possible. Once word gets out, there's always a chance of looky-loos coming around to see what they can find. I've been told that these days there's a hot market for crime-scene-related knickknacks."

Starting with a kid named Jack Carver, she thought.

"Exactly how bad are the roads?"

"Some of them are okay. Others are downright primitive. Four-wheel drive recommended."

Patricia sighed. "We and some friends have a time-share kind of arrangement on an EarthRoamer XV-LTS. Ever heard of 'em?"

"No."

"It's a four-wheel-drive RV that can get you in and out of otherwise impossible places. Most of the time, I'd suggest using that for this kind of trip, but it's almost Thanksgiving and our friends are off skiing in Colorado at the moment. We'll probably have to make do with the Sprinter and our old Jeep Wrangler. The problem is, we'll need a place to park the Sprinter while we're working the dogs, and the Sprinter is definitely not on speaking terms with primitive roads. If you can, please locate an

RV park that will let us bring dogs—big dogs. In this case we'll probably be bringing our two bloodhounds, Stormin' Norman and Big Red. When it comes to cadavers, they're the best."

"Look," Joanna said, "my husband and I have an RV hookup here at High Lonesome Ranch east of Bisbee, and we're definitely dog-friendly. Why don't you plan on parking your Sprinter here?"

"Good thinking," Patricia said. "Let me check with Dwayne, my husband, and make sure he doesn't have plans that aren't on the calendar. If he's good to go, I'll be back in touch to give you our ETA and get directions."

"Mommy," Denny demanded impatiently. Joanna looked up to find him properly shorn and standing directly in front of her. "Are you ready to go?"

Caught up in her phone call, Joanna had failed to notice that the haircut had ended, and now a bit of multitasking was in order. "Yes," she said, both to Denny and into the phone. "Yes, give me a call," she told Patricia Paxton, and "Yes, I'm ready to go," she told her son.

After paying for the haircut and bundling the kids back into the Enclave, she drove to Daisy's in Bisbee's Bakerville neighborhood, where Marianne was already tucked into one of the back corner booths awaiting their arrival. Denny made a beeline in her direction, threw his arms around Marianne's neck, and climbed up next to her while Joanna settled herself and Sage's infant seat on the far side of the table.

"Where's Ruth?" Denny wanted to know.

Ruth, Marianne's ten-year-old adopted daughter, often turned these Saturday lunchtime gettogethers into a foursome. Ruth and a twin sister, Esther, had come from an orphanage in China when they were a year old. Esther, born with a serious heart ailment, had died shortly after receiving a heart transplant at age two. Without her sister, Ruth had attached herself to her adoptive father, Jeff Daniels, becoming far more his shadow than Marianne's.

"They're off on a trip to Tucson, picking up their next project," Marianne told him. "They bought an old T-bird from a lady up there, and Ruthie and her dad are going to fix it up."

As a clergy couple, Marianne had always been front and center as the pastor with Jeff doing spousal duties—teaching Sunday school, singing in the choir, and running Bible school during the summers. In his off-duty hours, Jeff's sometimes profitable hobby was restoring old cars. He had started Ruth out restoring old Matchbox cars that they picked up from yard sales, but now she had graduated to helping her dad with the real thing and was, to no one's surprise, turning into a capable mechanic in her own right.

"Can I help, too?" Denny asked.

"Maybe," Marianne answered. "Ask Jeff next time you see him."

Sage began stirring now, and Joanna knew it was almost feeding time. Grateful for the privacy of a high-backed booth, she hauled out a receiving blanket for cover as she undid her blouse. By the time Liza Machett, the café's new owner, came around to take their order, a properly covered Sage was happily nursing away.

"So what will Master Dixon be having today?" Liza asked, handing Denny a kids' menu built for coloring, along with a slender pack of crayons.

"Mac and cheese, please," Denny told her without a moment's hesitation.

Liza turned to Joanna. "And you?"

"Do you have any pasties left?"

Cornish pasties had come to Bisbee in the late 1800s and the earliest twentieth century courtesy of miners imported from played-out tin mines in Cornwall, sometimes arriving in southern Arizona via stopovers at the mines in upper Michigan. Those hearty "hand pies" had been standard fare for Bisbee's hard-rock miners, and even though the mines in Bisbee had been closed for decades, pasties remained a local delicacy and a special treat. Daisy Maxwell, the café's previous owner, had served pasties at least once a week.

When Liza Machett had arrived in town as a refugee from Great Barrington, Massachusetts, she had known nothing at all about Cornish pasties. After taking over ownership of the café, however, she quickly discovered how popular they were. Now they were available every day rather than one day a week, and they generally sold out every day.

"You're in luck," Liza said. "I believe there's one left in the fridge, and I'm putting your name on it."

Marianne ordered a chili burger. Their drinks

came moments later—coffee for Joanna and Marianne and milk for Denny. Then, with the child seemingly totally occupied with his coloring, the two old friends settled in to talk.

"So how are you doing?" Marianne asked.

"Thanks for prodding me into leaving the house. Being out and about with one little one is complicated enough. Two is downright daunting."

As soon as Joanna spoke the words, she was sorry. The flicker of sadness in Marianne's eyes said it all. Yes, she remembered the complications of traveling with two babies, but even eight years later Esther's loss still hurt.

"That was thoughtless of me," Joanna apologized.

"No worries," Marianne said, managing a smile. "I'm glad you made the effort. Now, tell me about what's going on. I heard that your department is dealing with multiple homicides. Do you know how many?"

Since Reverend Maculyea functioned as the local fire and police chaplain, it was hardly surprising that she would be well aware of what was going on.

"I don't think the guys at the crime scene know for sure, at least not yet. So far they've found one body and skeletal remains for two more victims—however, that number may rise. Tom Hadlock is doing a great job. He's assembled a retrieval team and has it up and running."

Joanna glanced over at Denny. He was engrossed in his coloring. His struggle to stay inside the lines was so intense that she thought it unlikely that he would be paying any attention to what was being said.

"One victim is evidently very recent," Joanna continued. "The other two are from sometime earlier, weeks at least and maybe even months. I've been in touch with an organization up in Phoenix. We're hoping they'll be able to bring in a team of cadaver dogs tomorrow to help process the scene."

"Mommy, what kind of dog is that?" Denny asked without looking up from the paper. "Is it like a golden retriever?"

Marianne spluttered as she inadvertently sucked coffee from her cup into her nose. "It would appear that little pitchers have big ears," she managed, choking back laughter.

Joanna had always made every effort to answer Jenny's questions honestly. Caught out now, she felt she had to do the same with Denny. "'Cadaver' is another word for dead body," Joanna explained. "Some dogs are trained to track down crooks and some to sniff for drugs. Cadaver dogs are trained to locate human remains."

"You mean dead people like Grandpa George and Grandma Eleanor?" Denny asked.

This was not the way Joanna wanted the lunchtime conversation to go.

"Sort of," she said with a sigh. "These are bodies that have been left outside for some time. Scavengers like coyotes and vultures have probably scattered bits and pieces around in the desert. We need cadaver dogs to help find what's missing."

"Like bones and stuff?"

"Yes."

"Eeew!" Denny exclaimed. "That's gross."

"Indeed it is," Joanna agreed. "So can we please talk about something else?"

Marianne came to her rescue. "When will your daddy be home?" Marianne asked.

"In time to cook the turkey," Denny declared. "He says I get to help him this year. He says I'm big enough."

"What about your sister? Will she be home?"

"Which one?" Denny asked, frowning. "I have two sisters now."

"The one who's away at school," Marianne said with a smile. "Will Jenny be home for Thanksgiving?"

"I think so," Denny said.

Relieved that Marianne had succeeded in guiding the conversation away from murder and mayhem, Joanna nodded. "That was the plan the last I heard, and with any kind of luck, after lunch there'll be enough leftovers that I won't need to cook dinner."

ELEVEN

OUTSIDE, IT was still daylight, or maybe it was daylight again. As the endless hours ticked by, it was hard to judge, and with no one to talk to, there was nothing for Latisha to do but think. And wait.

She had always longed for a sister. She didn't know why. Friends who did have sisters didn't seem to like them much, and they argued, bickered, and fought about everything. But Latisha would've liked to have some other presence in Granny Lou's shotgun house—someone to talk to and share secrets with while Granny Lou was watching her soaps and her mom was studying.

When Latisha had asked about having a sister, her mother brushed the request aside. "For you to have a sister, I'd need to have a husband," Lou Ann had said, "and who has time for one of those?"

Of course, the girls Latisha knew who did have sisters didn't necessarily have fathers anywhere around, either, so that wasn't the whole answer. The real answer was that Lou Ann didn't want a second child. And when Lyle showed up, neither did he.

But now, as Latisha grieved for her lost

companions—Sandra, Sadie, and Amelia—she realized that she did have sisters. The other girls had become her sisters through incredible trials and appalling hardships. The only thing she could do for those lost sisters was grieve for them, pray for them, and remember.

Growing up, Latisha had known that her family was poor and that a lack of money had always been a problem. Still, even in Granny Lou's house they'd had a television set, air-conditioning, and indoor plumbing. It wasn't until Amelia showed up that Latisha had glimpsed what her version of poverty had entailed.

Amelia and her grandmother had lived in a one-room shack with no running water. Once a week a man with a water tank on his truck would stop by and fill the water barrel outside their house. Amelia didn't know exactly where the water came from. What she did know was that it had to be boiled—on her grandmother's makeshift wood-burning outdoor grill—before you could drink it.

"Even in the winter, my grandmother cooked over a wood fire outside," Amelia said. "But she made the best tamales. I got to help her sometimes. She taught me how to roll them into the corn husks."

"What's a tamale?" Latisha had asked.

Sandra was incredulous. "You've never tasted a tamale? Didn't you ever go to TacoTime or a taco truck?"

"East St. Louis isn't big on taco trucks," Latisha said.

That's what she said, but the real problem would have had more to do with the gang-fueled animosity that existed between the black and Hispanic cultures. They might have lived in the same geographical areas, but in terms of interaction and shared experience they might as well have occupied separate universes.

"So what's a tamale?"

Amelia had explained about making the masa dough, placing the dough on corn husks, and adding a filling made from a spicy pork-and-chili mixture before rolling up the corn husks and steaming the tamales in a vat of water—also on the fire outside.

Latisha tried to imagine why you would put some kind of corn bread and stew into a corn husk to cook it. Despite the fact that Amelia loved tamales and Latisha doubted she'd care for them, she had decided that if she ever did get away—if she managed to live—she would try at least one tamale, in memory of Amelia.

TWELVE

TOM HADLOCK had spent most of his law-enforcement career running the Cochise County Jail, functioning as an administrator rather than as a patrol officer out on the streets. It was a career path that helped him enormously in handling the paperwork aspects of serving as acting sheriff, but it had left him painfully lacking in terms of actual crime-scene expertise. When it came to examining the Peloncillos dump site, he was more than happy to take his cues from people who, although theoretically his underlings, were far more experienced in the tasks at hand than he was, and he was glad they were on the job.

After determining there were no usable footprints, Dave Hollicker settled in to study and photograph the crime scene. At the point where the body was found, broken grass stems running along the top edge of the wash and continuing down the bank seemed to indicate that something heavy—the corpse, presumably—had been shoved off the edge and left to roll down the bank. There was no other trace evidence to be found—no cast-off blood, no signs of a struggle. Nearby lay two large black plastic garbage bags that also appeared to have rolled down the bank. Once Dave had completed his crime-scene photos of the body, he approached the bags. They were securely tied shut, but the side of one had torn open, with an army of ants marching purposefully in and out.

The air was so thick with the odor of dead flesh that Dave approached the bags fully expecting to find another body. Instead he used the tip of his Swiss Army knife to pry open the layer of plastic. After peering inside, he stepped away.

"What is it?" Tom called down. "Another victim?"

"Nope," Dave replied. "Looks like somebody dumped a bunch of dead groceries. And considering where we found them, we're going to bag 'em, tag 'em, and drag 'em back to the crime lab."

He took a few more photos and then returned to the surface. "Okay, Doc," Tom said to Kendra Baldwin. "You're up."

While the M.E. conducted her preliminary examination, there was nothing to do but watch and wait. Dr. Baldwin and Ralph Whetson had just finished zipping the corpse into a body bag when Deb Howell returned with Detectives Carpenter and Carbajal in tow.

The group gathered near the loaded body bag as the M.E. stripped off her latex gloves.

"What can you tell us?" Tom asked.

"Female," Dr. Baldwin answered. "Most likely Hispanic, probably between fifteen and twenty years of age. It would appear that she was killed elsewhere and dumped here. No obvious cause of death at this time, but I can say she's severely undernourished."

"Do you think she's a UDA?" Tom asked.

"Maybe," the M.E. replied. "We'll know more when I do the autopsy and get a look at her teeth. If she's had dental work done, I may be able to tell if it's from here in the States or from somewhere else."

"Any items of clothing or personal effects?" Ernie Carpenter asked.

"Nothing," the M.E. replied. "Apparently she was stripped naked before being dumped. If she had any identifying markings—tattoos, moles, that kind of thing—the scavengers took care of those. There's a slim possibility that I'll be able to rehydrate the tissue enough to raise a fingerprint or two, but don't hold your breath, and even if we get a usable one, chances are her prints won't be on file."

"Do your best," Tom told her, and then he turned to the Double C's. "Here's the deal. In addition to Jane Doe, we've found partial remains of at least two additional victims, and there may be even more. I want us to scour this whole area on foot and put down evidence markers wherever we find anything resembling human remains. Sheriff Brady has contacted an organization that can have a pair of cadaver dogs on the scene sometime tomorrow. They'll be better at finding small stuff than we are, but let's take a crack at it ourselves before we bring in the dogs. Let's go back to the road and walk along it at three-foot intervals. Under the circumstances that's about as close to an organized grid search as we can manage."

Kendra and Ralph were loading the body bag into the van when a car showed up on the road. It slowed down and then stopped on the shoulder. A moment later a woman stepped out of the car and began waving frantically in their direction. "Whoohoo!" she called. "Chief Deputy Hadlock, do you have a moment?"

Even from a distance and despite the fact that she was wearing a golf visor, Marliss Shackleford's wild mane of bleached-blond hair was unmistakable to everyone present, including Tom Hadlock. He had failed to caution Tica about putting anything out over the radios. Obviously Marliss had been listening in on her police scanner, and now she was heading for his crime scene.

"Crap," he muttered under his breath. "What did I do to deserve this?"

"You're acting sheriff," Jaime Carbajal told him with a grin. "Did you maybe forget to appoint someone to take over at Media Relations while you're pinch-hitting as sheriff?"

"Shut up, Detective Carbajal," Tom groused at him. "Leave me alone and go look for bones. Otherwise you may end up stuck in Media Relations your own damned self."

Pulling himself together, Hadlock sauntered over to head the reporter off. "This is a crime scene, Marliss. You shouldn't be here."

"Is that a body bag they're loading?" she asked breathlessly.

"You know for a fact that I'm not able to comment on an active investigation. Once we're ready to do so, we'll hold an official press briefing, and you'll be notified."

"It looks like you've got the whole homicide squad out here working, and on a Saturday, too. That must be chewing up overtime like crazy, so whatever's going on must be serious."

"You're welcome to draw your own conclusions, Marliss," Tom told her. "Homicide is always a serious matter because people die. But it's an active investigation, and I'm not talking to you about any of this right now. I suggest you climb back into that little RAV4 and head straight back to town."

"Is the victim male or female?"

"Go!" Tom ordered.

"Is there any indication as to how that person died?"

"Get."

"Can you tell me who alerted you to the fact that a crime had been committed?"

Fortunately, none of Tom's interactions with the Carver family had been broadcast over the police-band radio.

"Ms. Shackleford," he said sternly, "my officers are conducting an investigation, and you are interfering with that process. We have work to do. I strongly suggest that you get the hell out of here."

"There's no reason to be rude," she told him. "And what about freedom of the press?"

"I don't have a problem with freedom of the press as long it doesn't interfere with our work. Now, are you going to leave on your own or do you want to spend the next half hour or so sitting in the back of one of our vehicles?"

"I'm going, Chief Deputy Hadlock," she said, backing away, "but you're not exactly winning friends and influencing people."

He turned back to the crime scene, muttering under his breath as he went.

"You know what? Ask me if I care."

THIRTEEN

BY MIDAFTERNOON Joanna had things fairly well under control. She had two batches of laundry going—one in the washer and one in the dryer. Miracle of miracles, she'd been able to get both kids down for naps at the same time. In between tasks she'd checked in with Tom Hadlock several times.

Based on what he'd told her, Joanna had struck a deal with Patricia Paxton and her bloodhounds to show up at High Lonesome Ranch sometime on Sunday morning. That wasn't exactly a huge contribution on her part, but it was something she could do while everyone else focused on the crime scene.

When Denny woke up, Joanna left the nanny cam to keep watch on Sage, sleeping in her crib in a room that was now half nursery and half mostly absent college student. Joanna whipped through the chores faster than she would have had Denny not been there to help. They started by feeding and watering the two horses—Jenny's retired barrel-racing gelding, Kiddo, and the blind Appaloosa rescue, Spot. Next up they fed and watered two un-named yearling calves and Dodo, the lone and now

118

fully grown and spayed female rabbit—an Easter Bunny adoption failure who three tries later had come back to High Lonesome Ranch on a permanent basis. The dogs, Lady and Lucky, who had accompanied them on their rounds were the last to be fed, and Denny handled that completely on his own. They were back inside before Sage let out a peep.

"Thank you," Joanna told him. "You've been a big help."

"Can I watch cartoons now?" he asked.

Fortunately, Butch had a complete catalog of recorded Scooby-Doos that filled that bill admirably. Joanna was folding clothes with Sage stowed on the living-room floor in her bouncy seat when Butch called.

"I finally have half an hour to myself before they pick me up for the evening event here in Dallas. Stacking two events and travel into the same day is too much. And if one more little old lady says men shouldn't write cozies or asks if my wife writes my books for me, or wants to know where I get my ideas, I think I'll go nuts."

"It's close to the end of the tour, so you probably *are* nuts," Joanna said. "And remember, Publicity crammed a three-week tour into two. Doubling up on travel and events was the only way to get it done."

"In other words, I should quit my bitchin'?"

"You said it, not me," she replied. "Are those little old ladies buying books?"

"Yes."

"Well, then?"

"All right," he said. "I'll get a grip. How are things on your end? How are the kids?"

"We're all okay. I got Denny in to see Eddie for his haircut. We've got leftovers from lunch for dinner, the animals are all fed, and I'm folding clothes. How the hell do you stay ahead of the laundry?"

"By doing laundry every day," he replied. "Either Carol does it or I do it."

"Point taken."

"Any news on the case?"

"The one body is at the morgue along with skeletal remains of at least three more. No idea when Kendra will get around to doing the autopsy. As far as I know, Tom Hadlock and the others are still out there working, but when the sun goes down, they'll have to quit for the day. Four homicides at once is a huge deal for someone as inexperienced as Tom Hadlock."

"How's he holding up?"

"All right so far."

"Your department's probably looking at another media firestorm," Butch added. "Who'll be talking to the press?"

"Beats me," Joanna said. "The last I heard, Tom was still in charge of that. We ended up at the hospital in such a hurry that I didn't think far enough in advance to appoint someone else to step into that role, and I doubt he did either."

"I half expected you to tell me that you'd packed

the kids in the car and taken off for the crime scene."

"I'm being a good girl," she said with a laugh, "but I was able to give Tom some behind-the-scenes logistical help." She went on to explain about the Paxtons and their traveling cadaver dogs.

A landline phone rang somewhere in the background. "Oops," Butch said, "that's the room phone. My ride must be downstairs. I have to go."

"Break a leg," Joanna told him, and he was gone.

Dinner was over, Denny was in the tub, and Joanna was loading the dishwasher when the phone rang, this time with Kendra Baldwin's name showing on caller ID.

"Hey, Joanna," the M.E. said. "Hope I'm not interrupting."

"Not at all," Joanna said. "What's up?"

"I know you're on leave, but I thought you should know."

"Know what?"

"Detective Howell followed me back to the morgue so we could get a head start by tackling that first autopsy immediately."

"It's done already?" Joanna asked. "That was quick."

"With several additional victims still at the scene, I needed to get that one out of the way. And that's what I need to talk to you about—the autopsy. The victim was female, and she'd had quite a bit of dental work done. I'd say some of it was done here in the States, some from elsewhere—most likely Mexico."

"So you think she was Hispanic, then?" Joanna asked.

"Yes, late teens, five-seven, ninety-five pounds, fifteen to eighteen years of age. Based on fly larvae found on the body, I'm estimating she was dumped two days ago at least, and maybe slightly longer."

"Have you checked with Records about any missing persons matching that description?" Joanna asked.

"Yes, I did," Kendra replied, "and came up empty. As I said, the older dental work would indicate she came from Mexico originally, but there are several newer fillings that were probably done stateside. She was also twelve to thirteen weeks pregnant at the time of her death. The unborn fetus was female."

"So Jane Doe and Baby Jane Doe?"

"Yes."

"Were you able to raise any fingerprints?"

"Nope," Kendra replied. "We tried, but it didn't work."

"If the victim is undocumented and there are no prints, chances are we'll never ID her," Joanna said.

"Don't be so sure," Kendra said. "Have you ever heard of something called the Banshee Group?"

"The what?"

"Banshee Group is a nonprofit operating out of the UK—an NGO run by a Brit named Kate Benchley. They specialize in using DNA analysis to identify skeletal remains. They started out working with victims found in mass graves in Bosnia. Now, with all the cartel violence playing out in Mexico and the discovery of mass graves there as well, Banshee Group is teaming up with the Mexican officials to do the same thing—ID remains.

"These days when someone comes in to report a missing person, they are encouraged to leave behind a DNA sample, a process that's creating a massive database of familial DNA. Oftentimes being able to zero in on even a distant family member can help lead to the identification of a specific victim. I'll be submitting a sample of Jane Doe's tissue to them for testing. I'm also going to submit her details, including DNA and dental charts to NamUs."

"What's that?"

"National Missing and Unidentified Persons System is a database containing the records of missing persons. The database includes medical and dental information, all of which is designed to be readily searchable by medical examiners and law enforcement."

"The information may be readily searchable, but getting results is still going to take time," Joanna concluded.

"A luxury we probably don't have," Kendra added.

"That sounds ominous. What do you mean?"

"As soon as I saw the body, I knew Jane Doe was severely malnourished. Now I know why. The only undigested food I found in her system was dog food—dry kibble."

"You're saying she was eating dog food?" Joanna echoed.

"Yes," Kendra replied. "It would appear she had a steady diet of it."

"Oh, my God!" Joanna exclaimed. "That's awful."

"And that's not all. I also found evidence of internal bruising on one leg just above the ankle. That kind of lower-leg injury suggests she'd been shackled for an extended period of time."

"You're saying she was manacled and starved?"

"Yes."

"Had she been sexually assaulted?"

"Highly likely," Kendra answered. "Tissue swabs tested positive for semen, so we should be able to come up with a DNA profile of the perpetrator. If the body hadn't been found when it was, that evidence would have been lost. So I guess we owe that creepy Jack Carver kid a debt of gratitude."

"What about cause of death?" Joanna asked. "Any visible wounds?"

"No potentially fatal ones—as in no gunshot wounds, no stab wounds, no blunt-force trauma."

"What did she die of, then?"

"Asphyxiation," Kendra answered, "but not manual strangulation. She had extensive injuries to her hands—injuries that occurred in the hours leading up to her death."

"What kind of injuries?"

"Contusions, multiple broken bones. Her hands looked almost pulverized—as though the victim had been pounding on something hard, and that made me wonder: What if she'd been shut up inside an enclosure of some kind and was trying desperately to get out? So I ran a specific test and took a look at her short-chain 3-hydroxyacyl-CoA dehydrogenase."

"Her what?"

"Never mind. The term is difficult to say and even more difficult to remember. In the world of M.E.-speak, we call that particular test SCHAD for short. The results I obtained suggest that Jane Doe was partially frozen before being dumped."

"Are you saying the victim was crammed into a freezer and frozen alive?"

"That's my theory," Kendra replied. "The wounds to her hands were self-inflicted."

Joanna Brady had been a cop for almost eight years, but news about this shocking manner of death left her horrified.

"That's appalling," she murmured.

"Yes," Kendra agreed, "isn't it just."

"Does Tom Hadlock know about this?"

"Not yet. As far as I know, he's still at the crime scene, and Detective Howell was on her way to tell him. As she was leaving, I asked her if she'd be informing you of my findings. Since you're officially on maternity leave, she said she'd have to go through channels. Seeing as how I don't work for the sheriff's department, I don't have to worry about going through channels. That's why I called. I figure us law-enforcement ladies need to stick together."

"Thank you for that," Joanna replied. "Is there any news on the other victims? Do you think they might have died the same way?"

"One for sure didn't," Kendra answered. "The partial skull that Tom Hadlock dropped off last night shows clear evidence of a single bullet wound to the back of the head. For John Doe I'd have to say gun violence is the most likely cause of death."

"Suicide?" Joanna asked.

"Not from that angle," Kendra said. "We're talking gun violence served up execution style. With the other two victims, until I have more bones to work with, I won't be able to tell, but if I were a gambler, I'd be betting money on the probability that we're dealing with several young women—marginalized women—who just happen to be the natural prey of serial killers."

"Any theories about who our perpetrator might be?"

"The level of malnutrition on the autopsied victim suggests that she had been confined for a number of months, so whoever this monster is, he's living far enough off the grid and with enough privacy that nosy neighbors aren't calling him out. My concerns are these: We've got three victims so far, but what if there are more? What if there are other victims still being held prisoner?"

Joanna took a moment to digest that. "Other living victims, you mean," she said. "That's what you were saying earlier about our not having the luxury of time."

"Right," Kendra agreed. "Let's bring this asshole down before he has a chance to kill anyone else."

"Believe me," Joanna said, "we're on it."

As soon as Dr. Baldwin hung up, Joanna tried calling Tom on the satphone. It rang, but he didn't answer. Knowing that a voice mail would show up once he was back in range, she called his cell phone and left a message.

"If it's not too late and if you don't mind, could you stop by my place on your way back to the Justice Center?"

As that brief call ended, Sage chimed in with an urgent newborn summons. She was hungry, and Joanna was more than ready to feed her. The rocker in the nursery had been Joanna's mother's. When the feeding was over, she sat with Sage nestled against her, thinking about another baby—a brutally slain baby—one who hadn't lived long enough to draw even so much as a single breath. Baby Jane Doe had never been wrapped in a soft blanket or held close or fed at her mother's breast.

It might have been nothing except raging hormones, but thinking about that poor lost child was too much. Tears trickled down Joanna's cheeks and dribbled onto the soft nap of Sage's pale pink receiving blanket. She was still weeping when Denny, wrinkly and damp from an extended bath, ventured into the nursery.

"Mommy," he said, touching her damp face, "what's the matter? Why are you crying?"

Joanna was grateful that her son had been out of earshot during that all-too-graphic discussion with Kendra Baldwin, but she was sorry to have been caught crying. For the second time that day, she forced herself to tell Denny the truth about what was going on.

"I'm sad," she admitted. "Two people were found murdered today, a woman and her baby."

"Are you going to catch the bad guy who did it?" Denny asked.

"Yes, I will," Joanna declared, wiping away the tears. "It's my job and my department's job, and that's exactly what we're going to do."

FOURTEEN

JAMES ARDMORE—Jimmy, as he preferred to be called—was pissed. The last thing—the very last thing—he'd ever expected to happen was to have one of his stalking victims turn the tables on him.

Once he'd dumped Amelia, he'd gone back to his truck, clocked in, and had driven to L.A., where he had unloaded the trailer at the warehouse. Then, instead of picking up his previously scheduled return load, he had driven east to the far side of Indio and parked his rig in the lot at the casino. It didn't matter that he'd be leaving it there for a couple of days. The guy in charge was a friend of his, who, for a few bucks in his hand, was generous with the guest passes that meant rigs could sit undisturbed in the parking lot for up to a week at a time, no questions asked.

Jimmy went inside to the car-rental desk. He would have preferred an SUV, but since none were currently available, he had to settle for a Nissan Altima.

Once in the car and headed back to L.A., he called his boss in Omaha. "Bad news, Jake," he announced. "I managed to get to the warehouse and unload, but when I went to leave again, my truck broke down and had to be towed. The mechanic here says it's going to take two days at least to get the parts in and another day to install them, so I'm stuck here for that long—three days and maybe more."

Naturally, Jake wasn't happy about that. It meant he'd have to send another driver to L.A. to pick up the load Jim was supposed to drive from L.A. to Dallas. The good news for Jimmy was that although Jake might be all kinds of pissed off right now, he was also desperate for experienced drivers and was in no position to give Jimmy his walking papers.

Had Jim Ardmore still been working for an actual living, he might have been more worried about such things, but his life had changed remarkably over the last few years. Now that he had unlimited access to his late brother's money, Jimmy had paid off his mobile home and treated himself to a brand-new also paid-in-full Peterbilt, leaving him free to call his own shots about working or not working—about taking trip assignments or turning them down. This was definitely one of the latter.

He drove to the Airbnb he'd rented in Venice. He had booked the place under the name of Arthur Ardmore and paid for it with an AmEx that had his brother's name on the account. Jimmy couldn't help but smile just thinking about that. Old stick-in-the-mud Arthur seemed to be doing a lot more traveling and having way more fun now that he was dead than when he was still alive.

As for the collection of girls Jimmy kept in the basement? He kept them for as long as he wanted—until he tired of them or they turned up pregnant, whichever came first. Which is what had happened to the little Mexican babe from El Paso. She must have gotten pregnant almost the first time he touched her. But what he was looking for now was a suitable replacement for Sandra Locke. She'd been a blonde, and that's what he wanted to bring back home—another blonde, preferably one with the kinds of curves he liked.

Jimmy wasn't in a big hurry. This was a vacation, after all. The weather in California was balmy compared to Arthur's drafty shack out in the Peloncillos or Jimmy's double-wide in Road Forks. He entertained himself by reading the restaurant reviews on Yelp and sampling the food, treating himself to upscale fare that wasn't generally available in the truck stops he usually frequented along the interstates.

By Saturday afternoon, though, his time off was coming to an end, and he was worried. Jake would want him back on the road by Monday at the latest, and time to find that missing blonde was running short. If he wasn't going to go home empty-handed, he would have to get a move on.

He spent the day strolling the beaches and the Santa Monica Pier, looking for a likely prospect. There seemed to be plenty of hot numbers to choose from, but the problem with the girls on the beaches and the pier was that they seemed to run in groups—in pairs at least. What Jimmy really needed to find was your basic one-of-a-kind—a loner—someone he could target without anyone being the wiser.

Earlier in the week, he'd done his due diligence by checking out the product on display at the various gentlemen's clubs around town, but the girls he found in those were all too old for his taste and too shopworn. He understood the trade-off. Women like that—the ones who'd been around the block—made for safer targets because they lived riskier lives. When something bad happened to a down-on-her-luck pole dancer, people in general and cops in particular tended to shrug their shoulders and act as if the victims involved had gotten what they deserved. The unexplained disappearance of a random prostitute here and there seldom caused a huge hue and cry. And most of the time, when one of them vanished without a trace, no one gave enough of a damn to go crying to the cops.

When Jimmy had plucked Amelia off that darkened street at the far end of El Paso, it hadn't occurred to him that he had just scored a virgin. That had been purely the luck of the draw, and one he was hoping to duplicate. So far he'd come up empty.

Late in the evening, tired and frustrated, he settled into a coffee shop at the corner of Pacific and Washington. When he ordered his tall, double vanilla blond iced latte, the young woman behind the counter—Megan, according to her name tag—turned out to be exactly what he wanted. Young, blond, blue-eyed, with no visible tattoos or piercings, and she came complete with a ready smile.

Drink in hand, Jimmy settled into a nearby chair, one that was close enough to the counter so he could hear the banter back and forth between Megan and her customers, most of whom seemed to be regulars. His eavesdropping provided him with several important pieces of information. Megan lived in the neighborhood, had recently broken up with a longtime boyfriend, was looking for a new roommate, was attending Santa Monica College, and wanted to get through school without a ton of student debt. Bingo.

Of all those tidbits, the most interesting was the fact that Megan needed a new roommate for an apartment that was evidently only a couple of blocks away. The coffee shop was scheduled to close at ten. By nine thirty Jimmy had moved the car from the beach lot to a spot next to the curb facing eastward on Washington. That way once Megan's shift ended and she was ready to go home, he'd be outside waiting, and she'd be ripe for the picking.

Except it hadn't worked out quite like that. Despite her age, Megan was evidently the coffee shop's manager, and she was the last one to leave, locking the door behind her. As Jimmy had anticipated, she walked eastward, away from the beach rather than toward it. Watching her go, he marked her progress along the sidewalk, delaying his attack until she was well away from the coffee shop's entrance and he could be sure she was alone.

Once she was halfway between two glowing streetlights and next to the end of an alley, he pulled up beside her and rolled down the window.

"Hey, Megan," he called. "Can you give me a little help here? How do I get back to the 10?"

Just as he expected, she came over to his vehicle and leaned down to peer into the window. "Oh, hi," she said. "It's you. Go back to Pacific and turn right on that. Follow that north to Rose. Right on Rose and then left on Fourth. Fourth will take you all the way to the freeway."

"Thanks for the help," he said.

"No problem."

"Can I give you a lift somewhere?"

"No thanks, my place is just a couple of blocks from here."

She turned and resumed her walk. He doused the lights, put the Nissan in park, and stepped out of the car. As he closed on her from behind, the last thing he expected was for her to fight back. She must have heard his footsteps because before he had a chance to lay hands on her, she stopped abruptly and spun around to face him. He barely caught a glimpse of the stun gun gripped in her fist before she zapped him with it, nailing him full in the chest and giving him a forceful shove for good measure.

Jimmy crumpled onto his back like a felled ox and lay there for a time, seeing stars and waiting for his head to clear. When he finally got his wits about him and struggled to his feet, Megan had disappeared into the night. Cussing her under his breath, he groped for his wallet and was relieved to find it just where it was supposed to be—still in his hip pocket. If the little bitch had rolled him and stolen that, he would have been up shit creek, with no credit cards and no money and with both his IDs—one for him and one for Arthur—loose in the world. That could have been disastrous.

As furious with himself as he was with Megan, Jimmy pulled it together and staggered back to his waiting car without making any attempt to follow her. She was gone. What he needed to do was get the hell out of the neighborhood in case she was even now calling the cops. Rolling down the window, he listened for approaching sirens before pulling in to traffic. Since Megan had given him directions for going north, he went directly to the first decent intersection and headed south.

As he drove, a still-dazed Jimmy tried to assess the potential damage. He had paid in cash at the coffee shop, so Megan didn't have any credit-card information that would be of use in tracking him. His biggest worry was that she might have been able to provide either a description of his vehicle or even the tag number. That meant he needed to get that Nissan back to the rental agency in Indio ASAP.

While on the hunt, Jimmy always kept his goods with him. That way once he had his target in hand, there was no reason for him to return to his lodgings. That was the case here, too. When he got to Venice Boulevard, he drove east as far as the northbound lanes of the 405.

Back on I-10 finally and driving eastbound still empty-handed, he pounded the steering wheel in a gesture that was equal parts fury and frustration.

How was it possible that he could have been taken down by a little slip of a girl who couldn't have been a day over twenty, if she was even that? What the hell was someone like her doing walking around with a goddamned stun gun in her pocket? How could that have happened? How could Jimmy have let that happen?

He was relieved to find, however, that there was no sign of any unusual police activity on I-10. He stayed in the middle lanes and stuck to the posted speed limits as he rolled past the long line of trucks waiting at the weigh station. By then he was relatively sure no one was looking for him, but he didn't want to take any chances.

Back in Indio he dropped off the car, gassed up his truck, and headed southbound on CA-86. Under the circumstances it seemed like a good idea to head eastbound on I-8 rather than I-10. What he really wanted to do was pull over, haul out a bottle of Jameson, and really tie one on, but he couldn't risk that. The last thing he needed was for some overly zealous cop to check out his vehicle and nail him on an open-container charge. That would be the end of his CDL and the end of his cover as well.

Once Jimmy finally had himself back under control, he used his cell phone to call Omaha. It was the middle of the night and the office was empty, so the call went straight to voice mail.

"Hey, Jake," Jimmy said. "Got my truck out of hock late this afternoon. I was planning to call in tomorrow to see if you had another load ready for me to take east. Problem is, I just had a call from home. My brother's health has taken a turn for the worse, and he's been transported by ambulance to a hospital in Tucson. I'm the only family he has left, so I'm going to deadhead back home. Sorry about that, especially knowing how shorthanded you are right now, but it's the best I can do. I'll let you know as soon as I'm available."

At Brawley he turned off the highway and tucked in among several other big rigs parked for the night on an empty lot behind a bustling gas station. Up in his bunk, he gathered the things he'd gotten out in advance of bringing his intended prize back to the truck—duct tape, tie-wraps, and a tarp. Once he had those properly stowed, he climbed into bed and tried to relax.

Lying there waiting to sleep, he noticed that he had a bit of a headache. That was unusual, and he wondered about that. Was it a residual effect from being hit by that stun gun or was it from the fall he'd taken? Except for those occasions when he cut loose and let himself indulge in more Jameson than was good for him, Jimmy Ardmore wasn't prone to headaches, but for the time being he decided that the best thing to do with this non-Jameson headache was ignore it and try to get some sleep.

FIFTEEN

BY EIGHT thirty Joanna had both kids in bed. Sitting in the quiet of the living room with the dogs at her feet, she gave herself the gift of settling in to read another entry from her father's journal:

I did it—filled out my job application and dropped it by the courthouse this afternoon after I got off shift and before I came home. Once I got here, you could say the crapola hit the fan. Ellie isn't speaking to me. The funny thing is, it's sort of like old Br'er Rabbit and the Briar Patch. I love it when she gives me the silent treatment. Sometimes it's only when she finally quiets down that I have a chance to think.

After reading that, Joanna had to look away from the text. Almost every paragraph contained a passage or two that would evoke a chain of powerful memories. Eleanor Lathrop Winfield's use of the silent treatment was something her daughter remembered all too well. Unbidden, a flashback came to mind as vividly as if it had been recorded on a DVR.

"Joanna, tell your father that I have a meeting after church today," Eleanor said over her shoulder. "He'll have to rustle up some lunch for both of you."

At the time Joanna couldn't have been more than eight or nine years old. That particular conversation had occurred early on a Sunday morning when all three of them were in the kitchen together—her mother at the sink doing the breakfast dishes and Joanna and her father seated at the kitchen table. Her mother went to church every Sunday. D. H. Lathrop was more of a Christmas and Easter attendee.

"Mom has a meeting after church," Joanna parroted dutifully.

"So I hear," her father said, giving his daughter a wink and a sly grin, thus turning the interaction between them into a private joke and leaving Eleanor on the outside looking in.

"How about if after church you and I hop in the car, run down to Douglas, and have ourselves a bowl of green chili at the Gadsden?" he suggested.

And that's exactly what they'd done. At the time, going to the Gadsden Hotel for lunch had been a big deal. There was an organ in the dining room where a man played music to entertain the diners. Sitting there eating and listening, Joanna had felt frightfully grown-up and sophisticated. When they returned home after lunch, Eleanor still wasn't back. When she finally did show up, much later, the silent treatment continued. She went straight into the bedroom without uttering a single word and closed the door behind her.

"Looks like we're on our own for dinner, too," D. H. had said, "but we'll manage. I won't let you starve to death."

There were plenty of other examples of the same thing, but that was the first one that came to mind. And although Joanna had no idea what had sparked this particular quarrel, she remembered that it had lasted longer than usual—for a number of days—and that it had ended as it had begun—for no discernible reason.

On the one hand, Joanna had enjoyed those little family dramas in which she was always allied with her dad—they'd made her feel both close to him and special. Even so, she had understood that it wasn't right for her parents to be using her as a weapon to score points off each other. And although it seemed clear that they were a devoted couple, that didn't mean they always got along.

At an early age, Joanna had determined that her mother's use of the silent treatment would never be part of her own emotional tool chest. When she and Andy married and had their arguments—which they did have—they were conducted out in the open. They were shouting matches—noisy confrontations conducted in front of God and everybody. Andy had sometimes referred to her as "his little red-haired spitfire," which usually only served to make Joanna that much madder.

But this round of silent treatment, the one referenced in the journal, was different. It was a pivotal one that had occurred when D. H. Lathrop had gone against Eleanor's express wishes and applied to work at the sheriff's department. Joanna wasn't even born at that point, making her wonder how long the periods of silence between her parents had lasted before she arrived on the scene and could be used as a pawn to intervene?

That realization set Joanna to wondering something else. Why had Eleanor been so opposed to her husband's change of job in the first place? Was she primarily worried about his safety, or was she more concerned that if D. H. left the mines, she'd lose some of her social standing in the community? How much did the potential wage cut have to do with it? Had she been concerned that the difference in pay scale would make it impossible for them to cover their bills or that maybe she herself might have to go looking for a job? And did the fact that Eleanor had been so opposed to her husband's becoming a cop play a part in her long-held opposition to Joanna's making the same decision those many years later? These were all good questions, and with Eleanor Lathrop Winfield gone there were no ready answers.

Lights flashed outside the window announcing Tom Hadlock's arrival. Both dogs went on high alert, barking like crazy before Joanna used the hand signal that Jenny had taught her to silence them. Hurrying to the door to greet her visitor, Joanna escorted Tom into the house. Stetson in hand, he was already apologizing.

"Sorry to show up so late," he said. "It's been a

long day. We'd all been out there in the boonies for hours on end with nothing to eat and not much to drink, either, so I had the whole crew stop off in Douglas on the way home so I could buy them some dinner."

"Good call," Joanna said. "You've got to keep your troops fed if you want them to deliver. How about you? Can I get you anything?"

"Some coffee would be good, if you don't mind," he said. "When I leave here, I have to stop by the department and work on the press release with Ernie."

Joanna did a double take. "With Ernie?" she asked.

Tom nodded. "This thing is gonna turn into a media shitstorm, if you'll pardon the expression. I can't run the department and handle a barrage of incoming from an army of reporters at the same time. Speaking of which, Marliss was out at the crime scene raising hell almost as soon as the detectives showed up."

"No surprises there," Joanna said.

"Anyway," Tom continued, "over dinner we had a chance to discuss the media-relations situation. I didn't exactly put it up for a vote, but close, and we came to the general conclusion that Ernie Carpenter is the best one to handle Media Relations. He's the only one who'll be able to hold his own with all those people. They'll eat everybody else alive."

"Can you afford to take him away from the investigation?" Joanna asked.

"Not really, especially since we don't have anyone else we can bring on board at homicide right now, either."

That was true. Joanna had once expected that Jeremy Stock would be the next deputy to get promoted into investigations. She knew now that would have been a disaster. In the face of this new crisis, having Ernie off the investigation team would make things difficult. Still, she had to agree that Ernie was probably the best choice to handle the press right then.

"Given what you're up against, sounds like you're making the best of a bad bargain," Joanna told Tom. "So have a seat. Coffee is coming right up."

Settled into the breakfast nook, Tom ran his fingers through his sparse hair in a despairing gesture that left his comb-over standing on end. It had been a long, tough day. The man seemed to have aged a year since Joanna saw him last.

"I hope you don't mind my coming to you for help," he said, "but I feel like I'm in over my head, and I hardly know where to start."

"Exactly where you started," Joanna assured him, "with the evidence. By the way, I had a courtesy call from Dr. Baldwin after the autopsy."

"So you know about the fetus and the freezer?"

"I do," she said. "It sounds like we're dealing with someone who's almost subhuman."

"That's my take on it, too," Tom agreed, "a serial killer with several victims."

"How many?"

Tom shook his head. "We're still not sure. In addition to the one body, we found two additional skulls and a whole mess of bones—whole bones and pieces of bones."

"So counting the one Jack Carver found, we're talking at least four victims."

Tom nodded. "I have no doubt that with the help of those cadaver dogs we'll probably find lots more bones, but telling which ones go together and which ones don't is going to be like putting together a giant jigsaw puzzle."

"And whoever's doing this has been doing it for some time."

Tom nodded again. "For months and maybe even years. Ernie says it's got to be somebody local, someone who can come and go without arousing suspicion. The idea that we've got a monster like that right here in Cochise County makes me sick to my stomach. Most of the folks who live out in the Peloncillos are ranchers who've been in this neck of the woods for generations. Some of them I've known my whole life. They're good people—honest as the day is long, salt of the earth."

"Most of them may be," Joanna observed, "but clearly one of them isn't. So tell me about the crime scene. You were out there all day. Did you do a grid search?"

"As best we could with the personnel we had on hand."

"Since one of the victims was a gunshot victim, did you find any shell casings?"

"Nope, none of those," Tom said. "The grass is too thick. To find shell casings, we'd need to search the whole area with metal detectors. All we found were bones and more bones, but no other usable evidence—no footprints, tire tracks, cigarette butts, or soda cans—nothing that would give us the possibility of a DNA profile or point us in the direction of a possible suspect."

"Frustrating," Joanna said.

"Yes," Tom agreed, "very. Since that new body is only a few days old, we can assume that the killer is still in the area and still active, but that may change. As soon as he gets wind that we've found his dump site, he's liable to take off."

"And if he's holding any other hostages . . ." Joanna began.

"They'll be dead, too," Tom said, completing her sentence for her. "So how the hell do we stop him?"

As the coffee finished brewing, Joanna rose, poured a cup, and brought it to him, thinking as she went. "Any ideas?" she asked.

Sitting there at the table, nervously fiddling with his hat, Tom reminded her of a little kid standing at his teacher's desk waiting to have his homework reviewed. At the end of this long, difficult day, he was in over his head. She needed a kind way to encourage him without undermining his confidence.

"I was thinking of calling in the FBI," he said.

Joanna had been thinking the same thing, but there was a problem with that. Tucson wasn't exactly a high-profile location when it came to FBI postings. During her tenure as sheriff, she had seen several special agents in charge come and go. The ones who were young and ambitious worked like crazy and quickly found ways to transfer out to places where career advancement was more of an option. Then there were the placeholders, the older guys on their way out, who were just counting down the days to retirement. Unfortunately, Tucson's current SAIC was one of the latter.

"Go ahead and call Ted Whipple," she said, "but I'm not sure how much good it'll do. I have it on good authority from my friend Robin that he's not much of a go-getter."

"Robin," Tom mused. "That lady FBI agent from up in Tucson who was here when Jeremy Stock went haywire?"

"The very one."

"So you don't think Whipple will go to bat for us and call in that team of people who ride around the country in a private jet in that *Criminal Minds* TV show?"

"I doubt it," Joanna said with a smile. "And even if he did, I'm not sure it would be helpful. Turning a bunch of visiting FBI agents loose in rural Cochise County might end up being counterproductive. What we really need is help from someone who can give us some context on a possible perpetrator."

"Like a profiler, you mean?" Tom asked.

"Exactly," Joanna agreed, "and our best bet for getting one of those would be appealing to the FBI, assuming you can get Whipple to go along with the program. In the meantime we need information from the people who actually live out near the crime scene."

"As in has anyone noticed anything out of line?"

"Yes," Joanna replied. "If our bad guy has been hiding right out in the open and coming and going from the dump site without arousing any suspicion, that most likely means he's somebody who belongs there—somebody no one is particularly worried about. But just because they're not worried about him doesn't mean he hasn't been seen."

"Too bad there aren't surveillance cameras out there," Tom muttered.

"But there are people," Joanna countered. "All we need to do is find the right one."

"How?"

"By talking to the neighbors, not just the near neighbors but the ones in the general area—people who might have noticed someone or something that was odd or out of place, a vehicle—maybe even a familiar one—coming or going at strange or unusual times. And for conducting those kinds of interviews, having locals do the job will be more effective than bringing in a bunch of outsiders. If you send in a troop of visiting feds, the people who live out there in the boonies—the ones you call 'salt of the earth'—are liable to clam right up."

"Are you saying I need to have our people hit the ground running and touch bases with everyone in the area?" Tom asked.

"Yes, that's it exactly," Joanna told him, "and the sooner the better. Once all of this hits the news, those folks won't be eager to talk to our people, either."

"How much territory are you thinking about?" Tom asked.

"The entire San Bernardino Valley for starters, north to south," Joanna said, "from the Mexican border north to I-10 and from Douglas east to

New Mexico. If this guy is a local, but a local with wheels, he could be from almost anywhere."

"That's a huge area to cover," Tom objected.

"Yes, it is," Joanna said, "but you need to get the job done—ASAP. Starting tomorrow morning, pull everyone you can off patrol and get them out canvassing."

"But the overtime—"

"Don't worry about overtime right now," Joanna advised him. "By the time that issue hits the fan, I'll be back on the job, and it'll be a lot easier to justify the extra expenditures if the serial killer is in custody rather than still on the loose."

"Okay," Tom conceded. "When it comes to dealing with the budget, better you than me."

"What about the crime scene?" Joanna asked as he rose to go. "Do you have someone posted out there overnight to maintain the chain of evidence?"

"Yes, ma'am, I sure do," he said, "Deputy Raymond from Elfrida. He showed up just as we were getting ready to come back here."

Deputy Garth Raymond from out in the Sulphur Springs Valley was a recent graduate of the University of Arizona, where he majored in criminal justice. Now twenty-three years old and fresh out of the academy, he was one of Joanna's most promising recruits.

When Tom Hadlock rose to go, he seemed to be in better spirits—as though the coffee and the pep talk from Joanna had given him a sense of direction.

"Deputy Raymond may be the new kid on the

block," Tom said, "but he's thrilled to have a crack at some overtime."

"I hope he came equipped with food, water, and blankets."

"That's right," Tom said. "I told him there's no such thing as a TacoTime in the Peloncillos. The weather report says it's supposed to get down to freezing out there tonight. I'll send someone out to relieve him first thing in the morning."

"What about chain-of-evidence coverage for to-morrow when the dogs are working?"

"I'll deal with that either tonight or tomorrow. Any idea when those dogs are due to show up?"

"The Paxtons expect to leave Phoenix first thing in the morning. They should be here right around noon, and they'll need someone to guide them to the crime scene."

"I'll see to it," Tom said, reaching for his hat. "Now I'd best get off my butt and head back to the department so Ernie and I can pull together that press release."

"What are you planning on saying?" Joanna asked.

"Just what you taught me," he told her with a grin. "We'll provide as much vague information as possible—enough to keep them happy without giving too much away."

"Sounds about right," Joanna said.

"You bet," Tom agreed. "I learned from the best."

SIXTEEN

AS THE long hours ticked by, Deputy Garth Raymond knew that guarding a crime scene in the middle of the night in the middle of nowhere was grunt work, but he didn't mind and was glad to do it. At least he had a job—a real paying job. Some of the guys and gals he'd graduated with last spring were still looking for work, hoping to get hired by one of the bigger departments, where the pay would be better than out in the boondocks. Not Garth. He had wanted to be back home, living and working in Cochise County, and he was happy with the pittance he was earning as a newly hired deputy in Sheriff Joanna Brady's department.

The money wasn't good, but Garth didn't need much. For one thing, as long as he lived at home in Elfrida with his grandmother, he didn't have to pay rent. After his grandfather's death, he had inherited Grandpa Jeb's elderly Silverado pickup, which still ran like a top. That meant Garth didn't have a car payment, either. When he was on duty and out on patrol, he traveled the county in the department's oldest and junkiest Tahoe, which he was able to drive home when he went off shift. So even though his take-home pay was low, he was nonetheless making good inroads on paying down his college loans.

Working in Cochise County allowed him to keep an eye on his widowed grandmother. The fact that Juanita Raymond refused to charge him rent was a side benefit, but he was determined to look after her. She was spry and in good health, but that might not always be the case, and since Grandma Juanita had looked after him for the past dozen years, Garth wanted to be there to return the favor should she need the help. None of that would have made sense to his unemployed classmates up in Tucson, but it made sense to him.

It was a cold, clear night, with uncountable stars glittering against a velvet black sky. Chief Deputy Hadlock had left the satphone with him, just in case, but he'd had no occasion to use it because nothing at all had happened. Some other officers might have been tempted to do a half-assed job by spending the night dozing inside the Tahoe. That wasn't for Garth. Staying awake was easier if he was outside, so he spent most of the time actively patrolling the area, walking back and forth along the shoulder of the road next to the crime scene. He had hand warmers in the pockets of his jacket, and those helped. Only when his feet got too cold did he climb into his vehicle again, fire it up, and leave it idling with the heater on high long enough for his feet to thaw out.

About midnight a double-curved moon peeked

out from behind the Peloncillos. As soon as he saw it, he was transported back to the first time he'd ever visited this small mountain range that straddles the Arizona–New Mexico border. It had been during white-tail season, and he had come here with Grandpa Jeb.

They'd camped out near a blazing fire on a late-October night similar to this one but not nearly as cold. Garth was twelve years old at the time, and it had been his first-ever hunting trip. They were curled up in their sleeping bags next to the fire when a moon just like this one made an appearance.

"What you're seeing right there is what they call a gibbous moon," Grandpa Jeb had said, pointing.

"A what?" Garth asked.

"Gibbous means more than half the moon is showing. It could be waxing or waning right now—hard to tell. 'Gibbous' comes from an old English word that means 'humpbacked.' And that's what they call moons like this in the book I'm reading—gibbous."

At the time Garth's mother, Betsy, hadn't been dead for very long, but what he remembered most about her was that she'd been sick for years and in and out of the hospital more often than he could count. "Cancer" was a word that was mentioned in hushed tones in their household, but only when Garth was thought to be out of earshot. His mother's mother, Grandma Peggy, had come to live with them early on, taking care of Garth when his mother was in the hospital and looking after both him and her daughter when Betsy was home.

Other kids had mothers who drove them to school and volunteered for the PTA and showed up at soccer games. In Garth's reality Grandma Peggy did the driving while his mother lived out her days in a hospital bed set up in what should have been the family room of their home in Tempe, Arizona. To Garth's way of thinking, that was how things were and how they would always be—with his father working, Grandma Peggy looking after the house, and his mother lying in the bed watching TV. Except that didn't happen. His mother died, and everything changed.

For a while things seemed to be the same. Grandma Peggy stayed on and made sure the household ran smoothly. That only worked until Laurie Magnussen appeared on the scene. Garth's mother had been ill most of his life, but she had also been naturally quiet and reserved. There was nothing quiet about Laurie. She was younger than his father. She was blond, loud, bossy, and flamboyant—from the tips of her brightly lacquered fingernails to the toes of her very high-heeled shoes. She had walked into his father's life and assumed total control.

Now that Garth was older, he saw Laurie for what she was—a gold digger who'd been looking for a free ride. Once she was ensconced in her new husband's house, after a surprisingly hasty courtship, her first order of business had been to get rid of Grandma Peggy. Laurie had declared war on the older woman, and it was only a matter of months before her incessant harping and constant criticism drove his grandmother out of their lives.

*   *   *

On the night of that first hunting trip, it had been five months since Garth's father and Laurie had effectively exiled *him* from their lives by shipping him off to his grandparents' farm near Elfrida. The original plan—at least the stated plan—had been for him to stay there over the summer while Laurie and his father finished remodeling their new place in Paradise Valley and got settled in. Somehow, once summer ended and it was time for school to start, the decision had been made—without any input from Garth himself—that he should stay on in Elfrida. Grandma Juanita had promptly enrolled him in Elfrida Elementary School, and that was that.

When his father drove him down from Phoenix, Garth had fully expected to hate being stuck on the farm. He was sure he'd be bored to death, thinking he would miss his friends, his video games, and his skateboard. Instead he spent the whole summer tagging along after Grandpa Jeb, who in short order taught him how to drive a tractor, plow a straight line, stack hay, and run the irrigation system, all the while feeding the boy little nuggets of wisdom.

Garth's twelfth birthday came along in mid-July. That evening after supper, once Garth had blown out the candles on his birthday cake, Grandpa Jeb had gone to his gun rack, taken down a polished .22 rifle—an old Remington—and presented it to his grandson.

"My old man gave me this on my twelfth birthday," Jeb had said, handing it over. "I'm giving it to you on the condition that you promise to take care of it and learn to handle it properly. If you do enough target practice between now and then, once white-tail season rolls around in October, we'll go hunting."

"Hunting?" Garth had repeated, barely believing what he'd just heard. "For reals?"

"For reals," Grandpa Jeb had replied.

Under his grandfather's supervision, Garth learned how to clean and load the weapon. Over the next couple of months, hours of target practice more than filled the void in Garth's life created by the absence of both his skateboard and his video games. And now here they were—hunting. The first day out, they'd seen several does but no bucks.

"That's okay," Grandpa Jeb had said. "If you're gonna hunt or fish, you need to pack along plenty of food and a full load of patience."

That night Garth lay on the hard-packed earth staring up at the rising moon. "How'd you know about gibbous moons?" he asked. "How come you know so much stuff?"

"I read about it," Grandpa Jeb said.

In the months Garth had lived in Elfrida, the only books he'd seen Grandpa Jeb reading out in the living room at night had been the King James Bible and the *Farmers' Almanac*. Garth was pretty sure neither one of those had anything to say about gibbous moons.

"I found it in your grandmother's *World Book Encyclopedia*," Grandpa Jeb replied.

"You mean those red-and-gold books on the shelf in your bedroom?"

"That's right," Grandpa Jeb said. "Those are the ones. Grandma picked them up at a church rummage sale a year or so ago. I'd always felt stupid because I never graduated from high school, but your grandmother's a wise woman. 'Jebbie,' she says to me, 'you don't have to have a high-school diploma in order to get an education. If you read a page or two of this every night, you'll be more educated than most of those tomfool, hotshot kids graduating from college these days.' So that's what I've been doing ever since, reading a page or two every night just before bedtime. I do my learning reading then, in hopes some of it will maybe soak into the old gray cells overnight."

"You read a page a night?"

"Thereabouts—sometimes more, sometimes less."

"How far are you?"

"I'm at the beginning of the N's now," Grandpa Jeb said. "Just finished the M's a couple of days ago. That's where I read all about the moon. And gibbous is one of those things that stuck with me."

Ever since it had stuck with Jebediah Raymond's grandson as well.

SEVENTEEN

AT FIVE o'clock in the morning, Garth climbed into the Tahoe and sat with the heater running while he ate the last of the ham sandwiches Grandma Juanita had packed and sent with him for this long, overnight shift. When the sandwich was gone, he polished off the last thermos of coffee, thinking about his grandmother with every sip. She had been the one unwavering presence in his life from the time he was eleven, and she still was.

On that first hunting trip, Garth and Grandpa Jeb never got a deer, but they did the second year, and the year after that, and the one after that as well. There was a guy in town who did the butchering for them, and Grandma Juanita always found ways to cook the venison they brought home, doing so without a word of complaint. Her rule of thumb was as follows: if you aren't going to eat it, you sure as hell shouldn't shoot it.

That was one of the interesting things about Grandma Juanita. She went to church every Sunday, but her pewmates would have been surprised to learn that at home she was the one who sometimes dished out the salty language.

When Christmas rolled around that year, Garth's dad, Cooper Raymond, came to fetch him and take him home to Paradise Valley, except as far as Garth was concerned, Paradise Valley wasn't home. The friends he'd had before still lived in Tempe, and even when he was able to connect with them, it wasn't the same. They'd all moved on, and he was an outsider. As for the few kids living in Cooper and Laurie's new neighborhood? They showed no interest in hooking up with someone who was there visiting for Christmas, especially not a hick who spent most of his time living on a farm in Elfrida.

"Where the hell is Elfrida?" one of the boys had asked him sneeringly. "Is that even in Arizona?"

Well, yes it was.

Being in Paradise Valley and under Laurie's thumb for two whole weeks felt like being in prison. She treated Garth like he was six instead of twelve. She expected him to be in bed by eight o'clock every night—in bed with no TV—while she and his father did whatever they usually did at night, which obviously included a lot of drinking and partying. At home with Grandpa and Grandma Raymond, everybody went to bed at nine. Laurie fixed him microwavable dinners to eat alone in the kitchen while she and his father ate their dinner at the dining-room table after Garth was tucked away in the "guest" room, and that's clearly what it was—a guest room. Boxes with his stuff in them, including the clothing he'd outgrown, were stored in the garage. There was no place in the house that had been designated as belonging to him. This was their house—Laurie's and his father's house—not his.

During his visit the only time Garth wasn't under her control was when he woke up in the morning. He was used to getting up early because that's when Grandpa and Grandma got up. The first time he went downstairs and found his dad drinking coffee at the kitchen counter, Garth had poured a cup for himself.

"Hey," his father said. "You can't do that."

"Why not?" Garth returned. "Grandma Juanita lets me have coffee in the mornings."

"Yeah," Cooper Raymond replied with a chuckle. "I suppose she does. She let me start drinking coffee when I was about your age."

Garth slipped onto the barstool next to his father's. "How come Laurie doesn't like me?"

"She's never had any kids of her own. I don't think she knows what to do."

They were quiet for a time. "I don't like this house," Garth said. "It's too big. I liked our old house better."

"That was Mom's house," his father said. "This is Laurie's."

"How come there's no carpet? There's carpet in Grandma's house."

"Laurie likes tile. I like tile."

But you don't like me, Garth remembered thinking.

For the next two weeks, he savored those early-morning hours when he was alone—after his dad left for work and before Laurie finally came out of the bedroom and started bossing him around. He walked the hilly, winding streets of Paradise Valley. They were all paved. The streets back home in Elfrida were mostly dirt. And that's where he wanted to be—back home with Grandpa and Grandma.

That was the only year Garth went to Paradise Valley for Christmas. Although his father was conscientious about sending monthly checks to cover Garth's upkeep, he came to Elfrida to visit on increasingly rare occasions, and when he stopped by, he never stayed long. From more than two hundred miles away, Laurie was still running the show, because, Garth realized now, his father had been pussy-whipped—he had always been pussy-whipped.

"I don't know why he never takes Garth home with him," Grandma Juanita grumbled to her husband one night after their son left Elfrida to drive back to Phoenix. "That's where he belongs."

"He says Laurie doesn't like kids and she isn't good with them," Grandpa Jeb had replied.

"That's a bunch of bull crap," Grandma Juanita snapped. "Since Coop already had a son when he met her, he should have figured that out before he ever married that awful woman."

Of course, Grandma Juanita never said anything like that directly to Garth. She and Grandpa had been having a quiet conversation in the privacy of their bedroom. Garth, sitting in the room next door, had overheard the remark and couldn't have agreed more. Obviously, Garth didn't like Laurie, either. That made them even, he supposed, and he was grateful for being able to stay on with his grandparents, with people who actually *did* like him.

He had graduated from Elfrida Elementary and gone on to Valley Union High School. Grandpa Jeb doted on his grandson, and Garth returned the favor. More than simply loving the older man, Garth respected him. His grandfather was a farmer, someone who lived close to the earth, and it was hardly surprising that Garth had planned on following in Grandpa Jeb's footsteps.

Garth got involved in 4-H his first year at Elfrida Elementary. By the time he was a senior at Valley Union High, he was president of Future Farmers of America. As far as academics were concerned, Garth was an excellent student, if not the top one. A Mormon girl named Anna Lee Smith beat him out as valedictorian, but being named salutatorian was enough to win him a full-ride scholarship to the University of Arizona. Garth's father had majored in business and become a CPA. Wanting a major as far away from his father's as possible, Garth signed on to study agriculture.

All that changed at the end of his sophomore year. Grandpa Jeb was out repairing a fence line one afternoon late in May when he'd been attacked by a marauding pair of UDAs, border crossers from Mexico, who had beaten him to a bloody pulp and left him to die before driving off in the old man's pickup. When her husband failed to come home at dinnertime, Juanita went looking for him. She found him lying near death and summoned help. He was airlifted to University Hospital in Tucson, where doctors worked feverishly to save him.

Grandpa Jeb was hospitalized in the ICU for the better part of three weeks, but he never fully recovered. When it came time to release him from the ICU, the doctors had given Juanita two grim choices, suggesting that she transfer him either to a nursing home or else to a brick-and-mortar hospice facility. Disregarding their advice, Grandma Juanita had elected to take her Jebbie home.

Back in the Sulphur Springs Valley, neighbors and friends from church had rallied around the Raymonds, taking turns bringing food and taking care of chores while Grandma Juanita and Garth, out of school on summer break, looked after Grandpa. Cooper and Laurie had made several brief appearances, staying long enough to murmur a few trite words of compassion, but without lifting a hand or offering to do any of the hard work that goes with actual caregiving.

Over the years Grandma Juanita had never knowingly said anything disparaging about either her son or his wife in Garth's presence. Coop and Laurie had enough good sense to stay in a motel in Douglas when they came to visit, but when they dropped by the house, they expected to be treated as honored guests, showing up at mealtimes and never seeing a need to do any of the cleanup afterward.

One day by the time they finally departed for Paradise Valley, Grandma Juanita had been pushed to the end of her endurance. She'd been washing the lunchtime dishes with Garth wiping them dry when she finally lost it.

"That no-good son of mine is worthless as teats on a boar hog," she had muttered fiercely, "and that wife of his is even worse. How dare she come around here sneering because we don't have a dishwasher!"

Then, much to Garth's surprise, Grandma Juanita burst into tears. It was the first and only time he'd ever seen her cry. Putting down his towel, he gathered her into his arms and held her while she sobbed against his chest.

"I didn't raise your father to be like that," she said at last, straightening up. "I raised him to be a good boy, and look how he turned out."

"How Cooper Raymond turned out is his fault not yours," Garth had told her. "Definitely not yours!"

Once back at home, Jebediah required round-the-clock care. The double bed the couple had shared during most of their married life was banished to a shed outside and replaced by a more functional hospital bed. Grandma Juanita had decamped to the bedroom that had always been Garth's, while he was reduced to bunking on the sofa in the living room.

One night when Grandma Juanita was taking the night shift, Garth ventured into the room to see how she was doing. He found her sitting next to her husband's bed with an open volume of the *World Book* resting on her lap—volume A, as it turned out. Afraid the book might fall off her lap and land on her foot, Garth attempted to remove it without disturbing her. Naturally, that didn't work. She jerked awake and then held the book to her breast as though fearing that he might tear it away from her.

"Have you started reading this, too?" he asked.

"I'm reading it to him aloud," Grandma Juanita said. "I'm not sure if he can hear me. I hope so."

Garth had hoped so, too. After that, whenever it was his turn to stand watch, he located Grandma's bookmark and he read aloud, too. These days after he got off shift, that tradition continued. Not every night, but often, when it was time to go to bed, he'd read a page or two as well, reading silently now rather than aloud. He was currently halfway through volume C.

When it came time to schedule Grandpa Jeb's funeral, there was no question that it would be held at Elfrida's First Baptist Church, where Jeb and Juanita had both been lifelong members, and on the day of Jebediah Raymond's funeral everybody in town turned out, packing the small white church to overflowing.

Cooper and Laurie were in attendance, of course, but when the service was over, Garth was the one Grandma Juanita asked to escort her down the aisle and outside to the waiting hearse. They were standing there in an unofficial receiving line, greeting people and waiting for the pallbearers to bring out the casket, when a tiny red-haired woman wearing a khaki uniform with a badge on the shirt appeared in front of them. A name tag identified her as Sheriff Joanna Brady.

Garth recognized the name, if not the person. In the aftermath of Grandpa Jeb's death and while working on his grandmother's behalf, he had dealt with any number of people from the Cochise County Sheriff's Department—with deputies and detectives—but not with the sheriff herself.

"Why, Sheriff Brady," Grandma Juanita said, extending her hand in welcome. "I didn't see you inside. It's very kind of you to come."

"I came to tell you that we got them," Sheriff Brady announced. "Our BOLO on your husband's pickup got a hit on a vehicle parked at a motel in DeKalb County, Georgia, yesterday afternoon. This morning an arrest team of U.S. Marshals picked them up. The killers are being held in the county lockup in Decatur, Georgia. Arlee Jones, the county attorney, is currently initiating extradition procedures. I thought you'd want to know."

"Thank you for coming to tell us in person," Grandma Juanita said. "That was very kind."

"It's my job," Sheriff Brady had said. "It's what the people of this county trust me to do."

That small act of kindness on Joanna Brady's part had stayed with Garth Raymond from then on, and it was one of the reasons, when school started back up in the fall, he changed his major over from the College of Agriculture to criminal justice. The other reason was the relatively swift and successful outcome of the case.

Because Grandpa Jeb had died during the commission of a felony—grand theft auto—the county attorney had charged both assailants with first-degree homicide. Faced with the possibility of a death-sentence conviction, they had seen fit to accept plea bargains of life without the possibility of parole. The agreement took lethal injection off the table, but it also denied them the right to initiate any future appeals of their respective sentences.

Originally, since the stolen pickup had been regarded as evidence in a possible homicide trial, it had been transported from Georgia back to the county impound lot at the Justice Center near Bisbee. Once Grandpa Jeb's killers were shipped off to the state prison in Florence, and with all further criminal proceedings canceled, the county attorney determined there was no longer any reason to continue holding the vehicle. The pickup was returned to Grandma Juanita, who promptly handed it over to Garth.

Given all that, it was hardly surprising that Grandpa Jeb's murder had changed the course of Garth's life and set him on his current path, one that had him spending this bitterly cold night out in the wilds, pacing up and down the roadway beside a field of bones. And because of that long-ago hunting trip, he spent most of that night thinking about Jebediah and Juanita Raymond, the people who'd raised him and nurtured him when his own father had turned away.

The traumatic events of that summer had forced Garth to grow up fast. In a matter of days, he was transformed from a carefree college kid without a care in the world to the man in his grandmother's household. Between then and the time school started, Garth did most of the chores around the place. In advance of going off to school, he helped his grandmother look for and find a suitable hired hand. And once school started back up, he came home almost every weekend to help out and make sure things stayed on track.

Within three months of Grandpa Jeb's death, Garth's father turned up with a ready buyer for Juanita's farm and a plan to move her out of her home and into an assisted-living facility in Mesa, where, as Coop assured her, he and Laurie would be able to keep an eye on her. Not wanting to be bullied, Grandma Juanita had turned to Garth for help. Garth, too, could see that running the farm on her own was too much for Grandma Juanita, but he also discerned that his stepmother's money-grubbing ways were behind his father's scheme to move Grandma to Mesa. Not only did Garth want to keep his grandmother from being dumped in among a bunch of strangers, he also wanted to help preserve her nest egg and maintain her independence.

To that end, although Garth might have changed his major over to criminal justice, he still had a few connections inside the College of Agriculture. One of his former professors was intimately involved with the burgeoning winemaking industry developing in southeastern Arizona. The professor put Garth in touch with an ambitious young vintner who was willing to pay almost double the lowball offer from the buyer Coop had located.

It wasn't until the day of the scheduled closing

that Cooper Raymond learned of his son's successful end run around him. Furious, he had shown up uninvited at the title company's office, barging into the meeting fully intent on getting Juanita to back out of the deal. When Coop started berating his mother in public, Garth grabbed his father by the arm and bodily escorted him from the office.

"You're behind all this, aren't you!" Cooper snarled accusingly, bristling with anger. "You're the one who got her to go with this deal instead of the one I found for her. How dare you pull an underhanded stunt like that?"

Standing under a warm October sun, staring into each other's eyes, Garth suddenly saw his father in an entirely new light. They'd never been close, not even when Garth's mother was alive. As a child Garth had regarded his somewhat distant father with a certain amount of awe. Cooper Raymond was a smooth operator, a sophisticated businessman who presented himself as the ultimate professional. Now Garth realized that entire persona was a fraud designed to smooth over who and what his father really was—a small-minded, weak-willed man who leaped to do his grasping wife's bidding.

For a long time, father and son stood there in a silent eyeball-to-eyeball stalemate. Back when Garth was a kid and his father had lit into him for some infraction or another, he remembered thinking, *Just wait until I get big and you get little*. And now that very thing had happened. Garth was a good two inches taller than his father, and years of hefting bales of hay and helping on the farm had made all the difference. He was taller and heavier than his father now and could easily have whipped his ass.

For a time it seemed likely that the situation might deteriorate into a physical confrontation. Instead, after several tense moments, Garth took a careful backward step. "You know what, Coop?" he said. "It was easy." With that he turned and walked away.

"Don't you turn your back on me!" Cooper raged after him. "And don't you go calling me by my first name, either. I'm your father, damn it. Show a little respect!"

Just outside the door to the office, Garth's forward progress came to an abrupt stop.

"Respect?" he demanded, spinning back around. "Are you kidding me? If I'd had a shred of respect left for you, it would have evaporated the moment you charged into this office and started yelling at your mother. And as far as being my father is concerned? Forget about it. That ended about the same time you brought me down here and dumped me off on your parents' doorstep. So good-bye, Cooper. May you rot in hell, and don't let the car door hit you in the ass."

With Cooper Raymond no longer in the middle of it, the real-estate transaction had moved forward without a hitch. Proceeds from the sale of the farm had paid off the remainder of the medical bills from Jebediah's three-week stay in the ICU with enough left over to allow Juanita to pay cash for a small two-bedroom home inside Elfrida proper, where she could live out her days in the same community that had always been her home.

The sun was well up, and Garth was back in the Tahoe warming his feet again when a marked patrol car, another SUV, pulled up behind his and flashed the light bar. Moments later a uniformed deputy tapped on the window, and Garth rolled it down.

"Deputy Hernandez," the new arrival announced. "You about ready to head home? I'm your relief."

"Thanks," Garth said, handing over the sat-phone. "Nothing much happened overnight."

"That'll change," Hernandez said. "I've heard there's going to be a big push today. Everybody will be canvassing the area looking for leads. If you want more overtime, I'd go home, get myself some shut-eye, and then turn up later to help out. According to the lieutenant, it's gonna be all hands on deck."

"Good advice," Garth told him. "I'm on my way."

EIGHTEEN

IN THE early hours of that Sunday morning, as the sun came up over Brawley, California, nearby rigs firing up their engines and heading out awakened Jim Ardmore from a sound sleep. The first thing he noticed was that his damned head still hurt. If he'd had an Aleve handy, he probably would have taken one. Instead he walked as far as the food mart at the gas station and grabbed some coffee. There was no sense in rushing. There was a decent Denny's in Yuma, one he visited often. He'd stop there, fuel up, have some breakfast, and do his shopping.

Although there was no indication that anyone was actively looking for him, Jimmy was still shaken by his near miss from the night before. Obviously he'd become complacent. That had to change as of right now, and next time he went hunting, he'd be more careful. As for doing that in California? Not anytime soon. Those fresh-faced California girls might be cute as all hell, but they could also be dangerous. When it was time to hit the road again, he'd ask Jake to assign him to trips that would take him east—back to Dallas or Houston or New Orleans or Atlanta, where the pickings might be easier. For right now, though, it might be a good idea to back off and consider keeping only one girl at a time.

Jimmy turned onto eastbound I-8 south of Brawley. As often happened when he was headed home, he thought about Arthur, his brother—his half brother, that is. Although he'd had his suspicions about that all along, it wasn't until Arthur told him about their mother's deathbed confession of infidelity that he'd finally learned the truth about his own parentage.

James Edward Ardmore had been the unfortunate by-product of an out-of-wedlock fling between his mother, Phyllis, and her husband's younger brother, Tim. Tim had died shortly thereafter in a fatal car accident, and Jimmy had been raised by Phyllis's husband, Harry (Harrison) Ardmore. Had Harrison known the truth about his wife's affair? Probably. That would help explain why he'd beaten the crap out of Jimmy on an almost daily basis.

As a result of the continuing abuse, Jimmy had grown up seething with hatred. He hated Harry, his presumed father, for the brutal beatings. He hated his mother for never sticking up for him and for not walking away from the marriage. But most of all he hated his brother, Arthur, for the unforgivable sin of being perfect.

Jimmy had been only eight and Arthur five years older when, at Sunday school, he'd first heard the story of Cain and Abel. Even then it was clear to Jimmy that Cain had a point. Abel was perfection itself, the kid who was the favorite and who did no wrong, while Cain did nothing right. That was the script for his and Arthur's lives, too. Arthur did everything he was supposed to do—he never talked back, studied, got good grades, went to college, and earned an M.B.A. He inherited Harrison Ardmore's wholesale auto-parts business just in time to make a fortune by unloading it to a group of investors.

Jimmy, in the meantime, did whatever it took to garner attention, and not in a good way. He acted out; he never did his homework; he bad-mouthed his teachers; he got into fights at school; he did drugs, drank alcohol, and raced hot rods. He got out of juvie on his twenty-first birthday, having been locked up for two years on a charge of involuntary manslaughter.

While driving in an illegal street race, he'd been behind the wheel of an out-of-control vehicle that had slammed into three innocent bystanders, fatally injuring two of them. Fortunately for the sole survivor as well as for the families of the deceased, Harrison Ardmore's insurance company had stepped up to the plate. Once the family's umbrella policy finished covering a fortune in ensuing liability claims, Harry'd had enough and washed his hands of this difficult offspring who was in reality his brother's son. By the time Jimmy emerged from juvie, Harry Ardmore was dead, Jimmy himself had been disinherited, and Arthur was richer than Midas.

The problem with Arthur and the thing Jimmy found so revolting about him was that, with one notable exception, he really was perfect. He was in fact a good guy. He had nursed their mother, Phyllis, through several bouts with cancer before her eventual death. He had sought out his dispossessed younger brother and did what he could to help him. Arthur made it possible for Jimmy to purchase his first big rig, allowing him to set himself up in the long-haul trucking business.

The only serious blot on Arthur's presumed perfection—the single unresolvable contradiction in his life—stemmed from the fact that he was gay. Try as he might, he was unable to reconcile those two polar-opposite realities. Homosexuality went against the grain of everything Arthur believed to be good and true. It was a glaring defect— something he refused to acknowledge, much less embrace.

In his late thirties, after a single exploratory same-sex relationship ended badly, Arthur had what he later referred to as his coming-to-God moment. Determined to live a simpler, more godly existence, he had sold out all his real-estate holdings back east in favor of taking up residence on a small section of Calhoun Ranch, a vast cattle-raising enterprise located in a sparsely populated corner of southeastern Arizona.

Throughout his life Arthur had been interested in the Old West. For him the major attraction of the Calhoun Ranch was that it contained the remains of a short-lived 1880s boomtown called Calhoun. Rather than constructing a modern-day ranch house, Arthur had chosen to use hand tools to refurbish a few of the ghost town's crumbling shacks, turning them into humble dwellings where he could live out the remainder of his days in monastic solitude and simplicity.

Over time that very solitude got the best of him and Arthur began to withdraw from the world entirely. As he morphed into being a hermit, Jimmy, by necessity, transitioned into the role of his brother's keeper. He stopped by regularly—bringing the mail, dropping off groceries, handling the finances, and making sure Arthur's bills and taxes got paid.

While Jimmy was doing this, he discovered that just because Arthur lived the life of an impoverished ascetic, that didn't mean he was broke, not by any means. Jimmy learned that there were comfortable sums of money stashed away here and there in banks and investment houses back east. Since there seemed to be plenty of cash to go around, and with no other possible heirs to gum up the works, Jimmy—under the guise of handling Arthur's financial affairs—began spending some of that excess cash on himself.

He paid off his rig so he owned it free and clear. When it came time to find a place to live, he settled on Road Forks, New Mexico—a dusty stopping-off place at the junction of I-10 and US Highway 80. His loads took him cross-country on I-10 on a regular basis, and Road Forks was the freeway interchange closest to Calhoun Ranch.

Using some of Arthur's money, Jimmy paid cash for several big-ticket items—a utility-equipped lot on the edge of town, a brand-new 24 x 50

double-wide mobile home, and an equally new
sturdy four-wheel-drive pickup that he could use
to ferry goods and supplies back and forth to Arthur's ranch.

By the time Arthur turned sixty-five, he was losing his grip on reality. His mental impairments included carrying on long, one-sided conversations
with personages as varied as God, Moses, and Wyatt Earp. He could be completely lucid one day and
totally out of it the next. He alternated between
unreasoning rages, where he threw things, ranting
and raging for hours on end about anything and everything, and periods filled with profound silence,
where Arthur sat in almost catatonic stillness, re-
fusing to utter so much as a single word, sometimes
for days at a time.

Jimmy was already contemplating the necessity
of hiring some kind of caretaker when, during one
of Arthur's relatively lucid moments, the patient
himself had first suggested and then outright insisted that Jimmy go through the process of obtaining a durable power of attorney so he'd "be able to
look after things when the time came."

It didn't take long for Jimmy to decide that "the
time" needed to come sooner rather than later. He
enlisted the help of a pair of brothers from Douglas, one a physician and the other an attorney. The
doctor diagnosed Arthur as suffering from some
form of early-onset dementia, and the lawyer was
happy to draft a durable power of attorney and put
it in place, leaving Jimmy completely in charge of
his brother's affairs.

Wanting to do bad things to women was something that had been part of Jimmy Ardmore's psyche for as long as he could remember. Top on his bucket list was having a place where he could take women, hold them prisoner, and do whatever he wanted. One of the falling-down buildings in Calhoun seemed to be just what the doctor ordered. And if he was going to go gathering women to bring back home, it occurred to him it might be handy to put Art out of his misery while at the same time maintaining a second identity—a variation on the theme of having his cake and eating it, too. The close family resemblance between the two men would make that plan entirely feasible.

First, however, Jimmy needed to establish a suitable home base. With Arthur's permission he took over the town's only remaining redbrick building. Back in the day, it had served as the Calhoun City Jail. When marauding Apaches had shown up from time to time, the basement under the jail had served as a community safe house.

When Arthur first arrived on the scene and while he'd been transforming one of the tin-roofed shacks into his primary dwelling, he had lived for a time on the ground floor of the jail. He'd piped in water and installed electricity, upstairs and down. Intent on having to make fewer trips into town for groceries, he'd dragged home a used freezer and hooked that up in the basement at the foot of the stairs.

By the time Jimmy came to Calhoun, the abandoned jail was empty once more, and that was where he decided to create what he liked to call his dungeon. His remodeling specifications were high on security and low on creature comforts. He left the earthen floor mostly as is except for a small concrete slab designed to hold a macerating toilet, one that flushed waste up and out of the basement and could be installed with only surface-mounted plumbing. Aside from the toilet, however, there was no other running water—no shower, tub, or lavatory. The toilet, a single bulb in the middle of the room, and a few glass blocks to allow a minimum amount of light were Jimmy's only concessions to the modern age.

Jimmy wanted a harem. That meant he needed to be able to control more than one prisoner at a time. After determining four to be the maximum number suitable for the space involved, he personally installed metal rings in the walls to secure his prospective captives. Carefully measured lengths of chain allowed each prisoner some freedom of movement. They could go as far as the toilet, yes, but that was it.

Only when the remodel was complete did Jimmy take the next step. On a warm May morning, while Arthur was sitting in the shade of a nearby cottonwood tree and carrying on a spirited conversation with someone who wasn't there, Jimmy walked up behind him and fired a single bullet into the back of his brother's head.

You could say Arthur Ardmore never knew what hit him.

As far as the neighbors were concerned—for people from the nearby towns of Road Forks, Animas, and Portal—Jimmy Ardmore was an outstanding member of the community, someone devotedly caring for an aging and unwell older brother. When Jimmy finally got around to mentioning that he'd had to place Arthur in what he called a "memory-care facility" outside El Paso, everyone who heard the story sympathized with him for having had to make and carry out such a difficult decision. No one ever once bothered questioning the validity of that placement. Through the years Arthur Ardmore hadn't ever gone out of his way to make friends with any of his neighbors, and none of them spent much time worrying about what might have become of him.

A few weeks after Jimmy dumped his brother's body out of the back of his pickup and left it to rot in an open field near Skeleton Canyon, a man who looked very much like Arthur Ardmore walked into the Department of Motor Vehicles office in Douglas to renew his Arizona driver's license. The woman who took his photo commented that life in the desert must be agreeing with him, since he seemed to be getting younger rather than older. They'd both had a good laugh over that little joke.

Arthur Ardmore's Platinum AmEx was the card that paid for meals and vehicles and rooms on Jimmy's occasional hunting trips. Jimmy Ardmore was the guy who lived in Road Forks, drove trucks for a living, and spent his spare time looking after the ranch that belonged to his ailing and now-institutionalized brother. No one anywhere had a clue that the two men were one and the same, and

Jimmy wanted to maintain that fiction for as long as humanly possible.

Over the years Jimmy Ardmore's antipathy toward his mother had always gotten in the way of his having any lasting romantic relationships. He'd had more than his share of encounters with the prostitutes who plied their trade along the various interstates he traveled, but because Jimmy liked his sex rough, he'd had very few repeat engagements. Now, with Arthur gone and the dungeon ready for action, Jimmy Ardmore had been ready to change all that. The girls who would be coming here would do whatever he wanted whenever he wanted. They wouldn't have any choice.

On that cold Sunday morning in November, more than two years after Arthur's death, Jimmy crossed back into Arizona and drove as far as the Fortuna exit before pulling off the freeway. Parking his rig behind the gas station, he walked as far as Denny's, where he indulged in one of their trademark Grand Slam breakfasts. Afterward he visited a nearby grocery store. Earlier his intention had been to buy a fifty-pound bag of dog food. Now, though, with only one mouth left to feed, he bought a twenty-five-pound bag instead, along with several plastic-wrapped packages containing multiple rolls of toilet paper. He supposed he could have bought the toilet paper anywhere, including closer to home. But the dog food? No way. Everyone in Road Forks knew damned good and well that Jimmy Ardmore didn't have a dog.

NINETEEN

A SQUAWK from Sage over the nanny cam brought Joanna wide awake at six the next morning. Once Tom Hadlock had left, she'd stayed up late enough for one more feeding, but given the fact that it had been nearly midnight by then, Joanna felt totally sleep deprived as she staggered into the kitchen.

Holding Sage in her left arm and pouring milk and cereal with the other, Joanna managed to get both kids fed at more or less the same time. Since Sage showed no inclination toward going back to sleep, Joanna wrapped her in an extra layer of blankets and then carried her outside in a sling while she and Denny did the morning chores. Afterward she sat down to enjoy a double miracle. Now that she was no longer pregnant, she could drink coffee again without turning green at the very thought of it. And with Sage finally back asleep and Denny playing outside, Joanna was able to drink it while it was still hot. That was when Butch called.

"How are you?" he asked.

"I'm feeling downright pioneerish," she told him with a laugh. "You should have seen me outside this morning, feeding the horses and cattle and carry-

ing Sage around in a sling. The only thing missing
was a sunbonnet, although it was pretty frosty here
last night, and it's way too cold for sunbonnets this
morning. How are things with you?"

"Wondering if I should tell you about this or
not," he said.

He sounded troubled, and Joanna felt a tug of
worry. "Tell me what?"

"The hostess who drove me back and forth to
the library last night tried to put the moves on me."

That wasn't at all what Joanna had been expecting, and she had to stifle the urge to giggle. "You're
kidding. Really?"

"Really," Butch replied, "and it wasn't funny, either." The way he said it made Joanna wonder if
maybe he'd heard a hint of that stifled giggle after all.

"All through dinner she was groping my thigh
under the table," Butch continued. "And after the
event she wanted to stop by the hotel so we could
have a beverage—wink, wink, in case I wasn't getting the message. I finally got rid of her by telling
her my wife had had a baby just two weeks ago. So
we're a real pair, Joey—you're a modern-day pio-
neer, and I'm a late-breaking sex object."

The words "sexual-assault victim" flashed through
Joanna's head, although she understood full well that
victim status in those kinds of situations was anything but a two-way street. Butch sounded genu-
inely troubled about what had happened, but since
he seemed prepared to take a light-handed approach,
so did Joanna.

"It was probably that shiny bald head of yours that got her attention."

"Maybe so," Butch replied. "But I'm guessing no male authors—young or old, bald or not—would be safe within reaching distance of that literary dragon lady. And, of course, if I tried to call her on it, the situation would immediately devolve into one of those 'he said/she said' things, and I'd end up being turned into the villain."

"Sorry," Joanna agreed, knowing all too well that what he said was true. No matter what, any kind of sexual interaction would be presumed to be the man's fault.

Once he finished letting off steam, they talked awhile longer, with Joanna bringing him up to date on the latest about both the kids and the case before Butch had to head for the airport to catch his flight to Albuquerque. As the call ended, another one came in—this one from Tom Hadlock.

"Struck out with the FBI's SAIC up in Tucson," he said. "Whipple gave me the runaround. Said he'd need to have more information before he'd be able to request the assistance of a profiler from D.C."

"What kind of information?"

"He was a little vague on specifics—autopsy reports, I suppose, along with crime-scene photos, notes from our investigating officers, that sort of thing."

"No real sense of urgency, then?" Joanna put in.

"Hardly."

"Did you mention our concern about the possibility of additional victims?"

"I did," Tom said dejectedly, "and it didn't make a lick of difference with the alphabet-soup guy. He said to send him what we have tomorrow. He'll make a determination at that time, which translates to when he's damned good and ready."

Just then Joanna caught sight of the book Denny had left lying on the coffee table. It was one of his favorites—*The Little Engine That Could*.

"Let me take a crack at it," Joanna said.

"Good luck," Tom countered, "but I doubt Whipple will listen to you, either."

"I'm not going to talk to Ted Whipple," Joanna told him. "Are you familiar with the story of the Little Engine That Could?"

"I guess," Tom admitted, "from back when I was a kid. Why? What does that have to do with Ted Whipple?"

"The train can't get over the mountain to Yon because its engine has broken down. Everybody else is ready to give up, except for the clown. He keeps right on asking one engine after another for help, until somebody finally agrees to give it a go."

"Who are you gonna call?" Tom asked. "Agent Watkins?"

"For starters," Joanna replied.

"Good luck, then," Tom said. "Let me know how it turns out."

It was almost ten in the morning by then, late enough on a Sunday for an incoming call to be considered civilized.

Robin answered on the second ring. "Hey, Joanna," she said. "How's it going? I just got back from my morning run and saw on the news ticker that you've had some excitement down your way—that your people are investigating a multiple homicide. You're still on leave, right?"

If the dump-site story was already showing up on a Tucson-based news feed, that meant word was definitely getting out. No doubt Marliss Shackleford had been working overtime.

"Correct on all counts," Joanna said. "I'm on leave, and my people have their hands full dealing with a multiple homicide. We've located a dump site that contains the remains of several victims."

"A serial killer, then?" Robin asked.

"That's how it looks," Joanna answered. "Most of the remains have been out in the elements long enough so all that's left is skeletal. One, however, is much more recent—a couple of days old at most. According to the M.E., we're looking at a Hispanic girl, most likely in her mid- to late teens who was thirteen weeks pregnant at the time of her death. Dr. Baldwin says she was severely undernourished and had evidently been subsisting on a steady diet of dry dog food."

"Cause of death?"

"Asphyxiation, most likely, combined with hypothermia. The M.E. found evidence that suggests the victim had been locked in a freezer."

Robin gave a low whistle. "What about the other victims?" she asked. "Did they die the same way?"

"One of them probably died of a gunshot wound to the head. Jury's still out on the other two. As I said, those are skeletal remains only, and the M.E.

is going to have to jigsaw the pieces back together in order to learn more."

"I'm betting that most of the victims will turn out to be young and female," Robin suggested.

"That's my guess, too."

"And you're thinking of asking the Bureau for help?"

"More than just thinking," Joanna replied. "The question has been asked and answered. Tom Hadlock already tried calling Ted Whipple and got nowhere fast."

"Not surprising," Robin replied. "Ted Whipple is one of those chain-of-command kind of guys who doesn't make a move until all the t's are crossed and i's are dotted."

"We weren't really looking for additional manpower," Joanna told her. "All we wanted was access to a profiler, someone who might be able to tell us what kind of person we're looking for and point us in the right direction."

"What do you have so far?"

"The dump site is in a remote location, one that would be known to locals but not so much to outsiders."

"You're thinking the perpetrator is one of your own?"

"Yes, someone who lives around here and can come and go and operate under the radar without arousing any suspicion. During the autopsy of the most recent victim, Dr. Baldwin noticed internal bruising to a lower leg that would indicate the victim had been held in restraints for a considerable period of time. Our biggest concern right now is that he might be holding additional captives. Once he knows we're working his dump site, chances are he'll—"

"Get rid of them and then bail," Robin concluded, "which means you can't afford to wait around for crossing t's or dotting i's."

"Exactly," Joanna said.

"You may have come to the right place," Robin said after a moment. "One of my good friends happens to be just what you're looking for—an FBI profiler. Her name is Rochelle Powers, and we were roommates back at the academy in Quantico. By some strange coincidence, she's currently in Arizona, visiting her folks, who live in Scottsdale. We were planning to get together while she's here. Would you like me to give her a call?"

"Would you?"

"I'm happy to, but how will this kind of back-door arrangement go over with your acting sheriff?" Robin asked.

"Tom Hadlock won't mind," Joanna said. "As I said, he already took his own shot at Ted Whipple and got nowhere."

"Tom Hadlock?" Robin inquired. "Isn't he the chief deputy who was running the show the night you were in so much trouble?"

"One and the same," Joanna answered.

"Cool guy," Robin said. "Everybody seemed to think he was in over his head, but he came through that whole mess like a champ."

"He's doing the same thing now," Joanna said.

"Sticking him with a multiple homicide means throwing him into the deep end. He's swimming like crazy, but he asked me for some logistical support, and that's why I called you."

"Fair enough," Robin said. "Is it all right, then, if I give Rochelle your phone number?"

"By all means."

TWENTY

WANTING TO be reasonably presentable by the time the Paxtons showed up, Joanna took a quick shower and dabbed on some makeup. While doing so, she toyed with the idea of maybe packing up both kids and driving out to the crime scene along with everyone else that afternoon—just to take a look at things and get the lay of the land.

In the quiet of her steamy bathroom, it seemed like a reasonable enough idea—tempting, even. After all, how bad could it be? She'd be driving her own vehicle, and if the kids were with her, she wouldn't hang around for very long. She *was* still on maternity leave. It wasn't like she intended to go out stomping around in the desert looking for evidence. She knew for a fact, however, that if Butch were home, he'd be firmly opposed to the idea.

Postponing a final decision, she went out to the living room, where, with a few quiet moments to herself, Joanna logged onto the *Bisbee Bee*'s Web site. As soon as she saw the lead headline, she knew exactly where the Tucson news feeds were getting their information.

CCSD Investigating
Multiple Homicide
by
Marliss Shackleford

Sources close to the Cochise County Sheriff's Department, speaking on the condition of confidentiality, report that homicide detectives are investigating a site in a remote area east of Douglas where evidence suggests the presence of several dead bodies in various stages of decay.

According to the anonymous source, the most recent victim is reported to be a young, unidentified Hispanic female. Her remains were located in the foothills of the Peloncillo Mountains on Saturday morning under what are described to be somewhat mysterious circumstances. Other remains found nearby are said to be skeletal in nature and are thought to belong to several other as-yet-unidentified individuals.

Currently all of the remains are being held at the Cochise County Medical Examiner's office in Bisbee, Arizona, where autopsies are due to be scheduled. As of this time, Chief Medical Examiner Dr. Kendra Baldwin has released no information concerning the incident.

According to the source, the cache of remains suggests the possibility that this is what homicide investigators refer to as a "dump site," a place favored by serial killers as disposal locations for the remains of multiple victims.

Newly reelected sheriff Joanna Brady is currently on maternity leave, so the investigation is being handled by her second-in-command, Chief Deputy Thomas Hadlock.

This is a developing story. A press briefing is scheduled to occur at the Cochise County Justice Center later today. Further updates will be provided as additional information becomes available.

Joanna finished reading and then sat staring at the words "Sources close to the Cochise County Sheriff's Department." *So who the hell are those sources?* she wondered furiously.

Which of her deputies or clerks or detectives had Marliss Shackleford on speed dial in order to spill the beans about ongoing investigations? Obviously someone either in or close to her department couldn't be trusted, and Joanna wanted to know who that person was.

Picking up her phone, she dialed Tom. "Who's the leak?" she demanded.

"I don't have a clue," he muttered. "That article is enough to piss off the Good Fairy. As soon as I saw it, I asked myself the same question. Problem is, Ernie's about to do his first presser. The conference room is full to the brim. We're going to tape it. Do you want me to send you a copy?"

"Please," she said.

She was just going to tell him about her back-door

approach on the profiler situation when the dogs set up a chorus of barking out in the yard. Seconds later Denny dashed into the house. "Mommy, Mommy!" he yelled as the door slammed shut behind him. "The people with the cadavel dogs are here. They're out front. Do you want to come see them?"

The dog people had arrived a good hour earlier than Joanna had expected. "I'll be right out," she told Denny. "Since there are other dogs, can you lock Lady and Lucky in the garage?"

"I think so," Denny said.

To Tom she said, "The Paxtons are here. I've gotta go."

Wrapping Sage in an extra layer of blanket, she stepped out onto the front porch. With the dogs successfully contained, Denny came racing back around the house in time to accompany his mother down the walkway toward the front gate.

The new arrivals consisted of an older, white-haired woman walking toward the gate with two enormous, wrinkle-faced, flop-eared hounds on leashes.

"Sit," the woman commanded, and both dogs instantly complied.

"Good dogs," Joanna observed.

The woman nodded. "It's a good thing, too. The leashes are mostly for show. They each outweigh me by twenty-five pounds. If they took a mind to, they could turn me into a flying human dogsled in a down-home minute. You must be Sheriff Brady," she added, offering her hand. "I'm Patricia Paxton. Most people call me Li'l Pat for obvious reasons."

The obvious reason had to do with the fact that Li'l Pat was tiny and probably didn't weigh ninety pounds soaking wet. All her life Joanna had been accustomed to being the shortest person at any given gathering, but that wasn't the case here. Even in cowboy boots with two-inch heels, Li'l Pat was at least three inches shorter than Joanna's diminutive five-four.

Patricia Paxton appeared to be somewhere in her late sixties or early seventies, with a suntanned, leathery complexion that spoke to lots of time spent in the great outdoors. Dressed in faded jeans, a plaid flannel work shirt, and worn boots, she looked ready to set off on a daylong trail ride at a moment's notice.

"And who might you be, young man?" Li'l Pat asked, turning a pair of intense blue eyes on Dennis and offering him her hand.

"I'm Dennis Dixon," he replied gravely, standing up straight and squaring his shoulders to return the handshake. "Everyone calls me Denny. Do your dogs have names?"

"Yes they do. This one is Stormin' Norman," Li'l Pat answered, nodding toward the dog on the right. "The one on the left is Big Red."

"Can I pet them?" Denny asked.

"That depends," Li'l Pat said. "Are you afraid of dogs?"

"No, ma'am," Denny said. "I'm good with dogs. My big sister showed me how to meet new dogs, by holding out the back of my hand for them to sniff."

"Sounds like your sister's got it just about right,"

Li'l Pat said. "If it's okay with your mommy for you to pet them, it's okay with me."

Dennis looked up at Joanna. When she nodded her assent, he let himself out through the gate and cautiously approached the dogs, carefully proffering the back of his hand. As he got closer, both dogs thumped their tails on the ground in greeting.

While Denny knelt to pet the dogs, Li'l Pat smiled reassuringly at Joanna. "Don't worry," she said. "They'll be fine. And that's one handsome baby you've got there. How old, and is it a boy or a girl?"

"A girl," Joanna replied, feeling instantly at ease. "Her name is Sage, and she's not quite two weeks old. Now, about your dogs. How are they around livestock—say, with cattle and horses?"

"They spend a lot of time on our ranch on the Hassayampa up near Wickenburg," Li'l Pat answered. "They're both accustomed to horses. As for cattle? A couple of years back, Stormin' Norman here got himself all tangled up with a Brahma bull we were boarding temporarily for one of the traveling rodeo companies. I'm afraid that one encounter cured this poor old guy of any interest in cattle whatsoever."

"You're welcome to let them off leash, then," Joanna said. "We've got our own two dogs locked inside."

"Where would you like my husband to park?"

Out in the driveway, a man sat behind the wheel of an idling Sprinter. When Joanna approached the vehicle, the driver rolled down his window and tipped a worn Stetson in greeting.

"I'm Joanna Brady," she said. "Welcome to High Lonesome Ranch."

"Good morning, ma'am," he said. "Dwayne Paxton at your service. Glad to make your acquaintance. Do you want me to stash this rig anywhere in particular?"

"Do you see that utility pole over by the barn?" Joanna asked, pointing. "There's an RV pad there equipped with both electricity and a water hookup."

"Sounds good. Once I get parked, I'll unhook the Jeep and get it out of the way so we don't take up too much room."

The Sprinter was shiny and appeared to be brand-new. The Jeep Wrangler it was towing was a battered old warhorse that clearly had seen plenty of hard use. After expertly positioning the Sprinter on the concrete pad, Dwayne switched off the engine, opened the door, unfolded himself, and stepped down to the ground. When he did so, Joanna found herself staring up at a man who was well over six feet. Considering how tiny Li'l Pat was, Joanna was surprised that her husband was so tall.

"That's right," he said with a grin, as though reading her mind. "Me and Li'l Pat there make for a regular Mutt-and-Jeff team. Now, if you'll just give me a minute, I'll get that Jeep unhitched."

As an embarrassed flush spread up Joanna's face, she was grateful that his attention was focused on the tow bar rather than on her.

"I understand the crime scene's some distance from here?" he asked over his shoulder.

"Fifty miles, give or take," Joanna told him, "and a lot of it on less-than-wonderful roads."

"Will you be leading us there, or will someone else?"

"I'm currently on maternity leave. I let Tom Hadlock, my chief deputy, know you're here. He should be sending someone to get you."

"Fair enough," Dwayne said. "We need to head out as soon as possible. With the days as short as they are, we'd best get started before we lose the light."

Once the Jeep was unhitched, Joanna showed Dwayne how to set up the utility connections while Denny bustled around helping Li'l Pat put out food and water for the dogs.

"When cadavel dogs find bodies, do they eat them?" he asked.

Li'l Pat shot a quick look in Joanna's direction, but she replied without making a fuss about the boy's mispronunciation.

"No," she answered. "When it comes to smell, dog noses are way better than human noses, and dogs can be trained to look for certain things— like drugs or bombs or runaway suspects. Cadaver dogs are trained to search out human remains, and they bark to let us know once they've found something so we can come tag it."

"You mean like evidence and stuff so Mommy can catch the people who do bad things?"

"Exactly."

About that time Tom Hadlock sped into the yard, kicking up a rooster tail of dust. Joanna had spoken to him by phone only minutes earlier. Walking over to greet him, she was surprised that he was there so soon. "Is the press conference done already?" she asked.

"Nope," he said. "I'm sure it's still going hot and heavy. We snuck out early and left poor Ernie holding the bag. I wanted us to be well on our way before he cuts loose that flock of reporters."

"Who's 'we'?" Joanna asked.

Tom nodded. "Dave Hollicker and I drew the short straws when it comes to working the crime scene. Deputy Raymond went home to grab some sleep while Deputy Hernandez is currently out there standing guard. Since we probably won't finish up processing the scene before dark today, I've asked Deputy Raymond to plan on being back on duty at sundown. In the meantime I've got everyone else hitting the bricks on the canvassing job. This evening the team will reassemble at the department for a debriefing so we can figure out what's to be done tomorrow."

With both Dave Hollicker and Tom Hadlock heading for the crime scene, there was no longer any valid reason for Joanna herself to show up there. Reluctantly letting go of that idea, she changed the subject.

"How's Ernie doing with the media assault?" she asked.

"Like gangbusters," Tom replied with a grin. "If you put the guy in front of a microphone, unlike me, he's a natural. You'd think he's been working Media Relations all his life. On the other hand, he's all thumbs when it comes to operating the electronic equipment, so I asked Kristin to come in and help out. She's spent all morning fielding phone calls from the media outfits that weren't able to have people covering the press conference in person. She'll be sending out copies of the presser to them and to you as well."

"Okay, then," Joanna said. "Let me introduce you to the Paxtons so you can get under way."

TWENTY-ONE

ONCE THE cadaver crew and Tom set off for the Peloncillos, Joanna returned to the house feeling like a star quarterback benched in the middle of a playoff game. This was obviously a major case, and even though her people were doing an outstanding job, she couldn't help resenting the fact that she'd been sidelined. She wanted to be in the middle of it rather than fixing a snack for Denny, feeding Sage, and starting another load of laundry, none of which improved her disposition.

Just after two her phone rang with an unfamiliar number in the caller-ID window. Thinking it was some kind of solicitation call, she almost let it go to voice mail. Then, after the third ring, she changed her mind and answered.

"Hello."

"Sheriff Brady?"

"Yes, who's calling?"

"My name is Rochelle Powers. I'm a friend of Robin Watkins."

"Oh, yes," Joanna said, "Rochelle. It's so good to hear from you."

"Sorry it took a while for me to get back to you.

I'm up at the Grand Canyon with my folks, and cell-phone service up here is almost nonexistent. The only place I can get even one bar is out in the parking lot. That's where I'm calling from, and I can tell you it's damn cold out here. This is Arizona. I thought it was going to be warm."

Not when you're close to seven thousand feet in elevation, Joanna thought. "Thanks for calling," she said aloud. "I hate to intrude on your vacation."

Rochelle laughed. "If you knew my parents, you'd know that having a vacation from my vacation isn't such a terrible idea. How can I help?"

"Did Robin bring you up to speed?"

"Only the basics—that your department may be dealing with a serial-killer situation and that you're having some challenges with bureaucratic stalling."

"That's pretty much the size of it."

"How about if you fill me in?"

"We've located human remains scattered across what we believe to be a dump site," Joanna explained.

"What kind of remains?"

"Mostly skeletal, although one body was recent enough that our M.E. was able to perform an autopsy."

"How many victims are we talking about?"

"That's unknown at this time. So far we've found evidence of four separate victims, but there could be more. My people collected a good deal of evidence yesterday, and we have a team of cadaver dogs and more crime-scene investigators on their way to the site today."

"So most of the bones have been there for some time and have probably been open to scavengers?"

"Correct."

"What about the body that was autopsied? How fresh was it?"

"Several days old at the time it was found."

"Who did the autopsy?"

"The Cochise County medical examiner, Dr. Kendra Baldwin."

"What did she turn up?"

"According to Dr. Baldwin, we're dealing with a young female, most likely in her mid- to late teens, who was thirteen weeks pregnant at the time of her death. Dental work suggests that she might have come from Mexico originally. There was internal bruising on at least one of her lower limbs that would indicate she was held in restraints for a considerable period of time. She was also severely malnourished. An examination of her stomach contents revealed dry dog food and nothing else."

"Dog kibble?" Rochelle asked. "That's all she had to eat?"

"I'm afraid so."

"Which explains her being malnourished," Rochelle observed. "What about sexual assault?"

"There were signs of a violent sexual assault recent enough that the M.E. hopes will provide enough DNA to establish a profile. Given the fact that the victim was pregnant at the time of her death, I think it's fair to assume that the sexual assaults had been ongoing for some time."

"Did the M.E. establish either a time or cause of death?"

"Dr. Baldwin estimates our Jane Doe was dumped on Wednesday, so the time of death would have been prior to that—the same day or earlier. Cause is listed as asphyxiation," Joanna replied. "In addition, the M.E. has established that at the time of her death the victim might have been locked in some kind of freezer."

"A freezer?"

Joanna went on to recount the other troubling details surrounding the victim's death. When she finished, there was a momentary silence on the line before Rochelle asked, "Have you found any matching missing-persons reports?"

"None so far," Joanna answered.

"What about the other victims? I know you mentioned we're talking only partial remains. Was the M.E. able to establish a cause of death in any of those?"

"One skull exhibited signs of a gunshot wound. The other two show signs of blunt-force trauma. Once Dr. Baldwin sorts all the pieces, she may find evidence of other wounds as well."

Rochelle fell silent again for a moment, as if sifting through her thoughts. "So we're dealing with an individual who abducts multiple victims, who has the ability to hold them prisoner for an extended period of time, who most likely subjects them to ongoing sexual assaults, and who murders them once he's had his fill."

"Yes," Joanna agreed, "those are our assumptions, too."

"All that being said, we can be reasonably confident that this is a well-established MO rather than a onetime thing, and with the likelihood of other victims no wonder you can't afford to wait to have your request for a profiler slow-walked through channels and across desks."

When the profiler fell silent yet again, Joanna held her breath, waiting to hear what would happen.

"I'm in, then," Rochelle concluded at last. "I'll do whatever I can to help, but I'll need information. If you can have your M.E. forward her autopsy results, I can run those through ViCAP and see if there are any other cases out there, solved or not, with similar characteristics."

"Wait," Joanna suggested. "Instead of my being in the middle, why don't you contact Dr. Baldwin yourself? Tell her I asked you to call. Once we're off the phone, I'll text you her numbers. I'll also send along the numbers for a guy named Ernie Carpenter. He usually works homicide, but right now he's holding down the fort at Media Relations. His information will be more current than anything I can give you."

"What about the detectives working the case? When can I speak to them?"

"Not anytime soon—they're all out working right now, most likely not in cell-phone range, either knocking on doors or examining the crime scene. There's going to be a debriefing later tonight when they finish up. Would you want me to see if we could maybe Skype that?"

"Don't bother," Rochelle said. "The Wi-Fi connection here at the hotel is useless. We're leaving in the morning, though, and heading back to Scotts-dale. Whereabouts is your department again?"

"We're located in the Cochise County Justice Center complex, a few miles east of Bisbee on Highway 80."

"My knowledge of Arizona geography is pretty limited," Rochelle admitted. "How far is Bisbee from Scottsdale?"

"Four hours, give or take," Joanna said. "Scotts-dale is more or less in the middle of the state. If you think about a map of Arizona, Cochise County is in the lower right-hand corner. The crime scene itself is only a few miles from the New Mexico state line."

"So we're not exactly right next door at the moment," Rochelle said. "I can probably show up there late tomorrow, but it would be helpful to know what's said in that debriefing between then and now. I'll be able to access whatever's in the re-ports, but I'd also like to hear everything else that goes on—the offhand hunches and theories people come up with, things that may not make it into any of the official reports but might prove useful in the long run."

"You're saying you'll need to speak to them di-rectly?"

"I will," Rochelle asserted, "but I can't stress how helpful it would be for me to have some inside ac-cess to that initial debriefing. That way I'll know where the investigation started and where it's head-ing. Would it be possible for you to record it and send me the file?"

"I can't promise, but I'll see what I can do."

"Even though you're supposed to be on maternity leave?" Rochelle asked.

"Theoretically," Joanna replied, "although I think people around here would tell you that I'm not very good at maternity leave."

Rochelle laughed.

"What about you?" Joanna asked. "Is doing something off the books going to land you in hot water back home in D.C.?"

"How long have you been sheriff?" Rochelle countered.

"Eight years or so. I won my third term in office a couple of weeks ago. Why?"

"In the intervening years, I have to assume you've had some dealings with the FBI."

"Yes," Joanna said, "some good and some bad, although I have to say, when it comes to dealing with field agents, Robin Watkins is my hands-down favorite."

"Mine, too," Rochelle agreed, "but do you know how she ended up being transferred to Tucson?"

"I seem to remember she got sideways with a supervisor back in D.C."

"That's correct," Rochelle answered, "and trust me when I tell you there are a lot of supervisors in the Bureau. The whole joint is top-heavy with them, and shit definitely rolls downhill. Robin got shipped off to Tucson—we like to say 'remoted' rather than 'demoted'—because she crossed a higher-up who happens to be a micromanaging jerk. I made the same mistake with someone else, and that's why I'm currently stuck on the bottom tier of the profiler totem pole.

"I didn't sign up for this job to push paper, Sheriff Brady," Rochelle continued. "I signed up because I wanted to catch bad guys, and you're giving me a chance to do just that. I have the skill set, but I'm lacking experience. I really want to work this case, but if I feel like I'm out of my depth, I'll let you know and you can call in someone else."

"That's more than fair," Joanna said. "Thank you."

TWENTY-TWO

FINISHED WITH the profiler call and feeling as though she'd accomplished something useful, Joanna sent the needed phone numbers to Rochelle and then sent texts introducing Rochelle Powers to both Dr. Baldwin and Ernie. After that she went back to the immediate task at hand—laundry—taking one load to the sofa for folding, transferring one load to the dryer, and putting one load—the last one for the day—in the washer. How did people keep from going nuts when they were washing, drying, and folding clothes day in and day out? How did Butch keep from going nuts?

Her phone rang with Sunny Sloan's name showing in the caller ID. "Sheriff Brady, so sorry to bother you at home."

Giving Deputy Sloan's widow a job in the department might have been regarded as an act of charity by some, but as far as Joanna was concerned, the young woman seemed to be doing an outstanding job. It bothered Joanna to hear Sunny sound so tentative—as though she weren't quite up to the tasks she'd been given.

"No problem," Joanna said. "You're saving me from folding onesies. What can I do for you?"

"One of your constituents is out in the lobby, and she's pretty upset."

"When you say 'constituent,' I'm assuming you don't mean in a good way. Did you tell her I'm on maternity leave and she needs to speak to Acting Sheriff Hadlock?"

"She doesn't exactly mince words. She said she voted for you, not some blankety-blank doofus named Hadlock. According to her, he's already screwed her over, and she wants to talk to you directly."

"Who is she, and what does she want?"

"Her name is June Carver," Sunny answered. "She says that when her son, Jack, came in and spoke to Chief Deputy Hadlock on Friday, Tom assured her that if Jack helped with the investigation, his name would be kept out of it. Today Mrs. Carver says that first thing this morning she found a reporter camped on her doorstep wanting to interview her son about his connection to a multiple homicide."

"Crap," Joanna muttered. "Marliss Shackleford rides again." After a pause she added, "How angry exactly is June Carver?"

"Very," Sunny replied. "Angry enough to show up here cussing a blue streak."

And angry enough for Sunny to have taken the precaution of moving out of June's line of sight before making her call to Joanna. Closing her eyes, Joanna envisioned the interior of that front lobby.

Nutcases occasionally turned up at police departments all over the country. If bad things ensued, there was always a chance that the women working there might find themselves on the front lines of some dangerous confrontation.

In Joanna's department that meant that the front counter in the public lobby was topped by a wall of bullet-resistant glass. The clerks communicated with visitors through speakers mounted in the glass and slid paperwork back and forth through narrow slots at the bottom of the barrier. That's where June Carver was right then, most likely pacing back and forth in front of the counter.

Recalling how easily June Carver had outmaneuvered Tom Hadlock in order to protect her son, Joanna realized that the woman had to be smart. But the real question Joanna asked herself right then had nothing to do with relative intelligence. Was Carver dangerous? Did she pose a viable threat to Joanna's people?

"Does she appear to be armed?" Joanna asked.

Sunny thought about that for a moment before she replied. "Not that I can tell, but since she's carrying a big purse, she might very well be."

It wasn't the answer Joanna had hoped to hear.

"Okay, this is what I want you to do," she suggested. "Go back out front. Turn your phone on speaker and offer it to Mrs. Carver via the pass-through. Tell her that I'm on the line waiting to speak to her. Under no circumstances should you go out into the open lobby. Once she has possession of your phone, direct her into the conference room so she'll have some privacy, while I see what I can do to straighten this out."

"Will do," Sunny said.

"And thanks for the way you've handled it, Sunny. Good job."

As soon as she said the words, Joanna wanted to retract them. It was the same kind of praise parental units heaped on toddlers when they started getting the hang of potty training. Not a smart thing to say to an adult employee, especially one with a young child, without sounding condescending.

"You handled what could have become a dicey situation in a diplomatic and professional fashion," Joanna added. "Keep up the great work."

As Sunny walked back to the front office, Joanna heard footsteps and the sounds of doors opening and closing. Moments later she heard an exceedingly angry female voice addressing Sunny.

"So that's how Sheriff Brady's department treats one of her voters?" she fumed. "You just turn your back on me and walk away? Where did you go? Was it time for a coffee break? Did you need to go grab a doughnut?"

"No coffee break, Mrs. Carver," Sunny replied reasonably. "I was trying to get Sheriff Brady on the phone for you, and here she is. You're welcome to take my phone into the conference room so you can speak to her. That way you'll have the benefit of some privacy and the conversation won't be broadcast to everyone passing through the lobby."

"Oh," June Carver said, sounding somewhat mollified. "All right, then, where's this conference room?"

"Back there and to the left," Sunny directed. "Just go inside and close the door behind you, but please remember to drop off the phone on your way out."

Joanna wanted to set the tone for this verbal meeting. It was important to make Marliss the bad guy here and take the focus off the department. Knowing some of June Carver's history, Joanna came out swinging.

"Marliss Shackleford is a piece of work," Joanna announced as soon as June's voice came on the phone. "Did you clean her clock?"

Clearly that wasn't anything close to what June Carver had been expecting.

"Since you already know it was Marliss, are you the one who told her, then?" June demanded. "It's bad enough that my son had to see that ghoulish sight yesterday, but to have her show up at my house first thing this morning, demanding to talk to Jack and implying that he maybe had something to do with a—"

"No," Joanna interrupted. "I told Marliss nothing. She's a busybody who's always poking her nose in where it doesn't belong. And I want you to know that both Acting Sheriff Hadlock and I are as upset about that article as you are. Once we figure out where the leak is coming from, we have every intention of shutting it down. Having unauthorized information out in public like that can sometimes be the one thing that screws up the prosecution of a case and keeps us from getting a conviction. So tell me, how did Marliss approach you?"

"Like I said, she showed up on our front porch

about the time I was putting breakfast on the table. She rang the doorbell and asked if Jack was home."

"So she knew his name."

"Yes."

"What else did she say?"

"She said that she was aware that there were multiple victims out there, and she wanted to know how Jack was connected to the case. I told her to take a hike, but what if she goes ahead and prints a story with his name in it anyway? You know how people are. Once they start thinking he's involved in something bad, his life will turn to crap."

"Mrs. Carver," Joanna put in, "we both know that what Jack did after finding that skull was undeniably stupid. He never should have picked it up and brought it home. He should have left it lying right where it was and called in law enforcement, but the truth is, his being stupid is part of what is putting my department on the trail of a serial killer in a timely fashion."

Joanna heard a sharp intake of breath on the line. "You said a serial killer?" June murmured.

"Yes, I did," Joanna confirmed, "someone who has most likely been operating unseen right here in Cochise County for an extended period of time, so let me be the first to say thank you for your son's involvement. Stupid or not, I'm very grateful that Jack led my investigators to that crime scene when he did."

"Oh," June said.

"How old is Jack?"

"Seventeen, why?"

"He's still considered a juvenile. When juveniles are involved in criminal proceedings, most publications—as a matter of courtesy—don't publish their names in print. When it comes to Marliss Shackleford, courtesy is in as short supply as common sense, but I'll be happy to have a chat with her, if you like. I'll let her know that if she so much as mentions your son's name in connection to this case—if she does so in a fashion that might somehow jeopardize his future—that you are fully prepared to take her to court."

"I'd rather punch her lights out."

"I'm sure you would," Joanna agreed, "and that makes two of us, but that would probably be a bad thing for you, for your son, and for my future as sheriff."

June actually laughed aloud at that. Hearing the sound, Joanna knew she had successfully defused the situation. For the first time in several minutes, she allowed herself to take a deep breath.

"So you'll talk to her, then?" June asked.

"With pleasure."

"Well, all right," June said. "You do that. And about what I said before? Since we're moving to Tucson, I won't be able to vote for you next time around, but I'm glad I did this time."

Which meant that June Carver's vote was one of Joanna's sixty-seven-vote margin.

"So am I," Joanna said. "Thank you for your support."

When the call ended, Joanna dialed Marliss's number—one she just happened to have in her phone. The call went to voice mail. She didn't bother leaving a message. Instead she dialed the number for Media Relations.

"Hey," she said when Ernie answered. "Tom told me that when he left the presser, you were doing a bang-up job."

"It seemed to go all right," Ernie said. "Did you listen to it? Kristin said she was going to send you a copy."

"It's probably in my computer, but I haven't had any computer time available. Did you talk to Rochelle Powers?"

"For a minute," Ernie answered. "She asked about recording tonight's debriefing. I told her I didn't think it was a good idea."

"It may not be a good idea," Joanna said, "but I want that debriefing recorded anyway. I want to be able to hear it, and I want Agent Powers to hear it, too. She's willing to help us off the books and in a hurry. That means she needs access to everything we have sooner than we could pass along reports."

"So you want me to bring in Kristin again?" Ernie asked, sounding less than happy. "It's all I can do to operate the fax machine. Recording stuff is way outside my wheelhouse."

"Call her in," Joanna ordered. "Everybody else is piling on the overtime. Why shouldn't she?"

TWENTY-THREE

WHEN LATISHA opened her eyes, she wasn't sure what had brought her awake, her aching tooth or her aching toes. The broken tooth hurt all the time now. She had tried pulling it out by yanking on it with her thumb and forefinger, but it wouldn't budge. In order to pull it, she'd need a tool of some kind—like a pair of pliers—and she didn't have one of those.

In this case, though, the real culprit was her toes—her big toes—coming in contact with the blankets. Her toenails hadn't been trimmed the whole time she'd been here. They were far too long, ingrown, and turned under. If she'd had shoes, she wouldn't have been able to wear them, and the weight of the blankets on them was absolute agony. Looking for relief, she poked her feet out from under the covers. That helped with the toenail problem, but not for long, because in this unheated basement the cold made her feet hurt, too.

So what time of year was it? As cold as it was, it had to be sometime in the winter, but when? Was Thanksgiving over and Christmas on its way? It

215

was maddening not to know what day it was, or even what month.

She lay there alone in the murky darkness that passed for daylight in the dungeon, wondering about the slow progress of time. How long had the Boss been gone? It seemed longer than usual, four or five days at least. There were dueling worries in the back of her mind. One said that he might never return and the other that he would. And if he did come back and brought along someone new, what was the likelihood that he would decide it was time to be in with the new and out with the old? What were the chances that sooner than later Latisha would be sent down the same path as Sandra, Sadie, and Amelia? As if to amplify her worries, from across the room, she heard the telltale click as the compressor in the freezer came on. Needing to keep that sound at bay, she got up and limped as far as the toilet, dragging her chain behind her.

Overnight the toilet-paper cushion she'd wrapped around the clamp on her ankle had come loose and disappeared. She sat on the toilet and made a new one—a thicker one this time—all the while trying not to think about what would happen if the Boss didn't come back. Eventually there would be no more toilet paper, no more food, no more electricity, no more water, and no more Latisha.

And maybe, at long last, that's what she really wanted. Maybe dying wasn't such a bad thing compared to wasting away in the darkness with no idea of what was going on outside. Maybe she should just stop forcing herself to eat the dog food, lie

down on her mattress, and wait to die. At least then
it would be over.

Then, above the steady humming of the freezer,
she heard the sound of an approaching vehicle.
She knew the sound of the Boss's pickup all too
well—all the girls recognized that one. This was
different. Either the Boss had changed vehicles or
someone else was approaching.

Latisha was in the basement, and that would go
a long way to muffle any sound she could make, but
the brick building upstairs was old and rickety. And
so she tried calling for help, but her voice, unused
for days on end, refused to cooperate. What she
hoped would be a piercing scream emerged as little
more than a pitiful squeak. Her cries of "Help, in
here! Please help me!" died away unheard, swallowed by the earthen floor of the basement and the
rough planks of the ceiling and the floor overhead,
along with the bricks on the outside walls.

The vehicle came, seemed to slow, and then it
went away. No car doors opened or closed, indicat-
ing that someone had gotten out. There were no
accompanying voices. No one pounded on the outside door upstairs, asking for admittance. Within
a minute or so, maybe less, she heard the vehicle
receding into the background, driving away, and
leaving in its wake one sound only—the hum of the
freezer.

Latisha cried for a while after that, shedding silent tears into the rough wool of the blanket that
formed her pillow. At last, though, she sat up and
reached for her food container. When she shook

it, she noticed that it was noticeably lighter than it had been. Even with Amelia's food added in, it was disappearing faster than it should.

She ate the kibble one piece at a time, chewing and swallowing and wondering about that strange vehicle. In all the time she'd been here—however long that was—no vehicle other than the Boss's had ever shown up. If someone had come here today, maybe whoever it was would stop by again. If that happened, she needed to make sure that her voice worked well enough so someone standing outside would be able to hear her. Maybe it was time to pray again, asking for a miracle. On this occasion and just for practice, she said the words aloud.

"Holy Mary, Mother of God, pray for us sinners now and at the hour of our death. Amen."

TWENTY-FOUR

SAGE WAS still young enough that she was asleep more than she was awake. Late in the afternoon, with the bed remade and with the last load of laundry in the dryer, Joanna turned once again to her father's journals.

Word is out that Sheriff Garner will decide next week who's in and who's out. I'm hoping for in. I haven't been doing much writing in this of late because I've been boning up on criminal justice in case I do manage to make the cut.

I went down to the bookstore at Cochise College and bought up all the books that are required reading for their criminal-justice program. I've been reading them through and making good progress, especially when I'm working night shift, because the house is quiet when I get home. If I do get hired on, I'll have to spend six weeks at a police-academy facility up in Phoenix, but I figure doing all this reading in advance will give me a head start.

That's just the course work. There's also a marksmanship component. When I work days,

*I've been sneaking out to the rifle range after my
shift and doing some serious target practice. I'm
still not perfect, but I'm a lot better than I was to
begin with.*

*The guys at work are razzing me about maybe
leaving. They keep putting doughnuts in my lunch
pail and telling me that the people who become cops
are either former juvenile delinquents or lazy.
It turns out that they've got me fair and square
on both counts, but I'll never admit it. I'd sure as
hell rather ride around in a squad car in a clean
uniform—eating doughnuts, thank you very
much—than be down in the dark mucking out
a stope. If that's lazy, then color me lazy. As for
the other? That's between me and my Maker and
nobody else.*

Once again something in her father's journal had
brought Joanna up short. D. H. Lathrop had been
in some kind of trouble as a juvenile? This was the
first Joanna had ever heard of it. Then there was
that disconcerting fact that much later on in life
he'd carried on a longtime affair with his secretary. Other than that he had always seemed like a
straight-up guy.

So what kind of trouble had he gotten into?
And had her mother known about that history?
According to the final sentence in that passage,
probably not.

The phone rang with the M.E.'s name showing in caller ID. "Hey, Kendra," Joanna said.
"What's up?"

"You're not going to believe this. I got a hit on Jane Doe. I've got an ID on her."

Joanna was astonished. "Already?" she demanded. "How is that possible? You just did the autopsy yesterday. I thought it took a lot longer than this to create a DNA profile."

"It does, but the tentative ID didn't come from DNA. It's from dental records."

"Are you kidding?"

"Nope, our Jane Doe is a sixteen-year-old girl named Amelia Diaz Salazar. She's from Juárez, south of El Paso. She was living illegally in the U.S. with an aunt, her mother's sister, a woman named Rosa Moreno. Amelia went missing the evening of July Fourth of this past year. She went out to watch the fireworks with some other kids from her neighborhood and never came home. Her aunt is the one who reported her missing."

"But how were you able to access her dental records?" Joanna asked.

"When Amelia came to the U.S., she had some tooth problems, so Rosa took her to a free dental clinic that works in conjunction with a homeless shelter in El Paso. Two months or so after Amelia went missing and with the investigation from law enforcement apparently going nowhere, Rosa entered Amelia's information—dental records included—into NamUs. Her entry is dated September seventeenth. As soon as I uploaded Jane Doe's information, I got a hit."

"And dental records don't lie?"

"No, they don't."

"Have you notified the family?" Joanna asked.

"That's why I'm calling you," Kendra said. "I tried to get a hold of Tom Hadlock so he could make the call. The problem is, he's out at the crime scene. He didn't answer, or maybe they're having some kind of technical issue with the satphone."

"It was working earlier," Joanna said.

"It doesn't seem to be now," Kendra told her, "so I was wondering if you'd like to do the next of kin."

"Like to do it?" Joanna replied. "Certainly not. Need to do it? Yes, absolutely. Do you have contact information for the aunt?"

"It's right here in the NamUs record."

"Does it include a cell-phone number?"

"Yes."

"Text it to me, along with the physical address."

"Are you going to make the call, or are you going to have someone from El Paso PD drop by to make an in-person notification?"

Joanna thought about that. Given some of the illegal-immigrant issues rampant across the country at the moment, there were a lot of places where having a cop car roll up to the front door of either a residence or a place of employment was not a good idea. But now that Kendra Baldwin had identified their victim, speaking to Amelia's family was also the next step in solving the case. Here was an opportunity to have whatever information Rosa could provide available in time for Tom's evening debriefing at the Justice Center.

"I'll probably handle it myself," Joanna said.

"I thought you might," Kendra said. "That's the other reason I called. I'm sending now."

A text alert came in on her phone. Off the line Joanna quickly scanned through the material, including the information Rosa had provided on the NamUs filing. Once she was finished, and with Sage still sleeping, Joanna dialed the number listed as Rosa Moreno's cell phone.

"Mrs. Moreno?" Joanna asked when a woman answered.

"Yes."

"My name's Joanna Brady. I'm the sheriff of Cochise County in Arizona."

"The sheriff?" Rosa repeated. Then, after a momentary pause, she added. "I suppose this is not good news."

"You're right, Mrs. Moreno, it is not. In fact, it's dreadful news. I'm sorry to have to inform you that your niece has been found."

"Is she dead?"

"Yes."

"How?"

Joanna had signed on to do the notification, but she wasn't required to supply all the sickening details. Those would come out eventually, but not right now—not in those first breath-robbing moments. Joanna had expected tears or hysterics. Rosa Moreno exhibited none of those. She had long since arrived at the awful conclusion that her niece was most likely dead. The call was merely a confirmation of what the poor woman already knew.

"Amelia was the victim of homicidal violence," Joanna explained carefully. "Her body was found at a remote location in southeastern Arizona."

"How did you find me?"

"From your listing on NamUs—more specifically, your niece's dental records. I have a small department, Mrs. Moreno, and at the moment my people are stretched thin. Right now all available personnel are out canvassing the area looking for the killer. There's a briefing scheduled for later this evening where we'll be trying to pull all the pieces of the investigation together.

"I'm not the detective assigned to the case, but I am a sworn officer of the law. I know you've suffered a terrible shock, and this is a distressing time for someone to be asking questions, but anything you could tell me about Amelia's disappearance would be a huge help. That way I'd be able to pass the information along to my investigators."

"Her death is my fault," Rosa said brokenly. "It's all my fault."

"Mrs. Moreno," Joanna said. "Were you in Arizona this past week when Amelia was murdered?"

"No, of course not. I was here in El Paso, working."

"Then how could her death be your fault?"

"Because I told my mother she'd be safer here with me than she would be back home in Mexico. It turns out I was wrong."

The sobs Joanna had been expecting earlier arrived now with a vengeance, bringing the conversation to a halt until they finally subsided.

"If you don't wish to speak about this right now, I can call you back later," Joanna told her. "But my people are working hard to solve the case, and knowing what you know about Amelia's activities and associates in the days leading up to her disappearance could be invaluable in tracking down her killer."

"Yes," Rosa said, taking a breath. "Give me a moment."

Joanna listened while Rosa blew her nose, then came back on the line. "I'm better now," she said. "I'll be glad to answer your questions. When I tried to talk to the cops here in El Paso, the detectives wouldn't give me the time of day. They said Amelia was a runaway, and that was that."

"How did you get hooked up with NamUs?"

"I kept calling and calling. The detectives kept giving me the runaround, but Mrs. Amado, the lady who answers the phones at El Paso PD, was very kind. I think she felt sorry for me. She's the one who suggested I put Amelia's information on the Internet. I don't have a computer at home. She met up with me at the library and showed me how to log on and create an account."

"Bless her," Joanna murmured.

"Yes," Rosa agreed. "I give thanks for her every day. When we finish talking, I'll need to call her and tell her what's happened. But for now what do you need to know?"

"Everything you can tell me about Amelia."

"Her mother, Andrea, was my baby sister. When she got pregnant, her boyfriend didn't stick around, and she and the baby ended up going back home to live with my mother outside Juárez. They needed money, so Andrea went to work for one of the *maquiladoras* in town, sewing children's clothing.

She worked there for almost three years while my mother took care of Amelia. And then one Christmas, when it was time for Andrea to come home, she didn't show up."

Rosa paused. "I suppose you heard about all the girls who disappeared in Juárez?"

"Yes," Joanna said. "I'm aware of that situation."

"Andrea was one of them, and my mother worried that the same thing might happen to Amelia. That's why I suggested that she come to El Paso to live with me." Rosa's voice broke. "I thought I could keep her safe."

"What can you tell me about her disappearance?"

"She was working with me at the motel—"

"At age sixteen? Shouldn't she have been in school?"

"She dropped out of school before she ever came to live with me. My boss was paying her under the table, but she was making a lot more money than she would have made back in Mexico, and she was able to send most of it home to my mother. Still, she was so young, and I thought it was important for her to have some fun—some time to be . . . well . . . you know, a girl. So when she made friends with some of the people her age from here in the neighborhood, I was very happy about that. And when she was invited to a party to watch the fireworks, I was happy about that, too. It was her very first Fourth of July. I wanted her to enjoy it."

"So she went to watch the fireworks and never came home?" Joanna asked.

"Yes," Rosa answered. "The next morning, when

she wasn't here, I called the two girls she had gone with. They told me that after the fireworks were over, she wanted to leave, because she had to be up early the next morning to go to work. They wanted to stay later, so Amelia left on her own and never made it home. When I called the police that morning to report her missing, they insisted she had probably run away."

"Did you talk to the kids from the party?"

"I did. One of the boys said he had noticed a strange vehicle driving around the neighborhood, an SUV of some kind. I passed that information along to the cops, but I don't think they followed up on it. And now she's dead. What happens next, Sheriff Brady?" Rosa asked. "How do we get Amelia home so we can bury her? And how do I tell my mother?"

Those were questions without easy answers.

A wail from the nursery announced that Sage was awake and tuning up. Trying to discuss those sensitive issues with a baby crying in the background wasn't a good idea. Just then Joanna had a moment of inspiration.

"As I mentioned earlier," Joanna said, "my investigators will be doing a briefing later on this evening. Under normal circumstances we'd probably send an investigator to El Paso to interview you, but these aren't normal circumstances. We're worried that there may be other girls out there."

"Others like Amelia?" Rosa asked.

"Just like Amelia, and if there are, they may be in danger. Having you speak to the investigators this early in the investigation might be a big help. Would it be possible for us to call you back then and put you on speakerphone so they could talk to you directly?"

"If there are other girls in danger, of course I will help," Rosa agreed at once. "Will you be the one calling me?"

It took no time at all for Joanna to make up her mind about that. "Definitely," she said. "I'll be the person on the phone."

Joanna was close to ending the call when Rosa spoke again. "Thank you for this, Sheriff Brady. Thank you so much."

Joanna was taken aback. *Thank you for what?* she wondered. *For telling you that Amelia is dead? For bringing you such terrible news?*

"Thank you for listening to me," Rosa said after a pause. "I'm just sorry Amelia had to be dead before anyone was interested."

"That makes two of us," Joanna replied.

When the call ended, she hurried into the nursery, scooped up Sage, changed her and fed her. Then, while Denny ate his traditional Sunday-night supper of cocoa, toast, and cheese, Joanna called Carol Sunderson.

"Something's come up," she said. "I can take Sage with me, but since tomorrow's a school day and I don't know how late I'll be, would it be okay if I dropped Denny and the dogs off at your house for a sleepover?"

"Sure," Carol said, "no problem at all, but what's going on? Are you going in to the office?"

"I am, and I'm taking Sage with me," Joanna declared. "Since I have it on good authority that babies are now welcome on the floor of the U.S. Senate, having one show up in my conference room at the Justice Center shouldn't be that big a deal."

"Hallelujah!" Carol exclaimed. "Praise be."

That wasn't at all the reaction Joanna had been expecting.

"Praise be?" Joanna asked. "You're that happy to be babysitting?"

"Butch and I had a bet," Carol said with a laugh. "He said you'd make it all the way through your month of maternity leave without going in to the office. I bet him ten bucks that you wouldn't make two weeks. It looks like I win and he loses."

The fact that Butch and the grandmotherly Carol were actually wagering money on the likelihood of Joanna's making a mess of her maternity leave was a bit perturbing.

"Right," Joanna grumbled. "You can hardly fault me for being predictable."

🌵 TWENTY-FIVE

RATHER THAN set up in the conference room off the public lobby, where stray reporters might wander in, Tom Hadlock had scheduled the evening briefing for the break room. When Joanna showed up with her diaper bag in one hand and Sage's infant seat in the other, people were milling around, but the briefing had not yet gotten under way. The countertop next to the coffee machine was covered with several open pizza boxes, and people were helping themselves.

Not wanting to make a grand entrance, Joanna sidled into the room and tucked Sage's infant seat away on a chair in the back corner. Her arrival didn't go unnoticed, however. As soon as she put down the diaper bag, Tom Hadlock appeared at her side holding a paper plate laden with pizza.

"If I remember correctly," he said, "pepperoni is your preferred topping."

"Thank you," Joanna murmured, "and thank you for remembering. I hope you don't mind my showing up like this. I don't want to interfere, but . . ."

"No problem," Tom said. "I need all the help I

can get. We're just waiting on Dr. Baldwin. Once she makes it here, we'll settle in and start. The M.E. called earlier and left word on my cell phone saying that she'd ID'd the one victim, but I didn't hear the message until I was back in town. She said she was going to call you about doing the next-of-kin notification."

"She did and I did," Joanna answered. "Our victim is Amelia Diaz Salazar, a sixteen-year-old illegal immigrant from Juárez, who was living with her Aunt Rosa and working in El Paso. Amelia went missing the night of the Fourth of July. She went out to watch fireworks with some neighborhood kids and never came home. When the auntie tried to report her missing, El Paso PD pretty much blew her off. Someone helped Rosa upload Amelia's information to NamUS, which is where Dr. Baldwin made the connection. The aunt is more than willing to help us, and that's why I came. It occurred to me that putting her on a speakerphone tonight and letting her talk to the detectives would short-circuit our having to send someone there to interview her."

"Great idea," Tom said. "Anything that will speed things up works for me."

"And since I was the original point of contact, I thought it might be helpful if I was the one who made the call."

"By all means," Tom said, "you should be the one doing the talking."

Someone summoned him from across the room.

As he hustled away, a text alert came in on Joanna's phone. It was from Rochelle Powers.

It's too cold to go outside to call, so I'm writing a text in my room and will go outside to send it.

I've spent the whole afternoon thinking about your case. Sounds like we're dealing with multiple victims abducted from multiple locations. When we've seen serial killers like this in the past, they usually have ready access to reliable transportation—like railroad lines or interstate highways. Since this guy apparently transports his victims from elsewhere and then holds them captive, train travel doesn't work.

Get someone to go through the rolls of your local CDLs. I'm betting the guy we're looking for is a long-haul truck driver.

Joanna responded immediately.

Got it. Thanks. Briefing will be starting soon. I'll let everybody know.

Just then Deb Howell, the lead investigator on the case, caught sight of Joanna and hurried over to her. "Hey," she said with a laugh, "you're on maternity leave. Are you even supposed to be here?"

"I can't seem to help myself," Joanna replied.

"So I heard," Deb said. "According to Tom you're the one who reeled in the Paxtons and their cadaver dogs, and he said that you might be helping in the profiler department as well."

"*Am* helping with the profiler," Joanna corrected. "Take a look at this." She turned on her phone, located the text from Rochelle Powers, and handed the device over to Deb.

As Deb read through the text, Joanna continued. "Her name's Rochelle Powers, and she's a friend of Robin Watkins from the Tucson office of the FBI. It just so happens that Rochelle is in Arizona on vacation at the moment. She's willing to help out, but more or less under the radar, because—"

"I know," Deb said, "because Ted Whipple wouldn't lift a finger to help us, but a serial killer who happens to be a long-haul trucker would make all kinds of sense."

Looking across the room, she caught Jaime Carbajal's eye and beckoned him over. "Hey, boss," he said, grinning at Joanna as he came. "What are you doing here?"

"She's helping us out by bringing an FBI profiler to bear on our case," Deb told him. "So how about seeing what you can do to locate the names and addresses of all the commercial driver's license holders living in Cochise County."

"The profiler thinks our killer might be a truck driver?" Jaime asked. Deb nodded. "Okay, then," Jamie added. "I'll get right on it."

As he left the room, Deb turned back to Joanna. "Did the profiler say anything else?"

"She's planning on driving down tomorrow, but in order to be of any help she needs to be in on the ground floor of the investigation—including tonight's briefing."

"We could Skype it to her," Deb suggested.

"We could, but we can't," Joanna replied. "She's staying at the Grand Canyon, and their Wi-Fi system is crap."

"Kristin is in the process of setting up a video recording. . . ."

"No," Joanna said. "A video file will be huge. How about we do it the easy way in audio only?" She held up her cell phone. "Jenny does this all the time. She records stories on her phone and then sends the files to me so Denny can listen to them before he goes to sleep."

"How about we do both?" Deb replied. "We'll make a recording on your phone to send, but we'll also have a video record for us to consult later as needed."

"Fair enough," Joanna said. "As soon as the briefing starts, I'll press Record. When it's over, I grab the file and hit Send. Rochelle probably won't be able to listen to it until she has a better Wi-Fi connection, but she should be able to download and listen to it before she gets here tomorrow night."

Tom Hadlock joined them. "Before who gets here?" he asked. "And what are we talking about?"

"We're going to do a recording of the briefing so we can send it to Rochelle Powers and she can listen to it before tomorrow night."

"Who the hell is Rochelle Powers?" he demanded.

"Our FBI profiler."

Tom turned on Joanna with a look of sheer wonderment in his eyes. "You got us one of those, too?" he asked.

Joanna nodded.

"You're a real miracle worker!" he exclaimed. "And now since almost everyone is here, how about we get started?"

When the briefing began, Tom opened the show. "We're happy to have Sheriff Brady and Baby Sage with us tonight. Sheriff Brady has been working behind the scenes and has managed to put us in touch with the cadaver-dog people as well as an FBI profiler named Rochelle Powers who's willing to work with us. In order to keep Agent Powers apprised of our progress in the investigation, we'll be recording tonight's briefing and sending the file along to her. Anybody have a problem with that?"

No one did, so Joanna brought out her phone, turned it on, set it to record, and placed it on the table for all to see.

"All right, then," Tom said. "Since Detective Howell is the lead investigator on this case, I'm turning things over to her."

While Deb stepped to the head of the table, three latecomers arrived: Dr. Baldwin and Joanna's CSI team. They paused long enough to help themselves to pizza before joining Joanna and Sage at the back of the room.

Noting their arrival, Deb nodded in the M.E.'s direction. "Since Dr. Baldwin has succeeded in identifying one of our homicide victims, how about if we start with her?"

Kendra put down her plate of untouched pizza and joined Deb in the front of the room. Everyone listened in silence while she related her findings—including the young victim's name and age; the fact that she was severely malnourished; the presence of those very disturbing stomach contents; the mangled bones in the victim's hands; the interior bruising on her tibia, just above her ankle, that was indicative of long-term confinement in some kind of restraints; indications of a recent sexual assault; and finally the grim likelihood that the victim had been confined in a freezer at the time of her death.

"Since we didn't find a working freezer anywhere near that field," Tom Hadlock observed when she finished, "that means we're not even close to finding the actual crime scene."

"Unfortunately, that's all too true," the M.E. agreed.

"Any way to establish a time of death?" Ernie Carpenter asked. He might have been sidetracked into Media Relations right now, but the man was still a homicide cop at heart.

"Because the body was partially frozen, it's difficult to establish an exact time of death. However, insect larvae found on the body indicate that she'd been left out in the open for a period of several days. I'd say she was dumped on Wednesday of last week at the latest. Since there are indications that her tissues weren't completely frozen through, I'd say that puts her time of death at sometime on Tuesday of last week."

Kendra paused for a moment before continuing.

"The cadaver dogs will resume their search tomorrow. As far as the skeletal remains are concerned, we've determined that we have three separate victims, one male and two female. The male, who suffered a gunshot wound to the head, would have been in his late sixties or early seventies, with a medical history of rheumatoid arthritis. The skulls of the two females both showed evidence of blunt-force trauma."

"What about DNA?" Ernie asked.

"There may be some good news there," Dr. Baldwin said. "The technology keeps moving forward, and there's a new DNA-extraction kit that can be used on skeletal remains. It's expensive, and I haven't used that technique before, but given the severity of this case, I believe the added expenditure is warranted. I've ordered the kits, and they're due to arrive at my office via FedEx tomorrow. Questions?"

There were none, so Kendra returned to her seat.

Deb consulted her notes. "As far as the canvassing is concerned, our people have covered a lot of ground, but I've been checking reports as they filter in from the field, and so far we've come up empty. Nobody has reported seeing anything out of the ordinary."

Just then the door opened and Jaime Carbajal entered the room carrying a sheaf of papers. "The CDLs?" Deb asked.

Nodding, he took a seat.

"How many?" Deb asked.

"Five hundred forty-eight," he replied, "all

of them registered to people residing in Cochise County."

"Wait, why are we looking at people with commercial driver's licenses?" Ernie asked.

"Because Agent Powers, the FBI profiler who's working with us, has suggested that our perpetrator might be a long-haul trucker, using his vehicle to transport his victims. Now that Dr. Baldwin has narrowed down the time of death, tomorrow we need to start talking to all these individuals and find out where they were on Tuesday of last week. It'll be another big needle-in-a-haystack job, but we should be able to verify their whereabouts using their logbooks and company GPS records. We'll put you in charge of that, Jaime, and if you need help, grab a deputy or two off patrol."

"Will do," Jaime told her, "starting first thing in the morning."

As nods of agreement went around the table, Joanna felt the attendees' sudden shift in mood. Coming into the briefing, everyone had been tired and dispirited. Now that the M.E. had established a time of death and Rochelle Powers had given them what seemed like a concrete lead to pursue, people were invigorated again. They had a renewed sense of purpose. Joanna suspected that some of them might even decide to go back to work when the briefing ended.

"Anyone else?" Deb asked.

Casey Ledford rose to her feet. "I've got something," she said, "and it may give us another break. Two loaded trash bags were discovered in close proximity to Amelia Salazar's body. When Dave brought them back to the lab, we found they contained packages of discarded food items—long out-of-date meat and vegetables. Unbelievably, the labeling on several of the meat packages was still faintly legible. It turns out they came from the Safeway store in Douglas."

"Wait a minute," Joanna objected. "Didn't that store shut down years ago?"

"Yes, it did," Casey said, "in 2011."

"Sounds like someone finally got around to cleaning out their fridge," Tom put in. "Come to think of it, there might be stuff that old in mine."

"More likely a freezer than a fridge," Casey corrected. "I think the killer chucked the food out of a freezer in order to cram Amelia inside. What's good news for us is that when he was dealing with the food, he must have been in a hell of a hurry, because he didn't bother using gloves."

"You've got fingerprints, then?" Deb asked.

"Lots of them," Casey answered. "I lifted them from the outsides of the garbage bags and from the food packages themselves. I ran the prints through AFIS and didn't get a hit, but I'm hoping there'll be enough cast-off DNA to get a profile. In other words, once we identify a suspect, we'll for sure be able to place him at the scene of the crime."

"At the scene of the dump site," Deb specified. "Unfortunately, as Chief Deputy Hadlock pointed out, we have yet to locate the actual crime scene. Anyone else?" When no one responded, Deb turned to Joanna. "Sheriff Brady," she said, "I believe you're next."

Joanna, listening to the briefing, had been feeling more and more ill at ease. These people were all professional law-enforcement types, discussing the nitty-gritty of terrible crimes in gruesome detail. Was it fair to bring Amelia Salazar's grieving aunt into this conversation? Rosa Moreno had expressed her willingness to speak with the investigators, but now Joanna had her doubts.

Leaving Sage and her infant seat in the corner, Joanna took her place at the front of the room, where, to her surprise, she was greeted with a round of enthusiastic applause. That was gratifying. It was good to be here in the department, even if it happened to be for all the wrong reasons.

"Thank you," she said. "This afternoon Acting Sheriff Hadlock was out of communication range when Dr. Baldwin identified our victim. With Tom unavailable, she asked me to do the next-of-kin notification. I spoke to Amelia's aunt, Rosa Moreno, in El Paso, Texas, and she expressed a willingness to speak to the investigators working her niece's case. I told her you were gathering here tonight and asked if it would be okay if I gave her a call. Since my phone is doing the recording, I'll need someone else's to place the call."

Deb handed over her phone. Joanna keyed in the number and then switched the phone to speaker and full volume. Rosa Moreno answered after only one ring.

"Hello," she said warily.

"It's Sheriff Brady," Joanna said.

"Thank goodness it's you. I was afraid it might be that reporter again."

"A reporter?" Joanna repeated. "What reporter?"

"I didn't catch her name."

Joanna didn't have to be told the name, because she was quite sure she already knew which reporter that was.

"We're in the briefing I told you about, Ms. Moreno," Joanna explained through gritted teeth. "Is this a good time to speak to you?"

"Yes," Rosa said. "I've been waiting for you to call. Once we've spoken, my cousin Ricardo and I will be leaving for Juárez to go tell my mother."

Even though Amelia's relatives were just being notified, Marliss Shackleford already had access to confidential information and was using that to nose around, yet another indication that the woman had to have an inside source. Fuming at the thought, Joanna fought to maintain a civil tone with Rosa.

"This briefing is being recorded on an open line," Joanna continued. "Is that all right with you, Ms. Moreno? Do you mind if we record what you have to say?"

"No, I don't mind at all. I'm happy to do whatever I can to help."

Over in the corner of the room, Sage uttered a small, preliminary whimper, one that boded ill for Joanna's ability to conduct an interview.

"I'm turning you over to Detective Deb Howell, the lead investigator on your niece's case. She'll be the one asking the questions."

With that, Joanna handed the phone back to Deb. She raced back to her chair, grabbed up Sage's infant seat and the diaper bag, and fled the room.

She managed to escape into the hallway before the whimper morphed into a full-throated screech.

Retreating to the privacy of her office, Joanna sat at her desk nursing Sage and fuming about Marliss Shackleford. By the time Sage was fed, changed, and rewrapped, Joanna was wondering if, on her way home, perhaps she should pay the reporter an unannounced visit.

Joanna was packing up to return to the break room when Kristin popped her head inside. "There you are," she said. "The briefing just broke up. I'm on my way home. I came by to bring you your purse, return your phone, and say thank you."

"Thanks," Joanna said, taking the purse and tucking the phone into her pocket. "These days I seem to be having a tough time remembering both the purse and the diaper bag, but what are you thanking me for?"

"For helping me win two hundred bucks," Kristin answered.

"How did I do that?"

"I won the pool," Kristin said with a grin. "The one about how long you'd be out on maternity leave. Today was my day, and here you are."

Yes, Joanna thought ruefully once Kristin departed, *when it comes to flunking maternity leave, I'm nothing if not consistent.*

TWENTY-SIX

IT WAS after ten before Joanna left the Justice Center with her baby, diaper bag, purse, and phone all safely in hand. She'd been sorry to be out of the room during the last half hour of the briefing, because she'd wanted to hear what Rosa had to say. Still, as she belted Sage's infant seat into the Enclave, she realized that as long as the audio file was on her phone, she'd be able to listen to whatever she'd missed at the same time she was sending a copy to Rochelle Powers.

Her initial intention was to go straight home. She was at the exit signaling to turn left and about to do just that when she changed her mind and turned right instead. With Sage once again fast asleep, now was as good a time as any for her to pay an unscheduled visit to Marliss Shackleford. And since Marliss had been up and out early in the morning in order to lay siege to the Carvers' house down in Douglas, it seemed only fair that somebody should return the favor that very night by keeping her up late.

Despite the thirty-year age difference between them, Marliss had always been bosom buddies with

Joanna's mother, Eleanor, but she'd never been a friend of Joanna's—quite the opposite, in fact. Marliss's column, "Bisbee Buzzings," often contained snarky comments about Joanna's department in general and her job performance in particular. It had always bugged Joanna that her mother had stayed close friends with someone who was clearly one of Joanna's top critics.

When Dick Voland, one of Joanna's original chief deputies, left the department, he and Marliss had struck up a whirlwind romance. They'd been married for a while, but that relationship, like Marliss's first two marriages, had ended in divorce, and Dick had left town shortly thereafter. Joanna supposed that Marliss had probably shared the gory details behind their parting with her good friend Eleanor. If so, mother and daughter had never discussed them, and that was fine. Whatever was going on in Marliss Shackleford's love life was none of Joanna's business.

Marliss had come away from her first divorce with custody of the family home on Wilderness Trail out in San Jose Estates, and she had hung on to it through thick and thin ever since. And that's where Joanna was headed at ten fifteen on Sunday night, turning onto Highway 92 at the traffic circle and driving out through Don Luis.

Wilderness Trail was the last street on the western edge of the development. As Joanna turned onto it, she was surprised to see a vehicle back out of the driveway at the far end of the street—Marliss's driveway. It came barreling toward her with its headlights on high beam. Joanna moved over to the shoulder to get out of the way, and that's where she was when the speeding vehicle, a small white SUV with a crumpled left front bumper, whizzed past. She had seen that vehicle before, parked in the employee lot at the M.E.'s office uptown in Old Bisbee, and she knew it to be a Kia Sportage belonging to one of Dr. Baldwin's mortuary assistants, Ralph Whetson.

It didn't take a lot of imagination to figure out why Ralph might be paying a late-evening visit to Marliss Shackleford. The moment Joanna realized who was at the wheel, she was sure she had also identified the person responsible for leaking confidential details of her homicide investigation to the media.

Ralph wasn't exactly the brightest bulb in the pack. He was overweight, not especially good-looking, and at least twenty years Marliss's junior. Still, in Marliss's manipulative hands he would be an exceedingly useful idiot. In fact, Joanna thought in a sudden moment of clarity, access to the inner workings of Joanna's department had probably been a big part of Marliss's intense but short-lived interest in Dick Voland.

Joanna pulled into Marliss's driveway just as the porch light blinked off. With her guest gone, Marliss was most likely intent on locking up and getting ready for bed.

"Not so fast," Joanna muttered aloud. "I believe you've got some explaining to do."

Shutting off the engine, Joanna looked in the

backseat to check on Sage, who was sleeping peacefully. "I'm locking up and leaving you here," Joanna explained. "Believe me, I won't be long."

There's a distinctive sort of police knock that is designed to intimidate and encourage unsuspecting people to open their closed doors. Joanna had never quite managed to duplicate that knock, at least not with her bare knuckles. To that end she dragged a Maglite out of the glove box and took that along with her, locking the car doors behind her as she exited the SUV.

"Police!" Joanna announced, hammering on the door with the flashlight. "Open up."

"Who are you?" Marliss asked a moment later. "What do you want?" She didn't open the door, but she was obviously standing on the far side of it.

"It's Sheriff Brady," Joanna said. "I need to speak to you."

"What about? It's the middle of the night. I'm not dressed. Can't this wait until morning?"

"Not dressed, really?" Joanna asked. "And with your gentleman caller just now leaving? Isn't that interesting! But no, I'm here on police business, and what I have to say can't wait until morning. Either you can open up, or I'll stand here yelling it through the door. I'm sure your neighbors will take notice."

The porch light flashed back on, a dead bolt turned in the lock, and the door swung open. Marliss, dressed in a robe, her makeup marred and her hair in more than its usual disarray, stood in the doorway with her arms folded across her ample chest.

"What do you want?" she demanded.

"How long have you and Ralph Whetson been getting it on?"

"That's none of your business."

"You're wrong," Joanna said. "It's very much my business. My department is dealing with a major incident, and confidential details of our investigation have been leaked to the media. Considering you and Mr. Whetson are clearly involved in some kind of romantic entanglement, it's not too difficult to determine who might be the source of all that unauthorized information."

"I'm a reporter. I'm just doing my job."

"No," Joanna said, "you're actually interfering with our investigation. So are you inviting me in or not?"

Grudgingly, Marliss stepped aside. "I suppose you can come in." She allowed Joanna into the house, but they went no farther than the entryway, and no invitation to have a seat was forthcoming.

"What's in your column for tomorrow?" Joanna asked.

"That's none of your business, either."

"Does it by any chance mention one of our homicide victims by name?"

"What if it does?"

"Does the publisher of the *Bisbee Bee* approve of revealing the name of a homicide victim prior to the notification of the next of kin?"

"But I thought . . ."

"Ralph told you that Dr. Baldwin asked me to do the next-of-kin notification, and you thought it was done. Unfortunately, Amelia's grandmother, the woman who raised her, doesn't have a telephone and has not yet been notified. If your column reveals our victim's name prior to that notification being made, I'll go straight to Richard Warren and lodge a formal complaint."

Not that that would do any good. Joanna knew Richard Warren to be a mealy-mouthed little wuss who let his star reporter run roughshod over him most of the time. Still, it was enough of a threat to get Marliss's attention.

"I'll take the name out," she conceded.

"Speaking of names," Joanna said, "Jack Carver's name better not show up there, either. He's a confidential informant whose contribution to our investigation has been invaluable. He's also a juvenile, and I have it on good authority that if you reveal his connection to this case in a fashion that in any way jeopardizes his future, his mother will take you to the cleaners."

"She wouldn't dare."

"Have you ever met June Carver?"

"Well, yes," Marliss admitted, "we spoke briefly, but—"

"She's not an attorney, but she's extremely conversant with the law and litigious as well."

"I had no idea."

"For the record, I believe that anyone dumb enough to tangle with her would do so at their own peril. Understand? As for Ralph, I'll be reporting your little dalliance to Dr. Baldwin first thing in the morning. If there are any additional instances of unauthorized leaks coming from that quarter, I'll see to it that he's terminated. Is that clear?"

With that, Joanna turned on her heel and took her leave. When she got back to the Enclave, Sage hadn't stirred. As she started the engine, however, her phone rang, with Butch's name in caller ID. She answered it through the audio system.

"Where are you?" he demanded. "Why haven't you responded to any of my texts?"

A glance at the face of her phone gave her the answer. Butch's thread of messages had all come in while her phone was recording the briefing.

"Sorry," she said. "I was at the office."

"I know," he fumed. "All I wanted was to tell you that the afternoon library event in Santa Fe was terrific. When I couldn't get you to answer, I finally called Carol. She told me you'd gone in to the department for a briefing. Did you really take Sage along for that?"

"I did," Joanna admitted. "I couldn't very well leave her at home, and I needed to be there. I was the one who'd done the next-of-kin notification, and it was my responsibility to introduce Amelia's Aunt Rosa to the investigation team. We were using my phone to record the interview when your texts came in. Sorry. I didn't see them until just this minute."

"Are you back home now?"

"Not exactly. I'm just leaving Marliss Shackleford's place in San Jose Estates. I stopped by to read her the riot act."

"About?"

"Somebody's been leaking information on our investigation, and tonight I found out who that somebody is. It turns out Marliss is having a fling with Ralph Whetson."

"Really? That roly-poly guy from the M.E.'s office?"

"One and the same."

"Okay," Butch said, sounding a lot less peeved and a whole lot more interested. "Now that you have my undivided attention, maybe you should bring me up to date."

TWENTY-SEVEN

JIMMY ARDMORE'S five-and-a-half-hour drive from Yuma to Road Forks had been uneventful, but it seemed to take forever. The headache was a killer and still pounding away. He got to his double-wide in midafternoon. He had planned on walking over to the café and having a bite to eat, but he felt too punk. Instead he went into the house and flopped down on the bed. Rather than simply rest for a while, he fell into a deep sleep. When he woke up, it was dark outside.

With a couple of nosy neighbors around, Jimmy needed the cover of darkness to transfer the dog food and toilet paper from his big truck into the smaller one, a beefy RAM 3500. He was surprised to find that moving even a twenty-five-pound bag was more of a struggle than it should have been. He seemed weaker somehow, as though his body wasn't quite right.

By the time he finished, it was almost ten o'clock at night—more than twelve hours since his breakfast in Yuma. The twenty-four-hour café at the truck stop was still open. He could have gone there and grabbed a burger, but the waitress who worked the night shift was an uncompromising bitch who reminded him too much of his mother. He raided his fridge for a bottle of beer and a couple pieces of string cheese. Then, with a bottle of Jameson along for the ride, he headed out.

Checking his jacket pocket to make sure he hadn't misplaced his car keys, his fingers landed on the packet of pills. There was a joint not far from the warehouse in L.A. where, for a price, you could buy pretty much any kind of pharmaceutical on the planet. Some customers were looking for meth or opioids. Not Jimmy. He'd gone there hoping to score some little blue pills.

He'd never expected that he'd be one of those guys who couldn't get it up. He was still shocked to realize that he hadn't been able to perform with Amelia, and he was going to do everything in his power to make sure that never happened again. That was the real reason he'd stuffed the girl in the freezer—because he hadn't been able to get an erection, and she knew it. Nothing he did or she did made it work. Using his leather belt to beat the crap out of a woman was usually enough to bring him to the edge, but not that time.

The unsatisfactory session had ended in total humiliation. When it was time for Jimmy to take Amelia back down to the basement, he was damned if he was going to turn her loose so she and Latisha could sit around talking about him and laughing behind his back. Being laughed at was something James Edward Ardmore did not tolerate.

He had bought the pills in anticipation of his

hunting trip, a hunting trip that had also turned into a complete bust. From his point of view, this had been a long dry spell, and he was ready for it to be over. That night, before he ever put the truck in gear to leave Road Forks, he shook three pills out of the clear plastic packet his supplier had given him, washed them down with a mouthful of Jameson, and got under way.

Jimmy headed for Calhoun just as the moon came peeking over the horizon. As he drove, he took the occasional swig of Jameson. On these back roads, the chances of having some cop picking him up on an open-container violation were next to nil. Had this been open range, he might have been more worried. The RAM was tough enough that hitting the occasional deer wasn't much of an issue, but hitting a stray steer or a cow was another matter entirely. Then you didn't just have to deal with cops, you had to contend with some pissed-off rancher. So yes, he drove along sipping his Jameson and appreciating that unending line of fence posts on either side of the road.

As a general rule, Jimmy Ardmore wasn't someone who believed in signs from above, but maybe that failed mission to bring Megan home had been exactly that—a message sent to him directly suggesting that it was time to consider putting his exit strategy into play—time to take the ghost of Arthur Ardmore with him, hang it up, and disappear.

He wasn't so egotistical as to think he'd never be caught, and he'd been putting pieces in place that would make it possible for him to vanish.

Arthur's passport still had eighteen months to go. Just as with the driver's license, the spooky resemblance between him and his late half brother made Jimmy's ability to use the passport to leave the country without detection entirely viable.

During his time on the road, he'd made the acquaintance of some pretty dodgy individuals, ones who had proved to be helpful when it came time to transfer sums of money out of the country and into numbered accounts where he alone would have access to them. That had to be done by dribs and drabs, because transferring large amounts might have raised too many red flags. He bought pieces of property on foreign soil—retirement condos mostly—and sold them again immediately, not caring if he took a loss. After all, the whole purpose of the purchases was to launder money. When the properties sold, whatever proceeds came in from the sale were already outside the country, and that's where they stayed.

By now he had enough of Arthur's money stashed away here and there that he would be fine no matter what, but the question was, where should he go? The near miss with Megan in Venice Beach still troubled him. It was possible that she'd reported the incident to the authorities and cops had launched a search for him. With that in mind, he needed to have a suitable destination in mind—a retreat the U.S. Marshals Service couldn't get to, somewhere that didn't have an extradition treaty. That way if the cops finally sorted things out and realized Arthur was dead and Jimmy was the one on the lam, there wouldn't be a damned thing they could do about it.

Time was when Venezuela would have been a good refuge of choice, but the government had pretty much wrecked that one. Jimmy didn't want to live in a place where people went Dumpster diving just to find food to eat. And it didn't seem to him as though any of those countries with "-stan" on the end of their names would be a good fit for him, either. Mexico was out, too. These days the U.S. Marshals and the *federales* were far too chummy. For proof positive of that, just ask Joaquín "El Chapo" Guzmán.

At the moment Jimmy's first choice was Cuba. He wasn't someone who cared about politics. If the people who lived there were all a bunch of commies, so what? Since planeloads of tourists were flying there from the States these days, getting there wouldn't be such a big problem. Staying there on a permanent basis might be, but if the people were poor enough, a little bit of money out there greasing palms would probably go a very long way.

Halfway to Calhoun, Jimmy began feeling agitated. The pill was starting to work. He put the pedal to the metal. He wanted to be home and have a go at Latisha before whatever was propping him up ran out of steam.

TWENTY-EIGHT

THIS TIME there could be no doubt. The aching tooth was what woke Latisha rather than her throbbing toes. The whole right side of her face felt like it was on fire. Maybe when she saw the Boss, she should ask him to pull it. After all, he liked to hurt her, didn't he? Surely pulling a tooth without benefit of novocaine would hurt like crazy, but she knew he wouldn't. If hurting her might somehow help her, he would refuse to do it.

She got up and made her way to the toilet. She was alone. There was no longer any need to check if anyone else was already there. Once the flushing tank refilled, she scooped up some water and drank it down. Then she refilled the cup once more and used that water to wash the sore on her leg. She wrapped the heavy metal clamp with another thick layer of toilet paper. She couldn't see for sure if it was helping, but the pain in her leg seemed to be subsiding.

She was on her mattress again, staring up into the darkness, when she heard the familiar sound of his approaching truck. The Boss was coming home. He was back. She hated it, while at the same time she was relieved and grateful. Roiled by a storm of countervailing emotions, her whole body began to quake. Now that he was here, he would probably replenish her dwindling supply of kibble. That meant she wouldn't starve to death. The power would stay on. The water would keep on flowing. She wouldn't die of thirst, either, but Latisha was pretty sure she was going to die.

If he had brought another girl home with him, chances were that he'd take her first. Sandy had told her that was how he usually operated. However, if he chose Latisha instead, at least she'd have a bath—at least she'd be clean—and whatever came after that would happen. Would he stuff her in the freezer, too? Not so long ago, she was pretty sure she wouldn't have been able to fit inside it. Now things were different. She had seen her sagging skin and sallow complexion in the pockmarked mirror up in the bathroom. For months she'd eaten nothing but kibble. Latisha was literally just skin and bone.

She heard the upstairs door open. Heavy footsteps pounded across the planked floor. They stopped moving on the far side of the room, and something heavy fell to the floor with an ominous thump. What was that? A body, maybe? Had the Boss carried the new girl into the room and dropped her on the floor rather than putting her on the bed? Had something bad happened to her on the way home? Was she already dead?

Latisha held her breath, listening for the sound

of voices or conversation—anything that would indicate if the new arrival was dead or alive. She heard the creaking of bedsprings, as though he had sat down on the edge of the mattress, but aside from that there was nothing. Yet then, after what seemed forever, the springs creaked again and footsteps thudded across the room, heading for the top of the stairway. A moment later the upstairs door was yanked open and the lightbulb flashed on.

Latisha had grown accustomed to the momentary blindness that always followed that initial stab of light. Once her vision returned, she saw first his work boots and then the legs of his jeans, slowly making their way down the stairs. When he got to the bottom, she saw he was empty-handed. If he had brought someone home with him, he hadn't forced her to go downstairs. That meant he was definitely coming for Latisha.

He took an unsteady step forward, but then he stopped and had to lay a hand on the freezer in order to steady himself. She knew he drank. She had smelled it on him sometimes, so was that what was happening here? Was he drunk?

"Hey, Latisha," he called. "Long time no see. Did you miss me?"

Drunk, she realized, most definitely drunk.

He let go of the freezer and staggered toward her. He always kept the key to the shackles in his right hip pocket. Usually he had no trouble locating the key or operating it, but this time he had difficulty extracting the key from his clothing and fitting it into the hole, cursing and swaying from side to side as he tried to do so. And yes, she could smell the booze on his breath. How drunk was he?

Latisha lay perfectly still while he struggled with the key. Any movement from her would be deemed resistance. Any offer to help him would mean she was belittling his efforts or making fun of him. In either case the punishment would be swift and severe.

As last he got the key to work. The lock clicked open, and the clamp came loose. "Okay, now, girlie," he said, tossing aside her blanket and then standing there leering at her. "Let's get ourselves upstairs. Daddy's got a surprise for you tonight—a big surprise."

Latisha struggled to her feet. Rising from the floor had not always been difficult, but months of disuse had robbed her of muscle tone, and that formerly simple maneuver was growing ever more challenging. Once she was upright, walking wasn't easy, either. Without the weight of the chain on her leg, it was as though she had to learn to walk all over again. Making her way across the room toward the bottom of the stairs, she realized she was probably staggering as much as he was, but for very different reasons.

Latisha had to use the handrail to help drag herself up the stairway. By the time she reached the top, she was winded and gasping for breath. Looking around the room, she noticed a bag of dog food lying on the floor just inside the door. It appeared to have fallen close to the same place where she'd heard that earlier thump, so maybe the noise had been the dog food falling, not a body.

He had gone hunting for another girl and had come home empty-handed. That meant there were just the two of them here now—Latisha and the Boss.

He brushed past her, stumbled over to the bed, sat down heavily on the bare mattress, and attempted to remove his boots. That was odd. Usually he walked her as far as the bathroom door and locked her inside. For the time being, she stood where she was and waited for him to walk her to the door. Instead, after untying his lace-up work boots, he made two halfhearted attempts to remove one of them. Finally, giving up, he looked up and glared at her.

"Come help me with these damned boots!" It was an order, one not to be disobeyed.

Each time Latisha approached that bed of horrors, she wanted to avert her eyes, but she couldn't help herself. The faded and filthy surface of the mattress was dotted with stains—some yellow and some rusty red. The original flower pattern of the mattress surface had long since faded into oblivion, while the stains seemed to grow ever more vivid. Latisha understood those stains because some of them belonged to her. Each of them offered mute testimony to some awful act of violence, and each of them was a visible reminder of terrible suffering.

"Well," he demanded, startling her out of her momentary reflection. "Are you going to take them off or not?"

Kneeling at his feet, she tugged the boots off one by one and set them next to the bed.

"Get going, now," he ordered. "Get yourself ready. You know what to do."

Latisha did know what to do. She let herself into the bathroom and closed the door. Knowing it wasn't being locked behind her made no difference—she'd never be able to get away.

She drew the bath and stepped into the tub. The hot water soothed her aching body, but her skin was so chapped and dry that the water stung almost as much as it helped. She examined the sore on her leg. The toilet-paper cushioning seemed to be helping. The last time she'd seen it, the wound had been an oozing open sore. Now at least it was scabbing over. She soaped herself down and shampooed her hair. It was an impossible matted tangle now, totally uncombable, but it least it would be clean.

She stepped out of the tub and dried herself on the communal towel. Next she brushed her teeth with the communal toothbrush. Finally, dreading what was to come, she squared her shoulders, opened the door, and stepped out into a whole new world.

The Boss was still on the bed—but rather than sitting on the edge of it, he was lying on it. He had undressed, dropping his clothes on the floor next to the boots. He lay there stark naked, obviously waiting for her, but to her amazement he was sound asleep and snoring like mad.

Latisha had prayed for deliverance for so long that when it was finally at hand, she was too astonished to move. She stood frozen to the spot, staring first at him and then at the door. Could she tiptoe out without waking him? But then what? It was clearly winter. As cold as it was in the basement, it would be colder outside. Not only was she naked, her hair was wet, and she had no shoes. Looking down at her bare feet, misshapen by those long curled toenails, she was overcome by despair. If she ran outside and he came after her, how would she ever get away, especially if he had shoes and she didn't? That would be hopeless. If she tried to run, he'd catch her and drag her back—back to the freezer, most likely.

Still unmoving, Latisha heard her stepfather's voice, as clearly as if Lyle Montgomery Richards were in this appalling room standing right beside her: "God helps those who help themselves."

Latisha had heard those words before, and more than once. He'd told her that when she'd been smarting off or arguing with him because the homework at Christ the King was too hard. His admonition came to her now like a bolt out of the blue, and that's when she saw the boots—his boots, the Boss's boots. They were still sitting next to the bed, exactly where she'd left them.

The Boss was a good five or six inches taller than she was. With any luck his larger shoe size would be able to accommodate her oversize toenails. So if she had shoes to wear, what about clothing? Even with shoes on, she couldn't very well go out into wintry weather bare naked. For clothing there could be only one answer—the army blankets on her mattress downstairs. She might still be naked underneath, but if she wrapped one around herself and wore it as a cloak, the heavy wool would help to ward off the cold.

Going back downstairs was the last thing she wanted to do. What if he woke up, followed, and trapped her there? But if she was going to get away, going down to grab that blanket was her only option. Holding her breath, she tried to tiptoe past the bed, but the muscles in her calves were too weak. She couldn't do it. Instead she had to walk flat-footed. Her heart pounded in alarm as one of the old wooden planks creaked under the weight of her body, but when she glanced over at the bed, the Boss hadn't moved.

She paused briefly at the foot of the bed, gathering her courage. And then, because praying had become a habit for her, she did so at that moment, moving her lips in a silent whisper to keep from waking the Boss.

"Holy Mary, Mother of God, pray for us sinners now and at the hour of our death. Amen."

At the top of the basement steps, she paused long enough to find the switch and bathe her hellhole prison in light. There were sixteen wooden steps in all. She took them slowly and deliberately, stopping on each one to recite the prayer once more. She didn't want to rush for fear she might stumble and fall and give herself away.

Down in the basement she made her way to her mattress. She collected the blanket she'd used for a pillow because it was already folded. After a moment's hesitation, she reached down and grabbed the container of kibble. She had no idea where she was or how far she would have to go to find help.

She was almost to the bottom of the stairs when she thought of something else—water. If she was in the desert, she'd need water as well as food. Hurrying back to her mattress, she located the container that had once held Amelia's kibble. She took that to the toilet and filled it from the water in the flushing tank. She didn't bother putting the tank lid back when she finished. If a rat fell in and drowned, it wouldn't matter now. One way or another, she wasn't coming back here—ever!

Overhead, the snoring continued. Climbing back up, she made it as far as the landing with her heart hammering in her chest and with her breath coming in short gasps, this time more from exertion than fear. Once again she forced herself to move slowly and deliberately across the room. She deposited the blanket and the two containers next to the door, then went to retrieve the boots, carrying them with her rather than putting them on. She was reaching for the doorknob when she noticed the jacket—a leather jacket—hanging on a hook next to the door. It had been there the whole time, but she hadn't seen it until just now. Wearing a jacket would make better sense than trying to run while holding a cloak closed around her. It would free up her hands. It would make it possible for her to bring along the blanket and the precious containers of food and water.

She eased the jacket down from its hook and shrugged it on. It was far too big for her. The sleeves were so long that the ends of them hung beyond the tips of her fingers. Compared to the scratchy wool of the blanket, the soft flannel lining felt heavenly against her bare skin.

She tried slipping one of the containers into a jacket pocket. It was too large and didn't fit, but in making the attempt she felt a small bulge at the bottom of the pocket. Curious, she reached in, pulled the object out, and was amazed to discover she was holding a key fob. Could it be the key to the Boss's truck? Was that even possible? Feeling as though Holy Mary, the Mother of God, had just granted her a miracle, Latisha slid the key fob back into the pocket of the jacket. She picked up the folded blanket and placed the two Ziploc containers side by side on that. Then she placed the boots on top of the Ziplocs. Only then did she turn the knob, open the door, and step outside.

A bitingly cold wind hit the bare skin on her legs and took her breath away. The hard-packed earth under her feet was shockingly cold, but she didn't pause long enough to put on the boots here, either. If she could find the truck first, she could put the boots on once she was inside that, and if she could figure out how to make it work, she could use that to get away. Using a vehicle would give her a far better chance of escaping than running on foot, boots or no boots.

Clutching her precious load to her chest with her left arm, she slipped her right hand into the jacket pocket, pulled out the key fob, and grasped it tightly in her fist.

It was dark outside. Coming from the unaccustomed light inside, she was momentarily blinded, but her eyes, used to months of almost total darkness, quickly readjusted.

She was standing on the street of what looked like a very old town, or maybe an old movie set. The brick building behind her, the one from which she'd just emerged, had the window covered with what looked like iron bars, making Latisha wonder if perhaps it had once been a jail. There were a few other buildings as well, some still upright and others tumbledown wrecks, on either side of the narrow dirt track. At first she saw no sign of any vehicle, but then, off to the side—parked between the would-be jail and the next building over—sat a huge pickup truck with the emblem of a ram on the hood.

She walked up to the door and tried the handle. The door opened as if by magic, and an interior light came on. She flung the boots and the containers inside ahead of her far enough that they came to rest against the passenger seat's armrest. Still clutching the key in her right hand, she used her left hand to reach for the grab bar. Scared of dropping the fob, she must have gripped it too tight. Somehow she activated the panic button. Instantly the horn began blaring and the lights flashed on and off.

Latisha plunged into despair. The noise was bound to wake him. *He'll come for me now*, she thought desperately. *I'm done. It's all over. He'll drag me back inside and kill me.*

And then she heard Lyle's voice again. "God helps those who help themselves."

There were buttons on the key fob. With the lights flashing and her hands shaking, she couldn't see the labels on the buttons, so she punched one at random. Mercifully, the alarm shut off. On the door she caught sight of the lock button. She pushed that, and the lock engaged. If he came outside with another key, he might be able to open the door and drag her out, but for the moment she was safe. With the lights still flashing, she stared at the dashboard.

Once, right after she and Trayvon left St. Louis, they had gotten into a fight. They'd been in a bar at the time. Latisha was underage, of course, but in the kinds of places where Trayvon hung out, being underage didn't matter. A few minutes later, when he'd gone to the restroom, he made the mistake of leaving his key fob on the bar. The one for the Cadillac had looked just like this one. Latisha didn't have a driver's license, but she knew that with one of those fobs all you had to do to start the engine was press a button on the dash. She had found the right button, but when she pressed it, nothing happened.

Trayvon had come roaring out of the bar right then and caught her in the act. Just like now she'd been smart enough to lock the car door behind her. She had thought she was safe, but one of his friends had handed him a baseball bat. He'd smashed the window to pieces, dragged her out of the car, and beaten her senseless. That was the first time he beat her and certainly not the last.

Later, after he'd gotten the window fixed, he'd laughed at her about it. "Stupid bitch," he told her.

"Don't you know nothing? Keyless ignitions don't do shit less'n you step on the brake at the same time you be pressin' the damned button."

She hadn't forgotten the beating, and she hadn't forgotten what Trayvon had said, either. His voice and his words came back to Latisha now almost as clearly as Lyle's had earlier. She put her foot on the brake and punched the ignition button. The engine roared to life, and the lights came on just as the door to the jail crashed open and the Boss bounded out into the street.

Latisha found the gearshift and moved the handle. On her first attempt, when the indicator landed on the letter R, the truck lurched into reverse and slammed into a corner of the building next door. By then the Boss, naked and barefoot, was barreling toward the truck. Instead of looking at him, Latisha tried again, moving the indicator until it settled on the capital N. This time the engine wound up to a full-throttled roar, but the truck didn't move. By then the Boss's furious face was just outside the window. He was yanking on the door handle and pounding on the window with his fist. Not daring to look at him, Latisha tried one last thing. This time the dial landed on the capital D, and the truck shot forward.

The unexpected burst of speed surprised her. She almost smashed into the building across the street before she managed to twist the wheel to the right. The truck wobbled from side to side before it finally got a grip, and she was able to point it down the street. The mirror settings were all wrong. If she'd been able to look back, she would have seen the Boss, as outraged as he was naked, standing in the middle of the dirt street shaking his fists in her direction and screaming at the top of his lungs.

Rather than try to look back, Latisha kept her eyes on the road, her foot on the gas, and drove like a bat out of hell.

TWENTY-NINE

"YOU LITTLE bitch!" Jimmy Ardmore screamed after the retreating vehicle as it sped off into the darkness. "You incredible bitch!"

Beyond furious and with his bare feet turning to ice on the cold, hard ground, Jimmy Ardmore limped back into the building. Twice in the process, he felt his head spinning so badly that he had to stop and grab something to steady himself—once by leaning against the doorjamb and a few steps later by grabbing on to one of the kitchen chairs.

Feeling this woozy made no sense to him. Yes, he'd had a few slugs of Jameson on the way down, but not enough to cause this. Eventually he made it back to the bed and sank onto it long enough to retrieve his clothing. When he went to pull his pants on, Jimmy discovered that his little blue pills were still working overtime, even though Latisha, damn her anyway, was well out of reach!

Not for long, he vowed. Latisha was running, but she wouldn't get far, and once he caught up with her . . .

Yes, she had taken his truck, but that didn't mean

he couldn't follow her. He still had the rattletrap 1998 Subaru Forester that Arthur had bought new and treated as his forever car. It was safely locked away in the garage right next door. Even with the power of attorney, selling and changing the title on the old heap over to someone else might have raised a few eyebrows and elicited some uncomfortable questions. So Jimmy still had the little green Forester. He started it occasionally and drove it some to keep it in good working order. So if Latisha was under the impression that she had left him stranded and without a useable vehicle, she was one hundred percent wrong.

It wasn't until he had his pants on and was looking for his boots that he discovered she'd taken those, too. Since he and his half brother had worn almost the same size shoes, that was a fixable problem. Padlocking the door behind him, he raced outside and hobbled to the garage next door, where he used a touchpad to open the rolling shutters. The Subaru was parked inside, surrounded by a dozen five-gallon fully loaded gas cans. The gas cans were there for a reason. When he was ready to leave Calhoun, there wouldn't be any evidence left behind.

He got in, started the car, and drove as far as the tin-roofed shack that had once been Arthur's pride and joy. The clamps on the girls' ankles had all been set to open with one key, and the padlocks opened with another. He opened the padlock on Arthur's front door and charged inside. Since he'd left Arthur's belongings just as they were, he had no problem locating replacement shoes. He dragged a pair of worn Johnston & Murphys—relics from Arthur's salad days—out of the closet. As Jimmy bent over to tie the laces, he was beset by yet another bout of dizziness. What the hell was the matter with him?

At the last minute, on his way out the door, Jimmy went back and grabbed Arthur's .22 revolver off the bedside table. Although Latisha wasn't in very good shape, she was a lot younger than Jimmy. In a pinch she might be able to outrun him, but she sure as hell wouldn't be able to outrun a bullet. Not that he wanted to shoot her. He had something better in mind.

At 4:45 A.M. on Sunday, a mere ten minutes after Latisha had raced out of Calhoun in his stolen pickup, Jimmy Ardmore set off after her. He stopped twenty or so yards short of the intersection where Starvation Canyon Road intersects with Skeleton Canyon Road. Exiting the Subaru, he walked forward along the shoulder, looking for tire tracks.

Jimmy had paid good money for the full set of oversize Nitto Terra Grapplers on the RAM. Yes, this was the desert, and relatively high desert as well. It seldom snowed, but when it rained, a thin layer of slime often coated dirt roadways, leaving the surfaces almost as slick as if they were covered with ice. Fortunately for him, his truck's all-weather tires left behind a distinct, telltale pattern.

Months earlier, when he drove Latisha to Calhoun from Road Forks, he'd seen to it that she was completely out of it. He doubted she had any idea about where she was, much less where she would need to go to find help or how to get there.

Jimmy couldn't remember where he'd heard this bit of trivia, but he was pretty sure someone had once told him that when people in unfamiliar terrain are frightened and trying to flee some perceived danger, they generally tend to turn to the right rather than the left.

Jimmy knew that a right-hand turn onto Skeleton Canyon would take Latisha back to Highway 80 within a relatively short period of time. Once she hit the paved road, she'd have a lot more options and a lot more opportunities to find help. If she turned to the left, however, she'd find herself in territory that was little more than empty wilderness. That would leave her almost entirely on her own. The roadway between Calhoun and Douglas made for especially rough going. An experienced driver might be able to make the trip in under two hours. An inexperienced driver would take much longer.

When Jimmy reached the intersection and saw the distinctive tire tracks make a wildly unsteady turn to the left, he couldn't help smiling. The arc of the turn said it all. Obviously Latisha wasn't a very good driver. In addition, she had no way of knowing that Jimmy, with another vehicle at his disposal, was already hot on her trail.

Jogging back to the Forester, Jimmy hopped in and hit the gas. The turn he made onto Skeleton Canyon wasn't much better than Latisha's had been. Her wobbling had been due to her being an inexperienced driver. His had everything to do with speed.

Jimmy Ardmore was coming for her, and she damned well wasn't getting away.

THIRTY

DEPUTY GARTH Raymond racked the driver's seat as far back as it would go and then leaned into it and relaxed. Leaving the engine idling for the moment, he let the heater warm his feet before tucking into what was now the next-to-last of the meat-loaf sandwiches that Grandma Juanita had packed for him before he left the house on Sunday afternoon. When he'd told her he had to go back out to the crime scene for another overnight shift, she had promised to make sandwiches for him to take along.

He awoke in the late afternoon to find she'd made meat loaf and was busy assembling a stack of sandwiches.

"I had to wait long enough for the meat loaf to cool," she explained, handing him a plate with a sandwich already on it. "I made five—one for now, one for dinner, one for a midnight snack, one for breakfast, and one for me. They're too good to pass up, if I do say so myself."

Garth took a first bite of his and groaned with pleasure. "Nobody makes better meat loaf," he told her.

"Maybe so," she told him, "but the next time we

have meat loaf, you'll be the one making it. I won't last forever. You'll need to know how to manage on your own. Besides," she added, "do you know where I got this recipe?"

"No idea," Garth answered, mumbling because his mouth was full.

"Handed down from Great-Grandma Raymond, who taught my Jebbie how to make it when he was just a kid. He brought it to a youth-group potluck at church. As soon as I took that first bite, I was hooked, and the rest is history."

"So you're saying I need to know how to make a decent meat loaf in order to find a girl?"

"It couldn't hurt," Grandma Juanita said. "You need to find someone to marry before you get too old and set in your ways."

"Grandma," he objected, "give me a break. I'm only twenty-three."

"That's two years older than Jebbie and I were when we tied the knot."

More than three years had passed now since they'd lost Grandpa Jeb. Garth knew that his grandmother still grieved for her lost husband, but when she spoke of him now, with humor and affection, it was clear her loss was no longer the aching black hole it had been to begin with. Garth was quite sure that the fact she still felt responsible for him was part of what made her keep on keeping on. Without her grandson's need for her, she might simply have given up.

When he finished the midnight sandwich, which had somehow turned into an early-morning sandwich, he opened the last of the three thermoses of coffee that Grandma had sent along. He wasn't sure why Grandma Juanita always sent three, but he wasn't going to argue with her about it. He poured the steamy liquid into the plastic lid that served as a cup and took a tentative sip.

Chief Deputy Hadlock had told him the previous afternoon that one more day of searching the site would probably be the end of it. That was disappointing. He'd been hoping for several more overtime shifts that would enable him to make a couple of extra payments on his student loans.

Garth moved the seat back to an upright position. His feet were warm again, and it was time to take another turn around the crime scene, just to be sure no one was on the prowl. The previous afternoon when he'd shown up for duty, there'd been a crowd of reporters gathered on the perimeter. Hadlock was worried that once he was gone for the day, some of them might return. That hadn't happened, at least not as far as Garth could tell. Other than a couple of Border Patrol guys stopping off to say hello, he'd been completely alone all night long.

Tonight, this far from civilization and beyond the reach of any streetlights, the glowing stars overhead had been spectacular. Garth had enjoyed the solitude and the wonder of it. With or without Great-Grandma Raymond's meat loaf, he couldn't imagine ever finding someone who would love the Arizona desert as much as he did. It just didn't seem as though meeting the right girl was in the cards. Garth suspected that he'd end up being a lot like

Tom Hadlock someday—a confirmed old bachelor
with no real way to explain why things had turned
out that way.

After first making sure the hand warmers were
still in the pockets of his jacket, he turned off the
engine and let himself out of the cab. He was well
away from the vehicle when he became aware of the
intermittent flashes of light that told him a vehicle
was approaching, speeding toward him on Skeleton
Canyon Road. What he realized about that vehicle,
long before he heard it, was that it was coming far
too fast. There was a sharp turn just ahead where
the road veered south and ran alongside a steep
ravine. If whoever was driving didn't slow the hell
down, they weren't going to make it.

And they didn't slow down. Garth stood transfixed, watching the scene unfold before his eyes—
knowing how it would probably end and utterly
helpless to do anything to prevent it. He could see
the individual pinpricks of headlights now and hear
the laboring engine—as though whoever was behind the wheel had shifted down into low and was
driving faster than the transmission could handle.

The headlights started into the turn. Garth
waited for them to emerge again on the far side
of the curve, but they didn't. Instead he heard
the sound of a distant crash and saw a headlight-
illuminated cloud of dust billow skyward.

Garth was a hundred yards away from the Tahoe
when the crash occurred. He sprinted back, climbed
into his vehicle, hit the light bar, and raced off into
the night. Trying to radio for help was useless. He

was out of range. That afternoon when he'd come on duty, Chief Deputy Hadlock had told him the satphone wasn't working and he was taking it back to the Justice Center to see if someone could fix it.

No, Garth realized, if people in that crashed vehicle were injured and in need of assistance, he was their only hope.

THIRTY-ONE

A DAZED Latisha came to her senses dangling upside down in the overturned pickup. She didn't remember fastening her seat belt. She had done it out of sheer force of habit, because that had been one of Lyle's inviolable rules—the car didn't move until everyone inside was belted in. Trayvon had always made fun of her for wearing a seat belt in his Cadillac, but given the reckless way he drove—routinely speeding and often driving under the influence—buckling up had been a matter of life and death. It was this time, too. That unthinking action on Latisha's part had most likely saved her life.

She remembered seeing a sign warning of an upcoming curve. She had slowed, but not enough. Partway into it she'd felt the tires veering off the road and skidding toward the left. She had pulled the wheel to the right, overcorrecting, and the next thing she knew, the truck flew off the road and tumbled down a steep bank into a ravine.

She was lucky not to have been thrown from the truck, but now she was desperate to escape it. Everything she knew about car wrecks came from movies and TV. There the cars always exploded into fireballs once they landed, so she needed to put as much distance between herself and the truck as she could and as quickly as possible.

The weight of her body against the restraining seat belt made it hard to breathe. After fumbling blindly with the release, she finally managed to unfasten the belt, sending her tumbling down onto the ceiling. The engine was still running. Fighting her way through a layer of deployed airbags, she located the ignition button on the dashboard and shut down the engine. In the process her searching hand landed on one of the stolen boots. If she was going to walk away from the wreckage, she'd need both of those boots. It took time to find the other one—time she didn't have. She discovered that both plastic containers had been crushed. While searching blindly for the missing boot, her hand encountered puddles of water dotted with mounds of wet kibble. But finally, just when she was about to give up, she found the boot.

Clutching both of them in one hand, she attempted to open the driver's door with the other, but it didn't work. The door wouldn't budge. Next she tried the window button, but nothing happened. The window wouldn't open, either. Crawling over a layer of shattered safety glass, she found that the passenger-side window had been blown out. Without even trying the door handle, she threw the boots out through the missing glass and then slithered after them on her belly. Just when she thought she'd made it—when she was safely away from the pickup—she came face-to-face with the toes of a pair of men's shoes.

"Well, looky here," the Boss muttered, grabbing Latisha by the hair and yanking her to her feet. "If it isn't my runaway bride! What the hell have you done to my truck?"

"How did you find me?"

"You think I'm stupid or something? How do you think I found you? I followed your tire tracks."

She tried to wriggle out of his grasp. He had seemed weak and dizzy before, but he wasn't now. He lifted her off the ground one-handed and shook her like she was a rag doll. That's when she spotted the gun in his other hand.

"Just shoot me, then," she whispered. "Shoot me and get it over with."

"I don't think so," he answered, pulling her so close that she could feel the heat of his breath on her face. "That would be too easy. You and me, kid, we're gonna go back home and have ourselves a little playtime. Afterward I've reserved a space in that freezer down in the basement. I'm pretty sure there's a spot with your name on it."

The freezer! Remembering Amelia's desperate plight, Latisha realized she had nothing to lose—nothing at all. Being shot would be better than being locked in that freezer. Anything was better than the freezer.

"Climb," he ordered.

"I'm barefoot," she objected. "Let me put on the boots."

"Bullshit," he told her. "You left me barefoot, and I'm returning the favor. I said climb! Do it!"

Left with no alternative, Latisha started to comply. Just then flashing lights appeared on the bank above them and a car door slammed shut.

"Police," a voice from overhead announced as a flashlight beam probed the wreckage of the truck. "Is anybody hurt down there? Do you need help?"

Realizing that the Boss was momentarily distracted, Latisha used the only weapon she had at her disposal. She was far enough up the bank by then that she was able to turn and nail him full in the balls with her knee. As he crumpled to the ground, she took off running.

Running for her life, she found herself in a dry stream bed with steep perpendicular banks on either side. The ground under her bare feet was mostly dry sand punctuated by occasional rocks.

It was still dark, but she had little difficulty seeing her way. The pale moonlight overhead provided plenty of illumination for eyes long since adjusted to the inky darkness of the basement dungeon.

Someone—the cop, probably—was stumbling down the bank toward them, creating a mini avalanche of rocks and dirt that landed on Latisha as she raced past. Instead of breaking her stride, she kept right on running. She darted around a slight curve and then ducked into a small indentation in the bank where a second dry stream bed emptied into the larger one.

She had just made it to cover when bullets began to fly. She counted off the shots in her head—one, two, three, four, five, six. It wasn't like the spray of automatic-weapons fire that you hear on TV. It was far more deliberate than that, with each shot followed by a distinct pause.

At first Latisha thought the Boss was firing the gun at her, but then she realized that wasn't the case. He was shooting at the cop, and so she resumed running, picking her way around boulders, sticking close to the shelter of the bank.

At one point she stubbed her right big toe on a rock that turned out to be the same color as the sand. A jolt of pain shot through her body, spreading from the ingrown toenail and traveling up her leg, but Latisha kept on going. Her lungs burned. Long-disused muscles ached, but she kept running until her legs literally collapsed beneath her. She lay prone in the sand, gasping for breath, unable to move, and waiting for the kill shot she knew was coming. And since she was about to die, and since she'd been saying the prayer for months now, she did so again, whispering the words. "Holy Mary, Mother of God, pray for us sinners now and at the hour of our death."

But then a car door slammed somewhere behind her and an engine started. Latisha sat up and looked back the way she'd come. The bank was somewhat lower here. She couldn't see over it, but she could tell that the blue and red lights on top of the cop car were still flashing. They hadn't moved. Meanwhile another set of headlights lit the nighttime sky as a moving vehicle executed a U-turn and sped off into the night—going back the same way Latisha had come, back toward the dungeon.

So had the Boss left her to live, then? Had he decided she wasn't worth killing? If so, why? And where was the cop? He had come to help her—would have helped her. What had happened to him? If the Boss had been shooting at him, what if he'd hit him? What if he was dying? What if he was dead?

Never in her whole life had Latisha Marcum thought of herself as brave, but the months in the dungeon had changed her. Running away from the Boss tonight, driving off in his pickup, had been brave things to do. Hitting him in the balls had been brave as well. Chained to the wall, she'd been able to do nothing to help Amelia or Sandy or Sadie, but if the cop was wounded and in need of help, maybe it was time for her to be brave again.

Slowly, still breathing heavily and hoping against hope that the Boss really was gone, she got to her feet and started back downstream.

THIRTY-TWO

NOBODY GOES through police-academy training without having the deadly risks inherent in traffic stops drilled into his or her head, but this wasn't a traffic stop. This was a motor-vehicle accident, and Garth was coming to offer assistance. As a consequence he was totally unprepared for the barrage of bullets that slammed into his bulletproof vest. They hit like hammer blows, knocking the breath out of him.

Looking for cover, he tried to retreat back up the bank. Instead he lost his balance and fell. As he plunged to the ground, the last shot came, and a searing pain shot through his body as a bullet penetrated his upper left thigh. He hit the ground hard and then lay there, dazed and unmoving.

Garth tried to make sense of what had just happened. He knew that his assailant hadn't used an automatic or a semiautomatic weapon. Fearing that the shooter might be reloading, Garth managed to extract his weapon from its holster, but by the time he had it in hand, his attacker had disappeared. He had gotten away clean. As for Garth? He was pretty sure he was dying.

Once when he and Grandpa Jeb had been out in the desert gathering up dead mesquite—sawing it and splitting it to sell—the head of Garth's hatchet had come loose, burying the blade deep in his upper thigh, only inches from where this bullet had hit him.

At the time of the accident, Garth and Grandpa had been miles from the nearest hospital or ER. Garth still remembered how Grandpa Jeb had whipped off his belt and wrapped it around Garth's leg, using it as a tourniquet.

"Cry if you want to, but don't you faint or pass out on me," Grandpa Jeb had ordered. "You've got to hold this tight long enough for us to make it to the hospital in Willcox."

Gritting his teeth, Garth hadn't cried. Later, after sewing up the wound and giving Garth a tetanus shot, the doctor told them that if it hadn't been for Grandpa Jeb's tourniquet, Garth would have died that day.

Lying wounded in the cold and dark, Garth decided this was the same thing.

At Sheriff Brady's insistence, these days all departmental vehicles were equipped with state-of-the-art law-enforcement first-aid kits—plastic pouches packed with all sorts of first-aid necessities, including tourniquets, pressure bandages, and packets filled with a powdered blood-clotting agent. All of that was right there in the back of the Tahoe, but from where Garth was at the bottom of the ravine with the Tahoe parked up top, it might as well have been on another planet. The only way to get to the kit was to climb up after it, and the tricky part was living long enough to make the climb.

Not willing to give up and die, Garth knew that he needed to stop or at least slow the bleeding. Recalling his grandfather's lifesaving actions, Garth attempted to remove his belt. Because he was lying on it, that wasn't easy. Once he did, when it came time to fasten the tourniquet around his leg, he was so shocked by the amount of blood he found on his pant leg that he had to fight to keep from blacking out.

"This is bad," he told himself aloud. "If I die, too, Grandma Juanita will kill me." The utter absurdity of that statement made him burst out laughing, making him believe that he was going into shock.

Just then a monster silently materialized out of the darkness and hovered over him. Standing silhouetted there backlit by the pulsing blue-and-red glow from his light bar, he could make out no facial features on the terrifying apparition. The creature boasted an enormous head and a bulky body, perched on top of what appeared to be pencil-thin legs.

Garth remembered one of Pastor Mike's long-ago sermons where he'd talked about the angel of death. That's probably what this was, Garth concluded now, the angel of death, sporting a huge explosion of hair instead of wings and come to collect Garth and take him home—not home to Elfrida and Grandma Juanita but home to heaven, where he'd spend eternity with Jesus and with Grandpa Jeb.

But then, to Garth's amazement, the disturbing figure dropped to the ground beside him and spoke.

"You're hurt," a woman said in a surprisingly gentle voice with a distinctly southern accent. "Please don't die on me. What can I do to help?"

He could see that she was a black woman, or maybe a girl instead of a woman. That's why he hadn't been able to make out her face. Now, though, the pain in his leg was so all-encompassing that it was difficult for him to speak.

"There's a first-aid kit in my patrol car," he managed at last. "It's in the back on the right-hand side, just inside the hatch. I dropped my flashlight. If you could find that . . ."

He'd been searching for it in the dark and unable to locate it. Without a word and with no hesitation at all, the woman walked a few steps away, picked up the missing flashlight, and handed it to him.

"I'll be right back," she said, "but give me your phone so I can call for help."

"The phone won't work," Garth told her. "We're too far out of town. No cell service. Hurry, please."

She left then. He switched on the flashlight to look at his blood-soaked thigh and immediately wished he hadn't. Just the sight of it sickened him.

Watching her climb the bank and feeling as if his very life were leaking out if him, the time it took seemed like forever. It wasn't that steep, and it shouldn't have been that much of a struggle, but it was, and although it might have been only a matter of seconds before she finally reappeared, for Garth it felt like a lifetime.

Trying to help her navigate the descent, Garth aimed the flashlight in her direction. His rescuer wore a leather jacket that was several sizes too big for her, but other than that she appeared to be naked. Her feet were bare, and she was so painfully thin that she reminded him of photos he'd seen of starving prisoners hanging listlessly on the fences of Nazi concentration camps.

"Turn off the light," she told him. "It's not helping. I can see better without it."

That surprised him. How was she able to see in the dark when he couldn't?

"Do you know anything about first aid?"

"No," she said. "Do you?"

With him giving directions, she used the scissors from the first-aid kit to cut off his pant leg. They replaced the belt tourniquet with a proper one. Latisha cut open one packet of the clotting agent and sprinkled the powder into the wound. Then, donning latex gloves, she applied pressure to the wound for the specified amount of time—a seemingly endless three minutes—before covering the wound with a layer of compression bandages.

During the entire process, it was all business between them—a period of total concentration with no small talk. By the time they finished, Garth realized that the sky was gradually turning gray overhead. His leg still hurt like hell, but thanks to her he might live long enough to see the sunrise.

As the light changed, he realized how very young and frail she was, and barefoot, too. And underneath that bulky, oversize jacket, she was entirely naked—an awkward reality for him but one she didn't appear to notice.

Once the bandaging was complete, she sank down onto the ground beside him with her whole body quaking. It was easy for Garth to attribute the chills to her state of undress. He had a spare uniform in the Tahoe. It would be huge on her, but no more so than the jacket she was already wearing. Still, he hesitated to mention it.

"Thank you," he said instead. "My name is Garth—Garth Raymond. What's yours?"

"Latisha Marcum."

"You're shaking," he said. "You're freezing, and you're probably in shock."

"I'm hungry," she answered. "I need some food, but I lost my kibble in the wreck. The container broke."

"Your kibble?" he said. "What's kibble?"

"Dog food," she answered. "I brought some kibble along, and water, too, but the containers either spilled or broke during the wreck."

"Wait, you eat dog food?" he asked in disbelief.

"It's all he ever gave us to eat."

"He who? The guy who shot me?"

Latisha nodded. "We called him the Boss," she said simply. "That's what he made us call him."

That was when the light finally dawned. Garth had heard some of the talk when he'd come on duty that afternoon—idle speculation that the field of bones might have something to do with a serial killer who first abducted young women and held them prisoner before murdering them. He realized now that Latisha had to be one of those, but instead of being dead she was a survivor.

"How long were you with him?" he asked.

Latisha shrugged. "What month is it now?"

"The end of November."

"Since March, then," she said. "He picked me up in New Orleans a while after Mardi Gras ended. He drugged me, put me in the cab of a truck, and brought me here. I've been here ever since."

Garth took a breath. "Thank you so much for the help," he said. "We've stopped the bleeding, but it hurts like hell, and I might still go into shock. We need to get me to an ER as soon as possible. Can you help me make it back up the bank?"

Without answering, Latisha got up and walked to the far side of the wrecked truck. She came back a few minutes later wearing a pair of boots that appeared to be at least two sizes too large. Then, with shoes on her feet, the two of them began the long, slow climb out of the ravine. It was a daunting struggle. The clotting powder seemed to be working, so Garth loosened the tourniquet, releasing a storm of pins and needles into his bloodless leg. When he tried to stand on it, though, the pain was excruciating. The only way to get the job done was for him to scoot along on his butt while Latisha guided him from behind, pushing him as needed.

They made it finally, but the superhuman effort cost them both. Crawling on his hands and one good knee, Garth made it as far as the Tahoe. There, panting and exhausted, he propped himself against one of the back wheels to rest and catch his breath.

"You're bleeding again," Latisha observed.

It was true. Blood was beginning to seep through the layer of bandages.

"Is there another packet of clotting powder?" he asked.

"Three more," she said, "but I left the first-aid kit down below. I'll go back down and get it."

Once again the trip down and back seemed to take forever. When she returned, Garth was redoing the tourniquet. After removing the bandage, he saw that the bleeding wasn't as serious as it had been before. Even so, together they repeated the entire process. The pressure Latisha applied during the required three-minute wait hurt like crazy, but Garth was grateful for that. You had to be alive to know that it hurt.

Initially his idea had been to head for the nearest ranch house and use the residents' landline to summon help. Now, though, he realized it would make more sense to drive west on Geronimo Trail until they caught a signal and could call for help from there. That way a 911 operator would be able to send an ambulance and EMTs to meet them somewhere en route. Closing the distance would mean saving time, but considering the amount of blood he'd already lost, there was still a very real possibility of his going into shock. Garth knew he was in no condition to be behind the wheel.

"Can you drive?" he asked.

"I suppose," Latisha replied ruefully, "but not very well. I already wrecked one car tonight."

"That's because you were going too fast for conditions," he told her. "We'll take it slow—slow and steady wins the race."

At last the three-minute hold time was up. With Latisha standing next to him, Garth occupied himself by applying the new layer of bandages. Not wanting to embarrass her, he was careful to keep his eyes focused on what he was doing rather than on her when he spoke.

"There's one other thing," he said.

"What's that?"

"We're probably going to run into some other people. There's an athletic bag in the back of the SUV, right next to where you found the first-aid kit. It's got an extra uniform in it. You might want to put some clothes on."

With a gasp of shocked surprise, Latisha scurried away from him. She reappeared a few minutes later wearing both the jacket and his uniform. She'd had to roll up the pant legs to keep them from dragging on the ground. One of the boots, now devoid of its shoelace, flopped loosely on her foot.

"I had to use the shoelace to hold up the pants," she explained. "They kept falling off."

"Okay," he said, "I think I'm better now. Let's do this."

Again it took both of them working together to get him up off the ground and boosted into the Tahoe's passenger seat. While Latisha went around to enter on the driver's side, Garth opened a plastic bag. As she slipped onto the seat next to him, he handed her a sandwich.

"This is one of my grandmother's meat-loaf sandwiches—the last one I brought along," he told her. "If you've spent months eating nothing but dry dog food, this is gonna taste like heaven."

He expected her to grab the sandwich and wolf the whole thing down at once. Instead she took a single careful bite, chewed it, swallowed it, and then put the remainder of the sandwich back in the plastic bag before handing it to him.

"Wait," he objected. "You mean you don't like it?"

"I love it," she replied. "I've never eaten anything better in my life, but I'm used to eating one piece of kibble at a time. If I eat the whole thing, I'll make myself sick, and I don't want to waste a single mouthful."

"Okay," he said, placing the bag on the console. "When you're ready for bite number two, let me know."

THIRTY-THREE

SPEEDING BACK the way he'd come, Jimmy Ardmore couldn't believe the catastrophe that had befallen him. Not only had Latisha gotten away, he'd killed a cop. It just didn't get any worse than killing a cop, but the guy had caught him unawares with the gun in his hand. And after that little bitch kneed him in the balls, he'd lost it—just flat lost it. Next thing he knew, the guy—a deputy of some kind—was shot to shit, lying on the ground and not moving. Where the hell had he come from?

Jimmy knew this area like the back of his hand. He was used to driving these roads at all hours of the day and night. He often encountered Border Patrol vehicles out here, but almost never anybody from the local sheriff's department—at least not in the middle of the night. So what was up? Was it possible somebody had located his burial grounds?

He had left Arthur out in the open for the vultures and scavengers as a sign of disrespect. He had disposed of the first few girls by burying them in shallow graves out behind Arthur's house. But digging in the hard-packed dirt had turned out to be too much like work. It wasn't as if he could hire some handy Mexican to do the job for him. He'd decided to leave the last few girls with Arthur, but what if somebody had found them? What if they'd found Amelia? It was time to put the exit strategy in motion, all right, and in one hell of a hurry, too.

He had always planned to burn Calhoun to the ground when he was ready to be quit of it—that's why he had all those loaded gas cans. Harrison Ardmore's final legacy would come crashing down in a firestorm of flame and ash—as close to hell-fire and brimstone as Jimmy could make it. Now, though, with a cop dead and Latisha on the loose, there was no time for those kinds of niceties. Besides, somebody beset with occasional dizzy spells had no business messing around with gas cans and matches. Nope, Jimmy needed to get away fast and clean.

Any trucker worth his salt and passing through El Paso knows the drill. Somebody strikes up a casual conversation in a truck stop or at a rest area and offers you a ton of money to deliver a load of "product" to someone somewhere else. It was always best not to know exactly what the problematic product was, and if you took the deal, you sure as hell better not renege on it. Mules who didn't make their required drop-offs tended to drop off themselves, usually sooner than later. It was risky, yes, but it was a way to make some money on the side that didn't have to go through the company's books and sure as hell didn't involve the IRS, either.

Over the years, in the course of running that

little side business, Jimmy Ardmore had made numerous connections with lots of useful people. And he had one in mind at this very moment—Tony Segura. Tony was a U.S.-based fixer for a network of Juárez drug cartels. If the price was right, he could book flights, obtain visas, create counterfeit documents, make real-estate purchases, move money from one place to another, and handle a myriad of pesky but vital details. For people interested in disappearing without a trace, Tony Segura was a one-stop shop.

But before Jimmy could avail himself of Tony's services, he had to get to El Paso. Now that he had killed a cop, that might not be easy.

Two miles outside of Road Forks was a failed and long-abandoned feedlot. Most of the buildings had been gone for years, but the concrete loading dock and the earthen chute they'd used to drive livestock in and out of trucks were still there. That's where Jimmy headed. The front gate was padlocked shut, but a bolt cutter from Arthur's ever-present toolbox made short work of that. Jimmy parked the Subaru out of sight behind the lot's sole remaining tin shed and then hiked into town.

Arthur's hand-me-down Johnston & Murphys were a little too big, and they weren't exactly built for cross-country hiking. By the time Jimmy made it to the truck stop, he had a popped blister on his heel and the soles of his feet were killing him— damn Latisha anyway! The grinding headache was back, too, but in all the excitement the bouts of crippling dizziness had mostly abated.

He got to the restaurant around eight and slid onto a stool at the counter just as Arlene, his favorite waitress, came on duty. "Hey there, stranger," she said, approaching him with a ready smile. "Coffee?"

"You bet," he said.

She took out her order pad. "What can I get you today?"

"My usual, the I-10 All-American, two eggs over easy with crisp bacon, hash browns, and pancakes instead of toast. I'm going to be heading out for L.A. in a little while, and I need to stock up."

"Isn't L.A. where you went last time?" Arlene asked. "Don't you get tired of driving the same old route over and over?"

"Not really," he said. "Once I got to L.A., they had me run a load up to Seattle, so I had a little side trip before I came home. I was planning on taking a couple of days off to do some chores out at my brother's place, but the boss called and needs me back on the road. Between time off or money in my pocket, money wins."

"Good for you," Arlene said. "You take care now. Your food should be coming right up."

Jimmy sat quietly, drinking his coffee until she returned with his order. "I noticed a lot of police activity out our way overnight. Any idea what's going on?"

Arlene was the closest thing Road Forks had to a daily newspaper. "The way I hear it," she said, "they found a whole bunch of bodies—seven or eight of them, maybe—out there by that dead volcano. The cops from Arizona are all over it."

I'm sure they are, Jimmy thought, *and that means I'm out of here!*

After breakfast he walked back over to his place. He felt no sentiment about leaving it behind. He took nothing with him, not so much as a change of clothing and most especially not his cell phone. He'd be starting over from scratch. He simply locked the door and walked away.

He started his rig and drove over to the diesel pumps to fill up. When he went inside to pay, he bought a pre-paid cell phone while chatting up the cashier, telling her the same thing he'd just told Arlene—that he was doing another back-to-back trip to L.A.

Jimmy knew the locations of the truck stop's security cameras, and there was one on the edge of the property that provided a clear view of the freeway interchange. He drove straight there and then up and over before turning onto the westbound entrance ramp with the security camera capturing his every move. What the security camera didn't catch was him exiting the westbound freeway three miles later, crossing the freeway, and then driving eastbound along the frontage road until he came back to the defunct feedlot.

He got out, removed the damaged padlock, which from a distance looked as though it were just fine. Backing up to the loading dock, he opened the door. Arthur's nimble little Subaru had no difficulty negotiating the livestock chute or bridging the six-inch gap between the end of the loading dock and the bed of the trailer. He drove the Subaru all the way to the front of the trailer, turned off the engine, and set the parking brake. Raiding his traveling tool kit, Jimmy located the adjustable straps that he used to stabilize loads. He crawled under the Subaru, secured straps to both the front and back bumpers, and then fastened those to the pins in the tie-down rails. Once the job was done, he knew that if he had to stop someplace in a hurry, the Subaru wasn't going anywhere.

He worked as fast as he could, because he didn't want to be at the loading dock of that deserted feedlot for a moment longer than necessary. One of the locals, someone who lived around here, might spot that distinctive blue Peterbilt and recognize it as his.

Once Jimmy finished loading, he closed the back doors and headed out. At 9:05 A.M. he paused long enough to replace the chain and the still-broken padlock on the gate. Then he drove westbound on the frontage road, returning to the place where he'd exited, and he entered the eastbound freeway there. By the time he drove past the Road Forks interchange, the guy who was supposed to be on his way to L.A. was definitely headed in the opposite direction.

He sincerely hoped that before anyone could figure that out, Tony Segura would have waved his magic wand and Jimmy Ardmore would be long gone. To that end, he picked up his brand new phone and called Tony. There weren't any numbers in his contact list, but that was OK—he knew Tony's number by heart.

THIRTY-FOUR

GOOD TO her word, Latisha drove with all the deliberate speed of a little old lady on her way to church. Once they hit the washboard surface of Geronimo Trail, every jarring bump was an agony. Garth knew that at this rate getting to Douglas would take forever, but he didn't criticize. Instead, in order to take his mind off the pain, he pulled a tiny spiral notebook from his pocket and dug out a pencil.

"We need to catch this guy," he told her. "Is it okay if I ask you some questions?"

She hesitated for a moment, but finally she nodded. "I guess," she said.

"You need to tell me everything you can remember," he said. "Once we get back to the department, the detectives will need to interview you as well, but anything you can tell me now will give them a leg up in identifying the guy and tracking him down."

Latisha nodded again.

"How did all this happen?"

"He found me in New Orleans," she answered. "I was standing right outside his car. He grabbed

302

me, drugged me, and tied me up in the bunk of a big truck. I don't know how long he kept me there. The next thing I knew, I was in the basement."

"In a basement, but where?" Garth asked.

"I have no idea. He kept us chained in the basement. There wasn't any light, and there weren't any windows. There were windows upstairs, but he kept them covered with blackout curtains."

"So you were in the basement of a building. Tell me about it."

"It was old and made out of bricks, with rough planks in the floor and iron bars on the outsides of the windows."

"But where was it located?" Garth asked. "Did you see any road signs?"

Latisha shook her head. "No, but when I took off, I noticed there were other buildings around. They looked like they might have been part of an old movie set."

"Calhoun, then, I'll bet," Garth said.

"What's that?"

"Calhoun is an old ghost town that dates back from the 1870s. It's located at the base of Starvation Canyon. Grandpa Jeb told me about it, but we never went there. By the time I came to live with my grandparents in Elfrida, some rich guy had come along, bought the town and acreage around it, and then plastered the whole area with No Trespassing signs. But back to the guy who kidnapped you. Did he live there with you?"

"No," Latisha said, shaking her head. "We called

him the Boss, because that's what he told us to call him. I don't know where he lived—just not with us. He'd come by, and . . . you know . . . do stuff. Then he'd fill our food containers and go away. We wouldn't see him again for four or five days."

Garth sensed there was a lot Latisha was leaving out when she said the words "do stuff." He could imagine what had gone on, but he didn't want to think about it.

"He went away and left you chained to the wall?"

"And in the dark," Latisha said with a nod. "The only time he'd unfasten the chains was when he took one of us upstairs, but we could sort of move around. The chains were long enough for us to walk as far as to the toilet, but that's it."

"The place had water?"

"Sort of," she replied. "There was running water upstairs, but down in the basement the only water we had was in the flushing tank of the toilet. That's what we had to drink."

Garth was appalled, but, afraid that any expression of sympathy might derail her, he asked more questions instead. "What can you tell me about him? What did he look like?"

"He was white with sort of a pinkish face and bad teeth," Latisha said. "He had grayish hair that was thin and kind of spiky."

"How old?"

"Sixty, maybe? It's hard to tell."

"And how big?"

"Taller than me—probably six one or six two."

"What did he weigh?"

"I don't know. He was big—a little pudgy, but very strong."

"Any scars or tattoos?"

"Not that I remember."

"Tell me about the other girls," Garth urged gently. "Did they have names?"

For the first time, tears sprang from Latisha's eyes. She had to wipe them away to see the road.

"Sandra Ruth Locke, Sadie Kaitlyn Jennings, and Amelia Diaz Salazar," she whispered hoarsely. "They were my friends. He took them away one by one, and I miss them. I know one of them is dead. I'm not sure about the others."

Garth, occupied with writing down the names, wondered what he should do. Latisha was telling him the truth. Didn't he owe her the same? "I'm sorry to have to tell you this," he said quietly, "but I believe the other two are dead as well. Do you know where they came from originally?"

The news that they were all gone landed as a terrible blow. More tears fell before Latisha was able to speak again. "Not really," she said finally, "at least not the actual towns. Sandy was from California, Sadie from North Carolina, and Amelia from somewhere in Mexico. I think she said Juárez."

"Where are you from?" Garth asked. "You said the Boss picked you up in New Orleans."

"I'm from St. Louis," she said. "I ran away from home with my boyfriend, Trayvon Littlefield, when I was fifteen. I thought he was a good guy, but he turned out to be a pimp. He took me to New Orleans. The next thing I knew, I was turning tricks."

She said it without any particular rancor. For her that was just the way things were, but Garth was shocked. "How old are you now?" he asked.

"I turned seventeen in October," she said.

Seventeen. That made her six years younger than Garth. He had always resented the way he'd been treated by his father and by Laurie, but what had happened to him was nothing compared to what had happened to Latisha.

"I'm so sorry all this happened to you," he murmured, "so very sorry."

"Thank you," Latisha said matter-of-factly, "but it could have been worse. If you hadn't come along when you did, he would've done the same thing to me that he did to Amelia."

"What was that?"

"He put her in the freezer and must have padlocked it shut." Latisha paused for a moment and took a deep breath before continuing. "I heard her pounding on the walls. It took a long time for her to die. I heard her, but I couldn't help her."

When the tears came again, Garth found himself tearing up, too. He couldn't help it. He couldn't imagine anything worse than standing by, helpless but listening, while one of your friends was murdered.

"I'm glad you got away," he said finally.

"Me, too."

While they'd talked, Garth had kept an eye on his phone, waiting for even a single bar of cell service to appear. Instead the radio on his shoulder suddenly chirped to life and the voice of Tica, the dispatcher, came through the speakers.

"Tica!" he exclaimed. "I've been out of range. Can you hear me?"

"Of course, Deputy Raymond, what's up?"

For a moment he wasn't entirely sure what to say. "Officer down," he answered at last. "Officer down and needs assistance."

THIRTY-FIVE

WITH BOTH hands on the wheel, driving along that dirt track, Latisha listened as Garth recounted everything she'd told him to somebody else—to his boss, she guessed. It sounded like a story someone would make up, as though it couldn't possibly be true, and yet it was true, and it was over. She was out. She was free. And somewhere along the line, she stopped listening.

The world outside the Boss's darkened basement was huge and beautiful and bright. Even driving away from the sun, there was so much light that it hurt her eyes. The landscape on either side of the road could just as well have been from a distant galaxy. They were traveling through a broad, flat valley with jagged pieces of distant mountain ranges scattered all around them and far enough away to be tinged a strange shade of bluish purple.

The weird, otherworldly plants she saw growing on either side of the road were fascinating and completely foreign to her. Even the barren trees with their blackened, twisted trunks were like no trees she'd ever seen back home. Still, strange as they were, those trees, set against a cloudless bright blue sky, were as astonishingly beautiful as anything she'd ever seen.

Traveling along, she took a few more careful bites from the sandwich. The softness of the bread, the taste of actual meat in her mouth, the ease with which she could chew and swallow it—that was amazing too. Yes, her tooth still hurt, but in the face of all this wonder the ache that had plagued her every waking moment had somehow receded into the background.

A series of pings broke in on Latisha's reverie. She hadn't heard sounds like that in months, but she instantly recognized them for what they were— text alerts on a cell phone. Garth was still talking on the radio, but the ping meant there was cell service now, too.

"All right," Garth said, turning away from the radio and speaking directly to Latisha. "The ambulance is on its way. So is Detective Howell, the lead detective on the homicide case. We should meet up with them soon. The dispatcher asked if I thought you needed an ambulance. I told her no, but Detective Howell will take you to the ER so doctors can check you out, if that's okay. After that she'll most likely need to interview you."

Latisha nodded, but she wasn't really paying attention. She was thinking about the phone. It hadn't been working before, but now it was.

"What day is it?" she asked.

"November twenty-first."

"No, I mean what day of the week is it?"

"Monday."

"And where are we?"

"Arizona."

The clock on the dash said fifteen past eight. "If it's eight fifteen here, what time is it in St. Louis?"

"We're on Mountain Time. St. Louis would be Central."

"Can I borrow your phone to call my parents?"

"What's the number?" Garth said. "I'll put the call on speaker. This road's too washboarded for you to drive one-handed."

Latisha recited the number for her mother's cell phone, then worried about what she was going to say. Instead the call went to voice mail. That probably meant her mother was already at work. At the hospital she always turned off the ringer and put her phone away.

"Do you want to leave a message?" Garth asked.

"No," Latisha said. "I need to talk to her in person."

"Anyone else?" Garth asked.

Nodding, Latisha reeled off her stepfather's number. Lyle was probably at work, too, but he went in early, and nine to ten was when he usually took his lunch break. Lyle answered on the second ring, and he sounded angry. "If you're calling to sell me something, don't bother," he growled. "Hang up now and don't call me again."

"It's me, Lyle," she said, her voice a tiny squeak. "It's Latisha. A cop rescued me. I'm safe."

The phone went dead silent. For a moment she thought the call had failed. "Oh, my God!" he exclaimed at last. "Is it you? Is this really true? Does your mother know? Have you talked to her?"

"I tried, but the call went to voice mail."

"She's at work," Lyle said. "I'll call the hospital and have someone give her a message. Can she call you back on this number?"

Latisha glanced in Garth's direction, and he nodded.

"Yes, she can call me back here."

"But where are you?"

"In Arizona."

"Arizona? How did you get there?"

"It's a long story."

"That worthless piece of crap Trayvon is responsible for this, right? If it's the last thing I do, I'm going to see that he ends up in jail."

"Lyle, Trayvon didn't do it," Latisha objected. "It's not his fault."

"The hell it isn't," Lyle muttered. "We'll talk about this later. Where are you in Arizona?"

"Bisbee," Garth put in, answering for her.

"Who's that?" Lyle wanted to know.

"A friend," Latisha said quickly. "Someone who's helping me out."

She didn't want to say anything more than that right then—she didn't want to mention that the deputy who had come to her rescue had been shot and that they were on their way to meet up with an ambulance.

"So if you're in Bisbee, Tucson's the closest airport, right?"

With Latisha at a loss, Garth answered for her. "That would be correct, sir, Tucson International."

"Okay," Lyle said, "I'll call your mom now. As soon as we can get plane reservations, we're coming to get you. It's so good to hear your voice, Latisha. I can barely believe it. Your mother and I both thought we'd lost you for good. We didn't think you were ever coming home."

"I didn't think so, either," Latisha said, speaking around the lump that had suddenly formed in her throat.

"We love you, girl."

"I love you, too, Lyle," she whispered back, but he had already ended the call.

"You call your father by his first name?" Garth asked.

"Lyle's my stepfather, not my father," she said. "I've never told him I love him before, and I don't think he even heard me."

"He may not have heard you," Garth said quietly, "but I'll bet he already knows."

A text alert came in, and then another call. "All right," Garth said. "Hold on, I'll have her take a look." After doing something to the phone, he turned to Latisha. "I need you to pull over and take a look at something."

"What?"

"Chief Deputy Hadlock just sent me a photo."

Once the SUV stopped moving, he handed her the phone. The image staring back at her from the screen took her breath away. Her fingers spasmed, and she dropped the phone.

"It's him," she whispered. "It's the Boss."

THIRTY-SIX

THE FACT that Joanna had gone to bed late and hadn't been able to fall asleep for a long time had no effect at all on Sage's preferred wake-up time, which was evidently permanently fixed at 6:00 A.M., come what may.

By 7:00 the baby had been fed, changed, and bathed. Since Sage didn't seem ready to go back to sleep, Joanna settled into the rocking chair in the nursery. In the ensuing quiet moments, with Sage's tiny fist holding Joanna's index finger in a baby death grip, Joanna sat studying her daughter's features. Like Jenny and Dennis, Sage had blue eyes and fair skin, but the older kids' hair had been blond from the get-go. Sage's wispy curls had a definite hint of red. So maybe Butch was going to get his wish and end up having a daughter who looked just like Joanna.

"But will you give me as much grief as I gave your grandmother?" Joanna asked aloud. "I certainly hope not."

Naturally, Sage didn't reply. Once the baby was asleep and back in her crib, Joanna treated herself to her second cup of coffee for the day. That was the thing about babies. They could always go down for a nap. As for mommies? Not so much.

Since Denny was leaving for school directly from Carol's house, Joanna booted up her computer, located the audio file of the previous evening's briefing, and fired off a copy of it to Agent Powers. Then she returned to the file and fast-forwarded to close to the end. After running the control back and forth several times, she finally located the spot where she'd taken Sage and exited the room.

Hitting the Play button, Joanna was able to hear the portions of the briefing she'd missed. Once she had handed Rosa Moreno off to Detective Howell, Deb had gently questioned Amelia's aunt, eliciting much the same information that Joanna had learned earlier in the day. She repeated the story about how Amelia hadn't come home after going out to watch the Fourth of July fireworks. She related her frustration with law enforcement's lack of interest in searching for the missing girl. She expressed her gratitude toward the one person who had reached out to help her—the lowly clerk/receptionist in the homicide unit who had pointed Rosa in the direction of NamUs. Only at the end of the recitation did she ask the question Joanna had been expecting and dreading.

"How did Amelia die?" Rosa asked.

At that point Deb deftly passed the buck. "Here's Dr. Kendra Baldwin, the medical examiner. I'd like her to address that."

"She died of a lack of oxygen," Kendra said.

A white lie if ever there was one, Joanna thought, a

lie that bypassed the ugly truth that Rosa Moreno's niece had perished after being locked in a freezer by a cold-blooded killer.

"Did she suffer?" Rosa asked.

Joanna was afraid Kendra would dodge that question, too, but she didn't. "I'm sorry to have to tell you this, Ms. Moreno, but I'm afraid your Amelia went through a terrible ordeal. We have evidence that suggests she was abducted and held prisoner, most likely from the time she went missing until her death. Unfortunately, she wasn't the only one."

There was a brief silence on the phone. When Rosa spoke again, her words were barely audible. "I'm sorry there were others," she murmured.

"We've located the bodies of at least three additional victims who are also deceased," Kendra continued. "Unfortunately there may be more."

"Did the other victims die the same way Amelia did?"

"One victim, a male, is thought to have died of a gunshot wound," Kendra answered. "Amelia's death was recent enough that we were able to autopsy her remains. The other two victims exhibit signs of blunt-force trauma."

Rosa took a ragged breath. "Will you catch the monster who did these awful things?"

"Believe me, Ms. Moreno, everyone in this room is fully committed to doing just that."

"What will happen to Amelia's body?"

"That is up to the family—to you, really," Kendra said. "At your direction we'll release the remains to a local mortuary, and they'll handle the arrangements from there."

"We don't have much money," Rosa said. "How much will it cost?"

"That depends," Kendra said uneasily. "Shipping a loaded casket will cost more than if they ship after cremation."

Joanna could tell from the way Kendra answered that the question had made her uncomfortable. Rosa and her family had lost a child. Now they were dealing with the unexpected, budget-busting expense of bringing home a body.

Joanna was pretty sure that she knew how George Winfield, her deceased stepfather and one of Dr. Baldwin's predecessors, would have handled that situation. He would have figured out a way to pay for the shipping and called it good.

Joanna was turning her attention back to the briefing when her phone rang. "Holy crap!" Tom Hadlock exclaimed. "You're not gonna believe what just happened!"

"What's going on?"

"Tica patched me through to Deputy Raymond. He's been shot."

Joanna's heart fell. Another one of her deputies had been shot? Losing Deputy Sloan had been bad enough. She didn't think she could bear to lose another one.

"An ambulance is on the way to rendezvous with him on Geronimo Trail, somewhere east of Douglas," Tom continued. "They'll transport him to the ER at the Copper Queen in Bisbee."

"What happened?"

"Garth evidently got into a shoot-out with the bad guy and took a bullet in his leg."

"What bad guy?"

"*The* bad guy," Tom replied. "The one we've been looking for."

"You mean the serial killer?"

"Yes, ma'am, one and the same."

"What about the shooter? Is he in custody?"

"No, ma'am, he got away."

"Tell me about Garth," Joanna said. "How bad is he?"

"Not as bad as it could have been," Tom replied. "He says that the clotting kits you bought probably saved his life. Like I said, I've got an ambulance on the way to pick him up. The EMTs should meet up with him somewhere between Douglas and the Peloncillos."

"You've actually spoken to him, then?"

"Yes, he's talking and making sense."

"And he's going to pull through?"

"Sounds like," Tom confirmed.

A flood of relief swept through Joanna's body. "And even though he's been shot, he's well enough to drive himself to meet the ambulance?"

"He's not doing the actual driving," Tom corrected. "A girl by the name of Latisha Marcum is at the wheel."

"Who's Latisha Marcum?"

"Someone who's spent the last however many months being held prisoner, chained to a wall in a pitch-black basement along with Amelia Salazar and two other girls. Latisha somehow managed to escape. When the bad guy came after her, he and Deputy Raymond went at it. Garth took a bullet, and the bad guy got away."

A wave of gooseflesh ran up and down Joanna's leg. Kendra Baldwin had worried that there might be additional victims, and she'd been right.

"What about the girl?" Joanna asked.

"She's not hurt, as in no gaping wounds," Tom told her. "According to Garth, she's not in very good shape, but she doesn't require an ambulance. I'm sending Detective Howell out to pick her up. Right now the only information we have to go on is what Deputy Raymond was able to pass along. I'm hoping that once Deb connects with Latisha, she'll be able to conduct a more formal interview."

"Was she able to supply the names of the other girls?"

"She was, and I wrote them down. In addition to Amelia Salazar, there was a Sandra Ruth Locke, who came from somewhere in California, and Sadie Kaitlyn Jennings, from North Carolina."

"Did you pass that information along to Dr. Baldwin?"

"Yes, ma'am, I certainly did. What I need right now is anything and everything Latisha Marcum can tell us about Arthur Ardmore."

"Who's he?" Joanna asked.

"Our killer."

"You've identified him? You've got a name? How on earth . . . ?"

"When Garth was a kid, he and his grandfather

used to go hunting out in the Peloncillos, so he's very familiar with that part of the county. From what Latisha told him, he was able to connect the dots and figure out that she and the other girls must have been kept prisoner in one of the buildings in an old ghost town over there, the one at the base of Starvation Canyon."

"Calhoun," Joanna supplied. "I went there once with my dad."

"Right," Tom said. "Calhoun's the one. So I ran a quick title search. It turns the whole town is owned—lock, stock, and barrel—by a fellow named Arthur Ardmore."

"I seem to remember hearing the name and something about him being a hermit," Joanna said. "Since he didn't seem to be breaking any laws, I didn't pay a lot of attention to the story."

"But he *was* breaking the law," Tom corrected. "We just didn't know he was doing it. I wanted to get the skinny on this Ardmore guy, so I called Kent Williams, and he clued me in."

That was a name Joanna did recognize. When it came to ranchers in the San Bernardino Valley, Kent Williams, owner of the Calhoun Ranch, was a major player. He also happened to be one of Joanna's political supporters.

"You know Kent?" she asked.

"Sure," Tom said. "He's an old buddy of mine. It turns out that the town of Calhoun used to be part of his ranch. A couple of decades ago, this Ardmore character—an odd duck with more money than good sense—turned up on Kent's doorstep asking to buy the parcel of the ranch where the ghost town was located. Said that's where he wanted to live—in a ghost town. Kent took the deal, and Ardmore has lived there ever since."

"In a ghost town?"

"Apparently," Tom said. "I would guess he's not what you'd call a sociable kind of guy, since it looks like he spends his spare time torturing and killing young women. I sent a copy of Ardmore's driver's-license photo to Garth's phone, and Latisha identified him from that. I didn't take the time or trouble to put together a photo montage, because I don't want him to get away. Detective Carbajal is off obtaining warrants, and I'm assembling the Emergency Response Team to go make the arrest. Since Ernie's a mainstay in the ERT, Media Relations is going to be offline for the time being."

"Marliss isn't going to like that."

"Screw Marliss," Tom grumbled. "The last thing I need to worry about right now is Marliss Shackleford."

"Do we know if Garth and this Ardmore guy exchanged gunfire?" Joanna asked. "If we're dealing with an officer-involved shooting, we'll need to bring in the Department of Public Safety to handle the investigation."

"Garth didn't say one way or the other," Tom replied, "and I didn't think to ask. I'll put you on hold and call him back."

A few moments later, Tom came back on the line. "Deputy Raymond says he drew his weapon but didn't discharge it. All the same, once he gets to the hospital, we should have his hands and clothing swabbed for GSR. We'll also collect his weapon. That way if an investigation of any kind comes up later on, we'll have our bases covered."

"Do we know anything about the vehicle Ardmore is driving?" Joanna asked.

"According to the Department of Licensing, the only vehicle registered in his name is a 1998 Subaru Forester. I've issued a BOLO on that and asked the Arizona Highway Patrol and the New Mexico State Police to be on high alert for it, especially out along US 80 and I-10. The Department of Public Safety is in the process of dispatching additional units to the area in case we need backup."

"Sounds like you've got things well in hand," Joanna told him.

"Not quite," Tom answered. "Dave Hollicker and I were supposed to meet the Paxtons at the Justice Center at eight to take one last crack at the dump site, but that's not going to happen, at least not today. Dave and Casey Ledford are on their way to the scene of the shooting. I was about to call Ms. Paxton and cancel, but I seem to have misplaced her number. If you could let them know that I need them to stand down today . . ."

"Of course," Joanna said. "I'll do that the moment I get off the phone." When an awkward pause followed, she sensed there was something Tom wasn't saying. "Is there anything else?" she asked.

"I'm out of my depth here," he said finally. "What the hell am I supposed to do? On the one hand, I've got a wounded officer on his way to the ER. By all rights I should be at the hospital to greet him. On the other hand, since I'm about to send people into harm's way, I should be with them, too. How can I be in both places at once?"

"You can't," Joanna answered, "so tell you what. You take charge of the ERT. I'll put on a uniform and be at the hospital when Deputy Raymond gets there. By the way, I don't believe Garth's grandmother drives."

"You're right, she doesn't," Tom said, "but I've got that covered, too. I've already dispatched a deputy to pick Mrs. Raymond up and bring her to the hospital. Oh, and one more thing. Your satphone was on the blink yesterday, but overnight some faraway wizard of a technician was able to reboot it remotely."

"Does that mean it's working again?"

"Yup. We'll be out in the middle of nowhere, but at least we won't be incommunicado. It seems to be taking forever to get those warrants. I hope to hell Arthur Ardmore doesn't give us the slip in the meantime."

"I hope so, too," Joanna said. "And since the phone is working again, please keep me posted."

Ending the call, Joanna sat for a moment lost in thought—thinking about both the distance and the difficult road conditions between the Justice Center and Starvation Canyon. A few months earlier, she had turned down a yearlong grant from an outfit called Police Our Borders, POB for short, that would have given her department a year's worth of access to a leased helicopter. On the surface it sounded like a great deal—it was a lot like one of those "free to good home" puppies. The front-end costs were low, but hiring a pilot and paying for aircraft upkeep would have had to come out of Joanna's budget. With the amount of money that would have cost, Joanna could have hired two additional full-time deputies. She had nixed the deal, and passing on the helicopter was something Don Hubble had used against her time and again during the election campaign.

Today, for the first time, Joanna found herself regretting that decision. A departmental helicopter would have made it far easier to transport key personnel and weapons to and from that remote location.

Too bad, she told herself. *What's done is done.*

Still in her robe, Joanna hurried outside to pass along Tom's message to the Paxtons. Back in the house, she pawed through her assortment of variously sized uniforms until she finally found a set that more or less fit her nonpregnant but still-not-back-to-normal figure.

She worried about taking a newborn along on a visit to the ER. Public areas in hospitals were well known for being germ factories, but gearing up to use a breast pump right that minute wasn't in the cards. She'd have to leave Sage here with Carol, and when it was time to feed her, she'd have to come home.

By the time Joanna was dressed, made up, and ready to go, Carol had delivered the boys to the bus stop and was in the kitchen loading the dishwasher.

As soon as Joanna explained what was going on, Carol came up with a better plan.

"Go grab Sage and pack the diaper bag," she said. "I'll take a book along and stay in the car with her while you're inside. When it's time for you to nurse her, you can do so in the privacy of your very own Buick."

"What an excellent idea!" Joanna said. "Why didn't I think of that?"

THIRTY-SEVEN

THE SHOCK of seeing the Boss's face left Latisha shaken, and it took some time for her to be able to put the SUV back in gear and drive. But still, if the cops knew who he was, maybe that meant they were that much closer to catching him. When the phone rang again, Latisha expected it to be her mother.

"It's my grandmother," Garth said. "Somebody must have called her." He took the call without putting the phone on speaker, leaving Latisha to listen in on only half of the conversation.

"Yes, it's true," he said, after being quiet for several moments. "I did get shot. They're taking me to the hospital in Bisbee, but don't worry. I'll be all right. We managed to stop the bleeding."

That statement was followed by another long silence. "They're sending someone to pick you up and bring you to the hospital? That's great. Okay, I'll see you there, but one more thing—do you happen to have any more of yesterday's meat loaf? You do? Great. If you could whip up a couple more of those sandwiches and bring them along to Bisbee, it would be terrific. I have someone here who thinks your meat-loaf sandwiches are manna from heaven."

The thought of having another meat-loaf sandwich was enough to make Latisha smile, and she treated herself to another bite of the one she had.

"Okay, Grandma," Garth continued. "See you there. And yes, I love you, too."

Some distance ahead of them, Latisha caught sight of a plume of dust, rising skyward and speeding toward them. "Is that them?"

"Probably," Garth said. "There's a wide spot just ahead at the turnoff to Slaughter Ranch. Pull in there."

Latisha was easing into the turnoff when another call came in. "Hello," Garth answered. "Yes, Mrs. Richards, your daughter is right here, but she's driving. As soon as she gets parked, I'll put her on."

When Latisha went to take the phone, her hands were trembling again. She knew what was coming and didn't want to go through it—didn't want to have to tell anybody else about what had happened to her, most especially her mother.

"Hello?"

"Latisha, Latisha, Latisha," her mother sobbed into the phone. "Dear God, is it really you? When Lyle called to tell me, I couldn't believe my ears. I thought I was dreaming—that I'd wake up, it wouldn't be true, and you would still be gone. Are you okay? Are you hurt?"

Latisha wasn't exactly hurt, but she wasn't okay, either.

"I broke a tooth," she said.

That broken, aching tooth was the least of it, but

it was one thing—the only thing, really—that she could admit to right then, as long as she didn't have to explain exactly how it had gotten broken. Would she ever get around to telling her mother and Lyle about having to eat kibble?

"Who's the man there with you, the one who answered the phone?" her mother asked. "Is he like a boyfriend or something?"

"He's not my boyfriend," Latisha answered. "He's a deputy sheriff, and he's my friend."

"Oh," her mother said. "Trayvon always claimed that you ran away from him—that you took off with someone else. But where have you been all this time, Latisha? We've missed you so much. Why didn't you ever call home? Why didn't you contact us and let us know that you were okay?"

At the moment those questions remained unanswerable. What was Latisha supposed to say—that she hadn't called home because she was being held prisoner, naked and chained to a wall, in some pervert's basement? That she'd been beaten and starved? That her friends had all been murdered? That she wasn't okay, not even close?

For years when she was a child, her mother had dodged Latisha's insistent questions about whether or not the Tooth Fairy and Santa Claus were real. Eventually Latisha had worked out the truth about those things for herself, and the same thing might need to happen here. For the time being, her mother would have to figure it out on her own, because Latisha was incapable of putting any of it into words.

"I couldn't," Latisha managed. "I just couldn't."

Her mother seemed to sense that she had pushed too hard, and she backed off. "The important thing is that you called today," she declared. "Lyle's probably on the phone making travel arrangements at this very moment. He says we'll need to fly into Tucson, but with him coming from one place and me from another, I don't know how long it will be before we see you."

"Wait," Latisha said. "Lyle's not in St. Louis with you?"

"No, he's down in New Orleans."

"New Orleans!" Latisha repeated in dismay. "What's he doing there?"

"Trying to get the goods on Trayvon Little-field," her mother said. "When we didn't hear from you, we were so worried that Lyle and I drove down to New Orleans and filed a missing-persons report. When we tracked down Trayvon, he swore that you'd run away. We didn't believe him, not for a minute. Lyle said he'd probably murdered you and dumped your body in a bayou somewhere.

"We tried telling the cops the same thing, but nothing came of it. After that we hired a private detective, but he didn't get anywhere, either. So for the past three months, Lyle's been working the case on his own, using his vacation time and days off to drive down to New Orleans and look around—talking to people, asking questions."

Two approaching vehicles—an ambulance with flashing lights and a marked SUV with a sheriff's-department logo on the door—ground to a halt beside them in a blinding cloud of dust.

"I've gotta go, Mom," Latisha said hurriedly as people piled out of the other vehicles and hurried toward them. "Someone's here. I can't talk right now."

"Please, don't hang up on me," her mother begged. "Is this your phone? Can I call you back at this number?"

How could Latisha explain that she no longer had a phone—that when she'd awakened in the bunk of the Boss's truck those many months ago, her purse, her phone, and all her ID had disappeared?

Latisha looked at Garth for help. "She wants to know how to call me."

"Tell her to contact the Cochise County Sheriff's Department," he said. "Have her ask for Chief Deputy Hadlock. He'll be able to tell her how to reach you."

"Did you get that, Mom?"

"Yes, Cochise County Sheriff's Department. Got it."

"Good-bye, Mom," Latisha said. "I love you."

Knowing that her mother would be even more worried if she heard that cops and an ambulance had just arrived, Latisha ended the call and returned the phone to Garth just as the first EMT tapped on his window. With a click of the lock button, the door swung open.

"Sir, are you Deputy Raymond?" the EMT asked.

Garth nodded.

"I understand you're in need of some assistance. Let's see about getting you out of there."

Meanwhile a woman wearing a navy-blue pantsuit and holding up a badge was rapping noisily on the driver's-side window. Latisha barely noticed. Overcome by what she'd just heard, she leaned into the steering wheel, buried her face in her hands, and sobbed.

The whole time she'd been locked in the basement—all those hours when she'd been sure that no one cared about her and that no one was bothering to look for her—none of that had been true, because her mother and Lyle had been out there spending time and money, frantically trying to find her.

In her mind's eye, Latisha tried to imagine straight-arrow Lyle prowling the streets in Trayvon's seedy, gang-infested neighborhood, looking for him and looking for her—for Latisha, for the stepdaughter who had given the poor man nothing but grief. Latisha wept about that—as ashamed as she was grateful.

By the time she regained her composure, the EMTs had Garth on a gurney and were loading him into the back of the ambulance. When the doors closed and the vehicle sped away, Latisha felt totally abandoned. The two of them had been through a terrible ordeal together, but in the course of those few desperate hours they had become friends. Latisha had already lost so much, and she was crushed to think that now she was losing him, too.

At last the woman outside, tired of knocking on the window, pulled open the door. "Excuse me, Ms. Marcum," she said. "My name is Detective Howell. I'm here to take you to the hospital so the doctors can check you out."

Wiping away her tears, Latisha started to hand over the car keys.

"Just leave them in the cup holder," Detective Howell said. "A CSI team is on its way to investigate the shooting incident. They'll be here in a few minutes, and they'll pick up Deputy Raymond's vehicle on the way."

Latisha started to get out of the vehicle. As she did so, she spotted that very last bite of sandwich, still in the plastic bag. She paused long enough to eat it, because she knew she needed to.

After months of enforced inactivity and days of endless silence, the intense activity and emotional upheaval of the preceding hours had left her feeling drained and exhausted. Stepping out of the car, she could barely stand on her own. She wobbled and would have fallen if the lady cop hadn't caught her and steadied her. Detective Howell led Latisha to the waiting SUV, helped her inside, and reached across to fasten the seat belt around her.

Spent and exhausted, Latisha leaned back in the seat and closed her eyes. The detective probably had all kinds of questions to ask, but Latisha didn't want to answer any more questions. It was one thing to tell Garth what had happened. He was a friend. From now on, though, she'd be talking to people who weren't her friends—first to a bunch of strangers and finally to her family—and what she had to say to all of them were things nobody would want to hear.

Just then she remembered that first day in the basement and what Sandy and Sadie had done when the Boss had come downstairs to get her. They'd covered themselves with their blankets, lying there side by side as still as death, hoping he wouldn't choose them.

Latisha no longer had her blanket, so she did the next-best thing. She sat with her eyes closed and her hands folded in front of her, pretending to be asleep. Once the vehicle started moving, though, and before they had traveled a full mile, she was no longer pretending.

THIRTY-EIGHT

THERE WAS no sign of an arriving ambulance when Joanna got to the hospital and parked outside. Carol had said she was bringing a book, but that wasn't entirely true. She had a book, all right, but it was on her iPad, and she was listening to it with a set of earbuds—a piece of electronic privacy that made it possible for Joanna to make some phone calls while she waited. The first one was to her department's chaplain, the Reverend Marianne Maculyea.

"Oh, no," Marianne said when Joanna told her the news. "Not Garth. He's such a sweet young kid. Is he going to be all right?"

"With any kind of luck, he will be, but he's on his way to the hospital in Bisbee right now. So's his grandmother. A deputy is bringing Mrs. Raymond in, but he won't be able to stay with her. I was hoping you would."

"Absolutely," Marianne said. "I'm caught up doing some wedding planning right now, but I'll be there as soon as I can."

Joanna's next call was to Kendra Baldwin. "I believe I know who's spilling the beans," she told the M.E. "Ralph Whetson and Marliss Shackleford have a thing going, and I'm pretty sure he's the one who's been leaking information about our cases—the Peloncillos cases in particular."

"You're kidding. Ralph and Marliss a couple?" Kendra asked. "I had no idea. How did you find that out?"

"I went to Marliss's house last night after the briefing. Ralph's car was pulling out as I was coming in."

"You went to see her? Why?"

"To have it out with her about doing interviews with victims' relatives prior to our completing the next-of-kin notifications. In the course of our conversation, I could tell she knew that you had asked me to do the notification. Who all was in the room when you called me?"

"Let's see," Kendra said. "Madge Livingston and Ralph Whetson would have been the only ones."

Madge was the tough-talking, chain-smoking, peroxide-blond receptionist who served as the M.E.'s gatekeeper. She'd been around county government in any number of departments over the years. Joanna knew from conversations with both her mother and with George Winfield that Madge and Marliss were oil and water.

"It wouldn't be Madge, then," Joanna said. "She and Marliss have been feuding for years."

"That leaves Ralph," Kendra agreed.

"So what do we do about this?" Joanna asked.

"I know what I'd like to do," Kendra said. "I'd like to fire his ass. I'm a doctor. The murder victims whose bodies come through this office are my patients. What goes on here is supposedly confidential, and if he's revealing medical records to an outside party, at the very least he's in violation of HIPAA regulations."

"You'd fire him?" Joanna asked.

"You bet, but not until I have some proof."

"How do you get proof?"

"I don't know," Kendra said. "Let me think about it. When I figure it out, I'll get back to you."

Joanna was about to call Rochelle Powers to find out if she'd listened to the recording, but a call from Butch arrived before she had a chance to dial the number.

"Guess what," he said when she answered. "I just got off the phone with my publicist. The weather report for Silver City tonight is crap. They're expecting a big snowstorm. The system was supposed to stay farther north, but now the radar's predicting a swing to the south. With a blizzard expected to start at about the same time as the meet and greet, the library board decided to cancel my reading as a precaution."

"So you're coming home today, then?"

"I've got a rental car. I can drive myself home from here in Santa Fe in a little over seven hours. That'll give me a whole extra day to shop and get ready for Thanksgiving."

"What about the weather?" Joanna asked.

"Not to worry. The storm's not due until later today. By the time it hits, I'll be home."

"I'm sorry about the cancellation."

"Don't be sorry. I'm more than ready to be home."

"I'll be glad to have you," Joanna told him, "and Denny will be ecstatic."

"I'll check out in a little while. In the meantime how are things on your end?"

Joanna was in the process of telling him when the ambulance from Douglas pulled up in front of the ER. She'd gotten far enough into the story that Butch knew that she, along with Carol and Sage, were all parked outside the hospital awaiting the arrival of her injured deputy.

"I've gotta go," she told him. "They're here."

Joanna hopped out of the Enclave and was standing next to the ambulance when the EMT opened the rear doors. As they rolled the gurney out of the vehicle, Joanna fought back tears. "Thank God you didn't come home in a body bag," she said.

Garth, pale as a ghost, still managed to give her a lopsided grin and a feeble thumbs-up as he rolled past. "And thank God for that clotting powder," he told her.

"That kid's tough as nails," the remaining EMT observed as the gurney moved away. "As much pain as he's in, I'm surprised at how well he's holding up."

"I'm not," Juanita Raymond said.

The old woman, arriving on the scene, pushed past Joanna and the EMT and followed the gurney toward the entrance. Pausing just outside the automatic doors, she turned back and added, "You should have seen him a couple of years ago when that fool kid tried to chop his leg off with a hatchet. He barely shed a tear then, either." With that, Juanita Raymond turned and marched inside.

"Who the hell was that?" the EMT asked, gazing after her.

"That would be Deputy Raymond's grandmother," Joanna told him.

"No wonder the kid's so tough."

"No wonder," Joanna agreed.

Joanna followed Juanita into and through the ER, stopping finally at a curtained cubicle where the head of the ER, Dr. Mallory Morris, aided by Eileen Hopkins—the ER's head nurse—and a pair of nursing assistants were easing Garth Raymond off the gurney and onto a bed.

When Joanna stepped through the curtain, Dr. Morris gave her an inquiring look. "What are you doing here?" he asked. "Aren't you supposed to be on maternity leave?"

It was annoying that everyone in town felt free to comment on Joanna's maternity-leave situation. In reply she took an evidence bag out of her pocket.

"I came to check on Deputy Raymond and to collect his weapon," she said.

Dr. Morris looked startled. "He's carrying a weapon?"

Joanna focused on the patient. "Hand it over, Deputy Raymond," she ordered.

Garth reached under the sheet and patted the holster where his .38 should have been and seemed surprised to discover that the weapon wasn't there.

"Sorry, Sheriff Brady," he said. "I don't remember dropping it, but I must have lost it when I fell."

Joanna shoved the unused evidence bag back into her pocket. "Not to worry," she said. "The

CSIs should be there any minute. I'm sure they'll find it. What's important now is to make sure you're okay."

"Which I can't do with everyone crowded around," Dr. Morris admonished them. "How about if we clear the room so I can find out what we've got here?"

Joanna started to comply but then stopped. "Be sure to swab his hands and bag and seal his clothing for us—at least his shirt and pants."

"Looking for GSR?" Dr. Morris asked. Clearly he knew the drill when it came to collecting gunshot residue.

Joanna nodded. "Yes, please."

"All right," Dr. Morris said, glancing around the crowded cubicle. "Nurse Hopkins stays. Everybody else out!"

Joanna did as she was told and retreated. Juanita Raymond held her ground and stayed where she was. "Garth is my boy," she said, crossing her arms and leveling a defiant look in the doctor's direction. "The only way you're getting me out of here is if you drag me out by the hair on my head."

Dr. Mallory nodded. "Yes, ma'am," he conceded. "In that case it looks like you're welcome to stay."

Joanna made her way through the ER, arriving outside just as Detective Howell's Tahoe sped to a stop next to the parked ambulance. As Deb climbed out, she greeted Joanna with a grin.

"Today's the day I chose," she said. "If you could have held off for one more day, I would have won the pool. Now, come around here and meet Latisha. After I make the introductions, the two of you can visit while I go get a wheelchair."

"A wheelchair?" Joanna echoed. "I thought she wasn't injured."

"She's not, but she's very weak. She's also mentally and physically exhausted. I'm not about to risk her trying to get inside on her own. I think she's probably had way more excitement today than's good for her."

Deb opened the passenger door. At five foot ten, she needed to lean over in order to see inside while Joanna did not. In the passenger seat, a young black woman, little more than a girl, stirred groggily as if awakening from a sound sleep. She was shockingly thin—a living, breathing stick figure—with an unruly array of uncombed hair stacked on her head like Medusa's crown of snakes.

"Latisha," Detective Howell said, "I'd like you to meet Sheriff Joanna Brady. Sheriff Brady, this is Latisha Marcum."

"I'm glad to meet you," Joanna said, proffering a handshake. "I understand you've had a rough time."

The fingers on the hand Latisha held out in return were skeletally thin. The skin of her palm was rough as sandpaper, her knuckles chapped and cracked.

"Yes," she said. "It's been pretty bad. If it hadn't been for Deputy Raymond, I'd probably be dead."

"From what I hear, the same might have been true for him if not for you," Joanna said. "So thank you for that, Ms. Marcum. Thank you very much."

"You're welcome," she said, "but you can call me

Latisha. Are you sure I have to go to the hospital? My parents are coming. Can't I just go somewhere and wait for them?"

"No," Joanna said firmly. "After everything you've been through, your health may be impaired. The doctors need to make sure you're okay."

"But I don't have any money," Latisha objected. "How will I pay the bill?"

Joanna knew that the same regulations that mandated hospitals to provide expensive medical care to seriously injured illegal border crossers would also apply here.

"Don't worry about the bill," she said. "That will be handled."

Deb arrived with the wheelchair in tow. Together they helped Latisha out of the Tahoe and wheeled her inside. At the admitting desk, Joanna stood by listening to the answers Latisha gave the clerk, including the contact information for her mother and stepfather. Joanna listened; Detective Howell took notes.

Once in yet another curtained-off cubicle, Eileen Hopkins helped Latisha up onto the bed. She knelt down and removed the boots. As she did so, an aghast Joanna caught her first glimpse of those grotesquely misshapen toenails. Next Eileen helped Latisha ditch the oversize deputy uniform and slip into a gown. At that point the newly revealed angry scab encircling Latisha's lower right leg just above the ankle told its own part of the story. When it came time to take the patient's vitals, the nurse said nothing aloud while looking at the blood-pressure reading, but her pursed lips spoke volumes. Clearly the numbers she was seeing were alarming.

"I'll be right back," Eileen said. When she returned a few minutes later, she brought along a rolling scale. "How tall are you?" she asked.

"Five-six," Latisha replied.

"And how much do you weigh?"

Latisha shrugged. "I used to weigh one-fifty to one-fifty-four. I don't know what I weigh now."

When Latisha stepped onto the scale, Joanna caught a glimpse of the numbers on the screen—108. Latisha Marcum really was nothing but skin and bones.

"When we found the other girl's body . . ." Joanna began.

"Amelia's body," Latisha murmured, interrupting. "Her name was Amelia Diaz Salazar."

"It appeared that the only content in her stomach was partially digested dry dog food," Joanna resumed. "Is that what you ate, too?"

Latisha nodded. "It's all he ever gave us."

Eileen shook her head. "All right," she said. "Dr. Morris will be in to see you soon."

THIRTY-NINE

AS THE ERT convoy barreled eastward on Geronimo Trail, leaving a vast plume of dust in its wake, Tom Hadlock was in the lead. It occurred to him that a troop of hard-riding U.S. Cavalry might have kicked up a similar cloud almost a century and a half earlier when they charged back and forth across the San Bernardino Valley on horseback chasing after Geronimo, the leader of the Chiricahua Apaches. Ultimately they caught the renegade chief. After being taken into custody somewhere near Skeleton Canyon, Geronimo and his band of warriors were loaded onto a train and shipped into exile in Florida.

Tom could only wish that today he had the cavalry riding backup. With every mile he drove, the chief deputy felt more and more as though he was leading his people on a fool's errand. Arthur Ardmore was a serial killer who had lost control of one of his captives and then shot a cop. Why would he stick around waiting for someone to come after him armed with warrants and weapons? By now Arthur Ardmore was probably in the wind.

Although it had seemed to take forever, the reality

was that Tom had managed to assemble his response team with lightning speed. Still, he doubted he'd been fast enough. Too much time had elapsed between Garth's shooting and now. Once they were ready to spring the trap on the killer, it might be too late.

As Tom drove, however, there was a second reason he was beating himself up, and that was the damn satphone. With a serial killer operating in the neighborhood, he should never have left Garth out there alone with no way to call for assistance. He could have stationed two deputies there rather than one. Barring that, he could have left somebody else's satphone there for Garth to use.

Deputy Creighton from San Simon had been out doing the canvass that day along with everyone else. His phone had been working just fine. Why hadn't Tom arranged for Garth to use that one overnight? If Deputy Raymond died or wound up being permanently injured, that would be on Tom—on his failed leadership.

Tom had driven this route so many times in the last few days that he almost knew the trip by heart. They were able to race along on the straightaway far faster than usual, but when they started up into the mountains, they slowed down. Once on the Forest Service road, they slowed even more.

They were picking their way along that and were well past the dump site when Tom spotted a traffic cone standing in the middle of the road. As he drew to a stop in front of it, Dave Hollicker came charging out of the undergrowth.

"What's up?" Tom asked, rolling down his window.

"Take a look at this," Dave said, handing over his phone.

"What is it?"

"A photo of the license plate from that wrecked pickup truck."

Tom pulled out his reading glasses and stared at the screen. "It's registered in New Mexico?" he asked in surprise.

"And here's the registration," Dave said, handing over the document.

"James Edward Ardmore, Road Forks, New Mexico," Tom read aloud from the document. "Who the hell is James Edward Ardmore?"

"Good question," Dave said. "More than likely he's a relative of Arthur's of some kind, but I thought you'd want to know about this before you and the response team turn up at Arthur's place in Calhoun."

"You've got that right," Tom told him. "I sure as hell do. Are you about done here?"

"Close," Dave said. "I've finished with the truck. We found out where the shooting went down. We found what we're pretty sure is Deputy Raymond's weapon, and Casey's combing the area for spent slugs. When she's done with that, we'll need to call for a tow truck."

"Yes, you will," Tom agreed, "and when you do, you can use this." He reached across to the passenger seat and picked up a satphone. "This was issued to Deputy Creighton. Since he's with the team today, he won't be needing it. Just be sure to get it back to him when you're done."

"Will do," Dave said.

Moving out, Tom reached for a second satphone. Since most of his key people were with him on the mission, there was really only one person left to call—Deb Howell.

FORTY

DEB'S PHONE rang. She went outside to answer it just as Dr. Morris popped into the room carrying an iPad. He nodded in Joanna's direction. "Your boy's off to X-ray and then to the OR. And now, what about you, Latisha?" he asked, reading her name off the chart. "I'm Dr. Morris. How are you feeling today?"

"I'm fine," Latisha said. "I want to go home."

"According to what I'm seeing here, young lady, you're anything but fine. Sheriff Brady, if you'll excuse us . . ."

"No, don't go," Latisha said, reaching for Joanna's hand. To the doctor she said, "I want her to stay."

"I'm sure you need your privacy," Joanna objected, "and Mrs. Hopkins will be here."

"Please stay with me," Latisha begged. "Please."

The visible panic and alarm on Latisha's face was obvious. Given her recent history, the idea of her not wanting to be left alone in a room—any room—with a strange man was entirely understandable.

"I'll be glad to stay," Joanna said.

And she did. Joanna remained in the cubicle throughout the entire examination. She learned about the damaged, bleeding gums and the abscessed tooth; she saw the crosshatches of scarring on Latisha's back left behind by the Boss's leather belt and buckle. She saw the ugly results of severe malnutrition—the protruding ribs, the distended abdomen, the brittle skin. What Arthur Ardmore had done to this girl was unspeakable.

"When was your last period?" Dr. Morris asked finally.

Latisha shrugged. "I don't know."

"Is it possible you're pregnant?"

And that's when it was all too much. Latisha burst into tears. "When Trayvon had me get that second abortion, the doctor said I'd never have kids," she sobbed, "never!"

It took a few minutes for her to quiet again. "Sorry," she said. "I don't know what's the matter with me today. Every other minute I start crying. I seem to cry over every little thing."

"You go right ahead and cry if you want to," Dr. Morris said. "Considering what you've endured, you're entitled. In the meantime, from what I'm seeing here, I'm going to admit you for observation."

"Admit me? You mean keep me here in the hospital?"

"Yes, in the hospital," he told her. "You're severely dehydrated and malnourished. Have you had anything to eat today?"

"Garth gave me a sandwich."

"A single sandwich isn't going to cut it," Dr. Morris said. "We need to hook you up to an IV and get some liquids and nutrients into your system. That broken tooth is infected and needs to come out, but it'll need to be treated with antibiotics before a dentist can perform an extraction. The toenails don't just need to be clipped. They're so ingrown and infected that trimming them will need to be a surgical procedure performed in the hospital and under sterile conditions. You need to rest and recover. We'll be supervising your food intake for the next several days. As for your emotional state? Given the circumstances, the outbursts you mentioned before are entirely understandable. I also believe that counseling of some sort is in order."

"Counseling," Latisha echoed. "I don't want counseling, I want to go home."

"Counseling may be the only thing that will make your going home possible."

Joanna left the cubicle while they were making arrangements to transfer Latisha to a room. She found Deb waiting just outside the curtains.

"I heard from Tom," she said. "The wrecked truck at the crime scene is registered in New Mexico to someone named James Ardmore. Dave thinks he must be related to Arthur."

"Sounds like," Joanna agreed.

"And I'm on my way to sort out how," Deb told her. "Tom wants me to send him whatever I find before the response team heads into Calhoun. It'll be easier to do research in the office rather than in my car, so my interview with Latisha will have to wait."

"Go do what Tom needs you to do and don't worry about the interview," Joanna told her. "Dr. Morris is admitting her, and she'll be here for a day or two. You'll know where to find her when you're ready."

Deb hurried out. Joanna was about to go to the OR waiting room in search of Juanita Raymond and Marianne Maculyea when a one-word text from Carol showed up on her phone: TIME!

That wasn't news to Joanna. She hurried out to the parking lot. Marianne's vintage Sea Foam Green VW Bug was parked next to the Enclave, but there was no sign of Marianne herself. Once Joanna was settled in the passenger seat, Carol handed off Sage and then beat a hasty retreat. "I need a pit stop," she said.

Figuring out how to nurse Jenny had been challenging, but Joanna was a lot younger back then. As a more experienced mom, first with Dennis and now with Sage, it wasn't a problem. Sage was an eager eater and immediately got with the program, so when Joanna's phone rang, once she wrested the device out of her pocket, she had no difficulty feeding Sage and talking at the same time.

"Your friendly neighborhood FBI profiler is calling," Rochelle Powers said with a laugh. "How are things?"

"You're not going to believe it," Joanna said. "We've identified the killer, and my people are on their way to make an arrest!"

"An arrest? Are you serious?" Rochelle returned.

"Way to go! But tell me about it. Who's the perp? What do you know about him?"

"Not much so far," Joanna answered. "He's a rich old guy named Arthur Ardmore who came out west with enough spare change in his pockets to buy himself a ghost town."

"To use as a torture chamber," Rochelle put in.

"Exactly. He kept girls—four of them at least—chained to a wall in some kind of basement. Last night the only one still alive somehow managed to escape. Ardmore took off after her and ended up getting into a shoot-out with Garth Raymond, the deputy Tom Hadlock left guarding the dump site. Deputy Raymond is currently undergoing surgery, but he should be okay."

"That's good to hear," Rochelle said, "but about this ghost town. Is it anywhere near the dump site?"

"Very near. The problem is, we've now discovered that there's a second individual involved—or who may be involved. His name is James Ardmore, and he lives a few miles farther east in Road Forks, New Mexico. We're thinking James and Arthur are related—brothers maybe, and the two of them are involved in this criminal enterprise together."

"That would make sense," Rochelle observed. "One to go after the girls and the other to keep them in line, but is either one of them a truck driver?"

The question was so simple it took Joanna's breath away. "I don't know," she said, "but I'm sure as hell going to find out. Hanging up now."

She ended the call abruptly and punched Deb's number. "Are you there yet?" she asked.

"Not quite," Deb replied. "Just pulling into the gate. Why?"

"Find out if James Ardmore has more than one vehicle and call me back once you do."

Joanna hung up. While she waited, she burped Sage and switched her from one side to the other. They were settling in for round two when the phone rang.

"James Edward Ardmore sure as hell does have two vehicles," Deb Howell announced breathlessly. "The other one's a Peterbilt."

"Does Tom Hadlock know?"

"That was my first call."

"Are you putting out an APB?" Joanna asked.

"Already done," Deb answered. "Suspects are to be considered armed and dangerous."

"You think they're together?" Joanna asked.

"Don't you?" Deb returned. "Tom tells me that the response team is just forming up to make contact. I told him I'd stay here in the office and do some Internet surfing to see if I can dig up anything else on these guys."

Once the call ended, Joanna sat for a moment considering that stunning news—news she needed to share with someone else. Still nursing Sage, Joanna used the mic on her phone to dictate a text for Rochelle Powers:

YOU NAILED IT. JAMES ARDMORE DRIVES A PETER-BILT. NOW ALL WE HAVE TO DO IS FIND HIM AND HIS BROTHER.

FORTY-ONE

BEFORE HEADING out, Tom Hadlock had gone to the supply room, grabbed a collection of walkie-talkies off their chargers, and then distributed them to all the members of the team. They came with a simple on/off volume control, a squelch knob, a channel selector, and a push-to-talk switch. Once they were all set to the correct channels, he could talk to his separate tactical teams or to the entire group as much as he wanted and the Marliss Shacklefords of the world wouldn't be able to hear a word of it, unless she or they somehow magically managed to get within a mile of Calhoun.

Starvation Canyon Road dead-ended in the canyon itself, a few miles beyond Calhoun. The plan was to lay down spike strips just east of the fence line. If Ardmore tried to flee the scene in a vehicle, four flattened tires would slow him down to a crawl. Because they expected to approach the ghost town itself on foot and with weapons drawn, Tom directed his officers to block the entrances with parked patrol cars in case the spike strips didn't do the job.

They'd all donned vests and Windbreakers and

were gathered in a huddle for a final briefing when Tom's satphone rang. Knowing the caller was Deb, he switched over to speaker when he answered.

"I've got news," Deb announced. "We now have two suspects instead of one, and they *are* brothers. According to their dates of birth, James Edward Ardmore, age sixty-six, is five years younger than Arthur. Both were born in Baltimore, Maryland. I'm looking at the photos on their driver's licenses. I wish you had an Internet connection so I could send you the photos. These guys look like twins."

"Good work," Tom said. "Anything else?"

"James owns a 2017 Peterbilt, an eighteen-wheeler."

Tom felt as though he'd been sucker-punched. "He's a trucker?" Tom asked despairingly. "If they took off with Arthur's Subaru loaded into the back of a Peterbilt, they could be anywhere by now."

"Not literally anywhere," Deb corrected. "Yes, they have a head start, but even a rig like that can go only so fast, and the distance it can cover is limited. I've already put out an APB. Somebody somewhere will spot them—an on-the-ball highway-patrol officer out on the interstate maybe, or else a sharp-eyed inspector at a weigh station."

Tom felt better. Maybe this wasn't such a lost cause after all.

"Okay, Deb," he said. "Thanks for the update. We'll still proceed with caution on this end, but you're probably right. I'm guessing the brothers Ardmore are long gone."

Then, breaking into four separate squads, the Emergency Response Team moved in formation with weapons drawn. Bill Creighton, the department's champion weight lifter, was the only one not pointing a loaded weapon. He was in charge of the battering ram they'd brought along in case they had occasion to bust down a door or two.

For the approach, Tom Hadlock, accompanied by the K-9 team, stayed in the middle and stuck to the road while the others spread out on either side. It was Mojo's first official operation with the department. He tracked along on his leash, alert and on the job.

"Looks like a good dog," Tom told Terry. "Acts like he knows what he's about."

As the town of Calhoun came into view, there were only a dozen buildings total. A hundred yards from the first one, Tom called for radio silence. The first one appeared to be an adobe structure minus a roof. When they reached it, they discovered that not only was the roof gone, so was most everything else. Two of the walls had melted away into nothing. Since only a single corner was left, clearing that building was no problem at all.

Next up came a tottering wooden shack that might have been part of a stable. It leaned drunkenly to one side, looking for all the world as though it would topple over at the slightest touch. Jaime Carbajal peeled away a loose plank and peered inside before giving the thumbs-up signal that meant it was clear.

The next building was not old at all. It was one

of those prefab Tuff Shed one-car garages that came complete with an automatic door. If someone was inside, the only way out would be to activate the door. Hopefully the team would hear the door opening in time to react.

On his way past, Tom saw that something—a moving vehicle, most likely—had slammed into the structure with enough force to shift it so it was no longer square with the concrete pad beneath it. There was no way to tell if the damage was recent, but a confusing tangle of nearby tire tracks suggested it might be. Wanting to preserve the tracks left in the dirt, Tom waved everyone away from the garage. They'd have to come back and look at that one later on, after Dave Hollicker had a chance to process the tracks.

The two most substantial structures in town came next, facing each other across the narrow dirt track. The larger of the two was constructed of faded red brick and looked like a fortress. The windows, largely intact, were covered by rusty iron bars, some of them hanging loosely on their mountings on the exterior of the building. The second structure was a dilapidated wood-frame storefront.

Ernie and his team quickly cleared the brick building, since the solid wooden doors to both the front and back entrances were padlocked shut from the outside. Once Ernie gave the all-clear, Tom walked up to the building and pressed his face against the window, attempting to peer inside. All he saw was a dense curtain that appeared to be nothing more than thick layers of black plastic garbage bags. His first thought was that they looked similar to the ones found filled with trash near Amelia Salazar's body.

This is where those girls were held prisoner, Tom thought grimly. *This is the real crime scene.*

By the time he stepped away from the window and back out onto the street, Jaime's team had cleared the storefront and then moved on, leaving behind what must have been the business part of town and progressing into the residential area. That consisted of four tin-roofed wooden shacks, little more than one-room cabins, all of which appeared to be in fairly decent repair. They all had glass in their windows, and their coats of exterior paint were probably only a few years old. They were no bigger than what HGTV often refers to as "tiny houses."

They reminded Tom of the old miner shacks that still clung like so many brightly colored burrs to the hillsides above Bisbee's Tombstone Canyon.

The first three were all padlocked shut and showed no sign of habitation. Up close, Tom could tell that the one on the end, the fourth one, was different. For starters it was half again as big as the others and had a no-kidding white picket fence around it. A lone cottonwood tree, leafless now, towered over the front yard. Beneath the tree sat an old wooden Adirondack chair. In the heat of summer, the tree would have provided a pleasant, shady retreat.

Tom spotted the fence first, then the tree, and

finally the chair. A moment later he saw something else—an evaporative cooler hanging on the sill of a side window. That suggested that the house was most likely occupied or had been occupied fairly recently. The front door was closed, but it wasn't padlocked shut, meaning that someone might be inside.

Tom motioned his team into a whispered strategy session on the far side of the fence. Then, with the others covering him and accompanied by Terry and Mojo, Tom walked up to the door and pounded on it.

"Police!" he shouted. "Open up!" But nothing happened. There was no sound from inside and no movement either.

Terry reached out and tried the doorknob. It twisted in his hand, and the door cracked open. "Should I send Mojo in?" he whispered.

Tom didn't want to send any of his team into danger, but with Deputy Raymond already in the hospital, putting the dog in jeopardy was better than losing another person. He nodded reluctantly. "Send him in," he said.

"Find him!" Terry ordered the dog, and Mojo sprang forward, slamming the back of the door hard against an interior wall and sprinting into the house. Tom held his breath, but nothing happened then, either—no shouts of alarm, no gunshots. Half a minute after Mojo charged inside, he came back. Wagging his tail, he went straight to Terry and was rewarded with a "Good dog!" pat as well as a suitable treat.

"Clear," Terry reported. "Believe me, if anybody had been inside, Mojo would have let us know."

Tom pulled out the satphone and an index card, squinting at the card until he located the number of Deputy Creighton's satphone. "Are you finished?" he asked when Dave Hollicker answered.

"Just about," Dave said. "The tow truck is on its way. Why?"

"Come on up to Starvation Canyon Road. I'll send someone down to move the patrol cars out of the way and pick up the spike strips. We're about to bust down some doors on a building or two, and I'm pretty sure you're going to have another whole crime scene to investigate."

FORTY-TWO

THEY ROLLED Latisha's bed from the ER into first a different wing and then a different room. A new doctor, someone named Dr. Lee, came in and introduced himself. He told Latisha he was prescribing antibiotics for the various infections and giving her something to dull the pain in her tooth.

"It might make you a little drowsy," he said.

The doctor seemed nice enough, but she was glad the nurses were still in the room while he was there, and she wished that little red-haired woman in the uniform would come back. She wanted to ask about Garth. She needed to know if he was okay.

The nurses covered her with a blanket, but that made her too hot. Her body was accustomed to the chill of the basement. In this very warm room just the sheet was all the covers she needed. But that sheet—that amazing sheet—was smooth and soft and clean. It felt heavenly. She kept running her fingers over the silkiness of it in sheer wonder. Someone—a nurse or maybe a nurse assistant, she wasn't sure—had rubbed lotion into her hands and feet. That felt heavenly, too. And then, even though there was an IV dripping liquids into her arm, they brought her a tray of food—a bowl of Jell-O and a bowl of chicken-noodle soup. It was a feast, almost as amazing as Garth's meat-loaf sandwich.

The doctor had said that the pain meds might make her sleepy, but they didn't—not for a long time. How could anyone sleep with all that noise going on? There were people talking and laughing out in the hallway, people rolling carts past her door, shoes squeaking on the polished tiles of the hallway floor. All that noise and all that light. There was blue sky showing outside her window—blue sky over what looked like a steep red mountain with a flat top.

Gradually the pain meds worked. The noise faded. Latisha drifted off, awakening with a start sometime later. It took her a moment to get her bearings—to figure out where she was. The Boss was gone. She wasn't in the basement anymore. And when she looked around the room, she found she wasn't alone, either. A blond-haired woman was sitting on a chair near the foot of her bed. She didn't seem to be a nurse—she wasn't wearing a uniform, and she was reading from a Bible.

"Who are you?" Latisha asked.

"My name is Marianne Maculyea. I'm a chaplain. Sheriff Brady had to leave, but she asked me to check in on you."

"How is Garth?" Latisha asked. "Is he okay?"

"He's okay, out of surgery, and just down the hall," Marianne said. "He asked me to give you this."

She handed over another one of Grandma Juanita's meat-loaf sandwiches. That time Latisha ate the whole thing.

FORTY-THREE

COCHISE COUNTY, Joanna's jurisdiction in south-eastern Arizona, is a square that's approximately eighty miles wide and eighty miles tall. The county line to the south is also the international border with Mexico, while the eastern county line is also the state line between Arizona and New Mexico.

The total area amounts to a little more than 6,200 square miles, with a population of approximately 126,000. Next door in New Mexico, Hidalgo County covers 3,400 square miles, with a population of 4,300. Where Cochise County is square, Hidalgo is skinny and tall. On the far side of Hidalgo is Grant County, a similarly sized—3,900 square miles as opposed to 3,400—with a population of 28,000. In other words, the two counties in New Mexico combined add up to an area a thousand square miles larger than Cochise County with only a quarter of the population.

That was the basic geography of the situation. Both Cochise County and Hidalgo County were located along the international border with Mexico and were beset with all the attendant complications of border security and lack thereof. Grant County's southern border didn't reach quite far enough to touch the Mexican border, but it was close enough to be affected by events and issues happening to the south.

A year earlier the Police Our Borders folks had come calling on affected counties with their offers of "free" leased helicopters. Over in Cochise County, Joanna had turned them down out of budgetary concerns. In New Mexico, however, the people calling the shots for Hidalgo and Grant Counties had arrived at an entirely different conclusion.

Hidalgo's longtime sheriff, Randy Trotter, was a good old boy if ever there was one. Somewhere north of sixty, Trotter was cut from the same cloth as Maricopa County's Sheriff Joe Arpaio and billed himself as a "toes-up sheriff," one who would die with his boots on, right along with his badge. Despite Trotter's annoying "sheriff for life" bravado, his constituents loved him, and when it came time for reelection, he generally ran unopposed.

With POB's generous offer of relatively free helicopters on the table, Sheriff Trotter had joined forces with Grant County's sheriff, Adam Yates, in an alliance under which the two counties shared the expense and reaped the benefit of having a single helicopter.

That was why, as soon as Carol returned to collect Sage, burp her, and change her, Joanna immediately pulled out her phone and dialed Sheriff Trotter's number. Much as she hated to admit it, today his shared POB helicopter might be just what was needed.

"Why, Sheriff Brady," he rumbled pleasantly when he came on the line. "How the heck are you, and did you ever get around to having that baby? The last time I saw you, you were big as a barn."

Randy Trotter was a lot of things, but politically correct wasn't one of them. He was known for putting his lizard-skin Tony Lamas in his mouth, sometimes both of them at once. The encounter he mentioned had occurred in the course of a late-night poker game while both he and Joanna had been attending the annual conference of the Society of Southwestern Sheriffs in Las Cruces.

When Joanna was first elected, SOSS had been something of a no-girls-allowed type of organization. They had let her in, but not without some sidelong glances and more than a few derogatory comments. Gradually her determination to be a law-enforcement professional had earned her a kind of grudging respect, but what had finally brought them around and given her real acceptance in the group was her ability to play poker.

Joanna had learned the game at her father's knee and over her mother's tight-lipped objections. D. H. Lathrop had been a wizard at Texas Hold'em, and he'd seen to it that his daughter was, too. The first couple of times she attended SOSS conferences, as the only woman there, she'd been self-conscious and out of her depth. She knew about the late-night poker parties—everyone did—but she wasn't sure she'd be welcome and didn't go. The games weren't officially sponsored events with posted times and invitations, but they were always held in one of the sponsoring hotels' larger suites. When ten o'clock at night rolled around, whoever wanted to play simply showed up.

The first time Joanna crashed an SOSS poker party was at a conference in El Paso. By then she'd already gained a bit of a reputation for beating the socks off her fellow sheriffs back home in Arizona. When she took a seat at the table, Hector Morales, from Greenlee County, had nodded in her direction. After only one hand, he winked at her and then politely excused himself from the table. It was a good thing, too. She'd cleaned everybody else's clock.

She wasn't snotty about being a winner, and she wasn't a sore loser when the tables turned. That qualified her as one of the guys. And the fact that she didn't take offense at every off-color remark didn't hurt, either, something that was especially useful in dealing with Randy Trotter. In fact, in Las Cruces—big as a barn or not—she'd pretty much set the old guy back on his heels.

"Yup," Joanna said now. "Had her a couple of weeks ago. Her name is Eleanor Sage after my mother, but we call her Sage. She's got red hair, and someday, when she grows up, she'll probably want to be sheriff."

"So a chip off the old block, then," Trotter observed. "Are you going to teach her to play poker?"

"I don't see why not."

Randy replied with a hearty laugh. "Good on you," he said. "Now, to what do I owe the honor? I heard about that dump site over on your side of the Peloncillos. Does this have anything to do with that?"

"It certainly does."

Not wanting to conduct confidential police business in the public square of a hospital waiting room, Joanna paced the parking lot as she briefed him about the case. By the time she finished, the phone was hot against her ear.

"Okay, my dear," Trotter said when she finished. "I've got some pretty good contacts over Road Forks way. Let me make a few calls and see what I can do. I'll be in touch."

As Joanna approached the hospital entrance, she was dismayed to find that Marliss Shackleford had spotted her and was lying in wait.

"What's going on?" the reporter demanded. "I know one of your deputies was shot and has been transported here from Douglas by ambulance. I believe it's Deputy Raymond from Elfrida. And there was something else happening as well—something about a woman or a girl—which makes me think this may all be connected to that crime scene over in the Peloncillos."

"I can neither confirm nor deny," Joanna said.

"You and everybody else," Marliss griped. "Nobody's home out at the Justice Center. I already checked. Hadlock is out. Carpenter is out. There's nothing coming through on my scanners, and no one seems to have any idea when they'll be back. Now here you are, back in uniform and hanging out at the hospital when you're supposedly on maternity leave. Something screwy is going on here, Sheriff Brady, something big, and I want to know what it is."

"My department is currently involved in a major

investigation," Joanna told her. "I'm assuming Acting Sheriff Hadlock's people are maintaining radio silence on account of people just like you. For the safety of my officers, I can tell you, Marliss, that anyone publishing premature information about that operation will be considered to be interfering with police business, which would be grounds for being banned from all future press briefings."

Marliss bridled at that. "That's not fair," she snapped. "You can't do that. I'm just doing my job—following the story."

"And I'm doing mine," Joanna countered. "It's my department, after all, and I'm in charge. If it turns out that one of my officers has indeed been injured, you can rest assured that his name, the circumstances surrounding the incident, and the extent of his injuries won't be released until Ernie Carpenter, our temporary Media Relations officer, is able to hold an official briefing. As for your finding me in uniform? I may be on maternity leave, but when one of my officers is injured in the line of duty, my place is at the hospital—no matter what."

With that, Joanna marched into the hospital. She found Juanita Raymond and Marianne seated together in the waiting room.

"How is he?"

"They just took him into the recovery room," Juanita said. "He lost a lot of blood. They had to give him two transfusions, but he's going to be okay."

"Thank God," Joanna murmured.

"Thank God indeed," Marianne agreed. She gave Joanna a searching look. "Are you okay?"

Joanna wasn't okay, but only a good friend would have caught it. She scanned the waiting room. "There's a lot going on," she said, "and with Marliss nosing around, I can't afford to be caught talking about any of it in public."

"Go do what you need to do," Marianne said. "I'll stay here with Juanita and Garth."

"And with Latisha, too," Joanna said. "Maybe you could call Deb. I believe Latisha's parents are flying into Tucson. Deb has their contact numbers. Maybe you could call and see if we can be of any assistance."

"Will do," Marianne said. "Go home and don't worry."

Not worrying was something far easier said than done.

FORTY-FOUR

WITH THE targets in the wind, the Emergency Response Team switched out of arrest mode and focused instead on crime-scene investigation. Now they would proceed with executing the search warrants, but because of the need to document and preserve evidence that part of the operation had to be conducted under the direct supervision of Dave Hollicker and Casey Ledford.

After hours of tension, the guys on the team were glad to push the Pause button. While everybody else was letting off steam and waiting for the CSIs, a bummed Tom walked away from the group, sat down in the chair under the cottonwood tree, and pulled out the satphone. The Ardmores had given them the slip. As near as he could tell, Deputy Raymond Garth had been shot right around 5:00 A.M. It was now 10:30—more than five hours later. The brothers Ardmore could be in Texas by now, or almost to California. Maybe Deb was right and someone spotting them at an inspection station or weigh station offered the best chance of catching them.

In the meantime the next piece of the investigation was obviously in Road Forks. In New Mexico. If it had been a hot-pursuit situation, Tom could have hopped into the Yukon, lit up his lights, and gone barreling across the state line. Only problem was, it wasn't a hot pursuit at all. Instead of calling Joanna to tell her they'd blown it, he got on the horn to Randy Trotter's office in Lordsburg.

It turned out that the woman who answered the phone was also the sheriff's secretary. "He's not in," she said when Tom identified himself. "I'm Connie, his secretary. I might be able to reach him by radio, though. Does this have anything to do with the situation out at Road Forks?"

"You know about that?"

"Sure do. We've got a deputy over there right now, talking to Arlene."

"Who's Arlene?"

"A waitress at the truck stop. She said Jimmy Ardmore turned up there for breakfast long about eight o'clock this morning. According to their security footage, he drove out headed westbound shortly after nine."

Tom swore under his breath. That was less than two hours ago. A two-hour head start was a big improvement over a five-hour head start, but it could still put the westbound Peterbilt well into Arizona.

"We were going to post an APB, but somebody from your office beat us to the punch. All the same, Sheriff Trotter and Donnie are in the helicopter right now, having a little look-see."

"Who's Donnie?"

"That would be Donald Dunkerson, our pilot. Can I have Sheriff Trotter call you at the number I've got on the screen?"

"That'll work."

"I don't believe I caught your name."

"Thomas Hadlock—Tom. I'm acting sheriff here in Cochise County."

"That's right, your sheriff just had her baby, didn't she? Okay, I'll let him know."

Dave and Casey showed up and went to work. While Casey made plaster casts of the tire tracks next to the garage, Tom and the Double C's trailed behind Dave to observe as he processed the scene.

In the interest of preserving evidence and wanting to be able to secure the property again after the search, Dave used a heavy-duty bolt cutter to slice through Arthur Ardmore's collection of padlocks. The three smaller houses showed no sign of human habitation and merited little attention. The one with the picket fence was a different story.

"Hold up, guys," he said, pausing in the doorway. "There's dust everywhere, and I can see two distinct sets of footprints, one coming and one going. When whoever it was went in, he was barefoot. Coming out, he was wearing shoes. I'll be right back."

Donning booties, Tom and the two detectives waited outside. "Here's the deal," Dave said when he returned. "The guy who came in the front door went straight to the closet, grabbed a pair of shoes, and went right back out. He knew what he wanted and where to go to get it."

Stepping inside, Tom, carefully avoiding the tracks in the dust, was struck by the utter emptiness of the place. It was like walking into a haunted house. If Arthur Ardmore had ever lived here, he didn't live here anymore.

"Come take a look at this," Dave said, snapping photos over by an old-fashioned Formica-topped kitchen table.

An old copy of an *Arizona Highways* magazine, dating from May two years earlier, lay on the gritty tabletop. Barely visible through a thick layer of grayish dust was an address label bearing the name Arthur Ardmore. Beside the magazine was an empty coffee mug with a stain in the bottom suggesting that the cup had been dirty but empty when it was abandoned. Nearby sat a French-press coffeemaker with moldy coffee grounds inside, but so much time had passed in the dry heat of the abandoned house that even the mold had died.

Ernie looked at the table and shook his head. "If Arthur gets up from the breakfast table, walks away, and never comes back, what does that tell us?"

"That he didn't know he was leaving," Jaime offered. "And since we've got no blood in here and no sign of a struggle, if something happened to him, it didn't happen here."

"But it did *happen*," Tom said, uttering aloud what everyone else was already thinking. "And I believe that means we're a whole lot closer to identifying the human skull Jack Carver dragged home—the one with a bullet hole in it. Instead of being on the lookout for two suspects, I say we're down to only one—James Ardmore."

When Dave was done with the house for the time being, they trooped over to the garage, where Casey was just finishing up making the plaster casts of the tire tracks. The side entrance to the garage was the only door in the place without a padlock, and it was the only one where they had to deploy Deputy Creighton and his battering ram.

Pushing past the shattered door, Dave stopped cold. "What the hell? Come take a look at what we've got here."

Inside the garage a dozen red gas cans were lined up against the side walls. "Full or empty?" Tom asked.

They were all wearing gloves, but Ernie was the one who walked over to the line of cans and hefted them one after another. "Full," he said. "They're all full—every last one of them. This much gas means we're dealing with a firebug who was probably planning on burning the joint down."

"So why didn't he?" Jaime asked.

"Ran out of time, maybe?" Ernie asked.

"Maybe," Tom said. "Let's go tackle that jail."

They'd known from what Garth had reported to them earlier that the brick building would be the crux of the matter and require the most attention, and that was why Dave had suggested they leave that one for last.

Because of the blackout curtains, the room was pitch-dark when Dave entered. Groping for a light switch, he tripped and fell. Tom, following behind, managed to locate the switch. When the light came on, they discovered that Dave had fallen over an unopened twenty-five-pound bag of dog food lying on the floor next to the door. Garth had reported that the girls imprisoned in the basement had survived on kibble. That unopened bag of dog food sent its own chilling message. Latisha, the last of the four, had somehow managed to escape, but the presence of that fresh dog-food bag suggested that James Ardmore had been planning to invite more guests into his private version of hell.

As Dave focused his camera on the horrifically stained mattress, Tom Hadlock stopped at the top of the wooden stairs that led to the stark dungeon. When he flipped the light switch, a single barren bulb lit up the bleak space below. Everything he saw testified to suffering and deprivation, from the four bare mattresses lying on the earthen floor to the various lengths of chain attached to the walls with eye bolts. And then there was the freezer, an old-fashioned chest-style freezer with an open padlock still dangling from a hasp on the lid. That one spoke of death.

Nowhere did he see any signs of faucets with running water. Instead there was a macerating toilet at the far end of the room. Walking up to that, he discovered that the lid to the flushing tank had been pried off and left on the floor. Inside the tank a single drowned rat floated in the water.

Tom Hadlock had spent years running the Cochise County Jail. He knew the realities of keeping people incarcerated, but seeing that dead rat and realizing the flushing tank must have been the prisoners' only source of water was it for him—as much as he could stand. He fled the basement.

The others were still upstairs. "Sorry, guys," he said on his way past. "That's it for me. I'm going to give Sheriff Brady a call. She needs to know what's going on here."

Wanting to put as much distance as possible between himself and the dungeon, Tom returned to the residential area and the house on the end, the one with the picket fence. Back in the chair where he'd sat earlier, he was about to dial Joanna's number when Deputy Bill Creighton showed up. "Hey, Tom," Bill said, "I think you're gonna wanna take a look at this."

The rest of the team had returned to Skeleton Canyon Road and retrieved the spike strips, as well as all the parked vehicles. Now they were waiting around to help pack and load whatever evidence Dave deemed necessary to take back to the lab.

Around the department Bill Creighton had the dubious honor of being labeled clown-in-chief, so the seriousness of his expression right then gave Tom pause. "Why?" he asked, putting the phone away. "What have you got?"

"Over here," Bill said. "Come with me."

Wearily and feeling his age, Tom rose to follow. Deputy Creighton led him from the clearing surrounding the house into a stand of mesquite, stopping only after the house had disappeared from view.

"I needed to take a leak," Creighton said, "but

Dave had given us strict orders to stay outside, so I went around back and came here. That's what I found." He pointed at what appeared to be a shallow grave.

"And that's not all," Creighton told him. "There are two more right over there."

Without bothering to go see for himself, Tom pulled out the phone and dialed Joanna. "Would you mind giving the Paxtons a call?" he asked when she answered. "We'll need to see if they can hang around a day or two longer. Looks like we've got another location that we'll need them to check."

FORTY-FIVE

SHERIFF RANDY Trotter had been all in when the Protect Our Borders people came along offering to hand out leased helicopters, namely Robinson R22 Beta IIs. Randy just happened to know an out-of-work helicopter pilot in need of a job. The guy, Donald Dunkerson, was also Sheriff Trotter's former son-in-law. He had come home from the Gulf War and landed a great job for an Albuquerque television station as their airborne traffic reporter—a job that had ended abruptly when he'd picked up a DUI three years earlier.

Donnie Dunkerson hadn't been anywhere near his helicopter at the time he was cited. He and his wife, Robin, had gotten into a terrible argument. He'd gone to a bar, tied one on, and was ticketed on his way home. The ticket, combined with his soon-to-be-former wife's very public allegations that he had physically assaulted her more than once, was more bad publicity than the television station could tolerate. Donald Dunkerson's employment had terminated shortly thereafter.

Sheriff Trotter's problem with the situation was due to the fact that he liked Donnie a lot better than he liked his own daughter. Robin was a bitch on wheels. On occasion the sheriff had been over-heard to say that if he'd been married to Robin, he would have been driven to drink, too. She was a micromanager of the first order, as well as a nagger and a constant complainer. As far as Randy was concerned, Donnie appeared to be a far better fa-ther to his kids, Kevin and Roxanne—Randy's only grandkids—than Robin was a mother.

Because he was a first-time DUI offender, Don-nie's conviction didn't require jail time, and he had complied with all the terms and conditions man-dated by law: he attended DUI school; he did the required screening for drug and alcohol abuse; he went straight to AA, did his ninety meetings in ninety days, and was still sober two years and nine months later; when random drug and alcohol tests were required, he passed with flying colors; he in-stalled the ignition/Breathalyzer interlock; he did his twenty-four hours of community service; and he paid all court and probation costs with a happy heart. His one big stumbling block had been the Victim Impact Panel, where Robin had gone on the record talking at tedious length about what an abu-sive, scary drunk he was and reporting that their kids were not only terrified of their father, they were also being bullied at school because all their friends knew what a failure he was.

Kevin and Roxanne were not called to testify before the Victim Impact Panel. If they'd been invited, they might have offered a different opinion, but since they weren't asked, they didn't provide one.

A few weeks later, when Robin filed for divorce, the family-court judge took her every word as gospel. With the DUI conviction hanging over his head, there was no way Donnie was ever going to get custody, or even joint custody. His parental involvement was dialed back to supervised visitation only. Not only that, the judge ordered him to pay child support based on what he'd formerly earned, which had been considerable, as opposed to what he was earning after losing his job, which was nothing.

The only way for him to remain even remotely connected to his children's lives was for him to stay in New Mexico—where he couldn't get work on a bet. As the unpaid child-support debt continued to mount, Robin threatened him with legal action that would have deprived him of even supervised visitations.

When POB's helicopter offer first surfaced, it seemed like the answer to a prayer. Had Sheriff Trotter gone out on a limb and hired Donnie on his own, it would have been deemed outright nepotism, but he and Sheriff Yates from Grant County were longtime pals, and they joined forces on the deal. As pilot bids came in, they were supposed to be sealed, and they might have *looked* sealed, but with Connie's help they weren't as sealed as they should have been. And when the bids were opened? Wonder of wonders, Donald Dunkerson's low bid won the day. That might have caused a few raised eyebrows in Hidalgo County, but nobody said a word, because everybody who knew Robin and Donnie Dunkerson figured the poor guy had gotten a raw deal.

That morning when Sheriff Trotter got off the phone with Joanna Brady, he called Donnie first thing. "Come and get me in that hopped-up bird of yours," he said. "You and I are gonna go out and find ourselves a bright blue Peterbilt."

Joanna had told him that there were APBs posted in both Arizona and New Mexico. Everyone pretends that in the world of cops all things are created equal, but they're not. For example, if you're a member of the New Mexico State Police, a crime committed in Arizona is far less interesting and urgent than one on your home turf in New Mexico, and when it came to the Arizona Highway Patrol, the reverse was also true.

The parking lot at the Hidalgo County Sheriff's Office was now completely paved—another of Sheriff Trotter's pet projects that had been accomplished in a somewhat good-old-boyish, tit-for-tat arrangement. Donnie brought the helicopter down there, and Randy jogged out to greet it.

"Who are we after?" Donnie asked, once Randy had buckled in and clapped on his earphones and mic.

"Some jackass who tortures and murders girls the same age as Kev and Roxie. He took off from Road Forks earlier this morning, and no one's really sure which way he's headed."

"So where are we going?" Donnie asked.

"They said he left Road Forks going westbound,

but I'm thinking he may have doubled back, so let's try heading east first," Randy suggested. "Either way I'm guessing he'll stick to the interstate. With any kind of luck, we'll find him before he crosses over into Texas."

Even then it wasn't a sure thing. Joanna had told him that two people were involved, two brothers. According to the security tapes at Road Forks, there'd been only one occupant in Jimmy Ardmore's bright blue Peterbilt when it took off earlier that morning. The truck had definitely entered the westbound lanes of I-10, but Sheriff Trotter was a New Mexico law-enforcement officer, and chasing a suspect across his own turf would make for better PR than doing an airborne pursuit into Arizona.

The whole time they were flying along, Randy Trotter was thinking that the situation sounded a lot like an old algebra problem, the kind he'd screwed up on while preparing for his SATs: If a truck leaves Road Forks for El Paso traveling at 75 mph, and a helicopter leaves Lordsburg thirty minutes later and flies at 100 mph, will the helicopter catch up with the truck before it reaches El Paso? He tried to work this one out in his head but gave up. He was too uptight. Besides, they didn't know for sure what time Ardmore took off, whether he'd be driving straight through, or even if he was heading for El Paso. There were too many unknowns.

But several of those unknowns also counted in their favor. According to Donnie, they had a hefty tailwind, which meant they were going faster than

100 mph—about 115 or so, he estimated. In addition, Jimmy Ardmore would have to stop for the Border Patrol checkpoint west of Las Cruces. They wouldn't. So maybe they'd catch him. Maybe they wouldn't. Or maybe the whole damned thing was a joke and the SOB was somewhere on I-8 by now and well on his way to sunny California.

They reached the I-25 interchange with no bright blue Peterbilts in sight. They had seen hardly any enforcement along the way. There'd been plenty of trucks tooling down the road at the 75 mph limit, but none of them were that distinctive color. As I-10 curved to the south after Las Cruces, Sheriff Trotter began to lose heart. Now two major interstates were involved, and Ardmore could be on either one of them.

"Which way?" Donnie asked.

Randy indulged in a mental coin flip. "Let's keep following I-10 for now," he said. "If we don't catch up with him before El Paso, we'll turn back and take a run up I-25."

"To do that we'll have to stop someplace and pick up more fuel."

Right, Randy thought, *just what we need. Why don't we run out of gas?*

"Hey!" Donnie yelled in Randy's ears bare moments later. He was shouting and pointing both. "Isn't that our guy?"

Randy looked where Donnie was pointing and saw that he was right—there it was, a bright blue Peterbilt.

"Where are we?" Randy asked.

"Just coming up on Mesquite," Donnie told him. "I need to call it in."

"Do you really want to do that?" Donnie asked.

"Do you have a better idea?"

"Actually, I do," Donnie said, grinning at him. "Back in the Gulf, they didn't call me 'Top Gun' for nothing. Watch this."

He put the Robinson into a steep dive, a hair-raising dive. It was like being inside a roller coaster, and Randy held on for dear life. A moment later they were flying over the trailer of the moving truck. For a time they simply kept pace with it, and then, without warning, Donnie upped his game, shooting them forward and bringing the helicopter down to a position that couldn't have been more than a couple of yards ahead of the speeding truck's windshield.

"Are you nuts?" Randy demanded with his heart in his throat, expecting the truck to crash into them from behind at any moment. "Are you trying to kill us both?"

"Naw," Donnie replied with an easy grin. "Just trying to get the guy's attention, and it looks like I did. He's going down."

Still coolly maintaining the distance between helicopter and truck, Donnie angled up, out of range, and slightly to the left. By the time Randy was able to see behind them, the Peterbilt's tractor was careening down the road, swaying drunkenly from side to side. Behind it the trailer whipped back and forth in a much wider arc, looking for the world as though it were about to go airborne.

"He's losing it," Randy murmured. "He's gonna jackknife for sure."

Other than the speeding truck and the hovering helicopter, there was no nearby traffic traveling in either direction when James Ardmore's bright blue Peterbilt came to grief. One moment it was moving forward. The next moment it had tipped over onto its side and was sliding off the roadway.

"That's how it's done," Donnie announced over the intercom. "Now we sit back and watch the fun."

"Fun?" Randy Trotter echoed. "You damn near killed us."

"What are you upset about—we got your man, didn't we?"

"Yes we did," the sheriff muttered, "but I believe I'm going to need to change my underwear."

❦ FORTY-SIX

JIMMY ARDMORE was driving along and carefully minding his own business. He'd been holding his breath as he approached the Border Patrol checkpoint east of Las Cruces, but the dogs hadn't alerted to anything in his truck, and they waved him through without a second glance. He'd seen a couple of cop cars in the course of the morning, but they'd been westbound and he was eastbound, and they had paid him no mind. He had bought that new phone in Road Forks. It was one of those cheap cell phones—a "burner," as crooks liked to call them, not that Jimmy ever considered himself to be a crook. He was far more talented than that. He had told the clerk that he'd broken his cell phone and he wouldn't be able to get it fixed until after he got back from this trip.

So yes, he wasn't supposed to be using a cell phone while driving, but he did anyway, keeping it on speaker and spending the better part of an hour on the phone with Tony Segura. During that long conversation he had been given the address of a place on the far side of El Paso, the site of a defunct crop-dusting outfit. He'd be able to pull his rig under the shelter of an old airplane hangar, a location where one of Tony's business associates ran a very profitable chop shop.

The part of I-10 between Las Cruces and El Paso was by far Jimmy's least favorite stretch of highway. There were all kinds of dairy farms in the neighborhood, and by the time he made it past them, he felt like he was breathing cow shit. He switched the cab's A/C over to recirculate, hoping to prevent the foul odor outside from permeating the interior.

He had just turned the control on the A/C when a helicopter appeared from nowhere, dropping out of the sky directly in front of him. At first he thought the guy was going to crash. He looked around, trying to find a place to dodge out of the way. He swerved, struggling to avoid it, and the truck lurched to the left. The helicopter was still there and still in front of him when Jimmy's overcorrection sent the truck speeding to the right again.

He fought desperately to regain control, but the Subaru in the back was a much lighter load than he was used to pulling. As the trailer began to sway from side to side, it felt more like he was flying a kite than driving a truck. He knew before it happened that he was going to jackknife, and there wasn't a damned thing he could do about it—not a single thing.

The next exit was coming up fast. The last thing he saw, just before he slammed into it, was one of those Gas, Food, and Lodging signs. The gas part was right at eye level as he creamed it, shattering the safety glass in front of him and taking out the windshield. As airbags enveloped him and slammed his head back against the seat, the Peterbilt flopped over on its side and slid, skidding across the dirt of the shoulder before crashing through a fence line and coming to rest at last in a steaming heap of cow dung.

When Jimmy came to, a guy in a fire-department uniform was speaking to him. "Sir," he said urgently. "Sir, can you hear me? We're here to help. We'll have you out of there in no time."

Jimmy heard the words and tried to make sense of them, but the only thing that really penetrated his consciousness was that he was covered in crap, head to toe.

FORTY-SEVEN

Joanna went home. She had raced off in such a hurry that she hadn't done the necessary chores. She made quick work of them now, hoping that the animals would forgive her for throwing them off schedule. By the time everyone was fed, Dwayne and Li'l Pat, bundled up against the cold, were out in the driveway playing fetch with all four dogs— their two and Joanna's two. It did Joanna's heart good to realize that although Stormin' Norman and Big Red were work dogs, they were also given the opportunity to play.

After showering, Joanna went to the kitchen for coffee and found Carol whipping out a batch of French toast. "A girl's gotta eat, you know," she said.

Truth be told, Joanna was famished. After that, she settled in to field phone calls, hoping to hear about what was going on. She wasn't actually at work, but she could just as well have been.

Tom Hadlock called first, his voice thick with disappointment. The arrest team had come up empty. The killers were in the wind, and they were waiting for Dave and Casey to show up to direct the collection of evidence. Joanna tried to assure Tom that whatever had happened wasn't his fault—that he'd done his best—but she could tell he didn't believe that for a minute.

Marianne called next. "I just talked to Lou Ann Richards. She said that she and Lyle could get better connections from St. Louis and New Orleans into Phoenix than they could into Tucson. They'll fly into Sky Harbor, arriving late tonight. They'll rent a car, stay there overnight, and then drive down tomorrow morning."

"That's good news."

"As soon as Latisha knew when her mom was getting here, she wanted to know if I could help her do something about her hair. I got her a comb, but when she tried to use it, the hair started falling out in big chunks. Eileen Hopkins from ER told us that losing hair is yet another symptom of severe malnourishment. Up to now the hair has been so matted that it couldn't fall out. Eileen suggested I call Eddie from the barbershop out in Don Luis. He's the hospital's go-to guy when someone needs what they call the 'Big C Hairdo.'"

"Which is?"

"A shave and a scarf. As rail thin as Latisha is, people will take one look at her and decide she's a cancer patient, but it's also the right thing to do. I believe that a drastic change of appearance will do her a world of good. When she sees herself in a mirror, she'll see someone entirely different from the person the Boss left behind."

"The Boss," Joanna repeated. "Does that mean she's been talking to you?"

"When Latisha's not sleeping, she talks non-stop," Marianne said. "She was so lonely after Amelia died that she's almost as starved for conversation as she is for food. And she asked me if I knew of a priest who would come see her."

"She's a Catholic, then?"

"She told me she's not—not yet anyway—but that her parents are, her mother and her stepfather. So I got a hold of Father Rowan from St. Dominick's. He said he'll stop by later on this afternoon to see her. How are things out in the Peloncillos?"

"The arrest team came up empty. The Ardmores had already fled the crime scene by the time they got there. They're all just hanging out right now, waiting to help process the crime scene once Dave and Casey turn up to supervise."

"Maybe I should take a run out there after I leave the hospital," Marianne said. "From what Latisha told me, it's likely to be tough going for everyone."

When the phone call ended, Joanna remained on the living-room sofa for a few minutes, just sitting and thinking. By rights she needed to let Latisha know what had happened, but she wanted to wait around awhile longer to see if maybe Sheriff Trotter had better news.

Joanna was alone. The house was quiet. Sage was asleep. Dennis was at school but was scheduled to go on a play date after school let out. The Paxtons had taken their dogs and gone somewhere. Carol was on her way to town to get the mail. Lucky and Lady, worn out from playing, were flopped down side by side on the living-room floor. Feeling suddenly beyond weary, Joanna allowed herself to kick off her shoes, lie down on the sofa, and put her head on a pillow. In a matter of minutes, she was fast asleep.

In the dream she was coming home from somewhere—work, maybe? Instead of driving into the garage as she usually did, she parked out by the gate and then walked up to the front door. She had opened the screen and was reaching for the knob when the door opened in front of her. A man, seemingly a stranger, stood just inside the door, holding Sage in one hand and a butcher knife in the other.

"Why, hello," he said to her, waving the blade of the knife in her direction. "Welcome home, Sheriff Brady. So what's it going to be today, you or this baby?"

She awoke with a start, gasping for breath and with her heart hammering in her chest. The danger had been so palpably real that for a second or two she had a difficult time grasping that it had actually been a dream. And then she realized that the stranger hadn't been a stranger at all. She'd seen that face before, twice—on both Arthur Ardmore's driver's license and his brother's.

Joanna wasn't even actively working the case—make that *officially* working the case—but it was still affecting her. If the horrors going on out in the Peloncillos were bad enough to haunt her from a distance, what would they do to her people—the ones who actually had to come face-to-face with such evil?

Tom called at a little past noon to tell her that the examination of the scene had turned up the likelihood that Arthur Ardmore was deceased. He also told her about locating what appeared to be three shallow graves out behind Arthur's house.

"How are you doing, Tom?" she asked.

He hesitated for a moment before answering. "It's been rough," he admitted, "on everybody."

Once off the phone with him, Joanna called the Paxtons to give them the news and to ask if it might be possible for them to stick around for a day or two longer. But the call she was waiting for, the one from New Mexico, didn't come in until slightly after 2:00 P.M.

"James Ardmore is dead," Randy Trotter announced. "He had a wreck on the I-10 between Las Cruces and El Paso. He was airlifted from the scene and died on the way to the hospital in Las Cruces."

Still rattled by her recent nightmare encounter with the man, the relief Joanna felt was overwhelming. "Thank God," she said. "How did it happen?"

"Not sure," Sheriff Trotter said. "My pilot and I were following him at the time, and suddenly he just lost it. Maybe he fell asleep."

There was something off in his voice, something that maybe wasn't quite right, but Joanna didn't pay that much attention. She was too busy being grateful. If James Ardmore was dead, Latisha would never have to face him across a courtroom to testify about what he'd done to her and to her friends. Joanna knew full well that nothing a judge and jury could dish out to him would be sufficient punishment for his crimes, but for now the fact that he was dead would have to be enough.

"Because my department was actively pursuing him at the time," Trotter continued, "my counterparts in Doña Ana County let me have a look at his personal effects. The weird thing is, he was carrying two very different sets of IDs and credit cards—one for James Ardmore and the other, including a current passport, for Arthur Ardmore. Any ideas about that?"

"Unfortunately, yes," Joanna said. "My people out in Calhoun are fairly certain that Arthur Ardmore is deceased. They found evidence to suggest he's been missing since May two years ago."

"That's interesting," Randy Trotter said. "We ran a credit report, and according to credit-card records the man's alive and well and living it up all over the country."

"It's more likely his remains are locked in a drawer uptown in our M.E.'s office," Joanna told him. "We believe the skull with the bullet hole in the back of the head belongs to him—or to one of them. Since they look so much alike, are you sure you've got the ID straight?"

"One hundred percent," Trotter said. "I had one of my deputies obtain a warrant and search James Ardmore's mobile over in Road Forks. We lifted some prints, sent them over to Las Cruces, and they check out. Our dead guy is definitely James Edward Ardmore. We're looking for other relatives, but so far none have turned up."

"I need to go let Latisha know. I've been waiting to hear from you before telling her the other news."

"What other news?"

"My people found three more bodies buried in shallow graves behind Arthur Ardmore's house in Calhoun."

"Three more?" Trotter echoed. "You're saying seven so far?"

"It would have been eight if Latisha hadn't gotten away."

"Go tell her, then, by all means," Sheriff Trotter urged. "It won't make things right by any means, but it might make her feel better."

Joanna packed up Sage to go deliver the news to Latisha. Father Rowan was in the room with Latisha when they arrived, so Joanna waited in the hallway until he was leaving.

The priest greeted her with a friendly smile. "I see that your bundle of joy has arrived. Congratulations."

"Thank you," Joanna said. It was refreshing for a change to hear a comment that had nothing to do with maternity leave.

When Latisha caught sight of Joanna, her face lit up. The IV bag still hung next to her bed, but already the liquids being pumped into her system had made her look less gaunt.

"I'm glad you came back," she said. "Thank you for staying with me earlier. And thank you for sending that nice Marianne."

"She is nice," Joanna told her. "We've been friends since seventh grade."

"And that's your baby?"

Joanna nodded. "Her name is Sage. We came to give you some news. I just got word from Randy Trotter, the sheriff over in Hidalgo County. He wanted me to let you know that the man you knew as the Boss, a guy by the name of James Ardmore, is now deceased. He had crossed state lines and was fleeing prosecution when he wrecked his truck. He died while being transported to the hospital."

Latisha's eyes widened. "He's dead, really?"

"Really."

"You mean I'll never have to see him again, and I won't have to testify against him in court?"

"It's over," Joanna answered, although she knew that wasn't true. Latisha Marcum would be suffering the aftereffects of James Ardmore's crimes for the rest of her life.

The young woman's tears came once again, as they had so often that day. This time they ended a little sooner than before. "Sorry," she murmured. "I just can't seem to stop crying."

"Under the circumstances I think you have every right. Later this afternoon my department will be holding a briefing about all this, and there's something you need to know before it becomes public knowledge. When my people were out at Calhoun today doing crime-scene investigation, they located at least three more sets of remains."

"Other girls like us?" Latisha asked.

"We're not sure, but I suspect that may be the case. The bodies are currently being transported to the M.E.'s office."

"Sadie always said there were probably others," Latisha murmured. "I should pray for them, but how can I? I don't even know their names."

"Do you believe in God?" Joanna asked.

Latisha thought about that before she answered. "I didn't used to," she said finally, "but now I do."

"You don't need to know their names to pray for them," Joanna told her. "He already knows."

A nurse came into the room. "Sorry to interrupt, Sheriff Brady. Latisha is due down in the OR to have her toes worked on."

"It's okay," Joanna said. "Sage and I have said what we came to say."

"Can you be here tomorrow when my parents come?" Latisha asked.

"Do you want me here?"

"Yes."

"All right, then," Joanna said. "You can count on it."

"And will you wear your uniform?"

That seemed like an odd request, but Joanna saw no reason to refuse. "I will if you'd like me to," she said. "But why?"

"Lyle, my stepfather, always used to try to tell me that cops were my friends. I want to let him know he was right."

"Fair enough," Joanna said. "A uniform it is."

On her way out, Joanna poked her head into Garth's room. He was asleep in his bed, and his grandmother, seated in a visitor's chair next to him, was sleeping, too. Joanna and Sage left without saying a word.

She had planned to pick Denny up from his play date just before dinner. When she showed up early, he wasn't happy.

"Do I have to go?" he grumbled. "Can't I stay just a little longer?"

"Nope," she told him, "Daddy's coming home from his book tour today, and I believe some welcome-home balloons might be in order."

FORTY-EIGHT

THE BALLOONS were a huge hit. So was the publication payment that Joanna had retrieved from Butch's office and had leaning next to his glass when he sat down at the table. Carol had made up a batch of green-chili casserole for dinner. Denny, thrilled that his daddy was home, spent the entire meal monopolizing the conversation, so until Denny was in bed, there was no opportunity for adult conversation. When Joanna was finally able to recount the deadly turn the Ardmore investigation had taken that day, Butch could only listen and shake his head.

"You've got a wounded deputy, a dead suspect, and now you've got three more victims. Could things get any worse?"

"I don't see how," Joanna told him.

Tom called at ten o'clock as they were getting ready for bed. "Just got home, and I'm beat," he said, "but I wanted to give you an update."

"How are things?"

"It was a hell of a tough day for everybody. The guys on the ERT worked their butts off. The M.E. came out and collected the remains of the three new victims, but it turns out she needed help with that from some of our guys because she's short-handed now, too. Seems like Ralph Whetson up and quit earlier today, right in the middle of his shift."

"He quit? Did Dr. Baldwin say why?"

"No, just that he was gone. Anyway, just because we couldn't see signs of more graves, that doesn't mean they aren't there. Did you update the Paxtons?"

"Sure did. They're still here and will be ready to deploy as needed whenever you give the word."

"Good. By the time we were headed back, it was too late for Ernie to do a presser. That's scheduled for tomorrow morning at nine. I'm tempted to bar Marliss from attending."

"Don't bother," Joanna told him. "For right now I'm pretty sure she's lost her inside track."

"Ralph Whetson?"

"You've got it."

"Fair enough, then," Tom said. "In the meantime I'm hitting the hay."

"Do that," Joanna said. "You've more than earned it."

The answer to Butch's earlier question came around midnight in the form of a phone call from the Copper Queen Community Hospital. "Sheriff Brady? Dr. Morris here."

Joanna's heart went to her throat. "Has Garth taken a turn for the worse?"

"No," Dr. Morris said. "As far as I know, he's doing fine. No, I'm calling about Thomas Hadlock. He insisted I call and tell you."

"Tell me what?"

"He showed up about an hour ago. He woke up with chest pains and was afraid he was having a heart attack, so he drove himself to the hospital. The damn fool should have called an ambulance, but it turns out he was right to get himself here in a hell of a hurry. He's in intensive care right now, but he insisted I call and let you know."

"But I just talked to him a little while ago. Is he going to be all right?"

"Our cardiologist will give him a full workup tomorrow."

"What's going on?" Butch asked when Joanna put down the phone.

"That was Dr. Morris from the ER. Tom Hadlock is in intensive care with a possible heart attack."

"I guess it's a good thing I came home early," Butch said. "It sounds like your maternity leave is officially terminated."

And it was. Early the next morning, Joanna nursed Sage, turned the baby over to Butch, donned her dress uniform, packed her breast pump, and headed for the Justice Center. It wasn't yet 8:00 A.M., but the parking lot was already filled to the brim with media vans, some from as far away as Phoenix. Ernie had billed the upcoming press conference as a joint one, with both the sheriff's department and the medical examiner's office participating, and Joanna spotted Kendra Baldwin's Honda CRV parked out front as she drove around back to her reserved parking place.

Once inside, Joanna found Kendra chatting with

Kristin, Joanna's secretary. They both seemed surprised to see her.

"What are you doing here?" Kristin asked. "Where's Tom?"

"In the ICU," Joanna answered. "He landed there overnight with chest pains. Drove himself to the ER."

"I wish I could say I'm surprised," Kendra said. "It was a hell of a day out there for everyone involved. I hope he'll be okay." Even Kendra, a person who was usually completely put together, looked surprisingly bedraggled. "I've got three sets of bones laid out on tables and three more sets waiting in boxes. My office is a mess."

"And Ralph quit," Joanna said.

Kendra nodded. "He certainly did. Right after I got the call from Tom about finding the graves, I caught him texting someone on his phone. I asked him what he was doing. He said it was private and none of my business. I told him what happens while he's on the job is most certainly my business. When he handed over his phone, there was a half-written text to Marliss, telling her he was headed to Calhoun to pick up some more bodies. I deleted the text—he hadn't sent it yet—and I would have deleted *him* on the spot, but he quit before I had a chance. Good riddance. He probably called Marliss afterward, because she was there waiting along with a bunch of other reporters as we were leaving the crime scene last night. She would have been there much earlier if she'd gotten Ralph's first message, and I'm sure she'll be front and center today."

"And probably more objectionable than ever," Joanna said, looking around. "But without Ralph feeding her inside info, I think she'll be less of a problem. By the way, where's Ernie?"

"Trying to figure out how to shoehorn more chairs into the conference room," Kristin said. "If the fire department shows up to do a head count, we'll be in big trouble. In the meantime here are some messages I had for Tom."

Joanna took the stack of message slips into her office. At the top was one from Ted Whipple, the FBI's special agent in charge at the Tucson office.

"Good morning, Sheriff Brady," he said when she returned his call. "I don't believe you're the one who contacted me originally, but I understand you folks down there are in need of our assistance."

"Actually we no longer are," Joanna said. "Or rather the assistance we needed has already been provided. A friend of a friend pointed us in the direction of Rochelle Powers, an FBI profiler who happened to be in Arizona on vacation. She was able to give us some pointers, and the individual involved has been dealt with."

"You went around me, then?" he asked, sounding offended. "I was simply following procedures."

"We didn't have time for procedures," Joanna told him. "We were afraid he was holding other victims captive, and without Rochelle's help he might have gotten away."

"He's in custody, then?" Whipple asked, sounding somewhat mollified.

"In a manner of speaking," Joanna replied. "He's

deceased. He died as a result of an MVA on I-10 in New Mexico late yesterday morning."

"Fleeing prosecution, was he?"

"Apparently."

"Well, all right, then. If you need anything else . . ."

"Of course," Joanna said cordially. "We'll be sure to give you a call." Adding under her breath, once the call ended, "Like bloody hell."

She was shuffling through the slips to see who should be next when a call came in on her cell phone from Randy Trotter.

"I've got some news for you," he said. "Based on the seriousness of the situation, I was able to get the Doña Ana M.E.'s office to move our boy Ardmore to the head of the line. Cause of death is a concussion. Manner of death accidental."

Joanna was incredulous. "They've already done the postmortem?"

"Yup, according to the doc here, Ardmore showed signs of having come in recent contact with the business end of a stun gun. He also had a slow brain bleed from a previous injury, so even the slightest blow to the back of his head would have killed him. When the airbags deployed and slammed his head against the back of the seat, he was done for. Incidentally, his death just happens to have spared Arizona and New Mexico huge amounts of money. Couldn't have happened to a nicer guy."

"Thanks for the info," Joanna said. "Since we're about to hold a presser here, let me go pass this along to our Media Relations officer."

She caught up with Ernie out in the hall, where he was raiding the break room for chairs and hauling them into the conference room off the lobby. "What are you doing here?" he demanded. "Where's Tom?"

"He's in the ICU. Chest pains."

"Are you serious?"

"I'm serious and I'm back," Joanna told him, "and I've got some important info for you from Sheriff Trotter over in Hidalgo County."

FORTY-NINE

THE CLATTERING of carts and trays out in the hall-way awakened Latisha. Because of her still-aching tooth, they'd given her something to help with the pain, and it had put her out like a light. For the first time, she'd slept without dreaming—without hearing the fading thumping of Amelia's fists pounding on the inside walls of the freezer.

The night nurse had warned Latisha that she was a falling risk and wasn't to attempt walking to the restroom on her own, so she pressed the Call button. She was still hooked up to an IV, and the nurse—her name was Barbara—had to escort both Latisha and the IV into the bathroom. When Barbara helped her out of bed, she stood for a moment and looked down at her feet. The gnarled toenails were gone. Her feet no longer looked like disfigured claws, and overnight the weight of the single sheet hadn't hurt. She suspected that was the other reason she'd slept so well.

After pointing out the grab bars Latisha could use if needed and directing her to press the Call button when she was done, Barbara left her there alone. Latisha stood transfixed in front of the mirror, staring at her own face. Without her hair it might have been her mother's face looking back at her, or even her grandmother's.

But seeing the face reminded Latisha that her mother was coming today—her mother and Lyle both. They had called and left a message while she'd been in the OR the previous afternoon. Their plane was due in Phoenix at midnight. They would overnight there and be in Bisbee by eleven that morning. And then, Latisha realized, she would need to find a way to talk to them about what had happened.

Would she be able to tell the whole story? Would they want to hear it? Would they be able to forgive her for the way she'd behaved toward them, the things she'd done? And if they couldn't forgive her, what would happen to her then? Regardless, when they got there, Latisha wanted to look her best. Marianne had stopped by the previous evening and dropped off a scarf—a bright blue scarf that she said was a shade called "Bisbee blue." By the time her parents showed up, Latisha hoped to be wearing it.

Before she left, Barbara had placed a little makeup kit on the counter next to the sink. Inside Latisha found a toothbrush—a brand-new toothbrush—and a tiny tube of toothpaste. She brushed her teeth, carefully avoiding the broken tooth. Her gums bled. Dr. Lee had told her that was to be expected. He had also told her that the dentist would be coming today to deal with her tooth. And a psychologist. She would be coming, too.

Dr. Lee had told Latisha that she might be suffering from something called PTSD. Latisha had heard about that before. She thought it was something that only happened to soldiers, but Dr. Lee had said she was a prime candidate. And he also said that talking with a stranger and telling her story might help her move beyond the hours and months of torture in the Boss's basement. And maybe he was right. She'd told the story twice now—first to Garth and later to Marianne—and already those dark days seemed to be receding, as though the terrible things that had happened to her back there had happened to someone else.

Latisha pressed the button, and Barbara reappeared almost immediately. "Are you ready to get back into bed?"

"Is Garth still here?"

"Deputy Raymond? Yes, why?"

"Can I go see him?"

"Let me get you a wheelchair."

"If you'll help me, and if it isn't too far," Latisha said, "I think I can walk."

Garth was sitting up in bed, eating breakfast. His grandmother was there, too. Latisha had already met Juanita Raymond. She had come by yesterday afternoon to say that her grandson was out of the operating room, in the recovery room, and that he was going to be fine. She had also delivered two more meat-loaf sandwiches, which Latisha had eaten slowly, over the course of the afternoon and evening.

"Good morning," he said, smiling at her. "I'm

glad to see you're up and around. They won't let me out of bed yet."

"I came to say thank you," Latisha said. "Thank you for saving my life."

"No problem," Garth Raymond told her with a grin. "On that score I believe we're even steven."

Barbara helped Latisha back to her room and into bed. She brought in a breakfast tray with scrambled eggs and ham and hash browns and toast and orange juice. It was a feast—more than Latisha could eat—and when she'd eaten her fill, she pushed the tray away and slept some more.

❦ FIFTY

JOANNA BUGGED out of the press conference a few minutes early, raced home, and spent half an hour feeding Sage. It turned out to be good timing for both mother and child, and a lot less complicated than using the breast pump. She showed up at the hospital a good fifteen minutes before Latisha's parents were due to arrive, so she popped into the ICU long enough to say hello to Tom.

"You gave us quite a scare," she said accusingly.

"I know. Sorry. How did the press conference go?"

"It was a three-ring circus. Marliss was surprisingly subdued, but Ernie did all right."

"See there?" Tom said with a smile. "I told you he's a natural."

"Enough about the case," Joanna said. "What about you?"

"I've got a blockage," he said. "I'm going to need a stent. I'm sorry about this, Sheriff Brady. I know you were counting on me—"

"And you came through with flying colors," Joanna said. "What you need to do now is concentrate on getting well."

"It was really rough," Tom said. "What he did to all those girls . . ."

Shaking his head, he left the rest of it unsaid, but Joanna knew that the mental anguish caused by what Tom Hadlock had encountered the day before would be far more difficult to banish than a chest pain which could be easily remedied with the simple installation of a medical device. One was a wound to the body, while the other had damaged his soul.

"By the way," Joanna added, "Deb told me to give you a message. You remember that chair you were sitting in yesterday, the one in Calhoun?"

"Right," Tom said, "the one under the tree. What about it?"

"She said that as they were getting ready to head out, she took a look at that chair and saw something that looked suspicious to her. She brought it back to the lab, sprayed it with luminol, and guess what?"

"What?"

"It lit up like a Christmas tree. She thinks Arthur Ardmore was sitting in that chair at the time someone shot him."

"So Jimmy assumed Arthur's identity and has been masquerading as him ever since?"

"That's how it looks."

Tom breathed a sigh of relief. "At least now we know where it happened."

Leaving Tom behind, Joanna arrived at Latisha's room a few minutes later, where she found the patient sitting up in bed with a bright turquoise blue scarf wrapped around her head. The improvement in Latisha's appearance between yesterday and today was nothing short of remarkable.

"You came!" Latisha said.

"Of course I came," Joanna replied. "You asked me to, didn't you?"

"But where's your baby?"

"Sage is at home today with her father."

"But she was with you yesterday," Latisha objected.

"Yesterday I was on maternity leave. Today I'm working."

There was a flurry of activity out in the hallway, and a man and a woman charged into the room. The woman raced past Joanna without a sideways glance and rushed straight to Latisha's bedside, smothering the girl in a heartfelt embrace, while the man hung back, as if uncertain of his reception. He was the one Joanna approached with her hand outstretched.

"I'm Sheriff Joanna Brady," she said.

"And I'm Lyle Richards, Latisha's stepfather."

"Your stepdaughter's one brave individual," Joanna said. "She escaped the clutches of a very dangerous man, and in the process she ended up saving the life of one of my deputies."

"Yup," said Lyle. "That's our girl."

"Lyle," a small voice called, summoning him from the far side of the room. Stepping away from Joanna, Lyle turned and approached the bed.

"How are you doing?" he asked, almost as though he were inquiring after the health of a total stranger. "I hear you've been out making like a superhero."

"I'm not the superhero," Latisha told him. "You're the one who saved me."

A look of utter astonishment crossed Lyle's face. "Me?" he asked in disbelief. "How did I save you?"

"I remembered some of the words you used to say to me, the ones I always thought were so stupid," she told him. "And remembering them gave me courage."

"What words?"

"'God helps those who help themselves.'"

"That one?" he asked with a chuckle. "If that's what did the trick, I'm not the one who saved you. My mother did, because she's the one who gave those words to me."

"What you said," Latisha told him, "and your pancakes. When we were locked in the basement and chained to the wall with nothing to eat but dog food, the other girls—Sandra and Sadie and Amelia—and me, all we did was talk about food. Sadie talked about her grandmother's fried chicken. Sandra remembered her foster mother's chocolate-chip cookies. Amelia was all about her grandmother's tamales. As for me? I told them about your Saturday-morning pancakes. Do you still make them?"

"I haven't made them in a very long time," Lyle admitted. "Not since you've been gone, but I will again, once you're home, I promise."

"Have you ever had tamales?" Latisha asked.

"Sure," he said. "Many times."

"Where did you get them? In St. Louis?"

"When I enlisted in the army right out of high school, I ended up being stationed just a few miles from here, at Fort Huachuca. I ate tamales all the time."

"Do you think I'd like them?"

"Your mom and I will go out later, find one, and bring it to you," he said. "That way you'll be able to decide for yourself."

"But tell us what happened," Lou Ann said. "From the beginning. You really had to eat dog food?"

As they pulled chairs close to their daughter's bed, ready to hear her story, Joanna realized that although Latisha had wanted her to be there to begin with, they were gathered as a family now, and her presence was no longer required.

"If you'll excuse me," she said, edging her way toward the door, "I'll be on my way."

She was gone seconds later, and it seemed unlikely that any of them noticed.

FIFTY-ONE

FOR JOANNA the next two days flashed by in a flurry of paperwork and complicated logistics with quick stints of motherhood squeezed in around the edges. She spent a good deal of time working closely with the M.E. At Joanna's suggestion one of the first things Kendra Baldwin did was contact a victims'-rights organization from Phoenix, putting them in touch with Rosa Moreno in order to facilitate getting Amelia Salazar's remains shipped home to her grandmother in Mexico.

At the moment it was far too soon for the M.E. to have established the identities of any of the three individuals whose bodies had been found buried behind Arthur Ardmore's place in Calhoun, although Kendra remained hopeful that the same kind of miracle that had allowed her to identify Amelia would happen again.

"Who knows?" she said. "Maybe lightning really will strike twice in the same place."

Unlike Latisha, neither Sadie Jennings nor Sandra Locke had ever been reported missing. Sandra's mother, Margo, was located living in a halfway house in Lodi, California. She was fresh out of jail, without a job, and completely broke. With no home of her own, she had nowhere to bring Sandra and no money with which to do so.

"I always figured Sandy was lying dead somewhere," Margo said, "so you could just as well go ahead and bury her wherever she's at. It don't matter to me."

"I'll talk to Norm Higgins over at the mortuary," Joanna said when Kendra reported what Margo had said. "I'll see what we can do."

Sadie's parents were both dead. Sadie's father had died of a drug overdose, and her mother had succumbed to hep C months earlier while still in prison, so Kendra was currently on the trail of a distant cousin in hopes that, if she could manage to get a genetic profile from the DNA-extraction kits, familial DNA would provide a positive identification.

The Department of Public Safety had launched an inquiry into whether or not Deputy Raymond's injuries were the result of an officer-involved shooting. The GSR tests Tom had ordered had completely exonerated the young officer on that score.

On Wednesday morning Joanna was present when both Deputy Raymond and Latisha Marcum were released from the Copper Queen Community Hospital. Raymond was going home to Elfrida to recuperate, while Latisha was scheduled to fly back to St. Louis with her parents. Since it was the day before Thanksgiving, the fact that they'd been able to find tickets to fly home at all, let alone three seats together, had been something of a miracle.

Before they left, Joanna managed to take Lyle

Richards aside. "From our preliminary survey of the situation, it looks as though there's a considerable amount of Ardmore money hiding out here and there. You might want to consider enlisting the services of a good attorney as well as a good forensic accountant. I'm a sheriff, not an attorney, but I think there's a strong likelihood Latisha could sue the Ardmore estate for damages due to wrongful imprisonment."

Lyle nodded. "Thank you," he said. "I'll look into it."

A few minutes later, as Juanita Raymond and Lyle Richards went about completing and signing all necessary release paperwork, Joanna noticed that Garth and Latisha were sitting off to the side, waiting to be wheeled out of the hospital. Joanna was gratified to hear them chatting away as though they were old friends.

"So what are you going to do now?" Garth asked.

"I want to go back to school," Latisha told him. "I think I want to become a teacher."

"Good for you," Garth called over his shoulder as a nurse grabbed the handles on his chair and wheeled him toward the door. "Stay in touch, and I'll be sure to send along Grandpa Jeb's meat-loaf recipe."

"Wait a minute, I thought that recipe was your grandmother's."

"It is," Garth replied, "but Grandpa is the one who gave it to her."

When it came time for Latisha to be wheeled out to Lyle's rental car, Joanna walked along beside her.

"I never knew that cops could be so nice," Latisha murmured.

She was settled in the backseat by then, but the car door was still open.

"We do our best," Joanna said.

"When you find out the names of those other girls, will you send them to me?" Latisha asked. "I'm praying for them without names right now, just like you told me. It may not make any difference to God if I don't know their names, but it would make a difference to me."

"You'll have those names as soon as we do," Joanna assured her. "I promise."

On the home front, Butch had been busy, too. He'd slipped back into his role of stay-at-home daddy as easily as putting on an old shoe. You would have thought he'd been taking care of newborn babies all his life.

On Tuesday he'd managed to get out of the house long enough to do all the shopping necessary to create their Thanksgiving feast. He had picked up a supply of new baby bottles and some formula as well. Joanna intended to breast-feed Sage as long as possible, but as the guy who'd be left holding a hungry baby if Mom couldn't get home in a timely fashion, Butch wanted to be equipped with a backup plan already in place.

As promised, Denny was fully involved in the preparations. By midafternoon, when it came time to bake pumpkin pies, Butch put Denny in charge of cleaning the pumpkin seeds so they could be roasted. While he was doing that, Butch went in search of Joanna.

He was surprised to find her standing in front of the bookshelf in his study, emptying the shelves of her father's journals and loading them into a box. "Hey," he said, "why are you boxing those up? I thought you were going to read them."

"I thought so, too," Joanna said ruefully, "but then I went to see Tom in the ICU. That business out in Calhoun really affected him. He's going to be carrying that burden around with him for the rest of his life. And I'm sure the same kinds of things happened to my dad. He confided in these books—he put his whole heart into them—the good stuff and the bad stuff. I'm packing these away, not throwing them away. Maybe someday, after I retire, I'll be able to read them, but not right now. I've got enough of my own stuff to carry around. I can't afford to carry his, too."

Butch thought about that for a moment before he nodded. "Gotcha," he said finally. With that, he turned and headed back toward the kitchen. "Hey, Denny," he called as he went. "Are you done with those seeds yet? We need to get them in and out of the oven so I can start on the pies."

Joanna had finished loading the books into the box and was taping the cover shut when the land-line phone on Butch's desk jangled awake. Plucking the handset off the charger, she picked it up and answered. "Hello."

"Joanna?" It was a woman's voice, one Joanna was sure she had heard before, although she didn't recognize it right off.

"It's Carole Anne Wilson," the voice continued. "How are you, and how's the baby?"

Of course. Carole Anne Wilson was Butch's editor in New York.

"We're both fine," Joanna said. "How are you?"

"I'm great. Is Butch home?"

"Sure, but he's in the other room," Joanna said. "Let me take the phone to him."

Out in the kitchen, Dennis was squatting in front of the oven, watching to see if his pumpkin seeds had started to burn yet, while Butch put the finishing touches on crimping a pair of piecrusts.

"It's Carole Anne," Joanna said, offering him the phone.

He dusted off his hands on his apron before taking the phone. "Hi, Carole," he said. "Yeah, I'm baking pumpkin pies. What's up with you?"

For the next several very long seconds—the better part of a minute—he listened, while a huge smile spread across his face. "You've got to be kidding!" he said at last. "That's great. Thank you so much for letting me know."

"Letting you know what?" Joanna demanded as he handed the phone back to her.

"I made the list!" he said.

"What list?"

"The *New York Times* Best Sellers list. I didn't make it the first week, but I did on week two. *Just the Facts* clocks in at number twelve on the combined hardback/e-book list."

Joanna was dumbfounded. "You made the *New York Times* list? Really? That's amazing!"

"Not really, because Gayle Dixon is the name on the list instead of Butch Dixon, but yes, we made the list. *Just the Facts* made the list!"

"What does that mean, Daddy?" Denny asked without taking his eyes off the pumpkin seeds.

"It means that maybe someday I'll be able to make enough money by writing books that your mom will be able to stay home for a change. She might even start running the household," Butch added with a wink in Joanna's direction.

"Are you sure?" Denny asked. "You're a better cook."

Joanna and Butch both burst out laughing at that. "Out of the mouths of babes," Butch said.

"That's all right," Joanna said. "Check with me four years from now. If you're making handfuls of money by the time the next election rolls around, maybe it'll be time for me to pull the plug, quit being sheriff, and learn to cook."

"Don't even think about it," Butch advised. "Given your recent history with maternity leave, you wouldn't last two weeks."

GRANDPA JEB'S SUNDAY MEAT LOAF

2.5 pounds ground chuck
1 cup oats
4.5-ounce can chopped green chilies
½ cup milk
½ cup minced onion
2 eggs*
2 teaspoons salt
2 teaspoons chili powder

About 2 hours before serving, preheat oven to 350 degrees. Bake 1½ hours.

Recipe compliments of Carl Bender and Barbara Brugnaux

_____

*(May substitute ½ cup Egg Beaters Southwestern Style for the eggs.)

A LOOK BACK

By J. A. Jance

WE'RE ON a cruise ship in the Mediterranean, docked at Civitavecchia, an ancient Roman port, but it's May 22, and I'm thinking about the tragic event that propelled me into my career as a writer— an encounter with a serial killer that happened near Tucson, Arizona, forty-eight years ago today. You might say that my starting to write some twelve years later was a bit of a delayed reaction.

From the time I read *The Wizard of Oz* in second grade, I had wanted to be a writer—dreamed of being a writer—but girls weren't exactly encouraged to become writers back in those days. In fact, when I attempted to enroll in the creative writing program at the University of Arizona in 1964, I was turned down on the basis that I was a girl. "Girls become teachers or nurses," the professor told me. "Boys become writers."

So I married a guy, Jerry Jance, who was allowed into the creative writing course that was closed to me, while I went on to earn first a teaching degree in English and later a master's degree in library science. By 1970 Jerry and I were teaching on what was then the Papago Reservation west of Tucson. We lived in what had once been ranch hand housing on King's Anvil Ranch—a humble one-bedroom brick house with a polished concrete floor, located on a volcanic knoll, thirty miles from town in either direction—Tucson to the east and Sells, where we taught, to the west. The Hill, as we called the place we lived, was two miles off the highway at the end of a rough dirt track and seven miles from the nearest telephone and/or neighbor.

On Friday, May 22, 1970, we went to school in Sells in the usual fashion. I was the junior class sponsor that year, and that Saturday happened to be the junior/senior prom. Because I was expecting out-of-town company to show up for dinner that night, the kids and I had arranged to do the decorating the following day. But when we arrived at school that morning, the principal, a retired army officer who brooked no argument, decreed, "You will decorate for the prom this afternoon after school!"

At lunchtime, Jerry and I discussed the problem. Since someone needed to be at the house to let the company in, we decided that when school got out that afternoon, he would walk over to the highway and hitchhike home. That way, when the kids and I finished decorating, I could drive home so we could all go into town for dinner.

There was no mass transit on the reservation back then, and that remains the case today. Hitchhiking worked, and even the nuns from Topawa hitched rides back and forth on occasion. So that's what happened. Jerry left to hitchhike home when school got out—around three—while I stayed on to help the kids.

It was about five when we finished decorating and I left for home. Driving past Law and Order, as the tribal police headquarters was called, I noticed that there were a number of unusual law-enforcement vehicles parked there. That told me I was free to drive whatever speed I wanted on the way home because every cop in the neighborhood was otherwise engaged.

Back at the house I met up with Jerry and our guests, and we headed into Tucson. Halfway to the trading post at Three Points, seven miles away, we were stopped at a roadblock. "What's going on?" we asked.

"There's been a homicide on the reservation."

"Indian or Anglo?" we asked.

"Anglo."

Figuring it couldn't be anyone we knew, we drove on when he waved us through. We stopped for gas at the trading post. While my husband pumped the gas, I went inside to pay, where I found a deputy talking to Shirley, the clerk. I overheard him say something about two little kids and something about a man in a green car. Back in our vehicle, as we headed into Tucson, I mentioned what I had overheard. A couple of miles later, my husband said, "A man in a green car. I wonder if that's the guy who gave me a ride home this afternoon."

We did a U-turn, drove back to the trading post, and told the deputy there who we were, where we lived, and that we didn't have a phone, but earlier that day, Jerry had been given a ride home by a man driving a green car. The next morning, at six A.M., there was a knock on our door, with Detective Jack Lyons, Pima County's chief homicide investigator, standing outside on our porch. He stayed for the next eight hours.

He told us that the previous afternoon, a twenty-eight-year-old woman had been on her way to spend the weekend in Rocky Point, Mexico, with her two young children—a four-year-old boy and a two-year-old girl. Ten miles beyond Sells, she was forced off the highway at gunpoint, shot, raped in front of her children, and left to die. An hour and a half later, some Indian miners, on their way home from working at the Hecla Mine near Casa Grande, came upon two little Anglo kids walking along the shoulder of the road, seventy miles from nowhere.

The miners stopped and asked what they were doing. "We're walking on the beach," said the little boy.

"Where's your mommy?" the miners asked.

"She's over there," he said, pointing. "She's dead."

She wasn't dead then, but she died before they could get her to the hospital.

The incident happened at twenty past two. An hour or so later, the man in the green car picked Jerry up and gave him a ride to our house—not just to the turnoff on the highway, but also up the two-mile dirt track leading to the house. "Do you leave your wife out here by herself much?" the driver asked.

"Well," my husband said, "she's got the dogs." For the next two months, those words hung heavy in the air.

I wore contacts in those days. Without them, I was virtually blind, and so that morning, I listened to that entire eight-hour interview between Jack Lyons and my husband with my whole being. The way Jack framed his questions was nothing short of fascinating. He got my husband to remember all kinds of telling details about the car and about items in the car—the braided strap on a pair of binoculars on the floorboard; the woman's name on a shredded check lying in the front seat; the bits of the driver's story about where he worked and what he was doing there that didn't make sense.

When Jack finally left that day, Jerry and I got dressed and went to the prom. On Sunday, we drove into town, where we met Jack and then traveled from car dealership to car dealership until my husband was able to say definitively that the man who gave him a ride had been driving a green Maverick. On Monday we returned to town once more so my husband could give the description for a composite drawing of the guy who gave him a ride. When Jack showed the composite to the little boy, he took one look and said, "That's the man who killed my mommy!"

Jack didn't exactly keep us posted on the progress of his investigation. He did mention at one point that it might make sense for us to consider living somewhere else for a time, but we were young and stupid. Besides, the Hill was our home. "What if they never catch him?" we wondered. "Are we supposed to run for the rest of our lives?"

School let out for the summer. My husband worked construction during the summers and was out of town during the week for most of the next two months. I had a twelve-month contract to work in the library, so I stayed on the Hill by myself. I wore a twenty-two revolver on my hip and was fully prepared to defend myself. One day, I did in fact fire the weapon, unloading all six shots at a rapidly retreating rattlesnake who was still laughing when he went up and over the wall and disappeared.

I was there by myself. I had no phone. When the rains came and the road washed out, I hiked in and out. Our well had a rope-pull pump. I was able to get the pump started. If you can get your own water in the desert, if you can handle yourself in the face of a very real danger, you earn a measure of independence that no amount of bra-burning can ever duplicate, and in the course of those sixty days on my own, I became a different person from the one I had been before.

In the meantime, Detective Lyons was doing his job. Armed with the details Jerry had provided—the woman's name visible on the shredded check; the make, model, and color of the car—he soon identified a suspect, but he also discovered something else. Jack realized that he was dealing with a serial killer, a man who shot people off moving vehicles at twenty minutes past two on the twenty-second day of the month. He had shot a forty-something-year-old man off a bulldozer, a sixteen-year-old girl off a bicycle, and the woman driving her car to Rocky Point.

So Jack knew who the guy was—where he lived and where he worked. He had him under surveillance, but he didn't want to make a move on him until he had all his legal ducks in a row. However, as the twenty-second of July approached, Jack was worried because the incidents had been getting closer together. So on the twentieth of July, he collected my husband and the two of them drove to San Manuel to pick the killer up as he got off shift. My husband identified him as he came through the gate. On the drive from San Manuel back to Tucson, the guy admitted that he had been to our house on three different occasions in the intervening sixty days. We had been scheduled to be July 22.

What happened then? Not much. There was no trial. We never had to go to court. My husband never had to testify. The guy accepted a plea bargain on one of the three charges with the other two still open should he ever be let out of prison on the first one.

Our lives went on. I still wanted to write, but my ambitions were put on pause. I wrote a children's book that had a positive reaction from an editor in New York, but when my husband saw the letter, he said, "There's only going to be one writer in our family, and I'm it." So other than writing poetry in the dead of night, I did nothing about my writing for the next dozen years. In one of those poems, written while I was living in Phoenix in the early eighties, I wrote about our years on the Hill.

Homestead Revisited
A windswept house on barren lava flow
Surveys the desert floor for miles around.
To this unlikely spot whose beauty none but we
Could well discern, we brought our new-made
  vows
And love.

We were each other's all in all.
It was enough, at least at first. Then small
  erosions came
To sweep us from our perch. The house still
  stands.
Only we are gone.

That first marriage ended in divorce in 1980 due to my husband's issues with alcohol, which would result in his death a mere eighteen months later. Worried that I might take him back, I decided that my best strategy was to put some distance between us, so I loaded up a U-Haul with all our worldly goods, and my kids, and I moved to Seattle. I was brokenhearted, but at the same time, I was determined to survive.

At the time I was working in the life insurance business. When my company offered to pay tuition costs for people taking the Dale Carnegie course, I signed up. I thought that taking a class in "winning friends and influencing people" would turn me into a better life insurance salesman. I couldn't have been more wrong.

Dale Carnegie turned out to be a course in public speaking. I didn't think I needed to learn about public speaking, but the only way to get my tuition money back was to stick it out, and so I did. Over the course of six months, Dale Carnegie students are required to give a number of talks, and one of those is supposed to be devoted to something that "changed the course of your life."

I thought about that—sat around wondering, "Whatever happened to me?" And then, finally, I remembered May 22, 1970. I remembered how I had carried a loaded weapon and gotten my own water, realizing in hindsight that the seeds of my divorce ten years later were sown during those lonely sixty days when I was there on the Hill by myself.

And so I gave my talk about that—about our brief encounter with a serial killer. After that talk, during the break, one of my fellow students came up and said, "Someone should write a book about that." And the words that flashed through my head at the time were these: I'm divorced. What have I got to lose?

That was on a Thursday night. I thought about it all day Friday and all day Saturday. It seemed to me that no one would want to read a book about someone who goes through a life-changing event and then finally gets around to getting a divorce ten years later. Sometime overnight on Saturday, I decided, "How about if I turn this story into a novel?"

And so I did. I started the next afternoon after church, writing by hand on yellow lined paper. The words spewed out. I remembered everything from back then about how things felt and smelled; the questions Jack asked during that eight-hour interview; the weight of the revolver in my hand; the loneliness of those long scary nights. I poured all of those memories into a book titled *By Reason of Insanity*, a thinly fictionalized version of those very real events.

If you're a longtime reader of my books, you may be thinking, "Wait a minute, I don't think I've ever read that book." You haven't and you won't, for the very good reason that *By Reason of Insanity* was never published and never will be. I wrote it in a frenzy, starting in the middle of March and finishing the first draft on—wait for it—the evening of May 22, 1982. Once the handwritten document was turned into a typed manuscript, it was 1,200 pages long, which is to say, approximately three times the length it should have been to be published.

I did manage to get an agent who advised me to cut the manuscript in half, which I did. Even then, however, the book didn't sell. The editors who turned it down told my agent, "The stuff that's fiction is fine. The stuff that's real is unbelievable and would never happen." (Even though it already HAD happened!)

My agent advised me to write something that was entirely fiction. *Until Proven Guilty*, the first Beaumont book, was bought and published by the second editor who saw it. Fifty-six books later, I'm still writing. Ten books into my career, my editor suggested that I consider reworking *By Reason of Insanity* so they could publish it as my first hardback. I had a problem with that, however, because the killer was then, and still is, alive and well in the Arizona State Prison at Florence. In the late eighties, when I was asked to rework the story, he had been a model prisoner, and they were thinking about letting him out.

At that point, my first husband—the witness in the case—was long dead, but I didn't want to write a book that would cause the killer to come looking for me. If I wasn't going to use the real killer as the bad guy, who would the bad guy be? I'm sure it's only the merest of coincidences that the crazed killer in *Hour of the Hunter* turns out to be a former professor of creative writing from the University of Arizona. And although nothing in that book has anything to do with the real homicides from 1970, everything in it is informed by what I learned back then.

I believe that one of the reasons I'm able to write police procedurals is that I know what it feels like to live through a shoot/don't shoot scenario and decide, in those bare seconds, that if it's between him or me, it's by God going to be him! You can't unring that bell. You can't untoggle that switch. You've changed something in the very depths of your soul, a reality law-enforcement officers have to live with every day of their lives.

Once *By Reason of Insanity* was turned down, I put it away and never touched it again. It's with my papers at the University of Arizona Special Collections, but as I said earlier, I don't expect it will ever be published. It was my on-the-job training for being a writer. It wasn't ready for prime time, but in all my writing since, I've deliberately stayed away from real crimes and real people. And I'm glad I did.

In 2001 I did a talk for the library in Pinetop, Arizona. As I was speaking, I noticed a woman standing at the back of the room. She stood with her arms crossed. She didn't smile or laugh at any of the jokes; she didn't nod as though she recognized something from my history turning up in the background of one of the stories.

In my thirty-plus years of writing, I've learned to recognize the people who come to signings with some other agenda in mind. Long before my talk ended that night, I was pretty sure she was the one. The "agenda" people always wait to be last in line, when they can isolate the author and trap them into a private conversation. And that was true that night, too. When the books were all signed and the last fan stepped away from the signing table, the woman from the back of the room was standing there waiting, and the first words out of her mouth gave me goosebumps.

"Was your husband a witness in a series of homicides that took place in Tucson, Arizona, in 1970?"

"Yes," I told her. What else could I say?

And then, without any further introduction, as though we'd been having the conversation for thirty years, she said, "My father was the man on the bulldozer. My mother was pregnant with me at the time. She would never talk to me about it. What can you tell me?"

And so I told her what I knew. But I learned a

very serious lesson that night. The people who are left behind by some act of homicidal violence never get over it. The idea of "closure" is a myth everyone makes up to make themselves feel better, but, for the families of the victims, their lives are forever changed. They number the days of their lives by how they were before that happened and how they are after that happened. As far as I'm concerned, that pain is nothing to be trifled with or turned into fiction for someone else's entertainment.

A few months ago, on a book tour in Mesa, I recounted this story. Afterward, a woman in the audience whom I had met before came up and mentioned that the killer is her first cousin. Her family's life, too, was irrevocably changed by those events. She went on to say that the two children trudging along the roadside after their mother was attacked have never truly recovered. And it is out of deference to them that I've made no mention of the killer's name or their mother's name in this piece. Those kids from back then are in their late forties or early fifties now, and I have no right to invade their privacy.

It's ironic to think that on this day, forty-eight years ago, a serial killer I never met in person lit a fuse that would result in my launching a writing career more than a dozen years later. In a very real way, I've benefited from his horrific actions.

And on days like today, I sometimes wish I hadn't.

"Homestead Revisited" from
After the Fire, *reprinted with permission.*